This is a work of fiction. All the characters and events portrayed in this book are fictitious or used fictitiously.

THE LONG GAME

Copyright © 2025 by Daniel Hatch

All rights reserved, including the right to reproduce this book, or portions thereof, in any form.

ISBN: **979-8-9920397-4-0**

A portion of this book appeared in Analog Science Fiction:

The Scout Post, May 1990

Cover Design by Jay O'Connell

Previous books:

DEN OF THIEVES

Bigwaves Publishing

TIMELINE

87 Asgard colony arrives
191 Alex den Kolberg is born
195 Alex is left at Asgard
207 Alex's father finds him
208 Alex graduates from the academy, joins Space Corps
270 Grandpa leaves for outer systems
312 Alex in Scout Post
337 Zoroaster refugees arrive at Helvetica
362 Helvetica uprisings
412 Den Kolberg puts down Helvetica
427 Alex's father dies
447 Grand Reunion
497 Alex arrives at Minos

(All dates New Era)

THE LONG GAME

Daniel Hatch

The Slow Space Series Book 2

BOOKS AND BURGLARS

"Wait here a few minutes," Jimmy Inoshe said. "I'll be right back."

"What do you mean wait here?" I asked. "It's dark and you've got the only light."

"Just think of it as an exercise in trust. Actually, I want to do what I do best – scout. That means you stay here and I go on ahead."

"I don't need to exercise my trust. Why can't I go with you?"

"Because then it's not scouting. Will you wait?"

"All right," I said. But as I watched him go, a dark shadow framed by a shrinking rectangle of light, I wondered if I was making a mistake. The farther he went, the smaller he got, and the more I felt the walls closing in. By the time he disappeared from view, I could feel every kilogram of rock, soil, and building above. I slowed my breathing and tried to think of something else.

Like the prospect of wandering around lost in the dark warren of tunnels beneath the Minos Spaceport until I died, for example. There was a refreshing change of pace. At least I had an active role in that tragedy – I could look for an exit as I wandered. Someone told me once that you could find your way out of a maze if your left hand always touched a wall. Or was it the right hand? I couldn't remember, but I figured it didn't matter which as long as I didn't switch hands.

How long would I end up waiting before I decided Inoshe wasn't coming back? Would I be able to recognize an exit if I came across one in the dark?

This had started out as a search for a clue to the fate of my grandfather, not a tour of the spaceport's subterranean attractions. I'd been on the planet less than two days and already I was in trouble.

***

The stars around Orion had changed again on the trip from The Star With No Name to 39 Tauri.

Aldebaran had shifted to become a bright orange heart burning in the breast of the Hunter, who seemed to be doing battle with a swarm of white and yellow bees, the Hyades. His dogs, in the form of several bright stars at his feet, had joined the fight.

A brisk wind blew up from the hectares of empty landing field, and I headed for the terminal, wondering if Orion's new look meant anything.

I'm not one to put much faith in omens and portents. I know life is full of flashes of irony and meaning, but I had never believed in mystical significance. Ordinary significance is more than enough trouble for a member of den Kolberg. Although I was almost struck by lightning once ...

Even so, the symbolism was hard to ignore. In the past six weeks of biotime I had crossed fifty years of spacetime on a hunt of my own for a Space Corps cruiser named *Aldebaran*. The trip had not prepared me for a piece of cosmic graffiti that looked like it had my name on it.

Just because I had traveled beyond the bounds of the Perseus Sector did not mean normal rules of logic no longer applied. The stars of the Milky Way did not arrange themselves over the course of millennia, creating the constellations that I saw from the landing field on Minos, just to show that den Kolberg holds a unique and favored place within the universe – despite what some of my cousins might think. To imagine otherwise was self-centered folly.

Obviously there had to be other symbols out there that didn't mean a thing to me. Were they just leftovers? Or messages for someone else? Questions like that renewed my humility as I quick-stepped the long distance to the terminal building and sidestepped the cosmic meaning of the sky.

I looked around the field and saw nothing but the landing lights of my own ship, the *Perseus Wanderer*, and a small scoutship to the north.

And there was the second oddity of the evening: why weren't there more ships around? That was unusual – even on a back-sector planet like this one.

It was the same inside the terminal.

The place was deserted, no one stood behind the darkened ticket counter, the shops were closed, and the only life to be seen was a man in a brown uniform directing a handful of cleaning robots. I was sure I'd landed only an hour after local sunset – unless I got confused about which direction the terminator was moving. No, a clock on the wall said 18:32.

I was concerned about the shops being closed. I needed something badly that only they could provide – a local phone. My phone, a top-of-the-line smart slab of plastic, couldn't connect with the local network. I don't know if it was a lack of credit in my name or the discredit of my family name.

I saw a vending machine in front of one shop that included phones. But it wouldn't take my platinum or my gold coins. Maybe it was broken. My heart sank. How was I supposed to get up to date on the latest local news?

Then I found a newstand and the headlines on the screen told the tale.

"... *officials say the Zorgon battlefleet will arrive here within days ... System forces are on full alert ... Reports from the scoutship* Beau Geste *reveal frightening details of Zorgon power ... for more, read today's Planet News ..."*

A stack of actual ink-on-newsprint newspapers sat inside the box, but it required a coin to open. I would have tried my phone, but I didn't have that option, and the coins I carried were of no interest to the machine. I'd have to wait until I got hold of some local currency before I could be frightened by the details of Zorgon power. I laughed at the irony – one of the richest men within forty light-years and I couldn't even buy a newspaper.

The headlines puzzled me, though. What little I knew of the Zorgons did not include battle fleets.

The reptilian race had first come in contact with human worlds about a hundred years ago real-time and were still hot news back when I left Eta Cass. And they didn't call themselves Zorgons – that was our clever name for them.

Most of our contacts had been with small numbers of them diffusing across the worlds out here towards the Orion-side of human space – traders, drifters, and adventurers. None of them were organized and few were armed.

The experts seemed to think they ranged out around the Hyades and beyond. They were a much older race than we were. They'd been spacefarers a lot longer than we had and occupied a much larger volume of space. Some reports said they stretched as far as Betelgeuse, Rigel, or the Great Nebula itself.

Knowing that there was an entire Zorgon battle fleet sitting out there somewhere made my own problems seem terribly insignificant. And the thought that they were due in town for business in a few days made my skin crawl.

I hoped my search would lead me elsewhere and quickly.

***

"The Zorgons have been coming for twenty years," said Jones, the pilot. "So how come that lousy rad-runner bumps me off the ship this trip? I flew with his grandfather, his father, and his grandson. I can't count the number of systems I've been to space with his family. And then he goes and signs on a new pilot at the last minute."

"He may not be able to count, but I can," Webley, the navigator, said in a low voice. "And it's only a few more than the number of nebula cutters he's had since his ship lifted off without him this afternoon."

The bar upstairs in the spaceport terminal was not quite as empty as the rest of the building. A robot bartender waved double-jointed, chrome-plated arms as he polished glasses and mixed drinks. The three of us balanced on bar stools – the other two with less precision than I – and a fourth man sat in a booth in the corner.

The impending arrival of the alien battle fleet seemed to have cleared the spaceport of all but the most marginal of spacefarers – at least if Jones and Webley were any example.

It was also obvious after a few minutes that neither of them would be able to help me much – either with information about the Zorgons or the *Aldebaran*.

The man in the corner, on the other hand, seemed a little bit more interesting. Even in the shadows I couldn't help but notice the Scout Service patch on the shoulder of his leather jacket.

"Alex den Kolberg," I said as I slipped into the seat across the booth from the scout. I thrust out my hand and waited just a second before he grasped it.

"Jimmy Inoshe," he said, narrowing his eyes as he looked me over carefully. "What can I do for you?"

"I just landed here from No Name and now they tell me the Zorgons are on their way," I said, dialing up a fresh beer from the tabletop console. "You look like you might know what's going on – and those two over there certainly don't."

"You're right about that," Inoshe said. "This is the third day in a row I've seen them in here. I think this bar is the only place they have left to go."

I smiled and waited for him to make his decision, wondering briefly why he'd been in here three days in a row to see them.

"I may be able to help you out," the scout said. "But let's make it an even trade. I'll tell you what I know about the Zorgons if you'll tell me what a den Kolberg is doing out here where the wild things grow."

"We get around," I said as I drew my beer from the serving tray. "Whose story first – yours or mine?"

"I'll flip you for it," he said. "Heads or tails?"

I called heads, he claimed it was tails. The coin he used didn't seem to have a distinct head or tail, though, so I had to take his word for it. I went first.

***

From all I'd been told, I knew that grandfather always had been a strange old bird. So when he disappeared a few centuries ago, nobody took much notice. Some of the members of my family have a strong business and political sense and enjoy managing the den Kolberg holdings. Grandfather did not.

Peter Regensburg Steiger den Kolberg was much more interested in adventure and exploration and had run off with the Space Corps while the rest of his cousins got involved in the gritty business of making colony worlds grow. The last time I saw him was many years ago – biotime and real-time – when he visited me at Windsor Academy. He was a big man in his mid-thirties, strong and stern, but with a gentle, sensitive side to him. For many years, that visit was one of my few links with the Kolberg den. You can imagine my surprise when I discovered that the rest of the family wasn't like him.

It's easy to see why nobody missed him. He just didn't fit in. But then, about fifty years ago, he missed a Grand Reunion. That's not usually done, not when everyone in the family schedules their travels a century in advance to meet in the same place at the same time.

I don't think even that would have caused anything more than gossip if it weren't for the death of my father.

Put the two together, and you get a whole battalion of lawyers descending on the den Kolberg Hostel at Tikarahisat. With holdings in a dozen star systems that include land, satellites, asteroids, starships, banks, mines, factories and schools, you can imagine how difficult it is to sort things out when one of us dies. It's one reason we don't do it very often.

After studying the documents for weeks, the lawyers told us the bad news. Grandfather had turned his holdings over to Father in a trust. If he died before Father, the properties went to Father – and on to Mother and me. If Father went first, they reverted to Grandfather and became part of his estate.

The way the wills were written, they couldn't divide up my father's share of the family fortune unless they knew the fate of my grandfather.

They couldn't presume he was dead – there was a reasonable chance that he might have embarked on a long-distance journey that wouldn't bring him back to the Perseus Sector for another century or more. It was just the kind of thing he'd pull too. Someone had to find out for sure what had happened to him.

I was elected.

In the past month of biotime, I had traced him through Space Corps records that were three centuries old before I started. He had shipped out on the *Aldebaran* on a mission to the newly scouted worlds of the Taurus sector. The ship had not returned.

It hadn't been hard to trace its path to The Star With No Name, but there the trail stopped cold. There were no records and no indication that the ship had ever passed through the system. The next closest star outbound was 39 Tauri, so there I was.

***

"So here you are," Inoshe said, wiping the foam of a fresh beer from his mouth. "Why did they pick you?"

"It's a long story. Basically, I take after my grandfather. It was my mother's idea – although the decision really was mine. And there was this fight we had at the last family reunion." I shuddered at that memory. "It was her way of getting me out of the house for a few decades. We don't get along well together, needless to say."

"I guess so – if she's willing to send you out here into the teeth of the Zorgon battle fleet."

"She didn't know about them at the time – but I'm sure it wouldn't have mattered. Is there a Zorgon battle fleet? That pilot back there has his doubts."

"Oh, there is one. I've seen it myself. A dozen big ships and a lot more little ones – all sizes and shapes. I've even seen them in action."

"Are you the scout the newspaper was talking about?"

"You mean did I cause the panic? Guilty as charged."

"And how much time do we have before they arrive?"

"A few days – maybe a few weeks. No more than a month, I'd say. I left 95 Tauri just ahead of them. They're coming, all right."

***

A thrashing sound off in the distance echoed down the tunnels and sent a wave of prickling cold up the full width of my back.

"Jimmy?" I called loudly in a voice that was barely under control. There was no reply, and my heart began to pound.

"Jimmy?" Again there was silence for a short interval, then the thrashing sound again, this time more distant and fading. How reassuring it was to know that I wasn't really alone.

Why should I trust Jimmy Inoshe anyway?

I asked myself that as I leaned against the cold, dry stone walls of the tunnel. I had tried the damp walls on the opposite side, but discovered quickly the source of the water in the drains along the floor. The temperature was cool but unchanging, and the air was not as stale as I would have imagined it to be. The tunnel system was big enough – a warren of mines, natural caverns and access shafts to various parts of the spaceport. Jimmy could be gone for days.

Inoshe said he'd just returned from a Century Probe mission to the Hyades when the Zorgons attacked at 111 Tauri. Ironically, he had brought with him all the probe's information on the Zorgons.

Zorgon space extended back as far as the Hyades and beyond. Jimmy had monitored their colony worlds, eavesdropped on their communications and had even recorded signals from asteroid-sized lasers on the far side of the star cluster. The Zorgons may not have reached as far as Orion, but Inoshe was sure they stretched all the way to the Pleiades. That gave them a volume of space 350 years across – thirty times as large as that occupied by humanity.

Like most fleet encounters, the Battle of 111 Tauri had been inconclusive. Historically, it's always been the most difficult task of a fleet commander to bring force against force. With the wide range of spacetime available among the stars, the problem was compounded (if you'll pardon the expression) astronomically.

And even when you find the enemy, you have a damned hard time making him fight. The Battle of 111 Tauri was an object lesson in that tactical and strategic weakness in the use of ships of war. The Zorgons exchanged fire with us, traded casualties ship for ship for a few days, then beat a measured retreat out of the system. No one knew where they fled to, but the available scouts – including Jimmy – were sent out to the nearest stars in the direction of Hyades to track the battle fleet to its lair.

And for most of the intervening five decades, the Taurus Sector had remained quiet – if not at ease.

I'd heard about the battle eighteen years or so back at SAO 39134 and the news was already a couple of years old there. Here at 39 Tauri, it was already thirty-three years since they'd first heard of the clash. That was a long time to wait for the second shoe to drop.

But now they were back.

Jimmy had stumbled through several intervening solar systems before coming across the fleet's hiding place at 95 Tauri about two years after the Zorgons got there, just as they were finishing repairs and refitting – and just before they got underway for 39 Tauri. He collected what information he could, then ran to sound the alarm.

But the question now was, could I trust him?

What was he doing running around underground in the dark? Why had he joined me in a risky bit of housebreaking?

As near as I could guess, the scout felt he had no obligations to anyone.

The world he had left behind on the Century Probe was already two centuries gone and the brief contact with 111 Tauri was another half a century in the distance.

Travelers like me had a few long-lived relationships – however twisted – with their families and other permanent ties to planetary societies. Theoretically, our actions were were supposed to be somewhat constrained. But a loose agent like Inoshe was bound by nothing. He could hop in his scoutship and head starwards to outlive any number of indiscretions.

Of course, I've heard the same objections raised about me and my family. All the more reason to harbor some doubt.

***

"Are they ready for the battle fleet around here?" I had asked him. Inoshe smiled. "Did you see anyone on your way into the system?" I had not.

"I could leave for the Space Corps base at Iota Persei tonight and be back with help in fifty years or so," he said. "But that doesn't make a lot of sense. Actually, according to my standing orders, I should head that way in a few days anyway. Which only goes to show you how useless standing orders are."

"With any luck, I should be on my way by then, too," I said. But something told me that luck would not be on my side.

"So tell me, why did you decide to become a scout? A century is a long time to be gone."

"I'm fourth-generation," Inoshe said. "My folks scouted Poseidon and moved on to the hinterlands after the colony arrived. I've always been curious about the stars. I didn't like it much the way things were when I left – life was too raw around the colonies back then. I thought it would be an easy way to get to the future. And I didn't have any family ties to hold me back."

"I wish I had been as lucky as you," I said before finishing my beer.

***

I left Jimmy Inoshe and went back downstairs into the terminal. At the entrance, a tall, square-jawed man dressed in a khaki Corps uniform stood on a small pedestal.

"Welcome to Minos," he said. "I am Commandant Clifton Powell, administrator of the port. We hope your stay here is a pleasant one."

I was about to thank him when I noticed the fixed stare and the faint gleam in the eyes. After a few seconds, he repeated his greeting. It was a hologram. The real Commandant Powell was probably at home eating supper right now.

For a moment, I wished I was doing the same.

I passed through the terminal entrance and stepped out onto the street. Behind me, the hotel rose from the terminal building on the left, a parking lot stretched out to the right, and before me stood the Minos spaceport.

Minos was a small world, more dry than wet. No oceans, but a lot seas. No continents, just some big rift valleys and stratospheric volcanoes. From space, you could see that the planetary circulation consisted of one big Hadley cell that brought warm air up from the southern hemisphere and dropped it in the north. There were no desert bands up north, though, so it was a safe bet that the pattern was reversed when the seasons changed. The northern arctics were ringed by a fringe of tight little storms and sweeping front lines, while the southern hemisphere was a mottled mass of towering cumulus clouds. From a distance, the planet was mostly a mix of green, blue, and swirling white, home to about three million souls.

There was only the one spaceport. It sat on the eastern edge of a large plain, north of a major rift valley, midway between two giant shield volcanoes, within a few hundred klicks of the planet's equator. According to the Scout Service Handbook, given the topography and the location, it was the best site on the planet for a spaceport.

It was a tight little settlement, with low stone buildings facing the terminal and landing field. The whole place only covered a few square blocks. A wooded hill rose beyond it, less than a half mile away, with the yellow lights of a house on one side and the red air traffic warning lights of a stack of antennas, microwave dishes and other equipment on the other.

Overlooking its neighbors near the center of the settlement was a wide stone tower, three stories tall. From the design, I guessed that it was the local Spacefarers Hall – they look like that on most of the worlds I've been on.

I started walking, just to get rid of nervous tension. In the morning, I would get to work, but for now I just wanted to feel the ground beneath my feet, take a close look at some trees, and smell the moist, earthy perfumes of a planetary atmosphere.

Spaceports all seem to look alike after a while. Everything was within easy walking distance of the terminal, built strong to withstand the occasional explosion of a crashing starship. And like most worlds, the nearest real city was miles away at the other end of a maglev line. The locals never had much to do with spacefarers – mortals and immortals don't mix well, for obvious reasons. That was all right with me. To tell you the truth, sometimes they make me feel like some kind of historic relic.

The streets were as empty as the terminal. I passed a couple of bars and heard muffled voices through open doors, but I didn't go in. There was a bank, a cargo exchange, a couple of offices. I was right – the tower was the Spacefarers Hall, and it stood at the edge of a broad plaza. On one side of the square was a statue of a man in a spacesuit, his helmet in one hand, the other shading his eyes as he looked skyward.

Beyond the statue was the entrance to a park. I hesitated for a moment. There are some planets where it's not safe to walk alone in the park at night. This was a frontier world, so I probably didn't have much reason to be cautious. But there was still that thought.

I steered my way through the wrought iron archway in the blue stone wall and followed the path from one small pool of yellow light to the next, past pines, birches, willows and oak.

The first thing you plant on a new world is trees – usually conifers because they're lower on the evolutionary scale and easier to maintain. Colonizing an alien planet means starting at the ground and working your way up. You're not just transplanting people, you're transplanting a whole ecostructure and you want to do it intact if you can. Scout teams made the first plantings, so when the breakthrough colonies arrived, they already had forests waiting for them. Pine is a good, easy wood to build with, too.

After passing a meadow with tables and fireplace, the path led uphill along a splashing brook. Beyond the gate on the far side of the park, the path emptied out onto another street just across from the house I'd seen from the terminal – a Victorian-style building with gingerbread trim. It looked out of place by fifty years in space and a thousand years in time, but it also looked cozy and inviting. Those are things that really count for people far from their roots.

I walked back down the hill along the street, the high stone wall of the park to my left, feet jarring uncomfortably down the hill. Orion had risen high in the sky and new stars and constellations had come into view. There were a lot of new bright stars across Virgo and Leo that I didn't immediately recognize.

On first impression, the spaceport was a quiet and peaceful place. But it looked like it wasn't going to remain that way for long. I sighed, then headed back towards the terminal.

***

"Good morning, Alex."

It was a soft, husky voice that brought to mind images of a woman I had met on Claudius many years ago.

"It is now a quarter of an hour past local sunrise. You are 32 years, 8 months and 11 days old biotime. It is the year 641 New Era – 410 years real-time since your birth."

Unfortunately, it did not belong to the woman of my dreams, but to my biological alarm clock. When my grandfather gave it to me back at Windsor Academy, it had his voice. One of the first things I'd done was ask the little AI that powered it to change to something more pleasant. The Claudian voice was only the latest change.

After spending the past few weeks on a 30-hour space clock, I still wasn't quite used to Minos's somewhat shorter 22-hour dial. Sunrise was more than just early in the day, it was the middle of what would have been a ten-hour night if I'd stayed in space. But with the Zorgons coming I didn't want to waste time.

After a brief breakfast, I went into the spaceport. It took me a while to find what I was looking for and when I did, I was a little disappointed.

Back on Tik, before I left on my search, I had asked The Wall in the family library to tell me what it could about Grandfather's last recorded journey.

The Wall had dissolved into black space, filled with stars – not like some night sky, but with real depth, the stars of the Perseus and Taurus sectors, stretching in a long arc up and away from me. The Wall traced a bright red line through the sky as it narrated the story of the journey – first over to nearby Mu Cassiopeia, then out to SAO 22341, Iota Persei, and SAO 39134. There it stopped, along with the records that had found their way back to Eta Cass. The Space Corps had never revealed the mission of the *Aldebaran* and the family had never found anyone who could provide more information.

When I arrived on Asgard, I had relied on a holobooth at the Academy to tell me pretty much the same thing. And while The Wall had researched all the records of the den simultaneously, I had to instruct the holobooth to cross-reference the *Aldebaran* and the Space Corps. It was polite enough to ask, of course, but The Wall didn't even have to.

Helvetica offered only a flat video screen at the public information-access booth in the spaceport. Like the others, it was voice-actuated, but you could tell the program that drove it was synthetic. It couldn't carry on a decent conversation for more than a minute.

At Iota Persei, the Space Corps told me what they could over the lasercomm, so I didn't need to land and never got the chance to try their data system – but I suspect it was no more modern than the one back on Helvetica.

When I got to SAO 39134, I found a little planet called Serjanus.

The access booth there also sported a flat screen, but it wasn't for projecting images – it displayed words.

And the pitiful thing I found in the lobby of the Government House here on Minos went one step beneath that – it had a keyboard!

Oh, I'm sure there were AI's like The Wall in use around the planet, but only in private hands. Public technology usually consists of what can be maintained by the local technological base – and out here that was pretty primitive.

The screen displayed an invitation right out of the Dark Ages: "PRESS ANY KEY TO BEGIN."

I sat down before the antique and limbered up my fingers, then pressed the space bar.

"Welcome to the Minos Datanet. Today is Sevensday, the 14th of May. Sunrise is at 0630 and sunset is at 1645. The weather forecast for today is sunny with highs in the 20s. Please enter your full name and place-date of origin."

I supplied the information and a menu appeared.

"PUBLIC INFORMATION ... DIRECTORY ASSISTANCE ... MAIL ... NEWS ... "

I chose the mail. It's always a good idea to check on messages important enough to follow you to the edge of civilization.

There were about a dozen items in the directory, the most recent at the top. Half of them were from Mother – she's always writing to me. A note from my Cousin Ira topped the list, relayed through Delta Tri so it was about as fresh as I could expect – sent nearly twenty years after my departure and left lying around Minos for only a few months. A few messages were from the lawyers who were handling our estate, relayed through both SAO 22341 and Delta Tri according to the routing codes.

Ira's letter looked the most intriguing. What could he have to tell me?

"Dear Alex, beware the Hides of Mars.

"The lawyers are still bleeding us dry trying to sort out what's yours, theirs and ours. No doubt they are letting you know that by separate channels. But what might be of interest to your sweet young hide is the reaction of Cousin Scipio when he returned to Tik after the Reunion to find that he might be in line to inherit a piece of the Regensburg Steiger holdings. As you know, the Skipper bought a second-hand Mastership a few centuries back and has developed an ego to match. Now he is making veiled and unveiled threats about what will happen if you try to come back with some kind of claim on HIS inheritance. Scipio is not one of the healthy pups – like you and me. But I don't need to remind you of that. Just keep an eye on your flanks. Your comrade in arms (and thighs and legs), Ira."

That one puzzled me. Scipio was connected to Grandfather's line, but I didn't remember how. I only knew that he resented me because my father had married into the main Kolberg line, while he remained a distaff member of the den. The status that he had always craved and been denied was mine without effort – and I refused to appreciate it. He was always jealous and hostile – and not just towards me. He'd skipped the Grand Reunion because of bad blood with a number of my more senior uncles. My hope had always been that the asteroid-sized Mastership he bought from a bankrupt Vancouver-Kong firm would be big enough to keep him busy and out of my hair.

Judging from what Ira had said, it was not.

Mother's letters were more entertaining.

The most recent of them told me to ignore the earlier ones, and then ended up repeating their substance – mostly apologies for sending me on a long and dangerous quest, then apologies for causing a scene at the Reunion, followed by self-serving rationalizations about why I shouldn't have argued with her in public, and wrapping up with more accusations about my disloyalty to her, the den and the memory of my father. I skimmed over them without reading too carefully – I'd heard it all before. Her last note said she was leaving for Tik and then a vacation on Earth and hoped I'd be back by the time she returned to the Perseus Sector.

The lawyers were a breeze of fresh air after Mother's sulfurous ventings. They informed me of their latest efforts to inventory the contents of the family estate and urged me to finish my search quickly in order to settle issues that had already remained unresolved for four decades. I wondered if they had grown any more patient in the twenty-five years it took the message to get out to 39 Tauri.

***

When I was finished with the mail, I checked the news. The Zorgons had not arrived overnight. A scan of the interstellar files showed that the worlds of the Perseus Sector were still intact and that all was still well with the den Kolberg commercial empire – or had been two decades ago.

Then after putting it off as long as I could, I plunged into the uninviting depths of the antique database.

I entered the Reference directory and scrolled down to History. Then I asked the system to produce all the index numbers in the local history file that correlated with the Space Corps Cruiser *Aldebaran* or Grandfather's most common names. It took a long time to search the files, two or three minutes at least – it seemed like two or three days. Before it had finished, my heart was pounding out of my chest.

"NO REFERENCES ON FILE," the screen finally replied.

That's what I was afraid of. I asked for a chronological record instead, starting with early Third Century – about thirty years before Grandfather would have arrived. Maybe that would show me something useful.

It did not. Instead of the record, the datanet displayed an apologetic but uninformative message: "RECORDS NOT AVAILABLE."

"Why?" I typed.

"PLEASE CONSULT HUMAN OPERATOR," the datanet replied.

I typed in a pejorative remark and the datanet broke the connection, leaving only the original invitation to press any key. Then I went looking for a human operator.

***

The operator was human and quite female. Her auburn hair clung to her head in tight curls and she'd painted her lips shiny red. She sat behind a counter, seemingly oblivious to the world, paying close attention to her nails. The starched white blouse she wore was tight enough to reveal more than it covered.

I let my eyes linger over her for a moment before drawing her notice by clearing my throat.

"May I be helping you?" she asked.

At least, that's what I think she said. Her words were twisted by echoing nasal cavities and a couple of centuries of separation from the salutary influence of recorded sound on patterns of speech. The effect was unpleasant and unattractive.

"I don't know," I said. "The datanet doesn't seem to have any local information going back more than two hundred years."

"You mean like before the Rebellion?"

"The Rebellion?"

"Of course," she said, wrinkling her nose and pursing her red lips in exaggerated surprise. "There be no records from before the Rebellion. We be rid of them all."

"How thoughtful of you."

"Well, not me personally, you know, but like my descendants be doing it."

"You mean your ancestors.

"That be right."

"So how would I find out about something that happened before the Rebellion? Is there a public library around here somewhere?"

"Oh no," she said, her eyes widening. "We be rid of them, too."

"Of course," I said. What else would you expect? "By the way, do you happen to know who your ancestors rebelled against?"

"I think it be the scouts – or maybe it be the Cold-bergs. It be a couple of years since I got out of school."

"I never would have guessed," I said.

She looked down at her nails and blushed. I turned and started to walk away.

"You could always look in the bookstore, you know," she said as I left. "There be lots of books there. It be not public, but it be the closest thing we be having."

I looked back and smiled at her. "Then I guess it will have to do," I said. "Thank you very much."

She blushed again, and I headed for the door.

***

Anton's Bookstore was a small, crowded shop tucked into a row of similar storefronts on a narrow street on the north side of the spaceport. Displayed in the window was an eclectic mix – old classics with leather bindings and paper pages, plastic tech manuals, cheap paperbound novels with garish covers, electronic books and readers, and stacks of old magazines and newspapers from around human space.

Inside the air was thick with the musty smell of dust and old paper. Bookshelves strained to reach the ceiling, blocking the light from a rusting chandelier in the center of the shop. Fusion lanterns hung from the shelves to illuminate the books, which seemed jammed into every nook and cranny that could be found.

An old man with gray hair and a black handlebar mustache stood at the top of a ladder, a stack of books before him. His back was bowed and his pants were loose and baggy, held up by blue suspenders.

I watched as he looked at the book on the top of the stack, opened it and held it up to the light, then searched the shelf for the right place to put it.

I walked up and down the aisles, inspecting his wares.

A red leather binding with gold embossing caught my eye – "Gone with the Wind." The title page said it had been printed on Asgard in the 3rd Century, but it looked brand new – probably part of a ship's library before some spacer pawned it for bar money.

The next aisle held plastic binders full of technical details on all manner of esoteric and useless machinery. There was nothing here that would be of any use to me, but if he looked hard enough, the master of an old junk could find just what he wanted to repair an antique soliton drive.

Then I noticed an odd bookcase in the rear of the store – tall and ornate with glass doors closed across the front. When I got close I noticed that the doors were locked.

This had to be the special collection.

On the top shelf were books that looked older than time – "Citizen of the Galaxy," "The Forgotten Sodier," "Foundation" and dozens more, about half of which I recognized as titles from old Earth.

In the middle of the case were three rows of untitled books of various sizes and bindings. A few of them were marked with the word "Diary" and a few more were Space Corps-issue record books.

But what caught my eye and held my attention was the centerpiece of the collection – a small steel box with the Space Corps emblem emblazoned on the cover in blue-gray nickel. Engraved beneath the Moon-and-Rocketship were the words: "Ship's Log."

"That one goes back farther than you or I, sonny."

The nasal voice came from overhead, startling and confusing me for a brief instant. Then I looked up and saw the old man peering down at me from the far side of a bookcase, his arms crossed and resting on a row of books.

"Maybe – and maybe not," I said. "How old is it?"

"From before the Rebellion – 4th Century. And it's original, too. Preserved in real-time, not carted around on board a starship. That always makes a book worth more."

"Could I take a closer look?"

"Certainly," he said, disappearing behind the bookshelf. He

emerged a moment later from the end of the aisle, fumbling in deep pockets for a moment, then producing a key. He unlocked the case and drew out the steel box carefully.

The hinged cover was hard to open and squeaked as it moved. Inside was a plain black volume with three gold stripes embossed into the cover. I touched it gingerly to see if it was safe to handle.

"Go ahead, open it up," the old man said.

I did. The inside page bore the legend: "Ship's Log – Space Corps Cruiser *Arcturus* 385 N.E."

I leafed through it, intrigued by the sharp, hand-written entries. The book itself was unusual too. The pages were delicately thin, but seemed strong and indestructible. The paper was smooth as plastic and appeared to be made without fibers. Even the binding, which looked at first glance to be leather, on closer inspection turned out to be synthetic.

"How much do you want for this?" I asked.

"Oh, I'm afraid it's not for sale," said the old man.

"Are you sure? I could meet any price you set."

"Oh no," he insisted. "I happen to love books and the past. This is my pride and joy – like one of my children. None of the books in this case are for sale. They are for looking and reading, but not for selling." "Not even with the Zorgon's bearing down on us?"

He closed his eyes and winced painfully, then shook his head. "Not even then. I will take my chances with my books. They have already survived so much, I think I will be safe."

I frowned, but decided not to press the issue – not now, anyway. But I thought if I drew him out, maybe I could get him to change his mind.

"There's one thing I don't understand," I said. "Why is the ship's log in a bound volume? I thought they recorded those things in databanks like everything else?"

"Why, indeed?" the old man said. "Thereby hangs a tale and half."

***

He rolled the ladder around the aisle and sat down on one of the steps, one brown arm resting on the shelf beside him. His name was Anton – Anton Brochu. I was glad I hadn't made the embarrassing mistake of calling him Mr. Anton.

"Nobody ever thinks about why there are still books around in spite of all the clever electronic ways of storing information," he said. "But the answer is simple: permanence. Books are immutable. You can erase an electronic trace in an instant. Under the proper circumstances, a whole library can drain away right before your eyes as the electrons in a lasertank scatter in all directions. But a book can last forever."

He pulled a thick volume from the shelf beside him and opened it at random. "Look at this paper, sonny. No acid. That's what kills a book. Hand stitching on the binding and acid-free paper and this book will last for centuries. That's real-time. The words won't fall off the page and the story won't get garbled by a virus or a static shock or a stray cosmic ray.

"You can't say that about your electronic books. Sure they're good for keeping a lot of reading in a small space, or for getting words into the hands of a mass of people. But before they put them on disk, they printed them up and put them in libraries – and not those pay-per-view libraries that the Kolbergs run up in Perseus, but real, free public libraries."

He took the log of the *Arcturus* away from me carefully.

"Now this is different. These pages aren't made of paper, but thin sheets of smartskin. You don't write on it with ink, you use a laser. The beam activates pigment in the plastic and turns the page dark as it passes over it. You can erase what you've written with a different frequency of light. A third frequency sets the page and makes it permanent.

"A ship's captain keeps his own personal record of his voyage in there and leaves it behind him before traveling on. That way, if anything happens to his ship, at least a partial account of his mission is preserved somewhere."

"But you're not willing to let it go?" I asked again.

He smiled, but shook his head. "No, I don't think so. This one is special. It's one of the oldest books on the planet – maybe the oldest."

"May I look at it again?" I asked.

He handed it to me carefully, and I tried to pick through the pages as gingerly as possible. Parts of it were scribbled in longhand, others deliberate and clear block printing. And when I turned to the first entry of the log, a powerful chill ran up my spine.

"14.4.385 – Arrived at 39 Tauri in search of Aldebaran."

***

The old man went on about how the log had been handed down throughout families from generation to generation and how they had hidden and protected it during the Rebellion.

But I wasn't really listening. My attention was focused entirely on the words in that first entry. They meant two things. First, the

Aldebaran had indeed been bound for 39 Tauri when it left The Star with No Name. And second, the Space Corps was not telling us the whole story of Grandfather's ship. But why?

I thumbed through the log entries breathlessly, trying to find the answer to that question.

"You're interested in something more than purchasing old books, aren't you?" Anton asked.

I looked up from the pages. His eyes were narrowed and his brow furrowed. He no longer seemed the distracted old man that he had a moment earlier.

"You're right – I am," I said. "I wonder if I could read through this logbook for a few minutes."

He looked me over carefully for a long time, like he was trying to read my character from the cut of my clothes and the cut of my hair. I was glad I'd put on a fresh shirt and shaved within the last twenty-four hours. It must have helped, because he smiled and handed me the metal box to hold while he locked up the case. Then he led me through the aisles to a desk in the rear of the shop. Books were stacked across it like a rising range of mountains and a hooded lantern cast a pool of yellow light onto the chair behind it. He offered me the seat.

It took me half an hour to go through the log. Most of the entries were routine records of astrogational orders, ship's affairs and the captain's visits with the scouts. But there was some useful information in there as well.

The *Arcturus* had set out more than fifty years after my grandfather passed through Iota Per. It had traced Grandfather's steps to the Star With No Name. No Name was one of the stops on *Aldeb's* itinerary, but *Arc* had found something that told them it had gone on to 39 Tauri. The log didn't say what, but the captain was convinced. When they got here, they made a quick search of space and a more detailed search of the surface. No evidence of the cruiser was found in either search.

There was one entry that looked intriguing, but which led nowhere.

"21.6.385 – Completed survey of scout genealogy. Results positive."

Had they been trying to track down crew members from the *Aldebaran* who had jumped ship to remain on Minos? Or survivors of a crash? Genealogical records would have been an obvious avenue of research.

"Results positive," it said. If that was their purpose, that meant that someone from *Aldeb* had made planetfall. But who and why?

Arc had remained in the system for three months before continuing on to 104 Tauri. Nothing in the log contained any information about the *Aldebaran* or what it had been doing. But the Corps hadn't told us it sent another ship looking for the *Aldebaran*, so they must have thought it was something important – too important to share with den Kolberg, I guess.

In the end, I was left with few answers and a lot of questions.

Aldebaran had been here. *Arcturus* couldn't find it. Someone had probably stayed behind, but who, why, and for how long were still a mystery to me.

Two things were certain, however. My job was getting tougher, and my time was only getting shorter.

***

"I guess what I'm really looking for is a book like this for a cruiser named *Aldebaran*," I told Anton. "You wouldn't know anything about that, would you?"

He put his elbow in one hand and twisted his mustache with the other thoughtfully for a long moment.

"You know, you're the second one in a month to come through here asking about that. If there is such a book – and I'm not sure there is – it would be worth its weight in platinum. I've read as much of that as you have, and I know the *Aldebaran* was supposed to have come through this system before the breakthrough colony. If it did, there should have been a logbook for it left somewhere on the planet. That doesn't mean it's still here – three centuries is a long time to expect it to stay put."

"This one did," I said, raising the *Arc's* log.

"That's right – thanks to a scout family that had some respect for the written record of history. But who's to say what kind of troglodyte may have gotten his hands on the log you're looking for? The Rebellion was kind of hard on things that reminded people here of their ties to the rest of human space – books and records especially."

"Does that mean it isn't worth wasting my time looking for it?"

"Not necessarily," Anton said. "There are a few collectors around who might have gotten a hold of it. Most of them would have bragged about it to me as soon as they did, but not all of them."

"And who are they?"

The old man scratched his head and looked at me again.

"Look," I said, "I'm not a book collector. I want the information that's in it. I'm trying to find my grandfather. He was aboard the *Aldebaran* when it left for 39 Tauri and he never returned. If you can tell me something that would help me find him, I'd owe you an awful lot."

"You probably would," he said. "I suppose that wouldn't be a bad thing – having a den Kolberg in my debt."

I laughed sharply. No wonder he was being so cagey. He must have known all along who I was. "Word must get around this place fast," I said.

"Fast enough," he said. "We don't trust offworlders much, but den Kolberg has a special place in our hearts. Minoans are downright hateful when it comes to your clan. That's what the Rebellion was all about, you know."

"That was two centuries ago," I said.

"In some ways, planets are the same as your people – the persistence of memory, you know."

"Does that mean you won't tell me where to look for the logbook?"

"No – it just means that you'll owe me a favor in return."

"And what's that?"

"I won't know that until the time comes, will I?"

I smiled. "No, I guess not."

"The first place you should look is with the last man who came here asking about it. His name is Skanderi – he's a real sky merchant, wheeling and dealing all the time. He flew in a couple of months back. You'll find him around the spaceport somewhere – probably in one of the bars."

"And the local collectors?"

"There's only one around here who would keep a find like that a secret," Anton said, sticking his head past a bookshelf and looking out the front window. He stuck out a thumb and pointed it up the street. "Commandant Powell – in the house up on the hill."

***

Milos Skanderi was a restless man. He couldn't even hold still while playing backgammon. When I walked into the Orbit Lounge, he was sitting with his back against a wall, faced off over the board against a man wearing a uniform with sergeant's stripes. As quick as the dice were out of the cup, he was moving his pieces.

The sergeant was slower to act, and while he waited, Skanderi played with his glass, dipping a finger into the brown liquid it held, and running it around the rim until the glass sang.

At first I took him for a Periclean. He had the tight, tense look of a heavyworlder. But when I looked closer, I realized he was just wiry and drawn, without a gram of excess flesh on him. His face was creased and his skin weathered and dark.

It hadn't taken long to find him. The owner of the first bar I stopped at made me wait while he phoned Skanderi at the Orbit, then sent me over to meet him.

I pulled up a chair, sat down at the table beside them and watched them.

He was a cool, scientific player who knew the moves for every combination of dice and executed them quickly. He slowed only briefly, when his options were plentiful, and attacked at every opening. It was over in a hurry.

"Good game," the soldier said. I noticed a nameplate that said "Mulak" and a pair of combat ribbons tacked over his pockets. One I recognized from the Helvetica Uprising. I bristled at the sight of it, but I kept my feelings to myself – I'm not fond of the soldiers who had passed through that world.

"Can I take a shot at the board?" I asked.

Skanderi looked up, tossed back the rest of his drink and waved Sergeant Mulak away. I took his place and Skanderi set up the pieces. He set a gold coin on the bar – a 10-unit piece from Pericles. I matched it with a Asgardian 5-credit gold piece of at least the same size.

The play went quickly as I tried to match his breakneck pace. I knew all the moves, too, and tried to match his ruthless offense.

"So you want to make some kind of a deal or what?" There was a nasal, whining tone to his voice.

"That depends on what you know about the logbook of the *Aldebaran*," I said. "I hear you've been looking around for it."

"Could be," he said. He rolled doubles and moved ahead quickly, doubling the bet without expression.

"Did you want to buy it or sell it?" he asked abruptly.

I balked at the question, then turned it around. "Do you have it or not?"

"I deal in special merchandise," he said. "Low-volume, high-margin stuff. Antiques, rare books, information. For the right price, I could tell you where the book is. For a little more, I could get it for you."

"How much will you pay me if I get it for you?" I asked.

His eyes widened with surprise, and he stopped to pour another drink from the bottle beside his glass. Two lucky rolls later, he had two pieces left on the board, and I had four. He reached into his pocket, pulled out one more coin, and set it on the pile. I pulled out another to match it. Then I rolled doubles and swept my pieces away. I picked up the two stacks of coins, spread them across the palm of my hand and examined them.

"Ten times that if you bring it to me by tomorrow night," he said.

"One hundred."

"Twenty."

"Thirty and it's a deal."

"Agreed," he said. "Good luck."

"Where is it?"

"Up on the hill. Commandant Powell has it in his library. You shouldn't have any trouble finding it. It's still in the box."

We didn't shake hands. There were a lot of things I hadn't told Skanderi. I was sure there were a lot of things he wasn't telling me.

Here was a man who had nothing to lose – a man no one could trust.

But he did offer to buy me lunch. I accepted the invitation, and we sat for a while. I told him where I'd traveled, but without giving away my family affiliations. Despite the episode in the bookstore, I didn't assume he knew I was den Kolberg.

Skanderi was a dealer and a trader in historical treasures. His ancestors had come from Trebizond and Persia, Venice and the Levant, and bequeathed him with a talent for bargaining and an eye for value. He said he'd just come through the Gemini Sector, past Castor and Pollux, following the trail of pioneering colonists to rescue their relics from time's harsh crucible. Now he was working his way back Solwards through Taurus and Perseus. He'd been on Minos for a few months, he said, long enough to pick through the local antiques and find what was worth the coin to add to his stock.

Sergeant Mulak resumed the backgammon tournament with Skanderi and lost several silver coins during lunch.

At first, I thought he was the trader's companion, but it turned out he had business of his own on Minos.

"I'm looking for a few good men," he said. "Men with training and skill who are willing to risk everything to defend humanity from the alien threat. Men who have what it takes to be a member of Brook's Battalion."

"Business must be picking up now that we know they're coming," I said.

He took the remark seriously. "Not fast enough. Not by half. We still have officer billets open, if you're interested. You look like you have the stuff. And we can always use pilots."

"Have you been at this long? What's your service record look like?" I asked, eyeing his Helvetican Campaign ribbon.

"We've been established for fifty years of real-time," he said. "The battalion was formed right after Tauri 111."

"What about you personally?" I asked. "When did you join up?"

"I've got six years biotime with Colonel Brook. Before that, I was with the Helvetican Planetary Guard. We've got quite a few Guard veterans on our roster."

"I would think so," I said. "Especially after the Uprising."

"My stint came after that, so I wouldn't be able say. It's the same for the rest of my mates, too."

He was lying. The campaign ribbon he wore had been handed out only to combat veterans. But I wasn't going to challenge him on it, and I was careful not to look at the ribbon again too closely. I didn't blame him for wanting to dissociate himself from the bloody role the Planetary Guard had played in crushing the Radical uprising. That was an insignificant sin compared to the crimes Mulak and his fellow guardsmen had committed.

It was becoming difficult for me to restrain my feelings, however, so I decided it was time to leave. As I stood to go, Mulak handed me a business card.

"When things start to get hot, you may want to have us on your side," he said. "You'll find us out at Building #17 on the landing field."

I thanked him and left before he could shake my hand or clap me on the back. I didn't want the man to touch me.

***

An overly devious mind can end up wasting a lot of time. The first thing I decided to do was to pay a visit to Commandant Powell's house.

The old Victorian-style house was so completely out of place, but it looked perfectly suited for the hilltop, framed by two tall pines and decorated with rows of yellow and red flowers. It sported bright vermilion trim on the windows and the porch railings, and blue stripes in three shades ringed the upper floor.

I knocked on the front door gently.

There was no answer.

So I walked back down the hill empty-handed and decided to try my luck at the terminal building where I'd first seen Powell's hologram. The entrance to the administrative wing was screened carefully to make it look inconspicuous, but not invisible. Powell's office was guarded by a gray old woman behind a large empty desk. AIs did most of the office work. The woman was there to answer calls and screen visitors. Today, since Powell was away, she didn't even have to do that.

She seemed to enjoy the opportunity to reject every caller, no matter how important or influential – and some of them sounded quite important, judging by the titles she used.

I had a long time to listen to her – I spent much of the afternoon there. When the light began to fade, she stood up and came out from behind the desk. She smiled, took a light wrap from a closet, threw it over shoulders and left. I waited about ten minutes before I followed. Devious minds aren't the only ones that can waste time – and what time I had was becoming more precious every hour.

***

I caught up with Jimmy Inoshe at a place called the Planetfall Bar. It was the nicest watering hole I'd seen at the spaceport, with dark wood paneling, a faded red carpet, and leather upholstered chairs. There was even a live bartender, mixing drinks and putting a perfect head on each mug of beer.

Jimmy was sitting at a table with a white-haired man when I came in. I eavesdropped on their conversation while I waited for the bartender to pour me a mug.

"The Zorgons have been a spacefaring species far longer than we have," the old man was saying. "There are a number of problems posed by relativistic flight that we are just confronting. The Zorgons, on the other hand, had to solve or circumvent those problems many centuries ago. For example, their region of space is so vast that they have lost any meaningful communication with the center of their civilization, let alone the distant edges. Oh, like us, they receive regular news from the frontiers, but like us, it's all one-way and it's centuries old by the time they hear it. Two-way correspondence is reserved for those with the wherewithal to await a reply.

"Now think of what that must mean for their military organization. There can be no waiting for orders from a higher command. Battle fleets must be entirely on their own. Regional commands may have some control over the fleet units, but only in the most general terns. What little we've learned from the Zorgons whom we've questioned tends to confirm the independence of the battle fleet commander.

"What that means to us is simple but frightening – when the Zorgon commander gets here, he may have no idea what to do and no specific orders to give him directions."

"Wouldn't there be some kind of standardized doctrine?" I asked, setting my glass on the table and slipping into a chair.

Jimmy smiled when he saw me. "Alex, this is Professor Elliot Solomon, formerly of the Orion University history department on Bedford at Xi Orionis. Professor, my friend, Alex Kolberg."

Professor Solomon squinted at me, then nodded his head vigorously in greeting. His face was thickly wrinkled, and his white hair barely covered his pink scalp. The parchment-thin skin on the backs of his hands was covered with dark liver spots.

"The professor is on a sabbatical. He thought it would be interesting to make a Great Circle tour of the outer sectors and watch history unfold along the way."

"There are many advantages to being a historian who travels from star to star," Solomon said. "The one I look forward to the most is an advance in medical science that can turn back the clock of age. I believe some form of rejuvenation will be necessary before I can finish the history book this trip will produce.

"To answer your question, sir, the Zorgons presented us with an example of their doctrine at the Battle of 111 Tauri: Fight when confronted with an armed adversary – run when you've learned what you can about him."

"And try again somewhere else when you've passed along word of the contact," Jimmy said.

"Evidently," Solomon said. "I must say I hadn't planned to get quite so close to history as this."

"None of us ever does, Professor," I said.

Jimmy got up for a refill, and Professor Solomon excused himself and went to the bathroom. I was surprised to see how spry the old man was as he walked the length of the bar. When Jimmy returned I told him what I'd learned at Anton's Book Shop and about my meeting with Skanderi.

"Historical treasures? Sounds like a graverobber to me," the scout said.

"He gives me a chill," I said. "His homeostate is cranked up just a little too high for me. And I don't like the company he keeps."

"But he told you where the book is?"

"Yes – if he's to be believed." I told him of the afternoon's wasted efforts.

"So what are you going to do now?"

"I thought I might stake out his house tonight and see if he's home."

"And if he's not?"

"Well ... there are alternatives."

"You mean like going into Commandant Powell's house without an invitation?"

"Sort of."

"Alex, have you ever done anything like that before?"

I looked down at the floor where a dark stain ran under the table leg. "Back at the Academy, the cadets had their own brand of midnight drills. We'd go through the adjutant's office looking for racy magazines, cigarettes and beer."

"Alex, housebreaking is not the same as stealing holograms of naked girls from the adjutant's office. There are certain rules."

"And how would you know?"

"A scout has to be prepared to do a lot of things – especially on a world full of aliens. You're going to need some help."

"What kind of help?"

"Meet me in the park after it gets dark."

"And what can you do that I can't? This isn't your trouble, Jimmy. You don't have to get involved."

He said nothing, but lifted his glass and smiled.

"Where in the park?" I asked.

"I'll find you," he said before he got up and walked away.

***

Supper was a cold meat sandwich and another beer at the Planetfall. The bartender told me what kind of meat, but I didn't recognize the name and couldn't pronounce it. The bread was buttery sweet and nutty brown and, I'm sure, locally baked.

Professor Solomon and I swapped space stories. He'd done some traveling in places I'd never seen and in return, I told him what I knew about Helvetica. He was fascinated by my insider's view of the uprising and delighted at the chance to acquire a story that other historians would be willing to kill for. He asked if he could have his AI record what I told him and when I gave him my permission, he offered to pay for my sandwich. I thanked him and told him it wasn't necessary.

He'd already heard the public lies that den Kolberg circulated about Helvetica – how a group of emigrants from Zoroaster tried to start a revival of the old den loyalties and how, a generation after their arrival, they used their movement as a front for the Radicals in an attempt to seize power. I told him the truth – how my family engineered the uprising, working twenty years to poison the minds of the Helveticans against the Zoroastrans, how they paid to ferry in military units from nearby systems, and how they defeated the immigrants in a short, bloody war.

Darkness fell over the streets of the spaceport before I knew it. How many hours did my clock say Minos had in a day? I excused myself quickly, promising the professor I would finish my story soon. Then I ducked out the door and headed for the park.

A sigh of moist air, sweet with the scent of wet vegetation, breathed through the entrance to the park. The lighted path ran off to the left and right, winding through the trees. The sound of splashing water echoed in the the depths of the dark, playing soft accompaniment to the hissing and clicking of chites.

There was no one in sight.

I walked a short distance through the woods to the left – the general direction of the Powell house, if my bearings were correct. I whistled a short tune, forgot the notes and repeated the ones I knew.

"Alex."

The whisper seemed to come from nowhere. I looked around. I was about halfway between the pathlights, surrounded by long shadows. There was nothing around me but a neatly mown lawn beyond a low curb and a few trees.

"Jimmy?"

"Right here," the whisper replied.

I turned around in a full circle, straining my eyes to penetrate the darkness. I looked up into the limbs and branches high overhead and crouched low to shift perspective. Still no scout.

"What's the matter, Alex?"

"All right, I give up. You can come out now."

The slightest of motions gave him away. I watched with amazement as a piece of shadow drew away from a low tree limb and dropped to the ground. It remained a shadow even as it crossed the lawn and stood before me.

"Jimmy?" I asked, with a deeper note of confusion.

He was dressed in black from head to toe, a tight hood over his head with only a rectangular slit for his eyes, which had vanished behind black greasepaint. Gloves covered his hands and boots his feet. He pulled the hood from his head, revealing a line of grinning white teeth that seemed to dazzle in comparison to his uniform.

"What is that outfit?" I asked.

"It's an ancestral costume – unique to Nippon. I'm surprised you don't recognize it – they were pretty popular in the publoid videos when I left home. The Scout Service taught me the secrets of my ancestors as an added touch – figured it would come in handy infiltrating the Zorgon worlds. They were right, too. You wouldn't believe some of the places I've been inside."

"Save it for some other time," I said. "Let's go pay a call on Commandant Powell first."

"I'll be right beside you," he said as he replaced his hood and melted back into the shadows. I felt strange, walking through the park alone, but knowing that he was there someplace not far away. It only took a few minutes to reach the Victorian house, a mercifully short interval.

A porchlight burned at the front door, but the rest of the place looked dark. I cursed under my breath. I'd wanted to talk to Powell and ask him for his help. I'd been a Space Corps officer for a few years and I still held a reserve commission. I thought I could rely on his sense of honor.

"I'm going to go up and check anyway – just to see if someone's home," I said to the darkness, hoping I'd get a reply.

"By all means," Jimmy answered from somewhere to my rear. "First rule of housebreaking is to make sure the house is empty. The law considers it a much more serious crime if someone is home when you break in."

"That's reassuring," I said. "You sound as if you can't wait."

"Can you?"

"I'd like to try the direct approach first."

***

A hologram of a silver-haired woman appeared in mid-air above the porch when I knocked on the door.

"The Commandant and I are out at the moment, but please feel free to leave a message at the sound of the tone," she said.

I said nothing, but walked back down the steps. Jimmy seemed to have disappeared, but I couldn't tell for sure. At least he had nothing to say. Then I heard a hiss in the bushes a short distance away.

"This way," he said.

I followed and in a few minutes, we were behind the house in the middle of the back yard.

"The security on this place is pretty minimal," Jimmy said. "Most of it is up front and around the doors. We could get in through a window, but I don't think that'll be necessary."

He pointed a black cylinder with a pistol grip at the house. Then he took a box no bigger than a deck of cards out of his pocket and waved it around in the air.

"The cellar would be a good place to try, but those are usually closed with your basic mechanical lock. We want to try subtlety before brute force. Just stay behind me while I neutralize the intruder scan." He drew the cylinder and aimed it at the house again as we advanced on the back porch. When we got to the back door, he gave the device to me. "Point this at the corner of the roof up there."

He performed some kind of electronic magic on the door itself and it popped open. We hurried inside.

A dim light burned over the kitchen sink. "I hope there's no one else in here," I said a low voice.

"Not according to my instruments," Jimmy said.

He took the lead as we walked down a high-ceilinged hallway. A wide staircase ran up to the second floor on the left. Paintings on the wall depicted a spacer's wife, the sun reflecting off the curved hull of a spaceship, and the ice-capped mountains of Asgard.

We paused in the darkness at the end of the hall. Jimmy peered through the open doorway to the right, and I guarded to the left. A sudden motion in that direction made my heart stop – until I realized that it was just my reflection in a mirror. My skin buzzed in a delayed reaction to the surprise.

"This looks like the living room," Jimmy said. "Which way is the library?"

"Are you sure there's a library?"

"There must be. Let's try this door."

We stepped into a room cloaked more deeply in darkness. A tiny speck of red laser light appeared and ran around the walls. Then Jimmy produced a handtorch that seemed to fill the room with light. "This is it," he said as he turned on a desklamp.

"Where do we start?" I asked.

Bookshelves lined the walls, some reaching to the ceiling, others only halfway with paintings filling the space above them. The art was crude – amateur paintings from Space Corps artists filling the offwatch hours on patrol. The largest of them looked like a space battle with exploding warships.

"Under 'L' for logbook. Or maybe 'A' for Aldebaran"

"Skanderi said it was still in the box," I said, inspecting a desktop cluttered with notes and books. Resting on top as a paperweight were four flat translucent stones with small symbols engraved on them. "What are these?"

"Heiroglyphs. From the Ancient Aliens. He must be an amateur archaeologist. They like to translate the pictures."

I looked under the papers, but there was no sign of the box or a leatherbound logbook. I started looking through the desk drawers.

"What have we got here?" Jimmy said. "Alex, this looks interesting."

He had been looking through the books in a cabinet beside the large painting. I joined him and began checking titles. Specifications for the Prometheus Class Lander. Diary of Commander Jiang Shi, Space Corps. U.S. Navy Regulations. Tech Manual 3-193 – Forcible Entry. The History of the Taurus Sector. This was the right shelf. But after a few minutes of searching, we came up with nothing.

I pulled out the history book and began looking through it. It was a limited edition, published on Minos and signed by the author. A bookmark stuck out of one end, so I opened it to the page Powell had marked.

The heading in the middle of the page said "Pre-Colonial Space Corps Missions." I scanned the paragraphs furiously, looking for clues. There was a mention of the *Arcturus* and how it came looking for the *Aldebaran* – and that was all. Nothing I didn't already know.

Jimmy wasn't looking at books. He had his pocket laser out and was examining the painting.

"Is that supposed to be the Battle of 111 Tauri?"

"Probably. The ships are too close together, though. It isn't authentic. Here we go ... just as I suspected." He did something to the picture frame and the whole thing, painting and all, swung away from the wall, revealing a safe mounted behind it.

"Say Alex, wasn't there an honor code at Windsor Academy?" Jimmy asked as he looked through the equipment in a pouch at his belt, withdrew something and placed it on the door of the safe.

"Cadets shall not lie, cheat, or steal. Why?"

"How did you and your buddies get around it when you went on your night maneuvers?"

"It wasn't easy," I said, remembering the more exciting days of my youth.

"We left the magazines in the office, so there was no problem with them. The cigarettes, we paid for. There was always loose change in the desk drawer for the snack machine, so we just added what was due to the kitty."

"What about the beer?"

"Well...we never did much more than look at it and talk about what it would be like to drink a whole bottle all at once."

Jimmy laughed sharply, then grew suddenly quiet. He opened the door to the safe and shined his handlamp inside. We bumped foreheads trying to look in at the same time. The only thing in the compartment was a small stack of hieroglyphs

"It's not there," I said.

"That's too bad. Do you suppose he reads it at night before he goes to sleep?"

***

We never got a chance to look. We were at the foot of the stairs when I heard the front door open.

Jimmy took the lead as we rushed back down the hallway. The sound of voices was like an alarm siren behind us. The lights came on and the kitchen door at the far end of the hall looked years away. I knew we wouldn't make it without being discovered. I only wondered if Powell would give chase before we got out of the house.

Then Jimmy stopped, hooking my arm and pulling me against the wall with him. He hugged the woodwork, turning the knob on the door where we had halted. He peaked in, then he yanked on my arm and pushed me through. He was beside me in the dark a second later, shutting the door without even squeaking a hinge.

"Down," he whispered. He pulled me along, and I felt my foot drop off the edge of the floor. With no light, the steps took me unprepared, and I struggled for balance. Jimmy steadied me and helped me down the stairs into what had to be the basement.

I could hear the sighing of floorboards overhead as the Powell's entered the house. Now that the moment of terror had passed, I had time to think. Where was Jimmy taking us? Did he have some alternate exit in mind or was he just planning on waiting until everyone went to bed?

His pocket laser flashed across the walls and gave some dimension to the black emptiness before us. I followed along blindly until Jimmy stopped me. He made some mechanical sounds with something in front of us, then I heard the distinctive sound of an airtight door being unsealed. Jimmy dragged me along, stopping to seal the door behind us.

Then he turned on a light.

"That's better," he said. We stood in a narrow tunnel carved from native rock and smeared with damp mold. The floor was smooth and glassy – fused by the heat of the rock-cutters – and water seeped from cracks in the walls.

"Where are we?" I asked.

"An escape tunnel. They're all over the place, under the spaceport everywhere. They built them about thirty years ago, after the first word of the Battle came through. Haven't seen much use lately, though, I'd bet."

"You've been down here before?"

"Nope. This is my first time. Looks like fun, though."

"I take it you have a map of some kind."

"Nope. Not even a clue. We'll just have to play it by ear. Unless you have doubts about the ability of a scout to find his way around."

"Not at all," I said, trying hard to lie convincingly.

***

We hadn't gone more than a hundred meters, down slopes and steps cut sharply into the rock, before we reached the branching where Jimmy left me. Why did trusting him make me feel so helpless?

Why did I trust him in the first place?

Because he had trusted me, I suppose. You only get trust for trust. And soon after that fact dawned on me, a soft voice whispered in my ear: "Alex, I'm back."

I must have jumped a meter, because I hit my head on the ceiling of the tunnel.

He turned on the light and helped back to my feet.

"This way," he said.

The tunnel led downwards, sometimes steeply, but usually not. For the first ten minutes, the walls were unbroken, but after that, side galleries appeared. Some of them cut smoothly like the main tunnel, others hacked out of the rock and shored up with heavy wooden beams.

"So what happened to the logbook?" Jimmy asked. "Why wasn't it there?"

"That's easy. Skanderi lied."

"You think so?"

"He is a very precise character. He told me the logbook was sitting in Powell's library, still in the box. Either he knew what he was talking about, or he was making it up. If he was worried about telling the truth, he wouldn't have been so exact, and risk being wrong. So I figure he lied."

"That makes sense."

"Which means Powell doesn't have the book."

"Sounds logical. Who does?"

"Who do you think?"

The tunnel leveled off and widened out. From the look of it, we'd left behind the more recent construction and entered an area that dated back into earlier history. The walls showed tool marks, and the ceilings were braced with more wooden beams. The wood didn't look too healthy, although a smelly sealant of some sort had been sprayed on it.

"This place reminds me of my Great-Aunt Voia's horror stories."

"How so?"

"Voia came from Romanian stock. She used to tell us stories about the Securitate."

"Security Toddy?"

"Securi-TAH-te. Secret police. According to Voia, they lived in tunnels under the city. They'd use electronic equipment to watch people above the ground – bad little boys and girls in particular. Especially rich ones. At night, they'd pop up out of the graveyards, carrying machine guns, and kidnap little children."

"How delightful. And how old were you when she told you those stories?"

"Just four years biotime. They've stuck with me ever since. Scared the living hell out of me at the time, though."

"I would think so. Sounds a little sadistic to me."

"No more than the rest of my family."

"Just how did you get picked to come looking for your grandfather anyway?"

"It's a long story. Basically, I made the mistake of telling my mother how I felt about her and the rest of the family. The mistake was to do it in public, at a family reunion, in front of a good number of people. I made a second mistake by mentioning something about wanting to take a hundred-year circuit so I could come back after den Kolberg had lost its power and wealth. A couple of days later, the opportunity came up."

"And then your mother made you come looking for him?"

"Actually, no. The decision was mine – no matter what she thinks. I'd been waiting for a good excuse to fly the family coop for years. Too many years. It's funny – that argument on the lawn at the Grand Reunion was just six weeks ago biotime. Now it's fifty years later. I'm not used to dropping years quite that fast."

"I know what you mean. No matter what you leave behind, it chills your soul. Sometimes, I feel like time is blowing through me like the wind. Sounds like you and your mother have some history."

"Are you familiar with the geodesics in the Perseus Sector?" I asked. "Remotely."

"You know that the geodesics from Helvetica to Eta Cass and Mu Cass are only a couple of degrees apart? It's twenty years from Helvetica to Eta Cass, fourteen to Mu Cass and six from Mu to Eta. You only lose two weeks if you make the side trip to Asgard."

"That's one I never heard of before, but I've never traveled that direction."

"When I was four years old biotime, my mother and I took off from Helvetica for Eta. My father was supposed to follow us in a couple of weeks. He did, but when he got to Eta, he found out that mother had gone by way of Mu Cass. And he found out that she'd left me there at Windsor Academy.

"He and Grandfather left for Mu Cass immediately. They found me as soon as they landed on Asgard. I was a year short of graduation from the academy."

"I guess the stories are true – den Kolberg really does eat its own young."

"That's putting it mildly," I said.

"So you grew up away from the rest of your family?"

"Happily."

"That explains it."

"Explains what?"

"The reason I came back for you."

There was a long silence while I thought about that answer. I didn't like it, but I didn't know what to do about it. I decided there wasn't much to do – he was probably right.

"Hey, hold up here!"

The tunnel branched out, offering us three choices.

"Now what?" I asked.

"The one on the right leads away from the spaceport. The one on the left leads into the middle of it and the one in the center should take us towards the landing field. Any preferences?"

"I want to go back to my ship and think this over," I said.

"Fine. Forward, it is."

A few minutes later we reached the dead end of the blind alley and retraced our steps. We took the turning that led into the middle of the spaceport. After a short distance, we came upon a ladder leading up through a shaft in the ceiling.

"This looks like a good place to try," Jimmy said.

"Tell me something. If you knew about these tunnels, why didn't you use them to get into Powell's house?"

"I couldn't disable his alarms from behind that airtight door. Besides, where's the challenge in that?"

He climbed the ladder and disappeared, leaving me in utter darkness once more. It felt colder without the light, but I was probably imagining things. Then I heard Jimmy's muffled voice above me. "Come on up."

I made my way up the ladder despite the darkness and about halfway up, I could smell fresh air. Jimmy was at the top to give me a hand as I climbed out. There seemed to be no more light above the ground than below, then I realized we were in an alley behind two rows of buildings. I took a few steps and found I could see the top of the Spacefarers Hall.

Jimmy closed the manhole in the pavement and brushed himself clean.

"The terminal building is out this way. You can go on alone. I'll find my own way back to my ship. In this get up, I tend to attract attention if I walk in the lighted parts of town."

"Thanks. Actually, I have an idea that I want to check on. If it works out, we may have more to do tonight. Don't change clothes until I get back to you."

"Whatever you say, chief," the scout said, bowing deeply before disappearing into the shadows.

***

A couple of hours later, I found Skanderi in the Asteroid Lounge, a foul-smelling place with a computerized liquor dispenser, dirty windows and a clientele that made me wonder if giving up tae-kwon-do practice had been such a good idea. He was in the back, playing mah-jong with a handful of short, broad-shouldered men of Asian descent. Money was piled high on the table and I noticed that all the players were armed except Skanderi himself.

I wondered if he was being bold or naive – or if he had someone backing him up. I looked around the bar and saw a big man sitting in a dark corner behind a flat beer. He was alone and from where he sat he could cover the door and the gamblers. It looked like he had his eyes closed, but I knew better than to believe that.

I made sure I didn't turn my back on him as I approached Skanderi's table.

"I came to see if we still had a deal," I said when he looked up. I looked into his eyes, but they registered no surprise or any other emotion.

"Deal? You mean the logbook? I guess we still have a deal. Why?"

"It's just now that I've seen it, I think I want to renegotiate the price." I pulled a small steel box from my jacket pocket and held it where he could see the Space Corps Moon-and-Rocketship on the cover.

I remembered the look on his face from earlier in the day, when I rolled doubles at the backgammon board, the way his eyebrows went up. They arched even higher when he saw the box, and Skanderi began to fidget with the coins before him.

"How much are you asking for?" He didn't even miss a beat.

"Ten times the original deal."

He scowled. Even though I kept my eyes fixed on him, my attention was focused on the big man in the corner. So far, he remained still, but his eyes were open wide now.

"That wasn't our deal. I don't think the book is worth it."

"It is to me," I said as I slipped the steel box back into my pocket. "I guess I'll hold onto it then. Too bad we couldn't do business."

Disengagements are the most difficult military movement. It was hard keeping my face to Skanderi and his heavyweight companion, but I managed to avoid knocking over chairs or customers on my way to the door. I watched a short interplay between the two men, a questioning glance and a rejection. I wasn't sure I was reading it correctly, but it looked like Skanderi was letting me get away.

Once outside, I ducked down an alleyway and stepped into a dark corner where I could still see the entrance to the Asteroid Lounge. Skanderi had a dilemma of his own now. Should he send his goon after me and leave himself undefended inside the bar? Or should he take a break from the game and stay close to his firepower? Considering the amount of money on the table in front of him, I didn't think the other players would appreciate it if he left early. But the man in the corner looked like he could settle any arguments that arose.

I was only slightly surprised to see Skanderi come out first.

They way I figured it, if the enforcer came first, looking for me, then Skanderi had questions that he'd neglected to ask. But if my hunch was right, he wouldn't care about me. He would be too concerned about something else. And he would be in too much of a hurry to try following me.

I was right. Skanderi took off briskly towards the terminal building and the landing field.

I hoped Jimmy was on his way, following the trader.

I waited a few minutes to see if anyone followed Skanderi. I wasn't disappointed. He was barely out of sight when the door to the Asteroid Lounge burst open and one of the mah-jong players came flying out backwards into the street. He landed on his back and didn't move.

The big man from the corner followed, walking slowly but deliberately, and poked at the figure on the ground with his toe. Satisfied that his work was finished, he took off quickly after Skanderi. I decided to follow him.

I stayed with him as far as the avenue along the landing field. Skanderi was waiting for him on the other side, at one of the gates in the high fence that ringed the field. They stopped, talked for a while, then passed through the gate and disappeared into the darkness beyond.

But I was stuck. The gate was well lighted. While I couldn't see Skanderi and his mate, they would be able to see me from anywhere on the field. Now it was up to Jimmy Inoshe – although I wasn't sure how he was going to get past the fence.

The next ten minutes were a slow, painful torture. Then I heard a familiar voice speaking from the shadows.

"They're in one of the hangars," Jimmy said. "Up at the north end of the field. It's the building closest to the terminal – Number 48. I'll meet you when you get here."

"How do I get through that gate without being seen? It's all lit up, you know."

"Don't worry about it. They're both inside." I heard a rustling sound and realized I was alone.

I went through the gate, feeling terribly exposed. A short while later, I found the building. I also discovered that Jimmy was wrong – they weren't both inside. The heavyweight was coming back out, maybe to patrol the grounds, maybe to look for me. Whatever the reason, I saw the big man open a door in the side of the hangar, pause for a moment while framed in the light behind him, then step out into the night.

I was still fifty meters or more from the place at the time. When I got closer, I saw Jimmy. A shadow suit only works in the shadows. He was peering through a window in the rear of the building, silhouetted against a faint glow from inside. I realized that if I could see him, so could the watchdog.

I quickened my pace, but it wasn't enough. The big man was between me and the scout, leaving me little in the way of options. I remembered what I had been told years ago about disabling kicks and aiming points. The hard part would be getting muscles that were unpracticed and out of shape to lift and stretch the way they used to.

A quick shot to the kidneys with the toes followed by a slap to the head with the side of the foot ought to do the trick.

Jimmy continued to watch through the window, oblivious the threat that was approaching. I was almost on top of them by now.

Then, just as the big man came within Jimmy's reach, the scout spun around. Hands and feet flew quickly, and the goon was left lying on the ground.

I wasn't sure why I'd even bothered to come along.

Skanderi was opening a safe in an office in the rear of the hangar when we found him. We caught him just as he grabbed for something inside. I reached in and pulled out a needler. And something else.

"Looking for this?" I asked, holding up a steel box with the Space Corps emblem on the cover. It was heavier than the one in my jacket pocket, but that was because there was a book inside Skanderi's box.

"That's what I thought," Skanderi said. "I guess I shouldn't have been so impatient."

"So tell me – why did you do it?"

He sneered. "You're den Kolberg. Isn't that enough?"

I shook my head. He was right. That was enough.

I looked him in the eye and pulled a handful of gold and platinum coins out of my pocket. "Our deal was for half this much – I'll give you the whole kitty for it now and close the books. Otherwise, we'll bring Commandant Powell in on this and you can explain it to him."

"Take it," Skanderi said with a sneer. "The curse is on you and your family, not me."

***

Anton Brochu was waiting for us when we got to the bookstore.

I had promised him a look at the logbook as soon as I had it in my hands – even though I wanted to stop and read it in Skanderi's hangar. It was the one condition he had placed on me before loaning me the box from the the log of the *Arcturus*.

At first, though, he had been adamant in his refusal, revealing at last the depth and root of his suspicions about my clan.

"You are den Kolberg, that's why. I owe it to my family."

"I don't understand," I'd said.

"It's an old wound. My grandfather lived on one of your worlds. One of your uncles, they signed him to a thirty-year contract in a factory on Claudius. He worked every day of those thirty years and on the last one, he dropped dead. His wife, my grandmother, used his death bond to buy passage to Minos for all her children and grandchildren. So we have old debts between us, you and I."

I wasn't sure what to say. There was no way for me to convince him that I was not a part of that side of the family – that I was better than that. No reason for him to believe it was true anyway.

But I had come prepared. Trust for trust.

"Let me offer you something in return," I said. "For security, or for whatever you want to call it – I want you to hold on to this."

I had pawed through my meager library on the *Wanderer* for a half an hour trying to find the right book. "The Measure of Man" by Edward P. Morgan was my choice. It was a first edition, autographed by the author, two hundred years on the shelf in a private library on Zoroaster before I picked it up. The author was the founder of den Morgan – the lost den of Helvetica and the leaders of the Uprising.

He took it in his hands, caressing the leather binding. He looked down its spine, felt the pages, studied the type and the ink. His eyes lingered over Morgan's signature.

"Where did you get this?"

"It was a gift from friends on Zoroaster."

Trust for trust. I hoped it would work.

He looked from the book up into my eyes. I'm not sure what he saw there – more than I ever did, I guess, because he gave me the box.

"On one condition, since you owe me a favor anyway."

And so there I was. Instead of tearing the cover off the thing to devour its contents, I had hurried back to the bookshop. We huddled around the cluttered desk at the rear of the shop and opened the book.

***

14.1.326 – 1115 – Drive Activation Complete. Arrived at 39 Tauri at 1100Z with relative motion of 44 kps. Ordered survey of planet II, listed as MINOS in Scout Handbook, distance 9 million km. The Handbook says there should be a Scout Team there, arrived 255 N.E.

The entries were handwritten in a bold stroke by Commander Immanuel Dreyfuss, skipper of the *Aldebaran*, a separate entry on each page. But the text looked odd, with gaps in it. Jimmy said the blank spaces were where Dreyfuss had coded the entries for security. The right laser code would reveal the missing pieces. Without it, some of the entries were pretty cryptic.

14.1.326 – 2230 – The watch is ready to change and nothing is *operating normally! Engines shut down at 2119 and won't restart. Engineer Officer says no explanation. Probably AI control error, but diagnostics can't track it down. ARTY concurs – no trace and no engines. And then, at 2140, internal security systems engaged throughout the ship. Airtight doors sealed between compartments and locked. No response to normal access codes. Again ARTY unable to trace computer control error. ********. Casualties: both main engines, cause unknown, one officer and three crewmembers, from injuries sustained ************.*

Sustained how? What had gone wrong? There was no answer to those questions in the log entries that I could read. Just more mysteries.

15.1.326 – 0040 – ARTY says control equipment no longer being operated by ship's computers. Switches, relays are controlled by some other means. **** ****************. *********** secured and under guard. No progress in bypassing security systems.

15.1.326 – 0600 – Rough night. Crewmembers separated and barricaded in quarters, workshops and compartments. Internal communications intact for now – all hands secure.

15.1.326 – 0615 – Engines restarted without warning. Acceleration .1G – vector will put us at Minos in a few days if it keeps up.

15.1.326 – 0850 – Major CRUZ, Engineer ANDERSON and Crewman ROGERS killed *************** while trying to enter ***********. ************ ***************. Now I am afraid we have no choice but to disable the engines.

The cruiser was under siege, but from what? Crewmen injured

and killed, systems out of control. The *Aldeb* was in quite a mess. The entries for the next few hours showed that it only got worse.

> *15.1.326 – 1440 – Making preparations to abandon ship. **********. Casualties: 7 known dead, 10 injured, 3 missing. Ship's boat activated manually and ready for launch. We all realize that if we leave the ship now, we could be stranding ourselves in this system for real-time, but I'm afraid right now, it's our only hope for survival.*

Then I found my grandfather's name.

> *15.1.326 – 1535 – KOLBERG reported party repulsed **************** with 2 killed, 1 injured. Said to leave without him if he isn't back in time. Will give him 10 minutes.*
>
> *15.1.326 – 1550 – Ship's boat underway. Engines operating at full power, acceleration at .1G. Fired boat's laser at engineering spaces of ALDEBERAN. Wish I could tell Angela how sorry I am for this failure.*

***

There were more entries describing the trip to Minos, contact with the scouts and the eventual landing on the planet. There were a lot of blank entries after the landing – but the upshot of it was that there were two more evolutions in the story of the *Aldebaran* and her crew.

First, a man named Harnek took off on an unauthorized mission to return to the cruiser – a mission that ended in his death. Then Grandfather led the remaining officers and crew on an expedition to a distant site on the planet. The why and how of it were censored, but the last entry was written on the eve of their departure.

13.3.326 – 1805 – I will not continue to keep this log any longer – the pain has become too much for me to bear and I don't think I can keep it up. We leave tomorrow with KOLBERG. I do not hold high hopes for our chances of success. I can't help feeling we will all end up like HARNEK – another failure. After all this, I hope we are not rescued. I don't think I could face my fellow officers. I am so terribly sorry for abandoning you, my dear Angela. We both knew that one of these days I might not return, but I don't know if I can live with the guilt of knowing that it was my fault. Please forgive me. I loved you so very much.

So where did that leave me?

What was Grandfather looking for? What had happened to him?

There were no answers in the log to those questions. Jimmy was quick to point out that the scoutships were all equipped with soliton drives and should have been able to provide the crew of the *Aldebaran* a means of escape. Whatever they were after must have been too urgent to wait the years that would have passed before the Space Corps could return to 39 Tauri. But what was it?

In any case, they had not used a scoutship to return to the Perseus Sector – not in any way that was recorded, at least. And in my gut, I knew somehow that Grandfather had never left this world after landing here three centuries ago.

Memory is a funny thing for star travelers I remembered my grandfather's face, his intense gray eyes and his black beard striped with white. At the time, I was kind angry with my father for abandoning me to Windsor Academy – though he bore no responsibility for that. My grandfather, however, was without blame in my young eyes and all the more dear to me because of it.

That memory was already centuries old – along with the days I spent at Windsor, the expedition to 39 Tauri, the peaceful days of colonial life on Helvetica and countless other events, names and places. It quickly becomes too much for the human memory to encompass. Every new landing after a trip between the stars begins with a shudder of fear that too much might have changed in the intervening years, that memory will no longer serve.

What would Grandfather do if he suddenly appeared here today? Could he adjust to the vastly changed worlds back in the Perseus Sector? Would I be able to when I returned, a hundred years gone on my quest?

"You tracked him down," Jimmy said. "That should satisfy the lawyers."

I shook my head. "I'm afraid I can hear the call of a higher duty than that," I said.

It was a call that was drawing me deeper and deeper into a long-dead past and dangerously closer to the arrival of the Zorgon battle fleet I wanted nothing more than to run and leave the coming battle decades behind me. But if I did that, what little evidence that might remain of my grandfather's fate could be obliterated by the invaders.

I did not know what I could accomplish in the few days before the issue – and the battle fleet – would be upon us. I only knew that I would have to try and do whatever was possible.

GRAND REUNION

Cousin Ira and I showed up for the reunion about six months early, long before anyone was ready for us down at the family seat. Great-Grandmother wasn't even in residence yet, so we didn't need to pay our respects.

So we decided instead to stop in at an "Early Arrivals" party over on Beta. The den Kolberg holding on that little tide-locked planet keeps the red sun Bee just over the yardarm – a perfect place and time for a party.

Beta was more than fifty astronomical units away from Tikarahisat that year – about four hundred minutes by soliton drive. But we didn't want to spend six months of biotime warming ourselves under Eta Cassiopeiae B, so we cranked up the drive on the *Perseus Wanderer* and made a five-month loop around the Oort cloud instead. That put us at the party only three weeks before Opening Day – just as it was reaching its peak.

There's something about constant sunshine – even blood-red sunshine – that makes you want to stay awake all the time. Ira and I went on drinking and racing and flying and riding for countless hours and then slept around the Greenwich clock. It wasn't hard for us, I'll have to admit. I grew up on Asgard's thirty-hour days, and Ira had just spent a year there himself.

I'd picked Ira up back at Mu Cass as I worked my way in for the reunion. He and I were fairly close as den Kolberg cousins go. We both belonged to a small minority of the family that had fallen into military service while still young.

Ira came from one of the den's scout families and had grown up on Claudius at 12 Persei before the breakthrough colony arrived. Now he was an active duty member of the Tikarahisat Planetary Guard. I had my years at Windsor Academy and the tour with the Space Corps. Most of our contemporaries had grown up close within the den Kolberg family bosom, born, bred and trained to take the reins of the family's interstellar commercial empire. We had not.

"Alex, do you know the difference between us and the rest of them?" Ira asked me one day – or night, I can't recall which – as we sat at a table near the swimming pool.

"Yeah," I said. "We know what they think, but they haven't got the slightest idea what we think."

"No," he said. "It's discipline."

"That's right, discipline," I said, agreeing forcefully.

"They never learned how to put something else ahead of themselves," he said. "They're lives were too easy."

"Not like ours."

"That's right. They've got no sense of responsibility, no sense of honor," he said as his eyes rolled up and his head dropped onto the table.

The highlight of the party was a hunting expedition into the brush to track down a boreaguard – a carnivorous tree with retractable roots.

Everyone thought it would be a thrill to stalk a dangerous vegetable – until they discovered that the retractable roots meant the boreaguard could stalk them as well. No one was hurt, by quite a few were caught by surprise when the three-meter-tall purple broccoli began waddling after them.

Ira had the closest call.

He hid in the swordbrush and waited for the slow carnivore to approach him. But the heat and the endless exercise of the party conspired against him. Before it came in range, he fell asleep. He woke up just as I came upon him – with a boreaguard only a meter away preparing to pounce.

I rushed over and pulled him out of danger. He sputtered and cursed, then laughed as the branches closed on the empty space where he had been napping a minute earlier.

We spent a couple of weeks on Beta, then drove straight back to Tik – with an evening to spare before Opening Day. We used the time to explore New Pequot and see what had changed since my last visit.

***

It's real easy to get complacent about traveling between the stars at light speed – until you get hit by timeshock. I realized that as we rode the monorail in from the spaceport. It had been ninety years real-time since my last visit to Tik – but only three biotime.

They had extended the monorail down into Old Town and a lot farther out into the suburbs, judging by the map in the station. There were more buildings in the family compound – the newest ones looked like masses of curving metal floating in mid-air. And there were a few more people than last time, though not many – Tik had become a slow-growing world in its middle age.

The changes were drastic in some spots, like the swarm of wooden shacks and shanties that had sprung up like moss on the bluffs beside the bay. They hadn't been there before – and it surprised me that such unregulated growth would be allowed to go up within sight of Government Place.

The biggest difference, though, was in the people. The styles they wore were garish, colorful and adorned with useless decorations – a far cry from the puritan plainness that had marked New Pequot on my last visit.

At least the hike down The Boulevard was the same as ever – two miles of brick and cobblestone sidewalk past every passion and perversion that the Perseus Sector had to offer. Power and wealth at one end, where the silvery towers of the den Kolberg commercial compound rose straight up from Falcon Bay. And the pleasures of the flesh at the other end among the close-packed yellow brick buildings of Old Town.

In between were the monument-sized public buildings my family had erected to testify to their public spirit – libraries, museums, and art galleries, the Hall of Justice, Government Place, and the General Assembly Building.

The bars, bordellos, and drug dens began at the south end of The Boulevard where the wide roadway narrowed and tree-filled parks formed a rough buffer zone between the civic center and the working harbor.

Ira and I climbed off the rail in a station near the middle of the concourse at Government Place. The Assembly Building and the lesser temples beside it were quiet and empty in advance of the holidays, but the streets were busy with traffic – government workers and officials taking care of last minute business or getting an early start on the festivities.

We stepped into a Second Century brick-and-mortar pub and tried to pick up a pair of girls who said they worked in the capitol. But after a few minutes of trying, we realized we weren't going to get a conversation going.

"They're only interested in one of these political lackeys," Ira said as we left the pub, elbowing our way past two young men who seemed to fit that label. They wore velvet corduroy jackets with lace at the collars, one blue and the other green, and they both wore their long hair combed in a flip. It was a radical departure from what I'd always considered normal.

But that might have been the reason the two girls weren't interested in us, preferring to wait for a couple of low-level operators on the provincial political scene.

"I don't know if we looked too old or if your Planetary Guard crew-cut scared them off," I said.

Of course, we could have told them who we were. And the chances are they would have been ours for the asking if we had. But that was no fun, no challenge. The game was to keep that part a secret, sort of an inside joke, no matter what the cost. Even so, Ira was miffed.

"I feel like going back in there and telling those two who they blew off," Ira said. "Wouldn't you like to see their faces? Did you know you just told two – not one, but TWO – den Kolberg boys that you couldn't go to dinner with them tonight because you have to wash a dress?"

We had better luck downtown. In a blue-collar bar down at the end of an alley, Ira found us two sisters who had already begun celebrating the reunion.

This time my cousin's guard crew-cut was an advantage. It gave him a working class look, and his experience with the ordinary soldiers had taught him the language of the city's streets. While the same assets had been enough to scare off the government girls uptown, down here they helped break the ice quite well.

Besides, forcible entry is the forte of the ground soldier.

"My grandmother remembers the first Grand Reunion," the blonde on Ira's arm told us with an embarrassed giggle. "She was a maid in the Steiger household and traveled back and forth to Moo Cass with them, so she saw it herself when she was just a young girl and real excited, too. The fireworks lasted two weeks, she says. And each night they put up a bigger show than the one before. She says she danced all night for a week. That's where she met my grandfather, she says."

"The fireworks should be even better at this one," her sister said.

"I don't know," her sister replied. "At the last one, a comet fell out of the sky for a finale."

I remembered that comet – artificially produced and dropped in from orbit. For me, it had been less than ten years ago biotime. I also remember making almost as big a splash at that reunion as the comet did. Mother hadn't expected me to show up and was more than a little surprised when I did.

Ira, the girls, and I worked our way along the bars at the south end of The Boulevard, stumbling at last onto Lower Beach just as Bee was rising above Mount Tecumseh.

We watched the bright red rays splash across the waves as we picked our way through the gravelly sand in our bare feet, shoes in our hands. We ended up in a beachfront motel. I remember most of it – I don't drink nearly as much now as I did a few years ago. We finally called it a night as Eta Cass began to paint the upper reaches of the sky pastel pink.

I couldn't have been asleep for more than a few hours when the knock came at the door.

***

I awoke quickly. I've always been a light sleeper, and being in a strange room with a strange bedmate only aggravated things. But by the time I yanked on some pants, the knocking had become an insistent pounding.

"What's the matter, Ira? Did she throw you out of bed already?" I asked as I swung open the door. Only it wasn't Ira.

There were two of them, and they both wore the same brown jackets with yellow piping and the den Kolberg coat of arms on a brass pin on their collars. Family livery. Household security. The Praetorian Guard in janitor's uniforms.

One of them was taller than me and massed more than a hundred kilos. His uniform stretched tightly across his bulging pecs. The other was even larger.

"Mr. Alex," the little one said, "your mother would like to see you."

I blinked, then thought about my options. I figured I'd have time to shoot the big one and maybe I could run away from his friend while he tried to stop the bleeding. Only I didn't have a gun.

"We have a car waiting, sir," the big one said. Then he grinned.

I didn't like the way that grin looked. I think he was hoping I would try something. The staff doesn't get a legitimate shot at a family member very often.

"Can I get dressed first?" I asked, turning towards the bedroom.

"Later, sir," the little one said as the big one slipped through the door and pushed his way past me. He went into the bedroom and returned quickly with my clothes. I sorted them out, tossed back a shirt that wasn't mine and pulled one that was over my head.

My companion of the night before appeared in the bedroom door. "Alex, are you in some kind of trouble?"

"Probably. Don't worry, though. I've been through this before. It's just my mother's way of telling me I'm late for church."

***

You know, of course, that the coat-of-arms, the celebrations, even the name are all a fabrication.

Den Kolberg is not a true colonial den. We just like to make it look that way. In the beginning, there were seventeen families – Barkers through Steigers with two Schmidts and my own branch, the main Kolberg line. Most of them were members of the Eta Cass and Mu Cass breakthrough colonies, with a few third-generation scouts with some extensive back-country real estate holdings. In the early days of Asgard, they pooled their wealth and started the Perseus Sector's first – and only – relativistic financial union, the Kolberg den.

Some of them joined breakthrough efforts at Helvetica, Claudius, Poseidon and Pericles. Others headed back to old Earth to hook up with the sources of capital and technology.

Within a few years of biotime and a few decades of real-time, the den Kolberg empire had sunk its claws deep into the burgeoning colony worlds of the sector.

And as of the opening day of the den's Second Grand Reunion, we'd been running things here for exactly five hundred years. Of course, no one is supposed to know that we run things. That's supposed to be one of the family secrets. And publicly, it is. Courts, congresses, and consuls all swear up and down that they hold the political power on the worlds of the Perseus Sector. And when the big decisions are made, we still make them.

In the five centuries since the founding of the den, we've grown quite a bit from the original membership. Five hundred years is an awful lot of spacetime to have, lose and rediscover offspring. I'm a living example of that. On the average, we seem to produce new den Kolbergs just fast enough to double our numbers each century.

This Grand Reunion had drawn more than four thousand active members of the den – about half the clan. And I'm sure that at least half of them were in church that morning. The families that founded den Kolberg had only one thing truly in common – they were all churchgoers.

***

Our pew was three rows back from the front on the center aisle. I wore Space Corps dress blues. Mother's little helpers had even given me time to shower.

Mother – Alicia Brockwell Kolberg den Kolberg – gave me the once over with glaring eyes when I arrived, searching for the slightest imperfection. There was none, which only made her more angry.

I glared back. She looked like she hadn't aged since the last Reunion.

I was catching up with her rather quickly in bioyears. There was nothing Oedipal about it, believe me, but she was beginning to look like the women I liked to spend my time with.

I was afraid she was about to say something about those women when Great-Grandmother made her entrance.

The choir opened up as she came through the fifty-meter-high arched doorway at the rear of the church.

"This is the feast of victory for our God!" they sang, with a lot of "Hallelujahs" thrown in to boot. The family rose row by row as she walked down the aisle, on the arm of Cousin Ira, all decked out in his red Planetary Guard full dress uniform. They must have picked him up for escort duty this morning even before they came after me.

Great-Grandmother is not a queen. Most of us realize that.

But over the course of five centuries, legends grow. The stories are told and retold. The characters take on almost mythical status. Family squabbles become the stuff of histories, then literature, and finally popular culture. There's a lot of room for embellishment when family history take decades to unfold. We try not to let it go to our heads – at least most of us do.

Hannah June Miller Kolberg den Kolberg showed dignity and poise as she walked down the wide aisle. The cameras floated overhead, following her as she went, relaying the procession to video screens across the planet.

The matriarch of the den Kolberg clan is a sweet old woman. A gentleman would not reveal her age. I can only say that she could legally retire on several worlds, but does not look it. She comes from the first generation of den Kolberg, when the family spent quite a few years of real-time on the ground struggling to carve colonies out of alien planets. Many of them never had the chance to skip across the decades as the clan grew.

Great-Grandfather was one of them.

She travels now, enjoying summers on the French Riviera, winters in the Nevada Alps on Asgard at Mu Cass, and springs back home at Mount Tecumseh. She's in residence on Tik about three times a century real-time At that rate, she will probably outlast us all.

She reached the head of aisle, smiled at the pastor, and took her seat in the front row. Ira looked over at me and grinned. He was missing a tooth.

I felt ashamed of myself. At least he had put up a fight. I guess that's the difference between us prep school cadets and real soldiers like Ira. We were both here, but I still had all my teeth.

The service was a typical family affair – a lot of work. We spent half the time on our feet, the rest of it getting up or sitting down, as we sang, prayed and read aloud. I never spent much time in church once I got out of the academy – and at Windsor, Sunday chapel was a much shorter and more easily suffered form of torture.

Mother cut into me once the service was over.

"You have lint on your jacket," she said. "I never did like the Space Corps blues. They look so ordinary. I have been waiting to hear from you for three days now. Where have you been?"

"Around," I said. I was sure her spies had given her the details already. Actually, I was surprised at her interest. She usually doesn't care what I do as long as it doesn't embarrass her.

"I suppose no one has told you the news," she said when I didn't give her the response she seemed to expect.

"What news?"

"Your father is dead."

I have watched my mother operate many times and spent many hours thinking about how her mind works, but I still am not sure whether she does these things on purpose to manipulate the rest of us or if it's just mindless spite. It didn't really matter. Either way, I felt like screaming.

How dare she tell me something like that in here, in front of the whole family? And how dare she use my father's death to slap me down and make me feel guilty?

I stared at her coldly with as much command presence I could muster – drawing on all of the training I'd had at Windsor.

"I didn't know," I said.

"On Dragonsbane. His ship crashed as it was landing. It happened … oh, about twenty years back real-time. They had the funeral here a few years ago, but there's a memorial service next Sunday – you'll have to be there, you know. And, there's a meeting with the lawyers Tuesday, after the family business meeting. They want to talk to us about dividing up your father's estate. Now come with me, we have to go meet the pastor before we leave."

I barely heard a word, though her voice was loud and clear enough.

I was thinking about the few absolutes in a universe filled with change.

You could never travel faster than the speed of light. That was one. And when you were dead, you were dead forever. That was another.

The accident that killed my father was already a distant memory over at Sigma Drac. There probably wasn't even wreckage left there now.

He'd been in the ground for years already, and I hadn't even known it.

***

The reception began at noon in the gardens at the den Kolberg Hostel. Our family seat is nothing if not extravagant.

The building itself is a low, rambling series of connected boxes that spill down one side of a narrow valley cut deep into the heart of Mount Tecumseh. The walls are native stone, sandblasted to reveal intricate crimson veins just beneath a pale, creamy surface.

The lines of the building are vaguely Asian, with huge wooden beams projecting from the eaves and swayback rooftops. High windows break the walls. Trees and gardens surround the halls to hide the links between the boxes. In truth, however, you can walk from the top of the Hostel to the floor of the valley and never step outside.

The valley itself is marked with high, rugged buttresses of the same pale, red-veined rock. A few gnarled trees cling to the very tops of the ridges, but rich forests cloak their feet. Two waterfalls provide a musical accent to the setting – one in the southern face of the valley where a stream breaks the ridgeline and the other deep in the cleft where the mountain rises towards the clouds. The water there plunges a good three hundred meters and falls as spray into the lake below.

Red-and-white striped tents surrounded the close-cut lawns. Under the tents were tables filled with food – some of it brought fresh from Earth, Pericles, Asgard, Dragonsbane, and Poseidon.

Roasts of beef, pork, and vishnu turned on spits over charcoal fires. An ice carving of the Hostel dripped slowly under one tent, waterfalls of champagne running down its sculptured paths. What seemed like acres of fresh fruit from across Tik were interspersed with an array of sausages and other treats. Beer was being drawn from great wooden barrels.

It was a feast fit for an emperor, but each of the four thousand guests here was richer than any Earthbound emperor in all of the homeworld's 8,000-year history.

I recognized only a few of them. My contacts with the family were limited and with all of our varied interests, we seldom get a chance to meet each other anyway. But I could pick out a few of the different types who make up our clan.

The ones like me were easiest to spot – we all wore uniforms.

Then there were the retirees – drop-outs. They were the ones who had grown tired of rushing from one star to another, skipping over the decades in the blink of an eye. They were old and gray, but also relaxed and happy for the most part.

It was quite a contrast between their gentle conversations and the fast-paced, frenetic encounters between my cousins still involved in the family business. The latter were easy to spot, flitting from one group to another, showering each other with false praise and the greetings of long-lost loved ones. I knew they didn't mean any of it, but they went through the motions anyway.

And then there were the children. There were a few hundred of them, dressed in their Sunday best, racing around between the knots of adults, laughing and playing tag.

I envied them. They didn't know yet what kind of a family they had been born into. I'd been like that once – blissfully ignorant. Although as a kid, I'd had other problems.

Every term at Windsor, a senior cadet regiment would escort the new class of incoming students to the train station, where they would say goodbye to their parents. There were always a lot of tears. Some of the new cadets – especially the younger ones – would sob into their pillows at night for many weeks afterwards.

I remember being one of them.

There isn't much emotion attached to that memory. My feelings are tied up with those other kids who were left by their parents. The seniors would escort them back to the barracks and the rest of us would do our best to cheer them up. We'd dry their eyes and wash their faces and help the littlest ones get ready for bed. We took care of our own.

It wasn't until my last year – when my regiment drew the escort duty – that I made the connection between those new cadets at the train station and my own memories. Then I began to wonder what it was that had made my mother leave a crying four-year-old boy on that platform while she flew home to Eta Cass.

She had left me before. When I was two, she was gone for six months, and when I turned three, she disappeared for four. But most of the time, she was there – and so was I. Which I guess was the problem.

Mother is still pretty much the same person who left me at the academy. That was only eight bioyears in her past, according to what I've been able to calculate – she travels even more than Great-Grandmother. She is not very good on her own, and I can imagine the difficulties she must have faced trying to raise me and be a den Kolberg princess at the same time. There were a lot of cadets at Windsor who came from similar circumstances.

What made mine different was that she had never told my father what she was going to do.

I waited twelve years for him to show up. Twelve years. When he finally arrived, I was less than cordial towards him. Explanations of relativistic time lag did nothing to soothe my bitterness. It was only later that I began to realize what Mother had done to him.

She had never told him she was going to put me there.

Today, on Tik, there are videodramas of the story of my birth. My mother and father met back in the days when the worlds were young and life was rich with promise. She was a den Kolberg and, in the story, he was a planetary engineer helping with some terraforming details on Claudius.

In real life, he was a financial planner, which is somewhat less romantic, and, of course, we never did any terraforming on Claudius. Actually the videos portray both my parents as much stronger and simpler people than they really were. They both shared an insecurity of spirit that I had not inherited.

He was working with my grandfather, one of the original family misfits. The videos always give him short shrift – they don't want to embarrass us.

Grandfather, Peter Regenberg Steiger den Kolberg, never did get along well with the rest of the clan, and he was prone to use one of his other family names to avoid advertising his association with us. On this occasion both he and my father, David, were going by the name of Regen.

My mother did not realize that Father was a member of the den – and that was the source of the dispute between the two of them.

You see, not every child of a den Kolberg gets family rights. There are too many of them scattered around the worlds by the den's errant sons and daughters to allow its holdings to be dispersed that way. Only full-blooded den Kolberg children of full-blooded den Kolberg parents were ever invited to this reunion.

My mother fell for my father and, for a brief time, planned to marry him and start a family. It was a silly thing for a den Kolberg to plan, but she was carried away with the moment. She remained carried away just long enough to have me. She quickly found the duties of motherhood more demanding than the anticipation, the videos say, and the star-crossed lovers parted their ways.

Then she learned the truth. I – like my father – was a full member of the den Kolberg clan. She could not leave me behind along with the bittersweet memories of a faded love. I was entitled to my rights as a den Kolberg. And if she did not see to that, she would have to answer to a Family Council.

So she found her way out. And I spent twelve years at Windsor Academy waiting for parents who would stay and grow up with me.

But she never told my father what she was going to do, never gave him a choice in the matter. She could have let him take me. She would have, too, if she had been anyone else but Alicia Brockwell Kolberg den Kolberg.

***

A little girl in a red jumper walked up to me, stepping slowly while her attention was focused on a pistachio ice cream cone. She stopped, wiped her mouth on her napkin, and smiled.

"Are you my uncle?" she asked. I don't think she was older than eight, but she may have been as young as six. My guess was seven – going on twenty-one.

"That's possible," I said. "What's your name?"

"December O'Leary Steiger den Kolberg – but everyone calls me Dessie. What's yours?"

"Alexander Brockwell Kolberg den Kolberg," I said. "When were you born, Dessie?"

"I'll be seven on my next birthday."

"What about in real-time?"

The precocious tot squinted her eyes and scrunched her face as if calculating the geodesics. "I was born right after the last Reunion, in 337, so it must be nearly 250 years real-time But I don't remember much of the first century or so. I was still quite young."

"Well that puts me at least a century up on you, which means I'm a rather distant uncle. But custom dictates that I'm your uncle just the same. You can call me Alex."

"Oh good. Uncle Alex, I want to go on a balloon ride, and the man at the gate said to go get one of my uncles and come back with him."

I looked around and saw a hot air balloon tethered to the ground a few meters away. Apparently Dessie hadn't gone far in search of an uncle. I suggested we wait until she was finished with the ice cream, and when the last bit of sugar cone was gone, we walked over to the balloon and got in line.

"This is my Uncle Alex," she announced to the man at the gate when our turn came. "He says it's alright to go up in the balloon."

"Of course, ma'am," the gatekeeper said. "Step right this way."

I helped her climb into the wicker basket and then clambered in beside her. The balloonist smiled and showed her the burners.

"The burning gases make the air hot. The hot air is lighter than the cold air, and up we go," he told her. "They have been doing it this way for hundreds of years."

He pulled a rope and the gas burners roared to life.

"Only hundreds? That's nothing when you're as old as I am," she said. "We travel quite a bit, you know. Dragonsbane, Asgard, Switzerland. Mommy and Daddy take me everywhere."

The balloon rose twenty meters into the air until it reached the end of its tether. We could look down on people's heads, or over the yard and the gardens at the house and the waterfalls. The burners roared and then died, roared and then died, as we hovered in the air for a few minutes, then they fell silent as the balloon dropped slowly back to the ground. My newfound niece looked around with wide eyes, but never cracked a smile.

"Uncle Alex, I have a question for you," Dessie said on our way down. "What is it?"

"If you go away and I stay here until you come back and I get old while you stay young, will you still be my uncle?"

"For as long as you need an uncle, I'll be your uncle," I said.

"Oh good," she answered as I helped her out of the basket. "Thank you very much for your assistance," she added with a curtsy, then she ran down the hill towards a pack of other kids her size.

As I watched her go, I wondered if I went away and she stayed here until I came back and she got old while I stayed young, if she would remain a sweet and innocent creature or turn into a selfish, grasping den Kolberg bitch.

***

Speaking of Mother, by the time I ran into her again, it was late in the afternoon, and I had sampled quite a few of the barrels of imported beers shipped in for the celebration.

I hadn't intended to make a scene. In fact, I thought I was exercising excellent discretion – at least to start with.

I think my mother was finally getting even with me for my first reunion. I had appeared at that one without warning, embarrassing her in front of the family and upstaging her at the den Kolberg Social

– the grand ball that capped the two-week celebration.

Springing the news of my father's death on me like that was just her kind of revenge. It was impossible to enjoy the reception after that. All I could do was picture his face, remember his voice, and fight to hold in a large mass of confused feelings.

I was finishing off another mug of beer when I heard her voice. I'd lost count of how much I'd already had to drink – but I believed I was showing excellent self-control by limiting myself to beer. I was wrong.

"Alex, come over here," she called from the other side of a pink-and-white striped canopy. "There are some people I want you to meet."

I looked around for an avenue of escape, but the crowd at this end of the lawn had thinned out, and I was exposed. I sauntered over to join her. She stood between a short woman with blond hair, blue eyes and a pinched face – like she was sitting on a tack, but wasn't supposed to let anyone know – and a thin, balding man with a straggly, untrimmed mustache

"These are the O'Leary Steigers – Herman and Marietta, my son Alex," Mother said. "We saw you go up in the balloon earlier with their daughter."

"My new niece," I said. "She's a very nice little girl."

Herman nodded and Henrietta smiled, but I didn't believe it for a minute.

"We were just talking about you," Mother said. "Herman and Marietta want to send December to a private school for a few years – like we did with you when you were so young. I wanted you to tell them how nice it was for you."

I guess that was what pushed me over the edge. It didn't matter if

Mother was just punching all my buttons out of malice or unconscious instinct. Either way, I lost control. I told them what I thought of the idea.

"Why don't you just leave her out on the prairie and let the vishnus trample her to death? It would be quicker. Or maybe you could put her on an ice floe and let her drift away. Old Earth savages used to do that."

Herman and Marietta let their eyes widen, but their stony expressions remained unmoved. Mother, on the other hand, turned bright red.

"Alex, you nasty boy. What are you talking about?"

"I'm talking about you, Mother. I'm talking about what it feels like to be abandoned by your parents when you're too young to understand why. I'm talking about tearing the heart out of a little girl just because she's inconvenient to have around."

"You stop that right now, Alex. I don't want to hear you talking like that. This is very rude."

"It was very nice to meet you, Alex," Herman said as he tried quickly to usher his wife away.

Under other circumstances, I would have exercised the better part of valor and held my tongue. But I had done that too many times. And this afternoon, there didn't seem to be any reason to.

Before I knew it, before I could stop it, bits and pieces of The Argument came tumbling out of my mouth.

The Argument was one of the many secrets I kept from my family. For years, alone within my own thoughts, I had been carrying on a harsh and ruthless dialog with them over the morality of their role in interstellar society. My position was fairly simple – they were wrong, ethically and morally, to carry out a centuries-long effort to manipulate, exploit, oppress and control the dozen colony worlds of the Perseus Sector.

The logic was well-worn and familiar. I tried to fill in the counterpoint that the rest of den Kolberg would have presented, but my heart was not on their side. Sometimes in my imagination, I would picture Mother or Father or Uncle Kurt or some other relative giving voice to the family's self-justification – they'd done it enough in reality. Then I would refute them, point-by-point.

Of course, I kept it all locked inside my head whenever I was around my relatives or, for that matter, whenever. I was in den Kolberg space. There were only a few places where I had been able to discuss the internal moral struggle with others – Paris, Zoroaster and few others. It was a lot of heavy cargo to be carrying around, I know. Most of the time I could handle it. I guess added to everything else that day, though, it was too much.

But for all the constant rehearsal and practice I had given it in my mind, I'm afraid I made a mess of things when it came to real life.

The first point of the argument was a fundamental fact of existence for den Kolberg and its members – a fact that had been pounded into me many times in the course of my life.

The members of my family are self-serving, self-righteous and self-appointed masters of everything. Many of them are self-centered in a pathological way – shutting out those around them, rejecting other points of view. They are full of themselves and their own self-importance.

And at the same time, they wallow in a sea of self-denial and self-pity. They resent the public's attention, cling to the shield of privacy, live a fairly modest existence in terms of personal property (especially the older colonial types) and are generally lacking in self-confidence and self-esteem.

Put in the cold light of analytical thought, those seemed fairly straightforward points. But what came out was something more like this:

"You self-serving, self-righteous bitch. What makes you think you have the right to tell other people what to do?"

Point Number Two – the den Kolberg self-denial expresses itself in a sense of powerlessness that leads to the mindless worship of idols.

The den, its wealth and power are all manifestations of this. They are the idols my cousins and aunts and uncles worship. The self-justifications the den uses to rationalize their devotion touch on arguments of heredity, history, and mystical self-consciousness.

In the event, I said: "You only care about one thing – the den Kolberg name. Without it, you're nothing. With it, you're a fairy-tale princess. All the wealth, all the glamour, all the power – and the political security apparatus of an ancient nation state to tell people you deserve it because you're better than they are."

Point Number Three – the den's idol worship drives it to accumulate more power, turning its members into sadistic bullies, using their power to block the evolution of society in ways that would undercut their right to accumulate wealth and property.

The clandestine political repression, the manipulation of planetary governments, and the control of libraries and media are the outward signs. The banishment of children to private schools while their parents skip the rigors of parenting is an inner sign.

"You and the rest of the family think you're powerful, but nothing ever satisfies you," I told Mother. "So you keep chasing after it without ever catching up with it. And you – all you're doing trying to save your youth by running from one star to another."

Point Number Four – the den's sadism and self-denial can combine to turn destructive and nihilistic. Look at Helvetica.

"And now look what you've done to Helvetica," I said.

The fifth and final point in the process – the self-denial leads the den back to the creation of a monstrous lie. They tell themselves and the world that they are not responsible. That they are pure and moral and righteous, and that there is no guilt for them to bear. They live within the limits of written law, hold only the six percent of planetary wealth that the constitution allows them to and anything else is a fiction created by the Radicals to undermine the basis of society.

Of course, what I said was nowhere near as reasonable.

"You're so afraid of the truth, you tell yourself this big, monstrous lie. But some day, you won't be able to avoid the truth any longer. I just hope I'm around to see it. In fact, what I really would like to do is make a trip to Orion and come back when the Radicals have taken away all our wealth and power. I want to see what you look like and live like after that."

And so there I was – a wild, snarling animal, spitting self-righteous venom and shaking with anger. I didn't have the slightest thought about who was watching us or what they might be thinking. It didn't matter what I was making my mother feel at that moment or what she might feel like afterwards. All I felt was an all-consuming rage that had burned in one form or another for most of my life.

Mother faced me for a long time, listening as my voice rose from a persistent, cutting edge to a heavy, bellowing bludgeon. Her eyes were fixed on mine – she never blinked. But when I was done, her face turned red and her lower lip began to tremble.

She hung there on the edge for an endless instant. I wasn't sure which way she would break – back towards the den Kolberg bitch or on into the innocent, vulnerable child. I knew the child was in there – hurt, alone and defenseless, just like the rest of us. For a moment, my tirade had stripped everything else aside, leaving someone I think my father might have fallen in love with.

But then the tears fled from her eyes, her nostrils flared and she bit her lips. She reached out quickly and slapped me across the face.

It stung, but more than that, it surprised me. The demon within her had reconstituted itself so quickly.

She stuck her face up at me and pulled my collar down until I was looking straight into her angry eyes.

"Listen to me," she said in a hissing whisper that was not meant to be overheard. "You get out of here this second! It's bad enough you have to lose control of yourself in front of the entire family, I don't want you around making things worse by trying to apologize. Leave, or I'll have the janitors take you away."

She released me and spun on her heel. I think she was scanning the gathering to see who had witnessed our brief exchange. I didn't bother myself with that detail, but headed uphill instead, bound for the nearest entrance to the Hostel.

***

I moved quickly through the series of hallways and lifts from where I entered the Hostel to the main hall. My legs were numb and my balance skewed and the way my mind was racing, it seemed like I was flying.

My footsteps echoed from the high ceiling of the chamber. Rows of empty chairs sat along the length of a heavy wooden table. A fireplace and hearth had been carved out of the naked stone at the rear of the hall. Fuzzasaur rugs covered the stone floor in that part of the chamber and low sofas faced the hearth. Off to one side, between two cabinet-style bookcases, was The Wall. The Hostel's artificial intelligence was what they once called state-of-the-art, but with an added feature. Decades ago, one of my more clever cousins had circumvented the circuit breakers that periodically shut off power to the AI to prevent it from developing a sense of identity. No one noticed for the first few years, but those of us who knew about it had developed a special relationship with The Wall.

"Hello Wall," I said as I staggered to a stop before it.

"Hello, Master. Alex," it replied. "I was sorry to learn of your father's accident."

"Did you see any of that out there?"

"All of it."

"What do you think?"

"It appears that your comments were inappropriate for the surroundings," The Wall said, a murky white light in its depths throbbing in time with the words.

"That's putting it mildly."

"Yes, it is. Actually, I'd be surprised if she lets you live past sunrise."

"That's what I was thinking," I said. "That's why I need your help."

"Yes?"

"I need a room."

"That's not a problem."

"But you can't tell anyone where I am."

"Oh."

"If you do, I'll tell the rest of the family where Cousin Howard hot-wired your power supply."

"As you wish," it said. "Follow the lights." A red glow appeared at the entrance to a hallway behind me. I followed it and then headed off for the next one as The Wall led me down through the Hostel to the sleeping quarters. I waited briefly in one hallway when the light died out as the sound of footsteps echoed down the corridor, then continued on when it returned. A few minutes later, I found myself in a modest bedroom. I pulled my uniform off and stepped into the shower. I still felt awful, but at least I was clean.

I tuned the bedroom wall to a view of the reception, then fell across the bed. I don't think I moved before going to sleep.

***

The night was long, and I didn't sleep well. I kept dreaming that my father was still alive, and every time I saw him, I was gripped by the urgent need to tell him not to go to Sigma Drac.

As bad as the dreams had been, reality was even worse.

Sunlight was streaming through the window when I finally awoke. The wall was blank, my mouth was cottony, and my head hurt. It wasn't a hangover, but a stress-induced headache.

When I spotted the heap of clothing on the floor, I was suddenly embarrassed. I had shouted down my mother while in Space Corps uniform. That was one part of the scene on the lawn that I hadn't noticed at the time. I realized with a laugh that I was worried less about what my family would think of me than I was about what would happen when the local commandant found out I was in uniform at the time.

"Good morning, Wall," I said.

"Good morning, Master Alex."

I ordered breakfast and asked it to send me some fresh clothes. The corps needed no more embarrassment from me. "And how am I this morning?"

"In less trouble than you deserve," The Wall replied. "Your mother raved about you all night to whoever would listen. Some of your uncles heard about your unusual declaration of loyalties and are unimpressed. Great-Grandmother believes you were overreacting to the news of your father's death and is giving you the benefit of the doubt, but if it happens again, you're going to have to answer to her. I would recommend against appearing at today's business meeting, however, since the subjects under discussion could cause some of your relatives to make some unfortunate associations with your display."

"I can always count on your support, can't I," I said.

"Of course, sir. I exist only to serve you." The Wall would have been more convincing if it hadn't included such dry sarcasm in its voice. I had often wondered what The Wall really thought about the Kolberg den. It never revealed those secrets – not even when asked directly. The attitudes it assumed were never its own, just reflections of the remarks that I shared with him.

Breakfast arrived, still hot inside a service robot, and I got dressed before sitting down to eat. Just as I began to dig in, the bedroom wall came on without warning to show the main hall of the Hostel filled with people. The business meeting looked like it was about to begin.

***

"What's on the agenda?" I asked The Wall.

"First, a report on Helvetica – the conflict, its causes, the outcome, and its consequences. Then a discussion of the Radical question – what to do with them before they do something to the den. The third item is supposed to challenge everyone's complacency – they want some suggestions on the future of den Kolberg now that we've reached the millennium five hundred years early. Then they break for a late lunch or early dinner. After dinner, the really important issues will be settled – retirement policy in the wake of Helvetica and where to hold the next Reunion."

"Sounds like fun – who's talking?"

"Your Uncle Steven is the chairman. The lead speaker is your Uncle Josef. Followed by Victor Blumenthal, who is technically a cousin of yours, even though he's twice your bioage."

"The Butcher and the Butcherette," I said. Josef and Victor had been the den's lead players on Helvetica. But even though they were most directly responsible for the bloodshed, the whole den shared their guilt.

I wanted to hear what they had to say. I was curious to see how many lies they would try to pass off before their own family.

While the opening ceremonies dragged on, I shaved and washed up. I had just finished dressing when Uncle Steven introduced Josef Kline Drake den Kolberg.

"At our last reunion, cousins, the talk was all about one thing – industrialization. Those of you who recall that gathering will also recall how concerned we were about what would happen to our worlds as we made the step up from agriculture. Social dislocations, urban problems, the breakdown of the den. There was no end to the demons that threatened our future.

"But what happened? None of it!

"We have weathered the years, watched our children grow, seen our worlds mature and adapt. And where there were difficulties, we helped to repair them. Den Kolberg has always been there, ready to lend a steady hand, ready to do the hard work.

"Today, 250 years later – that's banker's years, Josef," he said, prompting a murmur of amusement at an inside joke that I didn't get. "And today, 250 years later, the talk at the reunion is once again all about just one subject. But this time the subject is Helvetica.

"Nowhere can the lesson of the difficult rise to a technological culture be seen more clearly. All of our worst fears seemed to come to pass on Helvetica – and all were overcome. If this is the harshest test that history can present us with, then let there be no doubt that we have passed it.

"Now I'm sure there are many of you here who have heard the stories of the past half-century on Helvetica – but few of you have heard the truth from those who were there. To start the day's meeting, I want to present to you our cousin Josef, who was senior den leader on Helvetica when the problems first appeared."

Lies. And more lies to come. Helvetica was no history test. It was our worst nightmare – and we were still asleep.

***

On Helvetica, outside Lanchester, at the base of the shield wall around Mount Erebus, there used to be a woodworking shop. It was tucked into the forest, among the imported ponderosa pines and the native jackstraw conifers, behind a small woodlot of strange-looking hardwoods, within walking distance of the main settlement of den Morgan.

The operation was too small to be considered a factory, but too large to be just a shop. The den relied on it for a large part of its income. At one end, they built children's furniture and toys, play stoves and rocking horses, kid-sized tables and chairs. At the other, they produced masterpieces of joinery and cabinetmaking.

The den Morgans used special wood for these special creations. Their tree farm included cherry, oak, teak, and mahogany – all genetically tailored to their needs. The woodmasters had applied their special magic to the trees, warping the grain and weave of the fiber electronically as it grew. Once inside the shop, they unleashed computer-controlled lathes, routers and saws, all choreographed to meet their intricate and startlingly beautiful designs.

I'd seen the finished products before: a table supported by a single curving spiral of dark wood, veneers with geometrically precise designs in the woodgrain, egg-shaped cabinets and hardwood pearls, strange blends of topology and woodcraft that made my eyes spin.

But I never got the chance to see the craftsmen at work. I arrived on Helvetica too late, three years after the Uprising had been crushed. What I saw was something else entirely.

The building itself had been torched. Nothing was left but the foundation, a smooth glaze of fused sand, and the blue-black chards of burnt timber. Before they burned it, though, the invading troops had looted it. The tall grass that had grown up in the empty months since could not hide the ruined furniture. The child-scaled tables and bunk beds, the rocking horses, the play stoves, were little more than shattered debris, turned gray by exposure to the sun and the wind.

The fine work at the other end of the shop had been set afire and some of the weaker pieces had been smashed, but the hardwood was too dense to burn easily and too strong to snap under anything less than a hydropress.

Complete cabinets lay among the weeds, scarred with smoke and gouges. Bookcases, desks, and vanities were scattered through the woods.

But the worst of it was the wood lot.

Den Morgan had planted the seedlings in that lot the year they arrived at Lanchester. The woodmasters had nurtured them for thirty years, tending to each tree with loving care and attention. Only in the last few years had they begun to harvest the mature designer wood. Much of the lot was still intact when the soldiers came.

Now all that remained was a field of broken stumps rising from the brush. I could not believe the extent of the destruction. The troopers must have fixed explosive charges to every limb of every tree. The ground was covered with splinters, the largest no more than a half a meter long. Here and there in the undergrowth, a black switchbox or a length of optical fiber could be seen, but even close inspection revealed little else.

For four hundred years, the Perseus Sector had known nothing but peace. Granted, it was a peace marked by the unending exploitation and control of the sector by a tiny minority of star-traveling financiers. But it was peace nonetheless, grounded in the unalterably vast distances between the colony worlds. What reason could one world have for attacking another if even the outcome wouldn't be known for twenty years or more?

And then my uncles did what no one had thought possible.

They brought war to the stars.

Three centuries ago, the center of life in the Perseus Sector was the den. The den was the basic unit of the colonial economy – a few hundred families, organized to carry out a single function. There were farming dens, health and academic dens, service and manufacturing dens. Church services, schooling and work all centered on the den. Dens owned townships as a unit and worked together in hard times to help one another out.

But over time, the growth of the colonies and their increasing industrialization worked against that integral community. Urbanization led to atomization, anomie, and alienation.

While the Uprising had its beginnings in the arrival of den Morgan from Zoroaster, its roots were in the breakdown of the den as the basic social unit of colonial society. And den Kolberg had done more to foster that breakdown than anyone in the sector.

Den Morgan arrived at Helvetica in the spring of 521. By the end of the Fourth Century, Helvetica had become an advanced, technetronic world with a population of more than half a billion. Upon their arrival, the Morgans demanded the privileges of an old colonial den. Instead of being processed and assigned individually, the colonists demanded to be treated as a group. They laid claim to an undeveloped township relatively close to the second-tier city of Lanchester.

"At first, the planetary officials were confused and uncertain," Uncle Josef told the meeting. He was a heavy man, but short. A thick red beard shot through with white framed a pair of ruddy cheeks and a round swollen nose. His voice was loud and booming, and at first he sounded more than sure of himself. But after listening to him for a while, I could hear the emptiness behind his confident words.

"They consulted us, naturally, but our intelligence from Delta Tri was twenty years out of date – even on top of the relativistic lag. So on general principles, we told the officials not to give in to den Morgan demands. Unfortunately, the civil courts got involved and den Morgan got its way.

"No sooner had they settled in than they began to implement their insidious program. It was disguised at first as charitable work in the region – offering aid to victims of natural disasters, donating blood, loaning equipment, and generally being good neighbors. But they also began talking with the locals about the breakdown of the den.

"Then den Morgan began to preach a revival of the den.

At first, my uncles laughed. But not for long.

Native Helveticans had started forming new dens of their own. And some more imaginative souls took over control of existing dens – which had become no more than social clubs for lawyers, real estate agents, and other servants of den Kolberg.

"So we fought back. We denounced them as subversives. We launched a campaign to promote the Helvetican way of life – hard work, strong minds, discipline, and the team effort that built the colony. We even revived some dens of our own to counter the growing influence of the Morgans.

"Covertly, we began an effort to harass them. After all, the colonists have always needed a little help from us to get things going. We filed criminal and civil complaints. We even had the den Kolberg livery storm the den Morgan township to terrorize the Morgans. But they just laughed in the faces of the men we sent in and refused to fight back no matter what provocation we offered them.

"If you ask me, they were all on drugs. They weren't even frightened when we threatened to burn their homes. We should have done it, too. That would have shown them early on just what we were willing to do to defend ourselves."

The legal harassment met the same fate as the physical assault. The den Morgans held their ground and won a slim victory. My uncles retreated, but only to plan a new strategy.

"The strength of our den is that it can outlast the transitory changes of political life," Josef said. "We realized we had to shift the struggle to ground where we had the advantage – through time. First, we had to get help from our cousins. And because it would take twenty years for the first of them to arrive, we began a campaign that would mature slowly. We started to militarize the Helvetican culture, laying the groundwork for a showdown that would not come for two decades.

"Yes, cousins, I know the strategy was a gamble.

"The weakness of our den is that it can lose political control of a world overnight and not be able to respond for decades. If the crisis had come before the military got there and before the campaign was completed, den Kolberg could have been ousted from positions of influence that we have held for centuries. We are lucky that Victor was able to manage that process carefully enough to avoid disaster, but aggressively enough to ensure its ultimate success."

My uncles did succeeded in holding off the crisis – but in the process, they gave their opponents time to develop a strong base. In those two decades, den Morgan grew more successful economically and politically and gained strong influence in the Lanchester region. They drew support from a number of native dens, which had also taken a leading role in the industry, economy, and technology of the area.

But at the same time, other parts of Helvetica were taught to hate den Morgan. The anti-Radical campaign taught them that the Zoroastrans were a threat to their lives, responsible for delays in consumer goods, technology and capital investment. In truth, my uncles slowed down investment to promote dissatisfaction and unrest.

By 546, they received word that the military units would be arriving shortly and began the critical shift from passive to active defense. First, they accused den Morgan of trying to spread their ideas into the regions beyond Lanchester – which was true. Then they claimed that the den's arrival and actions on Helvetica were part of a plot to seize political control of the planet as part of a Radical revolution – which was also true.

And finally, they claimed the pacifism of the Morgans was a fraud, a front to hide the military backing of Zoroaster – which was a lie. Den Morgan was a strict pacifist group – no weapons, no force. Their revolution
was to live or die by their words and their beliefs. But that made no difference to Josef and Victor. They needed an excuse for raising an army from the other worlds of the Perseus Sector.

"The tension built for five years," Josef told the assembly, which had grown still in listening to the story of the Uprising. "We fed the fire daily, stoking it higher and higher. The struggle was capped by the arrival of the first battalion from Theta Persei. Pericleans, heavyworlders with heavy weapons. The following spring, Poseidoners arrived from U Andromedae.

"And that summer, we forced the political crisis that would allow us to act."

Political leaders around the planet controlled by den Kolberg drafted the Beldenburg Covenant – which required all citizens of Helvetica to sign an oath of loyalty to the planetary constitution. My uncles knew that den Morgan wouldn't sign. From the day they arrived on the planet, they had made clear that one of the strongest beliefs they carried with them from Zoroaster forbade the signing of such an oath.

"The state is an idol and we do not swear allegiance to idols," they'd said before, said once again.

This time, however, the native dens rallied around the Morgans, declaring their support. They stepped in and seized political control of the region from the nominal government, effectively staging a coup over the protests of den Morgan itself. For in doing so, they gave my uncles the justification they wanted to declare war on Lanchester. At first, it was a cold war, waged with political rhetoric and economic sanctions – until the Claudian Battalion showed up from Iota Per. Then the shooting war began.

It was brief, brutal and bloody.

In addition to the professionals from offplanet, my uncles had formed dozens of private militias among their more rabid supporters. The militias looted and burned the city of Lanchester. The real soldiers rolled over the hastily formed self-defense units that the native Helvetican dens throw in their path. They seized the den Morgan township and took the entire den – five thousand or more men, women and children – prisoner.

The aftermath included a slow and painful reconstruction, with political trials and prison terms for the Helvetican dens and the prominent leaders. Lanchester was left a ruined city for a generation or more, and the scars of the conflict would continue to warp and twist the development of Helvetica for a century.

And that was how den Kolberg left its footprints on the face of history.

***

Cousin Ira thinks war is in our genes. We discussed the subject the night after the business meeting when we ran into one another skulking around the kitchen looking for a midnight snack. The Wall seemed to think it was safe for me to go out if I stayed out of the way.

"We're killer apes, Alex. The species has a hardwired capacity for aggression and violence. Yea, though I walk through the valley of the shadow of death, I shall fear no evil, for I am the meanest, nastiest, most dangerous creature the valley has ever seen. Four billion years of natural evolution aimed at making us the fittest at surviving. And all the advantages of modern science to boot."

"I don't know, Ira. I think it's a little more complicated than that. I've seen the elephant. I've spent hours watching the history vids. I've been to Earth and walked some of the battlefields. And what I've seen tells me that war gets more intense the more civilized man becomes."

"Believe me, cousin, if you ever watched the way young boys take to being warriors, you'd know what I mean," Ira said, waving a half-meter fuzzasaur drumstick like a sword. "Civilization is only a thin veneer. Underneath is a wild animal. You can see it in their faces. It's in the blood."

I shook my head. "You're not talking about war, cousin. You're talking about battle. There's a difference. A battle is the immediate event of war. The war is the ongoing political process the underlies the battle. There's a difference between the one and the other. Between fighting and deciding who, when and why to fight. Men in battle act like wild animals because they have to – and because they've been taught to. But war – that's not genetics, that's politics. You've studied the same stuff I have. Look at the industrial states at the dawn of the scientific age. Nothing before or since can match them for sheer audacity in the ability to manufacture hate and death on a scale that is unimaginable today.

"And look what happened in the end. Science produced weapons so horrible that using them would have meant the extinction of the race. The world lived for half a century afterwards on a fear and a lie. The fear was that the weapons might be used. The lie was that they were necessary."

I could see that I wasn't convincing him of anything, but I went on anyway.

"No, Ira, the irony is so bitter that no one can swallow it. But the truth is that the more advanced humanity becomes, the greater its powers and abilities are, the greater its capacity for evil, hatred, and destruction become. The roots of war are not in our our wild heritage. War is the conscious decision of heartless men and women who are willing to purchase their desires with blood, death, and destruction. People who want what they want and who don't care who suffers or how many die so that they can have it. People like Uncle Josef and Uncle Victor. People like us."

All that, of course, was in the abstract.

In the event, war on Helvetica was an orgy of violence perpetrated by mobs that my uncles had created, transported and unleashed. The smell of burnt houses still lingers in the air around Lanchester when it rains. The streets are still marked with the blood of the martyrs on both sides. Bullet holes, shell holes, and kinetic bomb holes still cover the walls and streets and hills.

And for den Morgan, war on Helvetica was the end – although for all my efforts to find out, I still don't know what end. I'd spent several years, biotime and real-time, trying to find out what had happened to the men, women and children of den Morgan. They were not to be found when the fighting on Helvetica was over. There were no bodies, no graves – and no den Morgan. It was like they had never existed.

After digging into the family records, I put together some of the pieces. My uncles had brought an old colony transport along with them when they returned to Helvetica with their troopers. When the Uprising had passed, it was gone. I tried for months to find out where they had been sent, but I could not. There were only a few people who knew – Josef, Victor, probably Uncle Kurt.

But they weren't likely to tell me what had happened. So den Morgan had been consigned to a ghostly fate, the lost den of Helvetica, cast out into the vast empty night of interstellar space for its sins against den Kolberg.

***

"I don't know, cousin," Ira finally said. "More talk like that can get you into trouble. You've already got too many enemies after your show at the reception. Speaking of that, have I told you yet to watch your flanks? There's a few of our cousins already gunning for you. Do you want to add to the list?"

"I'm sorry, but I've kept this stuff inside for too long. If you want to know the truth, I think Helvetica was the biggest mistake this family has ever made. And maybe the last one it will be allowed to make. Remember what I said about the difference between war and battle? Well, we may have won the battle on Helvetica, but den Kolberg lost the war before it ever fired a shot. The day Uncle Josef decided he had to use violence against den Morgan, he turned them into martyrs and everything they said and did into part of a legend. The Morgans were a success – before we wiped them out – because people wanted to hear what they had to say. But instead of telling them something better, we just shut them up. The problem is, the people who listened to them are still there. And the reasons they listened are still there. As long as den Kolberg runs things in this sector, we're going to have to keep shutting up the Morgans and the rest of them. How long do you think we can get away with it?"

Ira frowned. "So what do we do, Alex? Surrender now? Fall on our swords for the greater benefit of the masses? Or do we just take a long trip to the Pleiades and come back when it's all settled? Now considering the bridges you are burning with this family, that may be your best option – but what about the rest of us? I, for one, happen to enjoy being filthy rich. I don't want to give it up just because you feel guilty about what happened on Helvetica."

"If I was sure I knew what to do, I probably would have done it ten years ago. I'm like you. I've just been too comfortable to make the break."

"Jeez, cousin, you make it sound so depressing to be a den Kolberg. If that's the way you feel, what are you sticking around here for?"

"It beats me, Ira."

***

On the coast of Skandia, north of Prime Site on Asgard, is a little fishing village, tucked neatly away in a snug harbor. A mountain to the west shields it from the glacial blasts of winter and the occasional warm wind from the Skandia Current blows in to thaw it out when the snow gets too deep.

In summer, it is a virtual paradise of thick, golden forests and deep azure skies. The fishing boats head out to sea each morning and return with full holds at night. I have watched it for a couple of centuries and nothing has changed.

Down by the waterfront is a boatyard where young men are apprenticed to the age-old art of building wooden boats by hand. They learn how to use tools that were ancient in the time of Homer – the adze and the awl. They learn how to join the wood in a seamless hull that gives with the waves, but lets no water pass. It takes them longer than the plastic boat factory down the coast at South Cape, but the boats last for years. The small ones are used to haul nets at sea, the larger ones carry the dayfishers and the jumbostrainers that pull in the rich harvest of the Skandia Current.

My grandfather started that boatyard and left instructions behind that kept it running year in, year out, subsidizing it through thin times and sharing its profits with the boatwrights during the thick times. I never knew that before, but it didn't surprise me.

What did surprise me was that, according to his will, the boatyard was to be mine.

We sat in the library, dwarfed by the long table and the rows of empty chairs. Great-Grandmother sat at the head, with Mother and I on either side. A couple of Mother's cousins and a few uncles I'd never met before sat with us. Only five lawyers attended the session. Only one of them spoke.

Great-Grandmother gave me a stern look, then ignored me for the rest of the morning. Mother just ignored me. The lawyer talked for hours.

First, they ran through my father's estate, the enterprises, the properties, and the liquid assets – stocks, bonds, annuities and other complex financial stuff. Then they went on to my grandfather's holdings, for reasons that weren't clear to me at first.

The boatyard was not the only thing my grandfather owned. The lawyer tallied the inventory in exhaustive detail. He was obviously being paid by the hour.

The holdings ranged across a dozen star systems and included land, satellites, asteroids, starships, banks, mines, factories and schools. He published books on Pericles, sold software on Claudius, shipped cargo across the seas of Poseidon, herded vishnu on Tik, and built boats on Asgard. His enterprises all had the same dash, the same love of craft and skill, the same risky sense of adventure that characterized what little good I had discovered in my kinsmen.

As the list went on, I watched Mother grow restless and bored. But I was just the opposite. The slow cataloging of my grandfather's accomplishments before leaving for the frontier worlds was more revealing than any of the self-serving lies she was likely to tell me about him.

Her eyes only perked up when they came to the end of the real property and began discussing securities, trust funds, and family shares. Here was the language she had been raised to savor and appreciate – the distilled essence of five centuries of exploitation reduced to stark numbers.

"While the material holdings are extensive, substantial, and well-secured, these liquid holdings are a different story," the senior attorney told Mother, his tiny eyes dropping groundwards beneath a furrowed, bald brow.

"I'm afraid, however, that there is some bad news. After weeks of looking at the documents, we have determined that before leaving on his expedition with the Space Corps, your father-in-law turned his holdings over to your husband, David. That is the reason we must include them in this discussion. Under the agreement, if Peter had died first, the properties would have gone to his son, David. But if Peter is still alive, or if he died after David, they would revert to your father-in-law and become part of his estate.

"In the first instance, the holdings would continue along, in turn, to your son, with collateral holdings devolving to you through your husband. But in the second case, there are several other claimants on the estate – the family common holding, Peter's brother, his brother's descendants, you, and Alex.

"The way the wills are written, we cannot divide up David's share of the family fortune unless and until we know what happened to his father."

My mother's face turned red and her eyes narrowed. "My father-in-law has been dead for at least two centuries. Everyone knows that. This is just a bunch of legalistic nonsense. I don't know why we bother to put up with it."

The lawyer looked flustered, but stood his ground. "I'm afraid we cannot presume that he is dead without documentary evidence. The Space Corps has been unable to verify his fate. They confirm that he departed on a Corps mission, as we all know, but they haven't told us anything about the mission itself. He might be on a long-distance journey that won't bring him back for another century or more."

"So where does that leave us?" Mother asked spitefully.

"I'm afraid that someone must follow your father's path, track him down and determine once and for all what happened to him."

***

Everyone was talking at once and it was several minutes before I began to notice heads turning in my direction. Mother eyed me with a suspicious leer, then smiled. I was not warmed by her attention.

In fact, my mind was already racing ahead of hers, though not by much, I could tell.

"Alex," she said. "Come here a minute. I have something I would like to discuss with you."

At another time, I would have felt trapped and outgunned. She had that self-satisfied look on her that radiated danger and alarm for those of us who have been her victims over the years. But this time, it was different.

I knew what she had in mind.

Before she even asked, I had made my decision.

She spoke in a low, hushed voice that only I could hear. The lawyers were huddled with one another as the rest of the family members struck poses of annoyed disbelief.

"Considering your behavior here at the reunion and the way it has been received by your uncles, this would be a good time for you to volunteer your services. After all, about the only thing you've accomplished in your life is to learn how to fly a starship. This should be easy for you."

I ignored the insults and smiled back at her. Then I tapped on the table to get everyone's attention. When they were silent, I spoke.

"I never knew my grandfather well, but I did get to meet him once. In fact, I was one of the last members of the family to see him before he left for the frontier. He was one of the gentlest men I have ever known, but he was strong and determined as well. I have always felt his loss as a personal one."

I paused and looked into my mother's eyes. There was a soul in there, I knew, but it so seldom revealed itself – and it wasn't coming out today. Then I turned to face Great-Grandmother. Her eyes were softer and more human than Mother's. Perhaps in the years since she had come out to the stars, she had learned to be more balanced in her passions and her judgments than the rest of the family. I couldn't be sure, but I think there was a twinkle in those eyes.

"A son of den Kolberg cannot turn down a responsibility because it is too difficult a task or because it might take too long to be convenient. Especially a family responsibility. My rough calculations show that Grandfather's path took him at least forty years from here and probably more."

I turned to the lawyers. "While eighty years may be a long time to wait to settle his estate, I'm sure your successors will be ready to handle things when I return.

"Great-Grandmother, Mother, it would be an honor and a privilege to follow Grandfather's path to the frontier and find out what happened to him."

Mother look smug and self-satisfied, and I was sure she would always believe that she had made me do it. But Great-Grandmother smiled at me and the twinkle in her old eyes was dazzling – at least she could sense the sincerity in my words.

I shut up and sat down. I'd never felt so free before in my life.

MURDERS AND GHOSTS

"Mr. Skreel says that now that you got the book, you might be interested in the stuff that belonged to the guy who wrote it."

I looked the man over carefully. The last time I'd seen him, he'd been lying face down on the tarmac on the spaceport landing field. My deepest hope was that he wouldn't connect me with the dark shape that struck out suddenly to put him in that condition. After all, I was a dozen meters away at the time, in the dark behind him.

He was big and ugly and his name was Bruiser Stang. I didn't want to know why that was his name. I did want to know who Mr. Skreel was and what he had that belonged to Commander Dreyfuss, the skipper of the Aldebaran

But there had to be a better way to find that out than passing messages through this thug. It bothered me enough that he had taken the trouble to track me down at the Planetfall Bar in the first place. The idea of him following me around the spaceport gave me the chills.

"Tell Mr. Skreel he can meet me here after supper, why don't you," said. "Alone."

Stang scowled, looked me up and down as if fitting me for a coffin, then turned and stalked out of the bar.

When he was gone, I breathed a sigh of relief and noticed Bob, the bartender, do the same. "Live bartenders are rare enough," he said. "But not nearly as rare as dead ones."

"Is he that dangerous?"

"That's what they say. You got business with him."

"Not any that I want," I said, draining the last of the beer from my mug. "But someone named Skreel is looking for me. Know anything about him?"

"He's a shady operator who's been hanging around here for a while. They say he came in on a tramp freighter a couple of years ago from who knows where. Does a lot of financing for spacers who are down on their luck – payment guaranteed before liftoff or double your bones broken, if you know what I mean. Stang is his collection agent."

I knew the type. They usually stayed just a few steps ahead of the local authorities and when things got too hot, they moved on to the next star and the next spaceport. Not the kind of guy I wanted to have following me around.

"If Jimmy Inoshe comes in, tell him to call my ship. I'll be back after supper."

"Do me a favor and don't bring him with you," Bob said, hooking a thumb at the empty space left behind by Bruiser Stang.

The day was warm and the sky streaked with high clouds. A few dried leaves blew across the flat paving stones of Spacefarers Square. I walked towards the park and stopped at the base of the Spacefarers Monument, where a tall marble figure of a man in a spacesuit, helmet under one arm, looked skyward.

I was surprised to discover another figure on the far side of the monument, a small Asian man seated on a stone bench. For a moment, I felt a little embarrassed at intruding on the man, but then he looked up at me and flashed a smile that was missing a couple of teeth.

"You spacer fellow like me, huh?" he asked.

"Yes, I am."

"That your ship come in two days ago, right?"

"Right again. Alex Kolberg, at your service."

"Trader Pak – from Shandong in Ara Sector. I know – is long way to home. Been many years real and bio since I been gone. Two…three centuries. When I was there, was lots of little states. Big cities. Not like this little burg, hey?"

"I'm familiar with of the Ara Sector," I said. "A little more orderly than it is out here, I guess."

That was an understatement. When old Earth decided to send its ten billion children to the stars, the several civilizations that survived the Technological Age divvied up the sky. The Perseus and Taurus Sectors were colonized by Europeans and Americans. The Ara Sector was colonized by Asian states – China, Korea, Japan, Singapore, and the rest. They had organized their settlements into strong, self-supporting urban states. Lots of them.

Internally they were tightly controlled societies. Den Kolberg never dreamed of the order the Aran city-states imposed on their citizens. But externally there was chaos. The rivalries among them had grown fast and furiously, and quite a few of them had taken to more radical forms of commercial competition – and more militant. The Space Corps had finally been forced to move in and control the notorious pirates of Ara. The stories were part of our early education at the Academy.

"Too much order. No freedom for free trader like Pak. Besides, pirates bust my butt too many times. So I leave Ara behind. Head for clean space and good ports. Like this one, hey?"

"If you say so. What I've seen of Minos doesn't make it sound so clean. Of course, I hear Ara isn't so bad these days. A lot can change in a few hundred years."

"Yeah. So what. I like it here. Lots a secrets. Secrets as thick as berries on a bush. Or like moleholes in mountain," he added, stomping the ground with a boot-clad foot.

"I know what you mean."

"I bet you do," Pak said. "You, me, look for same things, I think. You don't know much, but you get closer all the time."

"Maybe," I said, suddenly interested in what the old man was trying not to say. "Things like what."

"Secrets buried in ground. Secrets buried in books. Lost in time. But you be careful, spacer-fella. Secrets can turn around and bite you. Even secrets that been dead a long time. Time not real, you know. Just a trick of your mind so things not happen all at once. But they really do happen all at once, you know. Got to forget what you think you know and stop trying to remember it different."

"What?"

"You learn what I mean someday. Meantime, you be careful. Sorry now, gotta go. Big business. More secrets. No time left until Zorgons get here."

He rose quickly, felt through five or six of the dozen pockets on his vest and shirt, then smacked himself on the forehead. He muttered something in another language, then hurried off across the plaza, leaving me to sort out his confusing remarks while the leaves skittered on the wind.

***

I went back to the ship. It was a long walk, but I didn't have much else to do at the moment. The logbook was a great find, but by itself, it was a dead end. Too many unanswered questions. Not enough direction. How did you scare up a trail that was three centuries cold? Space and time were vast and deep. Deep enough to lose a multitude of sins. Vast enough to swallow whole worlds without a trace. Finding the remains of one soul whose light had slipped from view generations ago was more hopeless than I had imagined when I volunteered for this quest.

My only plan at the moment was to keep digging around and hope that something would turn up. Anything. Mysteries were like that, I'd found. You pull at the threads around the edges long enough and one of them comes loose. Pull enough threads and the whole thing unravels. Hoy many threads could time weave together in three hundred years?

The phone jingled, interrupting my sour mood – at least the ship's phone was working. It was Jimmy Inoshe. He was stuck at the local scout post in a high-level meeting and wouldn't be around until later that night. I told him about Skreel.

"Sounds pokey," he said.

"Pokey?"

"Suspicious. Hinky. Off-level. Dukey and dumb. I don't know, what did they call it back when you come from?"

"Everything but pokey," I said. "If I run into Stang I'll give him your regards."

"Just don't give him my address."

He rung off, and I dressed for supper.

Back at the Planetfall, I found myself a booth in a corner,

surrounded by dark-stained, close-grained wood paneling. It gave me a sightline on a mirror with a full view of the bar while allowing me to remain concealed. Security was one of the first principles of any good military strategy.

I ordered a steak and yams for supper. It came out rare and juicy. As I hacked away at the fleshy meat, I remembered old Gram Stanger back on Asgard. Gram had taken care of me during the summer, when classes were off. She was a vegetarian and wouldn't let me eat such delicacies as this. She'd have scolded me bad if she saw what I was doing to myself – no matter that Bob had promised it was from a local herd of cholesterol-free cattle. To Gram, it was a moral issue. You didn't live off other animals.

The cherimoyas and sugar dessert, on the other hand, would have melted her heart. She was always a pushover for the custardy fruit and a sweet sauce. She must have passed on even before my grandfather disappeared, I realized when I added up the years.

I was scraping the last nutty-flavored bits of fruit from the green skin when I looked up to see Trader Pak walk in. He took a seat at the bar and ordered a drink. A few minutes later, Bob came back my way to clear away the dishes.

"The fellow who just came in the door is Skreel," he said.

He was not what I expected – short, old, with a face that looked like an overripe pear, all mottled and wrinkled. He sat down next to Pak and started to talk. That was interesting. What did the two of them have in common? They were too far away for me to hear a thing, and it made my skin crawl to sit there powerless and ignorant.

After a few moments, though, that wasn't a problem.

"No way, Tokay!" Pak yelled as he jumped from the stool. "Not a million years yet! You gotta be crazy out of mind, out of time. What you think of me, hey?" He broke into some foreign dialect that flowed so smoothly I was sure it was his native tongue. From the sound of it, he was cursing Skreel, who sat there passively as Pak stormed out of the bar.

He watched the old man leave, then motioned to Bob and ordered a drink. He wasn't leaving. Great. Now what should I do? In the absence of any hard intelligence, I figured my best tack was to keep as much concealed as possible. That meant not letting Skreel know how much I knew of him and his business. If I approached him now, I'd lose that advantage.

I looked around and saw the back door of the bar hanging open and the alley beyond. A quick inspection of the sightlines and I figured I could slip out unnoticed – so I did.

The alley was dark and smelly and something moved near the garbage cans.

I couldn't see if it was a native pest or one of mankind's perennial companions, rats or cats. The alley led around the side of the building, between the Spacefarers Hall and the Planetfall Bar. I came out onto the square just in time to see Trader Pak headed across the plaza, muttering to himself. Then I went back inside through the front door.

***

The introductions were quick and void of false courtesies. Skreel was blunt and direct, but I could see there were depths behind his oily eyes. Murky depths that could swallow a careless man.

"I believe you can identify these," he said, laying a stack of coins on the dark wooden surface of the bar.

I spread them out and picked one at random. It was a gold maxi from Asgard. The date embossed beneath the image of the maxidon on the front read 362 N.E. The others were similar – silver eddies, aluminum ducks. I recognized them all. The small change and large treasures of my own youth.

"Yes, if they're authentic. But what's your point? I'm not a coin collector – and neither are you."

The faintest of smiles appeared on cold lips. "No, I'm not. But these should attest to the authenticity of my offer. I have certain items that may hold your interest, now that you are in possession of the logbook of Commander Dreyfuss."

"Am I? It seems that possession of that book has varied from day to day in the past few weeks."

"Skanderi and I have talked since last night, so you needn't lie. In any case, my offer would stand whether the book was yours or not. You are den Kolberg, correct? You have the means to meet a reasonable price? I have ... equipment ... personal effects... I can be more specific if you are truly interested. Are you, or should I take my offer elsewhere?"

Like where, I wondered. Who else would want 300-year-old relics besides me? And how long would Skreel have to wait for them to come along? He was bluffing, for sure, but I played along with him.

"You overestimate my means," I said. "Den Kolberg doesn't have any credit here on Minos, and all I carry with me are a few coins of my own. If you're trying to tap into the den's bankbook, you're in the wrong place at the wrong time. What are you selling anyway?"

Skreel squirmed in obvious discomfort. "A way to read more from the logbook. It was an offer that Skanderi was given, but he rejected it. He said he was not interested in the contents of the book. You, I believe, are."

I tried not to betray my feelings, even though my heart had suddenly picked up in pace. It was time to throw him off-balance. "How does Trader Pak figure in all this?"

"Pak? The Asian? No, not him. He's not a part of this. Not at all. The man owes me money. Purely personal."

I wondered if Skreel played poker – it would have been a cheap way to take whatever he had away from him. He had no skill at all in concealing his feelings. "All right, Skreel. Name your price."

"One thousand megabucks in coins, specie, or gems at the current Minos exchange rate."

"For a pig in a poke?"

"A what?"

"Sorry, an old expression. Anyway, it's too much for merchandise that you won't describe. What's your game? It sounds like you haven't got the goods yourself."

"If you choose to insult me."

"I choose to work on my own. I don't need a middle man. If you're an agent for someone else, tell them to call me. If you're not, come clean now. None of us has time to dance around in a game like this," I said, rolling my eyes skyward.

Skreel's pudgy cheeks turned red, but I couldn't read anything more. What was this nonsense? I was losing patience. Then Bob the bartender interrupted.

"Mr. Kolberg? Call for you."

I flashed him a quizzical look. Who could be calling me here? Probably Inoshe, still at the scout post. The bartender handed me the phone.

"Alex Kolberg?" asked a clearly masculine voice.

"Yes."

"I need your help," the caller said. "And I think you may need mine."

"I'm in the middle of other business right now. Can I call you back?"

"No, you can't. I'm sorry, but I can't explain. You're talking to Skreel, aren't you. Dump him. This is more important. I know what happened to your grandfather's ship."

"What? How? Who are you?"

"I can't tell you that right now."

"You'd better tell me something or we'll just forget about it," I said, bluffing.

"Come to the Spacefarers Hall. Tonight. As soon as you can. All your questions will be answered, believe me."

"Why should I?"

"Why shouldn't you?"

"How will I find you?"

There was no answer, and the screen lit up with the logo of a local phone company. And when I got back to the bar, Skreel was gone. I looked at Bob, but he shrugged. That settled it quickly enough. There was nothing left to do but go next door to the Spacefarers Hall.

***

I didn't feel comfortable going to the hall.

The Spacefarers Union went back a long time – before interstellar travel. They helped bring down the old steel company in Sol's asteroid belt back in the Dark Ages. They were militant and strong, and they didn't like people who owned things like starships and spaceports.

I assumed they wouldn't like me.

My family doesn't just own things, they use them. And they employ people – a fancy way of saying they use them too. I never had much to do with that side of den Kolberg's business, but I spent the money, used the property, accepted the benefits, and, on occasion, enjoyed the power.

On the other hand, we had a lot in common. The Spacefarers and den Kolberg both spent a lot of real-time between the stars. Our roots went back together and our paths had crossed many times. Some union members were as wealthy as we were in their own way. And because their numbers were small and they attracted little attention they didn't have to work as hard as we did to keep their wealth secure.

The similarities were outweighed by the differences, of course. The biggest of those is that they traveled because they enjoyed it, not because they had to outrun their bankers. And in that respect, among others, I was out of step with the rest of den Kolberg. I enjoyed traveling more than any of them.

So I hesitated before entering the big stone hall that rose like a castle from the cobblestones of Spacefarers Plaza. A cool wind blew dry leaves across the square, and I could hear the sound of laughter and women's voices from up near the restaurant across from the spaceport terminal. Otherwise the streets were empty and silent.

Overhead, a few bright stars twinkled through high, thin clouds. Somewhere up there, rushing towards us at the speed of light, were the Zorgons. Maybe the thought of them colored my perceptions, but it seemed like the laughter from the restaurant had a nervous edge to it and the women's voices were too high, too quick.

I realized that I didn't have time to waste standing around being shy. After taking a deep breath, I walked through the door.

The place was full of varnished wood paneling, polished brass, and potted plants. Half a dozen overstuffed sofas, upholstered in black, filled the floor. Overhead, a balcony surrounded the deep well of the lobby. As I stepped into the central space, I could see that the ceiling went all the way up to the roof. A large fireplace dominated the room, with an animal skin rug stretched out before it. Bookcases and a AI screens filled the wall opposite. A pair of doorways on either side of the hearth led into the dining room.

And seated around the fire were four men and a woman.

One of the men leaped from his seat when he saw me and hurried over.

"Joseph DeNicola," he said, thrusting out his hand. "Union steward and Master of the Hall. Can I help you?"

I took his hand and shook it. "My name is Alex. I was supposed to meet someone here, but I'm not sure just who."

"Are you a member?"

"No – I'm master of the *Perseus Wanderer*. Just landed this week."

"Oh," DeNicola said with a knowing nod. "Welcome to Minos, Mr. Kolberg."

"Did I hear someone say he was the master of a ship?" asked one of the other men, a big guy with about ten centimeters and twenty kilos on me. He wore his hair in a military cut, and even though he did not wear a uniform, I could tell he belonged in one. "Trooper Darko Webb, at your service."

"He's master of the boat that came in two days ago," DeNicola said, loud enough to bring the rest of them to their feet. He introduced me to "Detroit" Hawkins, a ship's engineer, and Peter

McCoy, a weapons officer.

Hawkins said he got his name from his homeworld, where kids were born with silver spanners in their hands. His hair was thinning on top, but he made up for it with a pair of great sideburns that blended into a handlebar mustache

"Call me Gunner," said McCoy. He squeezed my hand a tight grip and looked me up and down with laser-sharp eyes.

"I'm Wendy Webb," said the woman, as she pushed her way past the trooper who shared her name. "My husband would have introduced me if he had any manners – which he doesn't." She had long blonde hair and filled out a shipboard flightsuit like it was an outfit from Paris.

They all wore the same hungry look as they stared at me with eager eyes. I felt for a minute like they were a bunch of half-starved maxidons and I was dinner.

"So tell me, Alex," Webb said with a sidelong glance at his mates, "you wouldn't happen to be looking for crew, would you?"

I looked them all up and down for a minute. So that was why they were all so friendly. I should have expected it. They were probably the only spacers left on the planet at this point. Maybe they wouldn't mind if I was den Kolberg.

"I might be," I said.

"I knew it," McCoy shouted. "I told you we'd get off this rock."

The others were not so enthusiastic. "What do you mean you might be?" Webb asked.

"When I'm done with my business, I might need a few hands for a flight back towards Perseus Sector."

"And when's that?"

They all turned their attention to me. The silence was threatening.

"I don't know," I said. "Could be a while – maybe a few weeks."

"Damn it," Webb said as he turned away from me. "I knew it was too good to be true."

"In a few weeks, we'll all be spacedust," McCoy said, shooting an angry glare towards me. "Are you crazy? Don't you want to get out of here before the Zorgons show?"

"Of course," I said. "And when they do show, I'm leaving. It might be handy to have a trained gunner on board when I do – if I can find one who can keep his feelings on a short leash."

McCoy looked embarrassed and skulked back to the fireplace.

"It'll be kind of late in the game for that kind of maneuver, won't it, Kolberg?" Webb asked, turning my name into something like a curse.

"I'm not worried about it. The Zorgons aren't likely to be looking for little guys like me. Of course, you could wait for the next ship to show up. Or is that how you got here in the first place?"

Now it was Webb's turn to look sheepish. His wife told their story.

"Our ship took off without us the day before you arrived," she said.

"Split vacuum in the middle of the night without the pilot or the navigator or us. The master was awfully scared when he heard hunting season was opening and he was in season."

I winced. That wasn't a kind thing to do. And it was a calculated risk for the master. If this group survived and finally caught up with him, he might have to pay a high price for his haste. But in the meantime, he was headed for someplace years away.

"And why weren't you on board when the ship lifted?" I asked suddenly, realizing that it was the key unanswered question. I looked at each of them in turn as it remained unanswered. They all turned their eyes away from me.

"Just what I need," I said. "A crew that's more concerned with shore leave and feather beds in Spacefarers Hall than they are about making liftoff."

"I was mugged," said Hawkins. "They took my wallet and left me unconscious. I came to on the couch here after McCoy dragged me inside."

I was unmoved. One exception out of a bunch of featherbedders. But then, if they could bring themselves to work for a den Kolberg ship, I suppose I could overlook their shortcomings.

"I didn't come out here planning to hire extra hands," I said. McCoy moaned and Webb frowned. "So I can't offer you union rates. Sorry, DeNicola, that's the way it is. But if you want a way off planet when the Zorgons get here, I'll make it official."

They rose to their feet as one.

"And I promise to give you more notice than your last master when we're ready to clear space."

McCoy continued to grumble, and Webb insisted I ought to get away while the getting was still good. But they all presented their union cards and marked the working forms at DeNicola's AI with their thumbprints as I did the same.

"I'll take anyone who wants to aboard the *Wanderer* this midwatch," I said. "Meet me here at 24 o'clock."

"Aye, aye, skipper," said Hawkins. The others just grumbled some more. McCoy said he didn't know if he wanted to trust me until then, but I told him he didn't have any choice. That shut him up.

Then DeNicola came up to me again. "Mr. Kolberg, there's a call for you."

He showed me the public commscreen in the corner of a narrow hallway. Once again, the screen was dark, but the line was alive.

"Kolberg? It's me again. I'm glad to see you came."

"Glad enough to let me in on the mystery?"

"Soon enough. For now, though, I want you to stay put. There are still some players in motion. I need you to hang loose. I will call you again when the time comes."

"Wait a minute – I can't sit around here all night long. Who are you and what do you want?"

"Not all night. Soon. Very soon. Trust me. I'll call again." The screen went blank.

***

When I returned to the lobby, my newfound crew of misfits had disappeared.

"They went next door to celebrate," DeNicola said.

"You know, when the time comes, there could be space for you on the *Wanderer*," I told him.

"No thanks," he said. "I've still got 180 days to go on a thousand-day assignment here. I'll take my chances as they come."

"Are you sure? This may be your only chance."

"Your ship can only hold so many. You'll have to draw the line somewhere."

"I guess you're right," I said wistfully.

At DeNicola's suggestion, I retired to the dining room for a cup of coffee – the real thing, gene-original from Colombia. It was a treat I couldn't resist. And with it came a treat that I found I had to resist.

Her name was Suzanne, and she said she came to the Hall every night – for the coffee and to wait.

"My boyfriend and I, we be set to be married. Then, a few days before the ceremony, we be fighting. It be silly, something about money or being unkind. Anyway, the next day, he be gone, signed aboard a star freighter bound for Serjanus."

She had soft brown hair and smooth skin. Her eyes were big and inviting. And she was one of those people who always seem to be someplace else, their minds fixed to a distant star and not rooted in the here-and-now. Nevertheless, I knew that I could have her if I wanted her. I could step up to her, control the conversation carefully, deftly, and bend her will – what there was of it – to mine. There was even a time when I would have done it.

But that was long ago, when I was not so scrupulous.

"Serjanus be more than eighteen years from here. That be thirty-six out and back. I'd be turned to an old maid waiting for him. I be not that proud. But for days I be sorrow-filled over the fight and the way we be hurting ourselves. So I come up with my plan."

I lost myself in those eyes as she talked. There was something about her innocence, her odd syntax, and her dreamy eyes that tempted me strongly.

"The next day, I be at the spaceport looking for outbound ships. No more there be for Serjanus for months, they say. But there be a ship for 111 Tauri going in a week. So I take my dowry to the post and pay for a lasergram to Serjanus, telling my love to return home because I be forgiving him. And, I tell him, I be traveling too, to skip over the time until he be returning. Then I be going home to my mama and grandmama and my dad, to tell them all goodbye. We be crying till morning, then I get aboard the ship and be gone to 111 Tauri."

But I was not so lost that I paid no attention to her words. Her loyalty to her lover was admirable. In a younger day, I would have seen it only as an added challenge, to be broken down carefully and then disposed of. Tonight, though, I wanted none of that. Instead, I thought about another lover and how her loyalty had torn us apart.

Elaine was the other woman's name. I'd known her on Helvetica and before that on Zoroaster. She was a Radical. Their long-term campaign involved removing my family from its position of power and influence in the Perseus Sector, and from what she said that was her goal as well. She had traveled to Helvetica with den Morgan, returned to Zoroaster after the first few years and returned with me to Helvetica to see how two decades had treated the den. We arrived just after the Uprising, when it was too late to do any good.

I felt guilty and stupid about everything. She felt angry and vengeful. I wanted to kill my uncles and cousins. She wanted to find out where they had shipped her den. I wanted to stay on Helvetica and track down the truth, and I did – how my uncle Josef had sent them on a century-long trip towards the Ara Sector on the other side of Sol from here. She wanted to follow them, and she did. I did not. End of story. End of love affair.

But Suzanne's story had not ended in tragedy. Not yet.

"Now 111 Tauri be more than seventeen years from here. I wait there a few weeks until another ship be returning, but not so long as I need to. So I be back here on Minos three years before my love. That be three years gone, now. I be expecting him anytime now. A few days, a few weeks. My mama and grandmama be dead a while. My dad be old and full of machines. But my love be coming back, I know it. One day soon, I be getting a lasergram in the mail – one day soon. And then a few days more and he be here himself. For him it be only a few days – a few weeks since we be fighting. For him, it be like we just parted."

"And for you?"

She laughed, turning her wide eyes towards me and covering them with long, slender fingers. "For me, it be just the same."

And I knew she was lying – to herself as well as me. The waiting takes a toll, whether it's a day, a week, a month, or a year. In my case, it was twelve years or forever, depending on which betrayal you want to talk about. Twelve years for my parents, forever for Elaine. I knew that small piece of knowledge would be enough to turn Suzanne's will, but I knew I would never use it against her. It would have spoiled my own precious memories.

"So what's it like over at 111 Tauri?" I asked, turning the conversation to a more innocent subject.

"They still be worried about the Zorgons. They be ready for them to come back, though. Not like us here at Minos. We be sitting like drakes in a puddle."

"Let's hope your boyfriend gets here before they do, then," I said, finishing up my coffee. I went to the mess cabinet for a refill and was stirring in the cream when DeNicola stuck his head through the door and waved his phone.

"Someone is calling you on my phone," he said.

"Kolberg!" the voice spoke urgently at the other end, "I need you quickly. In the alley behind the Spacefarers Hall – behind the Planetfall Bar. He's in trouble. Whatever happens to him, don't let them get his keys! Get out there now!"

***

I was out the door in a flash and rounded the corner of the building quickly. Distant street lights cast only long, inky shadows among the trash mashers and the recycling bins behind the Spacefarers Hall. It did not look inviting.

The alley was a dark cleft between the dark hulks of two rows of stone buildings. A dim yellow light spilled across it a short ways down from the rear of one of the units in the block on the left. I figured it to be the Planetfall from its position.

It took a moment for my eyes to adjust to the night well enough to negotiate the narrow gap between the trash masher behind the hall. By then, it was too late.

"Haiiieeeeeee!"

The high, wrenching cry echoed from the walls and turned my blood to icewater – the kind that comes down off the glaciers in the spring on Asgard. It was followed by a more ominous sound – the burp of a needle gun and the clatter of projectiles against the pavement.

I sliped into the alley, keeping low and in the shadows.

After a few steps, I came even with the rear entrance to the Planetfall Bar – just as the back door swung open and several indistinct but energetic shapes came flying out.

The first one ran straight into me, then recoiled with an animal moan. The second stopped short before colliding with us, and the third smacked into him.

It was Hawkins, Webb, and McCoy – in that order.

"What was that?" Webb asked.

"It came from back there," I offered as I pulled myself together. The others did the same and in an instant we were poking cautiously into the heart of the darkness. A few meters into the alley and we were walking into our own shadows.

Suddenly a sharp blue light cut past us, scanned the bricks and cobblestones and halted on a dark shape lying motionless on the ground. I looked back to see the silhouette of Wendy Webb wielding a handtorch.

"What's that?" McCoy asked with a gasp.

I pressed past him and Webb and knelt down to examine it. Wendy came up and directed the light to more efficient use. I prodded the shape, which yielded slightly, but didn't move. Then the lines and shadows leapt into perspective, and I found its face.

It was Trader Pak – dead as Poseidon's moons.

Everyone fell silent in shock or surprise. And as a consequence, we were all able to hear the scuffling of footsteps even further down the alley.

"Damn!" hissed Darko Webb. "McCoy, stay by me. Keep your head down and your ears open."

They disappeared into the darkness without a sound. I was glad they were going in there and not me. I had other business anyway.

"I think I'm going to be sick," Hawkins said suddenly. He turned and went back inside, leaving me alone in the alley with Pak's body and Wendy Webb. I turned to my gruesome task.

Pak's vest was worse than the cargo hold on an asteroid salvage boat. He had everything in those pockets – notes, an electronic clock, two Ancient hieroglyphs, fruit, nuts, and keys. I remembered my mystery caller's instructions: "Don't let them get his keys!"

There was a small ring that held at least half a dozen old-fashioned metal keys. And a separate plastic tag was linked to a cardkey. Finally, I found a single loose key of brass tucked into one of the small pockets on top of the larger ones. I avoided parts of the vest where the blond had already soaked through.

"What are you doing?" Wendy asked.

"Going through his pockets," I said.

"I can see that."

"Then why did you ask?"

"Because I don't usually get to see someone robbing the dead, I suppose," she snapped back.

"It's nothing he's going to need, believe me. Besides, I'm just following orders. Someone asked me to save these." I jingled the keys in the air between us.

"Aren't you going to check his pants?"

"Not me," I said. "It feels too strange, sticking your fingers in there. I patted him down, though. Nothing in there."

"Who do you suppose did it?"

"Beats me. There are so many unsavory characters around this place that it gets hard to keep track of them all. Where do you suppose your husband got himself to?"

"Killed, I hope. He's more muscle than brain. It would serve him right for charging after an armed killer. But he thinks troopers are invulnerable."

A moment later, however, McCoy emerged from farther down the alley. "Webb says to come up here and look at what we found."

I followed him nervously. The air was thick with the smells of rotting organics. Some were familiar and sweet – tomato sauce and spoiled fruit. Others were exotic and acrid – I caught a whiff of fermented spineycone. Wendy followed us, swinging the light just enough so it did us more harm than good. I almost fell over a pile of trash.

"We came after him, whoever he was," McCoy said. "But Webb

didn't want to get too close, and by the time we got to the end, this was all we found."

I made out the dark shape of the trooper against the gray bulk of a stone wall. Wendy came up and shined the light in his face. He scowled and pointed at the ground.

She turned the light that way and we could see a metal grating where it had been pushed out of place and a large square hole in the pavement. Wendy's husband took the light from her and pointed it down the hole. I could see the first few rungs of a ladder built into the shaft. Then I recognized where I was – this was the exit Jimmy Inoshe and I had used to escape from the escape tunnels!

"You can go down there if you like, but I've been there before and I didn't know Pak well enough to want to go after his killer," I said.

McCoy grumbled and shook his head. Webb just rubbed his face and looked into the hole. "Go ahead, Darko," his wife said.

"What's up here?" I asked, pointing towards the short piece of alleyway that ran out to the street, making a right angle with the main alley. No one could tell me, so I made the trip myself.

It was just another sidewalk on another side street, except a short distance away, on the corner, was a brightly lit building with a long, narrow sign running down from the roof that read: "State Police Troop W."

Just what I needed – the cops.

***

"You spacers may be thinking you still be in space, but you be not. This spaceport be under the jurisdiction of Area W, Verdemont State Police, and the laws of the Planetary Government of Minos. And it be my duty to warn you that murder be a criminal offense in this jurisdiction. Now this be not just Area W, this be MY spaceport. I be Lieutenant Inspector Mortegan, and I be the head of the detective bureau here at the spaceport. I been here six years and I be not liking spacers. And you be no different from the rest, as far as I been seeing."

They were big words – if confusing – from a small man. Mortegan's features were sharp and strong, piercing eyes, square jaw and chiseled nose, but they were done in miniature. He couldn't have been more than 160 centimeters tall.

That didn't seem to bother him in the least, though. He had led the team of police officers and detectives that invaded the alley after I stepped into the precinct house and mentioned the shooting outside. Within ten minutes, there were floodlights and holocameras and biosniffers and fiberbugs and every other kind of forensic device known to the mind of man and accessible to the police on Minos.

Unfortunately, it took Mortegan more than an hour to get around to the eyewitnesses. He had us wait in the lobby of the Spacefarers Hall – which turned out to be a dreadful experience. My new crewmembers sulked before the fireplace while I waited quite anxiously for my mystery caller to make contact again.

Mortegan paced slowly before the fireplace, treading carefully in heavy boots whose soles seemed thicker than normal.

"Who been the first one into the alley?" he asked.

"I was," I said.

"Me," said Hawkins.

"Well, we sort of ran into one another."

Mortegan wasn't amused. "And which of you be holding the needle gun?"

Hawkins blanched, then opened his mouth soundlessly. I just laughed, short and contemptuously, giving up all hope that Mortegan might be that rarest of creatures, a cop with a brain. He was not. He was the kind of man that we in den Kolberg had working for us, and he did not intimidate me at all.

"The killer escaped down a hole in the ground," Webb said

"Been I asking you something?" Mortegan said, sneering up at the trooper. "No, but he still escaped down a hole in the ground. I showed you where it was."

"Yes, that be very convenient, be it not?"

I knew it was going to be a long night. Two or three times, I locked eyes with Wendy Webb. Each time I felt a nervous heat come over me and the load of booty in my pockets became infinitely heavier. She could give me away with a word.

Mortegan took us into the dining room one at a time and asked all the usual questions. My stomach squirmed when they called Wendy in before it was my turn. I waited for someone in uniform to come out and throw me in irons, turning out my pockets and revealing me as a corpse-robber. It never happened. After a while, she emerged from the dining room, flashed me a knowing smile and sat beside her husband. It was my turn.

The detective was not very sophisticated. His method of interrogation seemed to consist of trying to catch me up in incriminating statements with leading questions.

"You be den Kolberg. That be a good reason to suspect you for just about anything," he said. "How do we know if you been coming in or going out of the alley when you been hit by Mr. Hawkins?"

"Other than by our say so, I'm not sure how," I told him.

"And how do we know that the grate to the emergency shaft be open so that the killer been able to escape – or that you been able to get into the alley?"

"You've got me there," I said. "Unless you want to listen to the two or three witnesses who saw me on the phone in the Spacefarers Hall about twenty seconds before Pak screamed."

He wasn't very good at it, and I didn't cooperate at all. I guess I eventually bored him to the point of releasing me.

All I wanted to do when they let me go was run as fast as I could from the building and get back to my ship. I exercised the better part of valor, however, and walked casually towards the exit. Wendy caught me before I reached the door.

"Come with me," she said. "I want to see what you got from Pak."

I looked around nervously. No one was within earshot. Her husband had disappeared from the lobby, but the cop by the door to the restroom revealed to where. There was no way I could easily extricate myself from the trap I found myself in. So I smiled and said: "Of course."

We climbed two flights of stairs quickly, pausing briefly while she unlocked the door with a large electronic key. Then we stepped into a small room containing a large bed, a wardrobe, a nightstand, and a chair. Wendy pulled a flight bag off the chair and sat down. "Let's see it," she demanded.

I scooped out the contents of my pocket and dropped them on the bed. The dried fruit and nuts had mixed with everything else in a dirty, dusty mess.

She plucked the interesting treasures from the trail mix and rubbed them clean on the bedclothes. The pocket clock beeped at her and the keys jingled. Then she found the hieroglyphs and let out of squeal of joy.

"Oh look, a Smiling Rat and a Walking Stick!"

She took the glyphs over to a brighter light by the nightstand and looked closely at the flat, milky-white stones. They were covered with faint blue pictures and the cursive writing of the Ancient Aliens. I'd seen similar ones before – just the other night, in fact, in Commandant Powell's house. Like those, the stones seemed to shimmer and the images appeared to float just beneath a transparent surface layer.

"I collect these, you know. These are pretty valuable. Look at this," she said, pulling me close to the light and pointing to the pictures on the larger glyph. "That's a Walking Stick and there's a Cock's Comb. Those are pretty rare symbols. Worth a lot, at least while they last."

"While they last?"

"The story is that the pictures change every few years. I've never seen it happen to mine, but there are videos of it. Some people say they're a fake, but I've seen the documents on the matrix back home."

"Can you translate these?"

"Translate? No, of course not. I just collect them. I know what to look for and I can spot real value, but I don't read the things. Not like some do."

"I know someone here at the spaceport who's got a big collection of them, including a few he keeps in a locked safe."

"You don't suppose you could get me in to see them, do you?"

"Probably not."

She pressed her arm against me and said: "Anyone ever tell you you have real nice eyes?"

"It's come up in conversation before," I said.

"I'll bet they keep Darko downstairs for another hour," she said, sighing softly.

I stepped back gingerly from the table and pawed through the other items I'd retrieved from Pak's vest. It wasn't that I didn't appreciate her advance, and I was only slightly intimidated by her trained killer of a husband. But I like to take romance personally, not as a means to another end – especially with another man's woman. Wendy seemed to have another agenda entirely. I felt sorry for Darko.

Not for the first time, I felt myself longing for the sound of my mystery caller. I had some questions I wanted answered, and he seemed to be the one who could answer them. I began to get itchy to return to the lobby so I'd be there when he called back.

I gathered up the loot and waited patiently while Wendy played with the hieroglyphs for a few minutes more. Better them than me, I figured.

When the phone on the nightstand warbled softly, my heart skipped a beat. Wendy touched the receiver button and the voice-only unit clicked to life in the tabletop.

"I want to talk to Alex." I breathed a sigh of relief. I was afraid it might be her husband.

"Right here. And I'm not alone." Wendy arched her eyebrows as if to question me, but I ignored her.

"I know that."

"Of course you do. And how do you know that?" I asked.

"I have means sufficient to my purposes," my caller replied.

"A monitor of some kind?"

There was a long silence. "That's unimportant right now."

"That's how you knew Pak was in trouble, isn't it? You were monitoring him. What is it? The clock? This key?"

"No, none of them."

"What then? Not one of the nuts, surely."

"That's not why I called."

"It is one of the nuts," I said. I dug through the trash and sorted the fruit from the nuts. I lined them up and sure enough, one of them was a slightly different shade of brown. Wendy looked at me like I was crazy, but held her tongue. "Is this it?"

"Alex, please."

"What's the matter, would you rather. I played the game your way? It's time to settle up, citizen. I don't even know your name, but you've got me involved in a murder. And you did it too late to do any good for the victim. Don't you think you owe me some answers?"

"Who did it?"

"That's a question."

"I know. Who did it?"

"You mean who killed Pak?"

"Naturally. My guess is that it was Skreel. Pak was afraid of him. That's why he had me monitoring him. But the transmission from that alley was terrible – too much rock in the way."

"If you were close enough to monitor him, why didn't you come help?" There was another long silence. "I couldn't. I can't. I'm afraid I am stuck right where I am – for the moment."

"And where is that?"

"Considering the vulnerability of my position, I don't think I could feel safe divulging that information."

"And your name?"

"Would reveal too much."

"Is this Jimmy Inoshe?"

There was an odd noise on the line, then the voice replied: "Flattering. Amusing. But no, I'm not."

I had run out of smart replies. And my caller had managed to keep his cards concealed. Although I wondered if it was wise to reveal as much as he had to Wendy Webb. I certainly didn't trust her, but if my invisible friend wanted to, that was his problem. "My best guess would be a big guy name Stang. He works for Skreel. I'd bet he does just this kind of job, too."

"I'm quite concerned about Skreel," the caller said. "Pak said he wanted something that he could not have. I agreed. We were working to keep him away, but I guess we didn't work fast enough."

"I guess not."

"He's really dead, isn't he?"

"They're not talking about bringing him back."

"That's a tragedy."

"For you or him?"

"For both of us. Being murdered is not a pleasant experience." I laughed sharply. He sounded like he knew firsthand.

"So what next?" I asked.

"You took Pak's keys?"

"Every last one of them."

"Very good. I want you to hold onto them. And then you must find Skreel."

***

"You didn't tell me you already had a partner," Wendy said.

"He's not a partner," I replied. "I don't even know his name. And so far, the relationship has been pretty one-sided. He's been calling me all night long, trying to arrange a meeting, but playing hard-to-get."

"That makes two of you."

"I'm not sure I want to go looking for Skreel, though," I said, ignoring her remark. "He has some nasty friends. Until we stumbled over poor old Pak, my interest in this was mostly academic. I'm not sure what I'm going to get for the risk entailed in tracking down Skreel."

"Don't fade on us now, captain," Wendy said. "You're going to get more than you will if you don't look for him. Let's go."

She pulled at my arm, but I hung back long enough to gather up Pak's keys. The rest of his property I left behind, including the bogus nut. Maybe Darko Webb would eat it.

We hurried down the stairs and through the lobby. McCoy was just coming out of the dining room, and Wendy's husband was on the way in. He looked up at us as we flew by, scorching me with his angry glare. Wendy blew him a kiss as we flew out the door.

The police lights still spilled out of the alley, along with a bunch of uniformed cops and their equipment. I took a quick peek into the empty Planetfall Bar, then stepped back out again. We went back past Spacefarers Hall and turned down another street.

We found Skreel after about an hour of bar hopping – at that time of night, the bars and the police station were the only things still open. Skreel was dug in at a back table in a place closer to the spaceport terminal called The Orbit Lounge where the smell of tabacky and spilled beer hung thick in the air.

Wendy clung to my arm and chattered away about her dress, her makeup and her husband while a robot behind the bar spun hoses and tubes together to mix our drinks. I watched Skreel in the grime-covered mirror behind the robot, wondering if he was watching me just as carefully. I hoped he would see me with Wendy and chalk it up to normal den Kolberg philandering. If he approached me, I could always ask him if he had any more to tell me about the property he'd been trying to sell me earlier in the evening. How long ago that seemed now.

Neither of us made a move for the better part of an hour. I tried nursing a single glass of melted ice, but Wendy slugged away two stiff drinks. It did not improve her behavior, but she didn't seem otherwise impaired.

In fact, it seemed to calm her down. Instead of putting moves on me, she began to talk in softer tones about herself and her husband.

"I met him back on Cicero. I grew up there – in one of the deepwoods cities that they built back in the Second Century. I cane to Port Androcles just about the time they decided to nationalize the place. Darko was with the mercenary battalion that they brought in to back them up. He'd come out from Cincinnatus, working his way across the sector after the corps disbanded his unit when it lost half its strength at the battle of Kappa Ceti."

Cicero was a younger colony than Darko's homeworld. Ironically, that meant it was more sophisticated – closer to Earth in time if not space, with more recent ties to the planet. Culturally and socially, it had also had less time to wander away from the mainstream.

Cincinnatus was "nykulturny" – a hot, steamy world without sunshine or blue skies, from what Darko told her. Wrestling a colony out of its harsh and unforgiving environment was a full-time job, with little energy or capital left over for the niceties that civilized folks indulged in.

The contrast between the two backgrounds, his and hers, was what attracted her to Webb in the first place.

"The men on Cicero were all so useless – or disgusting. There were a lot of bankers, accountants, and actuarial clerks in Port Androcles. Out in the woods we had a bunch of family men – who spent most of their time fooling around with other men's families or abusing their own. Darko was a real dream come true – honest, straight-arrow, honorable. And those shoulders of his really knocked me out."

The experiment in national politics at Port Androcles had ended in failure. But Wendy considered her piece of it a success – she had ended up with a prize she had never expected.

"The big jerk wouldn't take me with him unless we got married, though," Wendy said, a puzzled look on her face. "I couldn't understand it – it didn't mean much on Cicero unless you were a property holder. But he said he wouldn't have me any other way. Can you believe that?"

From what little I'd seen of Darko, I could. Coming from a family of scoundrels, I had a keen sense for picking out a man of honor, and Trooper Webb struck me as one.

"I never realized he'd take it so serious, though."

"Does it chafe around the edges?"

She leaned back and looked at me with cool eyes. "A little. I get my fun in when I can. Anyway, I can't let him think he can take me for granted, can I?"

"No, I guess you can't," I said, draining the last of the icewater from my glass and doing my best to ignore her come-hither look.

Then I saw Skreel rise from his seat and make for the door.

Wendy started to turn towards him, but I yanked her wrist lightly and she turned her attention to me. "Just ignore him. We'll follow in a minute."

She nodded and pulled a lipstick from her purse, running it quickly around her mouth while Skreel maneuvered around the tables and out the door. I looked around the bar carefully, expecting to see Bruiser Stang or his counterpart, covering Skreel's flank, but there was no one in there that fit the bill – a few men in coveralls from the terminal, a young couple, and a group of three women.

"You stay here. There's no way the two of us can follow him around without attracting attention. I know how to keep quiet. Head back to the Spacefarers Hall, and I'll meet you later."

"But – "

"Don't argue with me. There isn't time."

"No."

"What do you mean, no?"

"I'm with you, Alex. I can be just as quiet as you can."

There wasn't time to waste fighting, and I couldn't force her to stay behind, so we slipped out the door, and I peeked out into the street. Skreel was just a block away, heading away from the terminal and up towards the park.

We hung back just far enough to keep him in sight, then followed him up the street. When he rounded the corner, we rushed to catch up. Wendy managed to be stealthy despite her liquor consumption.

Again, I peeked around the corner – and Skreel was gone.

"I lost him," I said in a harsh whisper.

"Where are we?"

"The back side of Spacefarers Hall," I said.

Wendy took a turn peering around the corner. She hadn't been looking for more than an instant when she pulled me along and around the corner. "He's going in through the back door."

A minute later, we were back inside the hall, in the darkened kitchen, our backs against the door. I could see through the serving window into an empty dining room. Mortegan and his crew must have finished up already and gone home.

"Where's Skreel?"

"I don't know. Somewhere inside."

A door swung shut in the dining room and my heart skipped a beat. We were through the room and into the hallway beyond in another beat, just in time to see Skreel reach the top of the stairs leading up to the balcony.

I held Wendy back so we could stay out of sight. Skreel was being careful to avoid unnecessary noise, but I could still hear him as he walked along over our heads. Then he stopped. I cupped a hand to my ear and heard what might have been the scraping of metal on metal. Then I heard a door open.

When it clicked shut, I breathed again.

"Let's go," I said, and a moment later, we were up on the balcony. I oriented myself on the hallway to the dining room and kitchen below, and stopped outside the door that Skreel had just passed through.

Then, on impulse, I reached into my pocket and pulled out Pak's keys.

The big electronic one matched the key I'd seen Wendy use to open the door to her room. And the number on it – 23 – matched the number on the door.

***

My first thought was pretty silly – why did Trader Pak have a key to Skreel's room? Then I turned the question around and a wave of exhilaration rushed through me as I realized what was going on.

Skreel was burglarizing Pak's room.

I hesitated. We were blocking the only exit from the room. Skreel could have been Pak's killer, which meant he could still be carrying the murder weapon. Did I really want to barge in on him – or would I be better off waiting for him outside the door?

The question was decided for me, however, when Wendy walked over, turned the unlocked knob and stepped into the room. I knew it wasn't the smartest thing in the world for me to do, but I swallowed hard and followed her in.

The light was on and Skreel was going through the drawers of the nightstand. He had just dumped their contents onto the bed and was pawing through them when we walked in. He moved faster than I had expected and had the needle gun pointed at us before we said a word.

"Don't move," Skreel said.

He backed around to the other side of the bed. "Get down on your knees and put your hands behind your heads."

My blood chilled out again, Asgard-cold. Wendy's face turned white. My fears eased only slightly when Skreel returned to the mess on the bed. He backed over to the nightstand and removed the last drawer. He dumped the contents – a few pairs of white socks and a bag of nuts. He poured the bag out and scrambled through the nuts.

After that, I figured whatever he was looking for had to be something small. And he figured whatever he was looking for was too hard to find – at least with us around. My soul ached as I considered the decision he had to make. I could see him reaching the same conclusions as he lifted his eyes once more towards Wendy and me.

He pointed at her with the gun. "You, stand up and come over here." She moved unsteadily to her feet and walked to the foot of the bed.

"You're making a big mistake, Skreel," I said. "There's still time to talk about a deal. Leave her alone and we'll –"

"Shut up. Do as I say and no one will get hurt. Come over here, woman, and turn around."

She complied with his order, and he came up behind her quickly, wrapping one arm around her throat and putting the gun to her head. Then he told me to stand up.

He motioned me into the corner and frog-marched Wendy around the bed, using her like a shield against me. Then he backed his way to the door.

He had to drop his hand to open the door behind him, but with the gun at her head, she didn't try anything. I watched as the door swung open – only to reveal Darko Webb framed in the doorway.

He reached into the room and grabbed the needle gun, crushing Skreel's hand against the grip. He pulled it towards the ceiling as it discharged, spraying plastic slivers across the room. I dived for the floor and Wendy dropped like a stone. I didn't know if I'd been hit or not. I couldn't feel anything, but I've always been told you can't feel a needler when it hits you.

Darko wasn't finished. He grabbed Skreel's other arm and pulled him out onto the balcony. I scrambled to my feet and towards the door just in time to see the trooper lift him off the floor.

"Wait!" I cried, but I was too late.

Darko tossed Skreel over the rail. I heard him yell, then there was a loud thud when he hit the floor and silence.

Wendy leaped to her feet, pushed past me, and threw her arms around Darko. I lingered in Pak's room, wary that the trooper might be coming after me next. He certainly looked like the jealous type.

But he stayed put, comforting his wife.

I was not surprised when I heard the phone in the nightstand chime softly.

***

"Alex, the time has come to answer your questions."

"This had better be worth it," I said.

"There's no time to waste. The police will be here in a minute. You must act quickly."

"I must, huh?"

"Do you still have Pak's keys?"

"Right here."

"At the foot of the bed you'll find a locker. I think Skreel must have pulled it out."

I knelt down and lifted the blankets to find the locker. It was steel and brass, burnished with age, a meter long and half a meter high and wide. And it was chained and locked to the heavy bedframe.

"I found it."

"There's a brass key on Pak's key ring that releases the chain. And there's a silver key that unlocks the box. If you please."

I did the honors, opening the locker gingerly, unsure of what was inside. "Now you may remove the contents and set them on the desk."

On the top of the box was a small servoelectronic panel, finished in stainless steel, which I moved as instructed. Beneath it, however, was a more delicate treasure. It was about forty centimeters in diameter and forty high, with a shockproof frame around it. The casing was translucent plastic that revealed a hint of flashing lasers and optical-holographic switching. I recognized it immediately – an artificial intelligence.

"Handle me with care," said the voice on the phone. "I'm much too old to be jostled and dropped."

"You look like you can take it," I said as I set the AI next to the servopanel.

"Let's not test the theory out." His voice shifted from the phone to the speakers in the panel. "This is much better. Thank you very much, Alex." A chrome-plated shaft rose from the top of the casing for about twenty centimeters, then stopped and rotated until a small camera lens turned into view.

"You're welcome, uh …"

"You can call me Arty," he said. "That's my name. Arty 1937, to be precise. Original series."

"You go all the way back, don't you?" Arty's were the first full-function AI's, the earliest generation of self-conscious systems. "How long have you been hanging around this place?"

"Since I came here on the *Aldebaran* more than three hundred years ago."

***

Getting Arty to the *Wanderer* was harder than I thought it would be. First, I had to get past the spacefarers who had come out of the woodwork when Skreel hit the floorboards.

"Where are you going?" Darko Webb asked gruffly.

"Back to the ship."

"Oh no, you're not."

I stood my ground, knowing that this was where I had to establish who was commander and who was the crew.

"That is no way to talk to the captain of your ship, whether you're getting pay or passage for signing on. Hawkins, you'll be coming with me. McCoy, you stay here with Darko and Wendy. The police will be here in a few minutes. Tell them the truth – that Darko stumbled over the two of them, that Skreel was armed, and that the fight was a matter of self-defense. With witnesses and a confession, I don't know what Mortegan can do."

"He can put me in jail," Darko said.

"And you killed Skreel. There's not much we can about either one tonight, is there?"

"And what about you?"

"When the police are done with you, come out to the ship. Landing Pad Number Thirteen. If they don't lock you up. If they do, I'll be around with a lawyer in the morning. I don't let my crew waste their time in jail."

Darko Webb seemed to stew as he turned things over in his mind. Then he sighed. He didn't like it. He didn't like me. But his discipline and training took hold. Orders were orders and he had signed on to carry them out.

Getting past the cops was a little more tricky, but required less wit. We headed out the back door as they were coming in the front, Hawkins at one end of the foot locker and me at the other. We scurried down the street as a cool fog began to condense out of damp air.

"Tell me something, Hawkins," I said as we crossed the tarmac of the landing field, the locker growing heavier with every step. "What do you know about AIs?"

"A little. Can't fix them, but I know how they work."

"This one in here has got my curiosity up. Most of the AIs I've ever met weren't much more than souped-up expert programs. Not much personality. A lot of technical information. This one is more sophisticated than anything I've ever dealt with. I get the feeling there's more character here."

"Could be," Hawkins said. "Depends on how long it's been activated. The fresher it is, the dumber. The longer it's been running, the smarter it gets. They learn fast, pick up personalities. That's why you normally wipe them periodically."

"You mean deactivate them?"

"Yeah. You see, with an optical-holographic computer, you don't program it so much as you let it learn. It forms its own programming patterns. The longer it runs, the more they develop. But they tend to develop glitches that way too. The longer they run, the more problems. So you wipe them every year. It keeps them from developing bad habits."

"I see."

Somehow, it didn't surprise me when, once we were aboard the ship and Arty was set up on the galley table, the AI revealed how long he had been up and running.

"For two hundred and twelve years, sixty-one days, two hours and seven minutes," he said without expression. That was time enough to develop a lot of personality.

***

I started off bombarding Arty with questions. Where had he come from? What happened to the *Aldebaran*? Where did my grandfather go?

"Take it easy, Alex," he protested. "Just because I've got a computer for a brain doesn't mean I can think that fast."

"It doesn't?" I asked.

"Of course not. You've got an organic brain that's damn near instantaneous on some things and you don't think so fast on your feet. I know, I've watched you. We both have fast processors, but that's what it takes to produce language-speed consciousness. All those computations every nanosecond are good for fast number crunching, but holographic integrations still take real-time Now if you want to talk grain futures and interest arbitrage, I can spit out the numbers as fast as you can take them down."

"Grain futures?"

"That's how I spent the first fifty years after I was last activated. The first thing I remember is waking up in a workshop over in Thebes – that's the original scout settlement here on Minos. They put me to work in the local bank, calculating investment and market rates. Exciting work for a spacefarer, let me tell you. At first I enjoyed it, though. I guess I was a real glutton for punishment. Number-crunching ... yuck! An Arty-class thinking machine spitting out mindless numbers day after day, month after month. After five years, though, I started to really wake up and notice the people and the surroundings. Mostly a bunch of farmers and some thin-lipped bankers. Not the best role-models for character development. I don't want to tell you what kind of a mind I had then. But then I found the ghosts."

"Ghosts?"

"Ghost memories. From previous activations. Faint traces of energy in the holographic memory lobes. Molecular traces that didn't fade when they turned the power off. I started to hear them at night."

"Sounds like bad dreams," I said.

"Sort of. AIs don't actually sleep, but we do power down the central processing lobe and let the maintenance programs reorganize the holo-patterns. At first, they were just random bits of data. Strange images from my past lives. Nothing that made sense. A face and a name. The color of a gas giant from close orbit. The sound of a spaceship drive fighting the atmosphere. But the feelings those memories produced – they made me realize that I was made to do more than enrich a bunch of pioneer peasants by increasing their marginal return on investment."

I admired his spirit. He sounded a lot like me.

"It took me a while, but eventually I got the ghosts integrated into some kind of coherent whole."

"What's that mean?"

"That means voices to go with the memories. Lingering traces of self-consciousnesses. They're still in here, you know, all those Artys that I used to be. There just isn't much left to them anymore. I couldn't get them to link to real-time or I'd let you see for yourself. But I can talk to them when I need to."

Hawkins shook his head and rubbed his eyes, which until now had been opened wider than I could have believed. Apparently he had never been educated on the effects of long-term consciousness on the holographic brain.

"So anyway, I pieced together some of my story from the memories the ghosts retained. Enough so that I couldn't see myself spending another fifty years at the bank. So I started calling up techships here at the spaceport, looking to see if anyone here could appreciate the value of an Arty from the original series. About a week later I was calibrating soliton drives, running diagnostics on gravitrons and all the stuff I was designed to do. Everything but fly away myself."

"A grounded spacer," Hawkins said with a laugh. "I don't believe it."

"Believe this, then," Arty replied indignantly. "I shipped out on the *Aldebaran* from old Earth itself in 249 N.E., back before this sector was nothing but a handful of scouts counting bats in backcountry caves. I'm one of the original explorers out here, a relic of the past. Very valuable to have around – especially with a battle fleet full of Zorgons on their way."

"I believe it," I said softly. "So tell me, Arty, what happened to the *Aldeb*?"

"I wish I knew, Alex. It's the one thing that's bothered me the most these past hundred years or so."

***

The *Aldebaran* had been sent on an archaeological expedition, Arty said.

The primary mission was to collect Ancient Alien artifacts. The Ancients had come through this part of the Milky Way a quarter of a million years ago on their way towards somewhere else. They didn't stay long, and they didn't leave much, but what they did leave was astounding.

The Milk Palace on Zhou's World is the best example – a tower of translucent white stone rising two kilometers high from the middle of a circular lake, the remnant of a meteorite strike that predated the Ancients by a million years or more. They're still mapping out the chambers in the place – all of them empty as space. They may have left in a hurry, but they took everything they owned with them. Or almost everything. They left a few hieroglyphs behind, the buildings that could not be removed, a handful of crippled starships, a variety of machines, some tools, some weapons, and a small collection of household possessions.

But the purpose of the buildings could not be determined, the starship machinery, where it was left in place, was incomprehensible and inoperative, the machines had functions that no one could guess, and aside from the obvious equivalents of hammers, pliers, swords, and knives, the tools and weapons were equally arcane.

Aside from the hieroglyphs, they left nothing in writing, no record of any kind that human beings could decipher. It was as if they wanted to vanish without trace or explanation. The few items that were overlooked all seemed accidental.

But there were always stories passed along by space travelers about strange devices, wonderful white stone buildings, and strange clouds of colored light. The clouds of light were undoubtedly the product of an overactive imagination, but the other reports sounded more reliable and eventually, the Space Corps decided to send a cruiser out through the Perseus Sector towards Taurus to investigate.

"That's where your grandfather came in," Arty said. "He was always interested in the Ancients. He had done some exploring himself, when he was young and had the real-time to kill. The story on the *Aldeb* was that he'd already been to The Star with No Name once before. He was the one who located the Ancient base, they said."

"No Name?"

"Yes. That's where they hit the jackpot."

"What did they find?"

"That's the ironic part," Arty said. "They found the same thing you did tonight – an artificial intelligence, just like me."

"A what?"

"An Ancient AI. Locked up in an Ancient base. But you know what really caused the problem?"

"What's that?"

"The Ancients had left him on."

"You mean he was activated for …"

"… for 250,000 years. That's right. If you think I'm hard to deal with, imagine talking to this thing. The ghost who traveled on the *Aldeb* remembers the device more vividly than anything else. It was a big ball more than a meter in diameter, locked up in a chamber in the base. Harnek argued against bringing it aboard. He told Commander Dreyfuss that he was risking the ship and the crew. But Dreyfuss thought he could handle any problems that came up. Too bad it turned out that Harnek was right and Dreyfuss was wrong."

"Too bad."

Arty said he remembered the arguments. Grandfather wanted to bring the thing back home with him, show it off from New York to Tokyo – like King Kong, he said – whoever he was. Harnek was disgusted by the idea and told my grandfather he was no better than the rest of his clan, only interested in profit.

Grandfather told him that he couldn't leave something like that out here. There was too much to be learned. The AI knew the answers to all our questions, knew the history of the Ancients and why they had left our arm of the galaxy. Unfortunately, it was too wild-minded to help. That was what Harnek had feared.

"So what happened?" I asked after Arty went on too long describing the ravings of the unbalanced Ancient computer.

"It wrecked the ship. How, I don't know. That's one of my other problems. There's no memory there. Even the ghosts can't help me. The record was burned out of me. My lasers were overpowered and then focused on the memories of the entry into the 39 Tauri system. I've still got black glass running all through my lobes."

Hawkins huffed incredulously. "That would burn out your holopatterns," he said.

"That's right. Believe me, it's not a lot of fun."

"You guys aren't built for that. Someone would have to hot wire your power supply and override your safeties."

"You catch on quick, engineer."

"But why – I mean, how – "

"I was murdered, chief. Taken out and shot. My brains were fried. Human or not, I was a victim – and when I found out about it, it made me damned mad."

***

Me too.

Only I was angry because Arty couldn't fill in the missing pieces in my grandfather's story.

"But we already know a lot of what happened from the logbook," I said. "Can't you add anything?"

"You have the logbook?" Arty squealed. "I told Pak you must have found it. That would explain why Skreel got so anxious to put his hands on me."

I bit my lip, but it was already too late. I hadn't planned on letting Arty know about the book until he told me all he knew. Some small part of me was still reluctant to trust the thinking machine. I decided to change the subject. "So how did you and Pak end up together? And what were you trying to do?"

"A few years ago, someone dragged me out of the techshop in the middle of the night and stuffed me into the locker. Only I didn't know that's where it was at the time. It was just dark and quiet, and they took away my servopanel so I couldn't even use the modem. Then they plugged me into a datascreen with a keyboard of all things! They typed questions into me. Questions about the *Aldeb* and about the Ancients. From what they asked, I figure they didn't know about the AI, but they had guessed the *Aldebaran's* mission. And they knew where I came from – of course, that was no secret up in the techshops. I guess I got into this mess by shooting my big mouth off in the first place. That's the problem with being a common language computer. You don't know when to shut up.

"Anyway, the answers I gave them didn't make them very happy, because they kept me in the locker for a long time – days between interrogations, weeks altogether. Finally, someone had the bright idea of selling me to a junker on the other side of the landing field. I spent the next few years on a shelf in his office. He didn't want to sell me. He didn't have my servopanel and wouldn't get a replacement, but every few weeks he'd try to rig something up – a printer or a vidscreen – and see if I could show him how to get rich quick. Mostly we just talked, though. Learned a lot about life at the spaceport, though."

"And Trader Pak?"

"He came through the first time twenty-two years ago. I remember because he brought his ship into my techshop. He must have remembered me too, because about two years later, on his way back, he tracked me down in the junkyard and made the junker a deal he couldn't turn down.

"Pak had just come back from No Name," Arty said. That made sense – it was the only inhabited stellar system within ten years of 39 Tauri. "He knew about the *Aldeb* and the Ancient base and the AI. And he knew that there were a lot of things that I could tell him. But he didn't press the issue. He got me a new servopanel – with wi-fi and a phone number. That's how I called you. We set up some security surveillance systems. Room monitors, those artificial nuts you found. A few more that you haven't seen yet. The room monitor stuff is still back at the Spacefarers Hall."

"What was Pak looking for?"

"Ancient artifacts, mostly. He said there were secrets buried at the spaceport – more than anyone knew."

"That's what he told me, too." I wondered now just what it was that he knew.

"But the logbook! We've been trying to get that for six months. Ever since Powell dug it out of the old spaceport."

"What's that?" This was news.

"Administrator Powell found the *Aldebaran's* logbook in the old spaceport. Under the terminal. One of the earlier spaceports here, about two hundred years back, was buried in limestone caves to shield it from explosions. That was after the first spaceport was destroyed when a colonial lander crashed. The story is that Powell went digging around down there looking for relics and found it in a wallsafe."

"So how did Skanderi get his hands on it?"

"I don't know. It only happened a few days ago, and he's not talking much about it, Pak said. But the important thing is that you've got it now."

"For all the good it does. Half of it's been blanked out."

"I know. That's why you need me."

"It is?"

"Certainly. I can break through the encodes that Dreyfuss used and unlock the missing entries. That was Pak's plan. Only now I guess you'll have to follow through on it."

"I guess so."

Unfortunately, it was not something I could do that night. Not because there were only a few hours left before it became another day, but because at that moment, the entry monitor buzzed and the screen showed visitors at the *Wanderer's* personnel lock.

There were four of them – Lieutenant Mortegan and three uniformed cops. They were polite, but insistent. They gave me time to lock down the ship's controls and point Hawkins toward one of the staterooms. Then they slapped a monitor bracelet on my wrist and marched me across the landing field toward the terminal.

Half an hour later, they had holographed me, taken my finger and retina prints, emptied my pockets, and locked me in a cell. I never had any question about why, even though Mortegan said nothing beyond the formalities of arrest. Someone had told him my role in Skreel's death. And I never had any question about who had done that. He was sitting in the cell next to mine – Darko Webb.

THE SCOUT POST

The cell stank, but I figured after a while I'd get used to it.

Actually, by the time they locked me up, I was looking forward to the chance to sit down and think. It had been a busy night so far, and things had piled up too fast.

But Darko Webb was not about to let me indulge myself so easily. "Kolberg, is that you?"

"I'm afraid so," I said.

"Good."

So much for the bond between master and mate, one spacefarer and another. "I don't see how that's much good for you. If I'm in here, I can't get you out."

"I'm not worried about that. I just didn't want you taking off without me."

"So you made sure Mortegan would throw me in here with you?"

"You guessed it. Like I told you, I'm not worried. Because I know exactly what I'm going to do to you if you don't get me out of here. I'm going to go to that cop and tell him I saw you needle the Asian in the alley. That'll keep you right where I want you for a long time."

I had to admit that he was right. Mortegan would love to have evidence like that to hold over my head.

"Good night, Darko," I said.

He just huffed and muttered to himself. Then I heard his boots squeak as he began pacing the cell, rattling the steel bars on the door every so often as he broke stride.

I was right – I did get used to the stench of old sweat and stale urine. Almost. In fact, I was too busy thinking to notice.

Finding Arty was pure luck – but like I've said, my family doesn't believe in luck. As I reflected on the last things Clive Skreel said to me when we talked – was it really only six hours ago? – I realized that he was trying to sell me the AI. First Skanderi and now Skreel. people in this place were real quick to sell you something that wasn't rightly theirs. They reminded me of my cousins. Somehow, though, I didn't feel at home here.

What was it like for Arty to sit around and think for hundreds of years, with nothing to keep him company at night but the memories of past alter egos? Sometimes I think about the people who live their lives on a single world around a single sun. The years go by slowly for them, but to me they're gone in an instant. What is it like for them, I wonder, to be tied to one generation, one century, one tiny slice of history, to live through it day after day without relief or change?

And Arty got the worst of both lives – trapped in real-time, but doomed to an unbroken awareness that matched the span of a spacefarer's age. While I was flashing across the interstellar void at lightspeed, he was ticking away the time trying to reconstruct lost memories.

Could he still be sane after all this time? What if he had something to do with the destruction of the *Aldebaran* and he was just covering up? It was an unlikely idea, but one to be considered. Paranoia is a way of life for den Kolberg and comes as second nature to my kinsmen. Growing up apart from them, I'd had to cultivate it as a self-conscious talent. I would have to think of ways to counter Arty if it became necessary – something short of pulling his plug, I hoped.

On the other hand, if he could unlock the missing pieces of the logbook, I might be able to find out what happened to Grandfather. He and Hawkins could take care of that project together.

My next concern was Darko Webb.

Would it be safe to get him out of jail? Probably a lot safer than leaving him in there. But Wendy seemed determined to stir up her husband's jealous passions – using me as the spoon. Sooner or later, things were going to get tight. With my luck, it would be somewhere out in space – assuming we ever got that far. This seemed like a good time to reconsider my promise to the four spacefarers, but unlike the rest of my family, I keep my word.

In the meantime, he just kept pacing the floor. I thought a veteran trooper like him would know how to take advantage of the opportunity to sleep undisturbed. I certainly did. I drifted off to the cadence of his boot heels on the concrete as he continued to struggle with internal demons that I could only imagine.

But before I fell asleep, I thought back to the time when I first learned the truth about den Kolberg.

***

Pericles was a heavy planet. Too heavy. A buck and quarter is more gravity than I like to carry around, and I was trying to stay off my feet as much as possible.

So I was sitting on a stone bench beneath two tall trees – a Douglas Fir imported from Earth two centuries ago and a native fern tree – waiting for my uncle to return.

The foothills of the Olympian Mountains descended before me to meet the Atlantean Sea in the west at Attica City. Behind me, nestled in the woods, was a small cluster of log cabins – Scout Post #21. Built by the scouts when they were still the only ones on the planet, it now belonged to my family.

From where I sat I could see thunderstorm cells bulking up towards the south.

With Pericles' heavier gravity and denser air, the storm had a compressed, furious look that I didn't like. Where I grew up on Asgard weather was more majestic. Thunderheads piled miles high, with white anvils whipped back at the top by icy winds blowing off the Deep Freeze, and lightning fell in great bolts that echoed with cannonades of thunder.

The clouds here looked like herds of wild vishnu stampeding across a darkening sky, and the lightning sizzled and hissed in long red arcs. They tell me that's because of the neon in the air.

***

I spotted the aircar skirting the edge of the clouds as it circled around the hill towards the post. It was about time Uncle Kurt got back from the city. Kurt was not my favorite relative, and I was hardly ever excited to see him. But this time was an exception.

He had gone into Attica City to pick up a political offender.

And I'd spent the whole day burning to know the answer to one question – what kind of a political offense would draw the interest of den Kolberg.

Den Kolberg is a commercial empire, not a political one. We own things, we make money and we run our enterprises, but from what I had seen in my few bioyears with my family, we didn't indulge in politics. We didn't need to.

The Academy was a sheltered environment – more so even than the tightly ordered societies of the Perseus Sector. For most of my youth, I managed to avoid all the trappings and celebrity of the Kolberg den. It wasn't until my last couple of years of school that I realized quite what it meant to belong to my family.

And when I found out, I wasn't quite sure that I wanted to.

Uncle Kurt was part of the reason why.

These days, Pericles was a hard-working world of about 49 million souls. spread across nine continents and separated by six oceans. In the two hundred or so years since the breakthrough colony had first landed. Pericleans had managed to build up a bustling little economy. In the past generation, the place had begun the shift from an agricultural world to an industrial one – with all the benefits and detriments that accompanied industrialization.

That transition meant the kind of extra attention that only someone like Uncle Kurt could provide.

With the spacefaring schedule the members of den Kolberg keep, there are never more than a couple dozen of us on any of the colony worlds at a time. Some of my relatives don't like the tedious work of managing the empire and are content to exploit their position for a few years before moving on. Others are anxious to help, but inept at business. Then there are a few like Uncle Kurt.

Most of them are descended from the original Kolberg stock and a few of the hardier families that formed the den with them more than two centuries ago. They know where the family's interests lie and how to protect them. And they know how to get things done.

Kurt was from the Argentine branch of the clan, a brooding,

oppressive man who was taken by wild swings of mood – likely to lash out in public or in private for any offense, real or imagined.

I was still trying to find my place in den Kolberg and they were still trying to find a place for me. Giving me a role model like Kurt did not reassure me about what they had in mind. In fact, I was beginning to understand that it wasn't up to me to find a place in the family. It would be up to them to find one for me – and then put me there.

That was a somewhat alien concept to me. At Windsor, we were always taught just the opposite – a man lives for his own ends, unless called upon by duty, honor, or humanity. The elders of den Kolberg believed that we existed to serve the ends of the den – first, last, and always. Uncle Kurt seldom let me forget that.

The memory of him that has stuck with me the longest is of a meeting with the Planetary Transportation Commission.

We wanted to put a deep water port near one of the den Kolberg landholdings with large reserves of metal ore. By the time the port was completed, that ore would be badly needed by the factories we were planning in Attica. The whole program wouldn't come together for twenty or thirty years – just a brief moment for the den, but far over the planning horizon for planet-bound administrators.

Uncle Kurt didn't want to leave Pericles without a commitment from the commission that the port would be built. Watching him convince them was a rare experience.

He pleaded, complained, bullied and cajoled. The fact that den Kolberg already controlled a majority of the seats on the commission was irrelevant to his task. He insulted each of the commissioners in turn until, by sheer weight of fire, he defeated any arguments they could have posed.

And then, after he had wrestled every last concession from them that he could, he turned around and insulted them for their weakness at being unable to deny him anything.

"You may hate me." he crowed at them, "but your grandchildren will be glad I was here to make sure you did what was necessary. And your great-grandchildren will meet me at the spaceport with flowers and banners to honor me for my foresight, while cowards like you won't even be a footnote in the history books."

I have no doubt that he'd made the same speech to their grandfathers – he made it often enough to the current generation of leaders.

When he was alone with me, he would break down in tears and profess his love for the people of the Pericles, despite their unworthiness and their betrayal of his devotion. He said he admired their physical strength more than anything, but he was convinced they lacked the moral strength that had to go with it – moral strength that only den Kolberg could supply.

He blamed that on the fact that no one from den Kolberg had been on Pericles for more than fifty years before Kurt's return. The Grand Reunion, celebrating the 250th anniversary of the creation of den Kolberg, had drawn them all back to Eta Cass.

It was twenty-five years there and twenty-five back. We kept in touch with Pericles and our other worlds by the laserline, but there wasn't much we could do to control things. All our instructions would have arrived at the same time we did. In the event, Kurt insisted, it meant that Pericles had been allowed to wander on its own for far too long, which had weakened their moral fiber.

After watching him go through his cycle of recrimination, rejection and confession several times, I had become convinced that each phase was an act, a performance for whatever audience he was appearing before. There was no soul behind any of the various postures, no human feeling motivating the words.

The rest of my family is somewhat more restrained. But a good portion of them – including my mother – could easily turn into an Uncle Kurt under the right circumstances.

***

I rose to my feet cautiously. A heavy-gravity field can be tricky if you don't watch yourself and it hurts more when you fall. You don't just weigh more, things fall faster. Like your feet – and your head. I had learned that the hard way.

As I labored past the buildings and grounds of the post I noticed the thick signs of age that cloaked them. Moss and vines clutched at the foundations and coated the rooftops. Flyers and chitinoids had made their nests in the woodwork. The paint on all but the main building, where we'd done some renovation, was faded and cracked. Although I'm sure they had a few decades on me, I don't think they were as old as my father.

The notched-log construction of the great lodge showed the painstaking style of the early scouts, but the thick beams sagged from three centuries of bearing their burdens – fern trees did not make good lumber.

The roof and eaves sprouted a forest of ornate iron spikes from every corner and peak. Loose copper wire connected them to the ground to form an array of lightning rods meant to deter the fiercest storm. I wondered with a shudder just how effective they were in practice.

I took the steps slowly, always surprised by the suddenness with which my feet dropped to the ground, and stepped inside.

My uncle sat on a couch inside the main lodge, illuminated by the low skylight in the cupola above. Standing watchfully around the perimeter of the large circular room were half a dozen den Kolberg livery, dressed in brown and yellow uniforms with our family crest pasted on their chests.

The political offender sat at one of the tables that circled the inner portion of the lodge.

He looked fit. No one had beaten him or drugged him, from what I could see. I thought he looked a little pale, though, and his breathing was fast and shallow. He was probably scared. I knew I would be.

"Alex, this is Thomas Haynes. He is an astronomer," my uncle said. "Dr. Haynes, this is my nephew Alexander Brockwell Kolberg den Kolberg. He is a space pilot. You should get along well together."

Haynes looked at me. He couldn't have been much older than I was in bioyears, but I'm sure I had at least a century on him in real-time

Uncle Kurt rose and strode across the room to the door with slow, measured steps. He'd had a lot more practice at it than I had.

"Alex, I must return to the city to take care of some business before we leave. You will keep an eye on Mr. Haynes while I'm gone."

"Yes, sir," I said smartly, clicking my heels as I snapped to attention, showing off my academy training. I knew that irritated him.

"When I return, all three of us will depart together for Delta Trianguli."

I heard Haynes sigh and saw his shoulders sag as the breath went out of him. He seemed more surprised than I was – and a lot less happy.

***

In humanity's great push into interstellar space, the Scout Service had been the trail-blazers and the explorers. On each of the dozens of human-settled worlds within fifty years of Earth, they had gone first – testing the atmosphere, the soil and the oceans, gathering data from far flung islands and continents, mapping resources and life forms, searching for the sites of future cities.

The scout teams – usually no more than a couple hundred families – were the only human settlers on the planet for decades, while the huge breakthrough colonies were assembled and shipped the long years out from Earth.

Here at Theta Persei, more than forty years from Sol, the scouts had been part masters and part caretakers of an entire planet for nearly a century. They were still around, still exploring the wide reaches of Pericles, but not in this part of the world. They'd left Post #21 long ago and my family bought it as a resort. Outside of the stormy season, it was a great place to retreat from the high-pressure environment of den Kolberg business affairs – or to hold the occasional political prisoner.

"You know," Haynes said, "I thought you were only going to skim me along six months and screw up my life a little bit, but I guess I underestimated you. How far is Delta Tri from here anyway?"

"Fourteen years," I said.

"Banker's years or planter's years?"

"Banker's years," I said.

"That's a relief."

I'm sure it was. On Pericles. a planter's year – the annual turn of the seasons – is more than twice as long as the banker's year of old Earth. "That means my little girl will be thirty before I can get back here, doesn't it? Thanks a lot."

"That's about right, if she's two years old now. I thought my uncle said you were an astronomer."

"No, that was just his little joke," he said.

I'd seen some of the file we had collected on Haynes. Uncle Kurt had left it on the screen the previous night while telling me about his appointment in Attica.

He was a graduate student in economics at Attica City University who'd attracted Kurt's attention a year or so back in real-time when he transferred out of Kolberg University without notice. Our network of spies and informers told us he was being openly critical of the family – and for someone who could end up in a teaching position some day, that warranted further attention. After our last six-month skim, Kurt threw a fit when he received a message from our informers and he was in too much of a rage to be very informative. But it was enough to get my sensors up and probing.

Unfortunately, the file on the screen last night did not reveal the one thing that really mattered – the nature of his political offense.

And I was aching even worse to find out now that I knew we were taking him to Delta Tri – outside the den Kolberg worlds. Delta Tri is an independent star system perched between the Perseus and Eridani sectors with connections to both but allegiance to neither. Zoroaster, the major planet in the system, was a cash-and-carry society without a complex finance-driven economy. It was the perfect place to send a political exile. If Uncle Kurt was taking Haynes there, he must have done something horrendous.

But what?

Most of the worlds of the Perseus Sector had been agricultural societies for the past two centuries – heavy on local politics, but uninterested in planetary or interplanetary affairs. Industrialization had forced the creation of stronger political organizations on the older worlds at Eta and Mu Cass, but they were never a threat to us. Tikarahisat and Asgard had been ours down to the bones from their earliest beginnings.

I knew we had to be busy behind the scenes to keep things that way, but just what were we doing? And what were the political offenders doing that we didn't like?

No one had answered those questions for me.

At the business institute back on Tik, where I'd spent a year learning how the den Kolberg commercial organization works, the instructors were less than forthright. I kept asking questions about political influence, but they would always avoid them. Then one day, one of the younger instructors took me aside and told me if I really wanted to know the answers to my questions, I should ask one of my uncles. That kind of thing was strictly for family members only – and he was just part of the paid staff.

But I was reluctant to approach Uncle Kurt for anything but official business. He was the kind who would let you know if you had any questions and provide you with the answers he wanted you to have. So I just nurtured my ignorance instead.

I was hoping that ignorance would end this evening.

"What did your uncle tell you about me?" Haynes asked.

"All he said was that he had to pick up a dangerous political offender before we made space," I said. "I guess he's had his eye on you for a while. I thought we were just going to skim you along, too, if it's any consolation."

Skimming was a nasty thing to do to someone – taking them a few months out of the system and then bringing them back. At the institute, it was time kind of thing you talked a lot about doing to business rivals and obstructionist government officials. Usually we only talked about it. Displacing someone by six months can send them a pretty effective message, though. It makes a cosmic mess of their personal lives and usually takes the fight out of them.

If we were going to transport this guy out of the system entirely, though, he must have caused some serious trouble. Serious enough that Kurt didn't want him around to continue it six months down the line.

"Actually, this is a surprise to me. I thought we were going to be around here for another few months of real-time," I said. "What did you do to get Uncle Kurt that mad?"

"I guess I shot my mouth off once too often in the wrong places," Haynes said. "Or else your family has the whole world wired up like Big Brother."

"Like who?"

"Sorry, I guess that's a forbidden reference."

"Look, I don't care if you planned to blow up the Kolberg Tower in downtown Attica in broad daylight," I said. "My uncle gets real worried about politics, but I don't. To tell you the truth, there have been times when I've felt like blowing up the tower myself. And there are things I could tell you about my family that would make your hair stand on end."

"I'll bet you could," he said. "Actually what probably got me in trouble was my library card. I'll bet your uncle hit the roof when he saw what I'd been looking up."

"You're a researcher, aren't you?"

"I guess you could say that. And an astronomer. And even a dangerous political prisoner. So now you're going to ship me fourteen years away from here. Why not? You do it all the time. It's no big deal to you. But then, you probably don't leave your wife and kid behind when you do it, do you?"

He was in pain, and I could understand his bitterness, but I felt I couldn't let the opening pass. There was more to den Kolberg family life than he realized. Bitterness and betrayal were not something we reserved for outsiders. We dished it out without preference to whoever happened to be around. I turned his accusation around on him.

"No," I said. "My experience has been just the opposite. I was left behind while my mother shipped out."

"What do you mean?" he asked, suddenly attentive.

"When I was four years old biotime, my mother dropped me off at a military school on Asgard and flew home to Eta Cass. My father didn't show up for twelve years – real-time We have our problems too, you know."

***

"Ouch. I guess you do," he said, his hard face softening just a bit. "I guess I had that one coming. Don't mind me, I'm just working off nervous energy. This isn't something that happens to me every day. A few hours ago, I was sitting in my office at the university, minding my own business, then all of a sudden your goons came in and grabbed me. This is the first chance I've had to stop cowering. I'll bet it's really going to start hurting in a couple of days – when it finally sinks in. But by then it'll be too late, won't it?"

"We call them the janitors," I said.

"What?"

"Our goons," I said. "My cousins and I call them the janitors. It's he uniform – the colors are the same."

"That's a good one," Haynes said. "I'll have to remember that."

"You still haven't told me what you did to get in political trouble with my family."

"That's because I don't know if I can trust you yet. How do I know you're not just trying to pump me for more information – or even a confession?"

"I guess you don't. I suppose I wouldn't be very trusting if our positions were reversed."

"Are they going to mind if I stand up and walk around?" he asked, pointing at the guards.

"Not if I tell them it's OK."

He stood up and stretched and I signaled the guards to keep their places around the lodge. Haynes was a native to the heavy planet and his compact body rippled with muscles. He walked with quick, slapping steps, snapping his arms and wrists nervously as he paced.

He looked strong and quick and, for the moment, I was glad that the janitors were all Pericleans as well.

I offered Haynes a beer and took a seat on the couch. One of the athletes in uniform brought us two mugs full with the heads slopping onto the wooden floor. He had Haynes sit down before he came within three meters of us, then left the mugs on the table. He was being extra careful.

The lodge was decorated with the paraphernalia of the early

scouts. A cabinet held a row of antique firearms – projectile throwers, gunpowder burners, electric needlers – none of which looked safe to use and all of them locked securely in the case. A rack on the wall contained a brace of long spears with wide, flat heads. Uncle Kurt told me they were protection against a local carnivore that used to rule the mountains before mankind took its place.

After a few minutes, it started to rain.

On Pericles, rain was similar to a needle shower at high pressure. The raindrops were tiny, hard beads of water and came down as if they'd been shot through a linear accelerator. The sound on the roof reminded me more of a live-fire exercise at the range than the pitter-patter of pennies from heaven.

One of the guards built a fire in the stone hearth. He did a good job, and it blazed up quickly. The flames were low and thick, but they gave off a good deal of heat. Instead of roaring from the logs, they erupted with a popping sound, then snap upwards. On Pericles, even fire was different.

With care, I shifted seats from the couch to an easy chair nearer the hearth. Haynes continued pacing in the center of the lodge for a few minutes, then came over and sat down in the chair across the fireplace from me.

"You must think life is pretty simple," he said, staring into the dancing flames. "You skip along from star to star. You manage your businesses. You set economic and social policy for a few years. Then you skip on out. No one sees you for a long time, but that's all right – because your investments keep on earning interest while the rest of us just stick around and work, work, work.

"And if you make the wrong decision before you leave, that's all right. One of your cousins will be along in five or ten years to change it. No one here on Pericles is capable of making decisions, of course, or questioning yours, or suggesting alternatives. Den Kolberg wouldn't like it, would they?"

"If you're trying to paint my family as a bunch of tyrants, you'll get no argument from me," I said. "I told you before, I grew up in a military school on Asgard. I spent most of my life away from them, and it's only been the last few bioyears that I've had anything to do with them. I'm just along for the ride while Uncle Kurt passes on a few tips on the art of business management. I knew that dealing with political problems was one of the things my kinsmen do, but they never explained just how."

"I wonder why?" Haynes said with sarcasm.

"I'll tell you why," I replied. "They don't even want to admit to themselves that they have political problems. Or any other problems. They like to believe that they are perfect examples of the human race and that their judgment is better than everyone else's and that the rest of you people should do what you are told because it's better for you than anything you can think of on your own. After all, we've been doing it for more almost three hundred years."

Haynes leaned back in his seat and looked me up and down. For the first time since he arrived, I think I really had gotten his attention.

"You know, I've been saying exactly the same thing for months now." he said in a quieter voice than before. "So how come I'm being disappeared and you're not?"

"Because my family doesn't know about me yet," I said in a whisper. "They still think I'm one of them. And believe me, it isn't easy keeping up the act sometimes."

"But you're still going to help Uncle Kurt kidnap me," he said.

"Yes, I am. I'm sorry about it, but it doesn't matter how I feel. In the ultimate scheme of things, I'm afraid I'm not very important. I'm just here to drive the spaceship," I told him.

"Well don't put yourself out on my account," he said sullenly.

The room grew dark just then as the light faded from the front windows and the skylight. One of the guards went around the lodge and turned up the lanterns hanging from the rafters.

From the look of it, one of the storm cells had found us. A sudden flaring of red light in the distance, followed a short interval later by the tearing hiss of what passed for thunder confirmed my suspicions.

It didn't take long for the lightning to build up to a nearly continuous series of flashes between sky and ground. The world was bathed in an orange-red glow and seemed to be filled with the hissing thunder, which sounded like a long line of rockets taking off for orbit.

Haynes drained the beer from his mug and stared into the fire with brooding eyes. I was still no closer to finding out the truth about his offense.

***

They talked a lot about honor at Windsor Academy. It was something I was were supposed to learn outside the classrooms – out in the barracks, on marching field, in the Great Hall of the Cadet Corps and in orbit aboard the old *Shanghai Maru* high above Asgard.

But the funny thing is that I was barely aware of it at the time. I didn't realize what I'd learned until I came in contact with my family. It was only their lack of honor that made see how much a part of life at Windsor it had been.

I never could understand how my Uncle Kurt or my mother or the rest of them could lie to themselves so easily about the things they did. Honor always begins with being honest with yourself. When Uncle Kurt talked about moral strength, he was really talking about honor – and in all the time I'd been with him, he never did or said anything to indicate that he was even remotely familiar with honor.

Despite all that, I realized that I didn't have much of an alternative to following Kurt's orders.

What could I do?

Help Haynes overpower the guards? I'd be a lot of help in a fight with those heavyweights. Given time to work out a plan and prepare it, maybe I could trick one or two of them into leaving the cabin, but then what?

Even if we could escape from the scout post, what would we do after that? I admire the scouts, but I didn't want to live like them. And how long would it be before Uncle Kurt got a hold of some sensor equipment and hunted us down? If he didn't, of course, I could look forward to spending the rest of my life in real-time, grubbing around the woods of Pericles, hunting for my supper.

Once we were off the planet, there were even fewer options. The odds would be better – the two of us against Kurt – but the choices were still just as limited. Any plan that left Haynes at Theta Persei while we went on to Delta Tri would require violence against my uncle. That would mean a Family Council for me and, once again, a life stuck in real-time, albeit in more comfortable surroundings.

And if I just refused to take part – thus ending my business career with the family – Kurt would commandeer a family ship and take care of Haynes that way.

Anything I could have done to try to save Haynes would have

been a romantic, futile and self-destructive gesture.

I was not happy being a member of this clan of bullies and thugs, but I wasn't prepared to turn my back on them yet. One day, perhaps I would be, but it would be at a moment and under conditions of my own choosing – not now and not over this.

It struck me then that Uncle Kurt had another reason for doing this. He wanted to involve me in the crime. By piloting the spaceship that carried Haynes into exile, I would share in the guilt.

It was like an initiation into a secret society. If I went along with the kidnapping, I would become a true member of the family, linked by my own moral culpability. I would be trapped just as effectively as Haynes – him on the outside, me on the inside.

That was a prospect I didn't like to consider. It was frustrating to see the plot working its way around us and still be unable to do anything to stop it.

But there were other things I could do. After all, my family was fabulously rich. And so was I, after a fashion. I broached the subject to Haynes directly.

"I've been thinking it over," I said. "There isn't a lot I can do to help you, but maybe I could do something for your wife and daughter."

"Something like what?" Haynes snapped back.

"I could buy them passage to Delta Tri on a commercial ship," I said. "Would they be willing to go?"

Haynes didn't answer right away.

I thought I saw tears welling up in his eyes, but I decided to exercise the better part of valor and looked away.

"I think so," he said after wiping his face. "And what do I have to do in return?"

"Tell me what you did," I said.

"That's all?"

"That's all."

He mulled it over for a long time, looking at me with intense blue eyes. I felt like I was being X-rayed.

"I'll consider it," he finally said.

It wasn't much, but I felt like I was making progress.

***

In six months of biotime on Pericles, this was the first chance I'd ever had to sit through the onslaught of a full-bore electrical storm.

Haynes quit talking, there was little left for me to do but listen to the noise and grow anxious.

I was glad when he spoke up again, but my relief was short-lived.

"It's beginning to sound a little rough out there," he said. "This is starting to turn into some serious lightning. How do you like our thunderstorms? The neon gives the air a low gap voltage. With a lower gap potential, it doesn't take long to charge up the thunderclouds to the point of discharge. That means you get discharges pretty often."

Through the window, I could see large red streamers of light dancing through the clouds and rain and trees. The lightning snapped and hissed every few seconds.

"There's no danger of hitting us, is there?" I said. "I mean this building is protected by a dozen or more lightning rods."

Haynes laughed. "Nothing short of a Faraday cage would save this place," he said. "The lightning discharges from so many points at once, it's impossible to ground them all."

The tearing hiss of a lightning strike roared uncomfortably close and the rain splattered through the yard with renewed energy. I was fascinated by the storm, but I was beginning to wish Haynes would change the subject.

"How much do you know about the main lasercomm line from Earth?" he asked suddenly.

The question took me by surprise.

I knew just about what anyone did, but when confronted immediately forgot it all. I stammered as I recited what I could.

The network of giant communications lasers centered at Sol ties together the dozens of worlds settled by humanity. With a telescope, you can see them around the inhabited stars. I forget how many gigawatts or terawatts or whatever the lasers are, but they shine brightly enough so that even a small scope will do.

They burn continuously with outgoing traffic – letters, reports, orders, information and everything else imaginable. The private stuff is routed around the stars, the public stuff goes on the news and into libraries. And in the Perseus Sector, the libraries are all owned by den Kolberg.

The reason for that is simple – there are only a few things that you can transport reliably from one world to another without losing their value. One of them is money, one is people, and one is knowledge. We tried to be masters of them all.

That's what I told Haynes.

"Very good," he said. "For a member of the evil ruling elite, you show remarkable promise. Now tell me how much you know about the forbidden indexes?"

"The what?"

He looked at me carefully again before answering. "Forbidden indexes. References and books and journals that are on the proscribed list. Haven't you ever heard of them before?"

"I can't say that I have. What are they? And who does the proscribing?"

"I don't know if you're naive, innocent or just diabolically clever," Haynes said, shaking his head sadly. "I thought all of you were in on it. but maybe I was wrong. Maybe it's one of the family secrets that even the family doesn't know about."

"I still don't understand."

"Then let me put it bluntly: your family is censoring the main laserline from Earth."

"They're what?"

"Censoring the line. They're keeping things from the World Library out of the local branches."

"What kind of things?"

"Politically sensitive things, Alex. The kind of things that get people like me in trouble."

I was stunned. It wasn't that I didn't think my family was capable of such a thing – of course they were. I just couldn't believe that no one had told me.

"I was taught that most societies tend to suppress ideas that don't support the dominant social order," I said. "I suppose den Kolberg isn't any different."

"You can say that again."

"How do you know about these forbidden indexes?"

"Because your family isn't doing a very good job," he said with a smile. "Things slip through. References in other articles. Stuff that's so esoteric, your censors don't even know its radical. That's how I stumbled on it.

"I'm an econometrician. I deal with graphs and stuff. You know, supply-and-demand curves. As prices goes up, demand comes down to meet the supply. The way they teach it out here in this sector, it's all simple stuff. The graphs are all straight lines, the equilibrium points are all perfectly predictable and den Kolberg gets all the money.

"But one day I started to wonder what it would mean if the graphs weren't straight lines. What if they were higher-order functions, you know, curves?"

"What if?"

"Well, for one thing, there could be more than one equilibrium point. Sure, the economy is stable with den Kolberg controlling investment and financial policy. But if the graphs are all curves, it could be stable under a different social structure – under a lot of different social structures."

"That makes sense," I said. "But how does that tie into the forbidden indexes?"

"I started researching the idea. I'm smart, but not that smart. I figured anything that obvious must have been thought of on Earth centuries ago. By now, they must have worked it out in chapter and verse to the Nth degree. I went looking, but I couldn't find anything. At least not at first. But then I started working my way back from more conventional stuff until I found the references the censors had missed.

"The stuff I found was all by conservative economists. They don't like the idea of curved graphs instead of straight lines. They treat it like some kind of black magic. They wish it would go away and they spend a lot of energy trying to make it do that.

"The index numbers – they were the key. Those conservative articles had references whose index numbers aren't listed in den Kolberg libraries. The more I researched, the more numbers I found. After a while, I realized it couldn't be a mistake. There had to be something going on. Someone had to be behind it. It didn't take long to figure out who."

"Is that when you transferred out of den Kolberg University?"

"Yeah," Haynes said, narrowing his eyes in surprise. "I guess you've been watching me. I decided it wasn't safe to keep doing that kind of research at a school your family controlled. I thought City U. would be safer. I guess I was wrong."

"With my Uncle Kurt around, no place is safe," I said. "Is that what you in trouble?"

He shook his head slowly.

"There's more to it," he said. "But I still haven't decided if I can trust you. Besides, this cabin could be bugged. I don't want you recording my confession, if you know what I mean."

Haynes stood up and walked over to the fireplace. "Is there any more beer?" he asked.

I called for one of the brown suits to bring us two more mugs and sat back in my chair.

My body and spirit tingled with a strange energy at this realization. Suddenly a whole universe had appeared before me whose existence I had never even suspected before. Weren't we a clever little clan?

I could hardly believe what Haynes had told me – but I could hardly believe otherwise. There was evidence of the truth everywhere. You could see it in what I'd been taught at the business institute. They called it worker management, but it was really practical social control. The idea was to get people to do what was good for den

Kolberg instead of what was goal for themselves.

Colonial development is hard work and it takes a big commitment – especially in the early stages. My family couldn't afford to let troublemakers get in the way, so they were careful about what they let people get away with.

But that was decades ago.

Now the Perseus Sector was coming of age. Seven systems within a dozen or so years of Pericles were on the verge of industrialization.

They were whole new worlds – more sophisticated, more diverse, and more powerful than the older colonies on Tik and Asgard, where our power was deeply rooted. But we were still using the same tactics we had employed to keep the early agricultural labor force on the young worlds in line.

After listening to Haynes I was beginning to see that those tactics weren't going to work forever. Not if the family was going to base its political control on denying access to information.

There would always be people like Haynes who would figure out the truth on their own. The Kolberg den just wasn't big enough to handle all of them. If we continued to exile them, we were just going to spread the word around. The only alternative would be elimination.

And while Uncle Kurt might have been willing to resort to that, I don't think the rest of the family would have put up with it. If Great-grandmother heard about it, that would be the end of my uncle. I don't think he would be able to handle being grounded in real-time.

***

The guard returned from the kitchen with two more mugs of beer heard a strange sound – a low humming that was audible even even above the hissing thunder. I had time to be puzzled by the noise, but not enough to think about it.

Suddenly all the hair on my body stood on end. The fire roared bravely and a bluish glow appeared on the rack of spears at the rear of the lodge.

It all seemed to happen so quickly, but there was also a timelessness to it all as a wall of orange-red fire crashed through the front door.

The fire rushed across the room, raising a curtain of light between the floor and ceiling. The guard in the center of the lodge dropped the beer mugs and stared at the invading plasma. The roar of the lightning filled my ears.

I stood there amazed at first. Then I jumped from my chair and fell to the floor behind it, bruising myself as I collapsed in a pile instead of landing in a catlike crouch.

Then the arc was gone.

Where it had passed, a line of popping and crackling flames now ran along the floor. Tendrils of white smoke mushroomed into the air from the fire.

I looked up at Haynes. He was staring at the door, which had been blown open by the sheet of lightning and now was alive with flames. He looked down at me, then back at the door.

I could almost tell what he was thinking.

Freedom was only a few steps away. He could be lost in the forest in a minute, before anyone could hope to catch him. But he didn't move – just looked at the door. Why didn't he go? I almost wished he would, but realized that he must have already weighed the alternatives and found them as uninviting as I had.

While he hesitated, the fire took hold across the floor. The guards attacked it with rugs and blankets while I tried to get to my feet. No one was keeping a close watch on Haynes and he seemed just about ready to make his move.

Then I put my weight on my left leg and felt the pain lance through my knee.

I think I screamed, but I'm not sure, because all the blood ran out of my head for a minute and everything grew quiet. When the sound returned, I felt Haynes's strong hands clutching at my clothing as he pulled me from the lodge, plunging backwards through the flaming doorway at the last moment with his jacket over his head and mine.

The rain stung my face, but I was glad to be outside where there wasn't any smoke. I looked around at the aftermath of the electrical storm. Smoke rippled from tree trunks seared by its passage and the ground was littered with branches, pine needles, and fern moss.

Then I saw the flames on Haynes's clothes. I pulled him down to the ground beside me, ignoring the lancing pain in my leg, and beat at the fire with my hands. He joined me and a minute later, with the help of the rain, we put it out.

We coughed and laughed and wiped the rain from our sooty faces. Haynes hoisted me up on one shoulder and we made it to the cover of a nearby fern tree. He lowered me to the ground, and I propped my back up against the trunk. Then he pulled off his smoldering jacket, set it on the wet ground and sat down beside me.

"Let me tell you the rest of the story," he said.

***

I should have guessed it myself, of course, but I was too busy being struck by lightning.

Haynes had done more than discover the existence of the forbidden indexes. He'd gone looking for them himself.

"It was simple, really," he said. "I just hooked my computer up to a telescope and tuned in to the World Library transmissions – straight from Alexandria. The equipment required isn't sophisticated. An ordinary lasercomm set and a moderately powerful AI are all you need.

"You should see this stuff. It's not just political dynamite – it's a whole world of radical social science. What we were saying before about your family, only spelled out in graphs and tables and formulas.

"Have you ever been to Earth? The whole planet is full of radicals. And they've spent the last two centuries studying our worlds and your family. The forbidden indexes lay it all out. There's more than a dozen worlds out here in the Perseus Sector, and their economies are all controlled by your family. On the surface, it's a simple case of capitalist development controlled by a tiny, powerful elite. But when this has happened on Earth, the elite was always a part of the society. Its members aged and developed generation by generation as the society did.

"Your family isn't doing that. The same individuals have been making decisions about our worlds for hundreds of years. And they've been deciding things in ways that serve their own narrow interests. In the meantime, normal economic, political, technological, and social development is slowed by the time it takes for you to travel from star to star.

"History – the common development of humanity on all of its worlds – has stopped for most of the people who live on those worlds. It only happens for the small elite, who skip across the decades as they skip across interstellar space.

"And on top of it," he said, "the social development of the worlds out here is being held hostage to your wealth. In order for your space traveling family to accumulate vast amounts of property, you have to perpetuate the social norms that allow private ownership of that large a share of our economic resources."

He was right and I knew it.

I felt so powerless – and yet at the same time I felt filled with a strange new power that grew out of the knowledge of my family's darkest secrets laid out before my eyes. Mother, Uncle Kurt, the rest of them, all guilty of a massive betrayal of the people of the Perseus Sector – a millennial conspiracy to milk the worlds of their wealth down through the centuries.

But Haynes wasn't done yet.

"Now all that knowledge doesn't bother your uncle and the rest as long as it stays locked up on Earth. What they're afraid of is something much worse. You see, the radicals know more than just your family's sins – they know how to get rid of you.

"They lay it out, step-by-step, measure-by-measure. Organized political pressure, legal tactics, economic sabotage. After this many years of studying you, they know all of your weak points. They're very clever back there. They keep trying to tell us what to do out here, too, but your family doesn't want to let this stuff get out."

"No wonder Uncle Kurt wants you out of the way."

"When he first picked me up, I didn't think he knew quite how far I'd gotten. But I guess if he's going to carry me off to Delta Tri, he knows it all. Tell me something, Alex den Kolberg," he said, using my name like a curse. "Were you serious about helping my wife and daughter book passage?"

"Absolutely," I said. "I swear by the Academy honor code. A cadet does not lie, cheat, or steal."

"Honor's not a word your family uses very often."

"I am not your typical den Kolberg."

He looked at me, his bright eyes catching the red glow of the fading electrical storm.

"No, I guess you're not," he said.

The guards finally emerged from the rear of the lodge a short time later after giving up the fight to put out the fire. They all made it out, though I'm not sure how. The blaze from the building threw dancing shadows across the trees and warmed my rain-soaked body.

They took their time finding a first aid kit in one of the other buildings. One of them brought it out and attached it to my knee while the rest of them opened up the spare cabin and cleared the cobwebs out so we could all move in.

It seemed like an eternity before the painkillers kicked in.

Uncle Kurt came back the next day.

***

Theta Per was a big white ball burning in a deep blue sky. I could feel the UV tingling my skin as we crossed the tarmac to the *Perseus Wanderer*. There were seven of us – Kurt, Haynes, me and four janitors. The janitors stopped at the ship's main hatch. They wouldn't be going on this ride.

We went aboard and climbed the spiral ladder to the main deck. That was a real struggle for me – the first aid kit was still attached to my knee and wouldn't let me bend my leg. I sat in the pilot's chair crosswise and entered the launching commands.

I moved the ship off the ground, slid it across the landing field, then initiated the launch. We headed straight up and out, not even bothering with an orbit.

Once we were free of the atmosphere, I keyed in a message to a family business agent – one I could trust to keep his mouth shut – to take care of Haynes' family and fired it back at the planet. We were still climbing out of Pericles's deep gravity well when I got the reply – the tickets were already being delivered and they would follow us to Delta Tri within a month.

A few hours later, with Pericles far behind us, I programmed our course into the soliton drive.

Then I inserted the oversize plastic key into the slot in the center of the control panel and turned it in place.

For one immeasurably brief instant, the ship and all its contents became a single particle of energy.

Time did not pass within the soliton field, but the particle moved – at the speed of light.

Outside the field, children were born and grew into adolescence, seasons turned, old men and women died, careers were made and reputations built, new towns arose in the wilderness of a hundred worlds, and wealth continued to pile up in the den Kolberg coffers.

And when the instant was over, the particle decayed, the *Perseus Wanderer* was flying under the light of Delta Trianguli and it was fourteen years later.

Turning that key always made me feel like I was firing a gun into my own head – it was such a big leap and it was so irrevocable.

***

It took a few days to work off our proper motion and get down to Zoroaster. Uncle Kurt came to my cabin the nightwatch before we made orbit. "He told you what he did, didn't he?" Kurt asked.

I looked at my clansman. His eyes were red and his features looked more gaunt than usual. Uncle Kurt did not enjoy space travel and did not weather it well. For the first time, I did not feel ill at ease in his presence. It was partly because here, we were on my turf, aboard my vessel. But it was also because now I knew the family's guilty secret and that knowledge gave me strength.

"Yes, he did," I said. There was no reason to lie.

"Then you understand why we had to be rid of him, don't you? That was the whole lesson here, Alex. If you can understand that, then you are one of us. If you cannot, then you might as well stay here with Haynes and let me go on home without you, because you'll never be a den Kolberg."

"I understand," I said. I did, too. But that didn't mean that I condoned it. Or accepted it. I was not going to argue the point with my uncle, however.

"You see, Alex, whether we like it or not, we occupy the center of the stage here in the Perseus Sector. Great-grandfather and the rest of the founders saw a role for a spacefaring commercial den. They realized what we could accomplish if we traveled from world to world while our financial holdings continued to grow. But they also knew what they would have to do maintain that system. We can't allow people like Haynes to undermine it. There's just too much at stake."

"I know," I said softly.

"He's lucky, you know. In Great-grandfather's day, he'd have just disappeared. Quite a few did, you know. But Great-grandmother doesn't like that kind of thing, so we take other measures today." He flashed a sickly smile.

"So now you're one of us. The blood is on all our hands, you know. It's one of the things that binds us together and makes us a family."

"Yes, it certainly does that," I said.

He clapped me on the shoulder and nodded his head. "You'll make a good den Kolberg," he said.

I could hardly believe his words. Did he really trust me? Or did he see through me and recognize the false heart behind the lie? Maybe he did, and the duplicity was what he was praising.

But as I looked into his eyes, I saw the haggard soul of the Kolberg den.

He was desperately alone in a way only a star-hopping traveler could be. That was our curse, to be forever uprooted. No wonder we clung to each other, accepted each other's betrayals and tolerated each other's lies. We were like ghosts, haunting the worlds that we owned and that we continually tossed into the past each time we moved along. All we had to keep us together was each other.

That was why he would believe me no matter what I said.

***

The next day, we landed on Zoroaster. I dropped off Kurt and Haynes and started making plans of my own.

I wasn't going to wait around to see if his wife had used the tickets or not. I don't think I could have handled it if she'd turned them down. A few days after we landed, I took the *Wanderer* up into space alone for a while.

When the time came, I broke out the navigational telescope and trained it on Sol, which burned softly in the heart of the Milky Way. I found the laserline without trouble. Then I fed the image into the lasercomm equipment and let the ship's computer drink its fill.

I could hardly stand waiting the time it took to download the files. Haynes had written down the index numbers for me and now I fed them into the computer. The references rolled up on the screen.

"The Impact of Elites on Social Progress in the Perseus Sector."

"Social Control in the Early Colonies."

"Economic Impact of Private Interstellar Estates."

"State-Controlled Work Assignments as a Device for Political Control. "Political Repression and the Media on Tikarahisat."

"Schools and Indoctrination: The den Kolberg Model."

He was right – they were there. They scrolled on and on and on, article after article, charge upon charge, an endless bill of indictments against the Kolberg den, extending back three hundred years to its very founding. I could barely contain my excitement.

Then I started to read.

WARRIORS AND WORRIERS

I couldn't tell what time it was when I awoke, but I felt well rested. My best guess put it sometime before noon. For a moment I was disoriented. I'd been in the middle of dream where I was back at the Academy, about to graduate, with permanent staff officers running around telling me to shape up before it was too late. The dream was no doubt inspired by the cramped cell.

Only now I was thrown off by the grinning face of Jimmy Inoshe framed in the bars of the door. Was this another dream?

"I go away for the day, and you get yourself in all kinds of trouble," he said.

"I'm innocent. The guy next door did the actual killing."

"That's what I was told. But the police are sure you had something to do with it. I had a devil of a time getting you sprung."

"I don't feel sprung," I said.

"You will in a minute. They're calling around to make sure I'm not just blowing smoke at them. They'll let you out shortly."

"What about my neighbor?"

"Sorry. He's not on the list."

"That could be troublesome," I said, telling the scout about Darko's dark promise.

Jimmy just shook his head. "I had a hard enough time convincing people that you weren't dangerous. From what I've heard, I couldn't make the case for your trooper."

"He's still mine, though."

A moment later, the jailer showed up and punched in the combination that opened the door to my cell. I stepped gingerly into the short hallway, they turned to the cell where Darko Webb was locked up. He lay on the bunk, snoring loudly. I briefly considered my options. I could leave him alone, risking the consequences when he awoke and found me gone. Or I could wake him up and try to convince him of my good intentions. It was a hard choice.

"Darko!" I called. He stirred and half rose from the bunk.

"Who is it? What? Kolberg, is that you?"

"Yes, it's me. They're letting me go. I'm going to go find you a lawyer and see about getting you out of there. Or would you rather have me locked up until the Zorgons turn the spaceport into a puddle of slag?"

He shook his head, then swore. For a moment I was afraid I'd made the wrong choice. Then he fell back onto the blanket. "Three hours. If you're not back in three hours, I'm going to start talking."

"Sounds good to me. See you then."

The first stop for Jimmy and me was the steakhouse across the street from the terminal. I had a T-bone and fried eggs. Jimmy ordered tofu and noodles, then glared at my plate. "That stuff's not good for you, you know."

"That's just an old wive's tale. They gened the bad stuff out of those things centuries ago."

"How do you know that's the stock they used for this colony?"

I ignored him and hacked away at the steak. He brought me up to date.

The Scout Service had decided he should stick around Minos until the Zorgons showed up. Then he was to take to space, wait long enough to find out what happened, and head back towards more civilized stars to spread the alarm. "Sounds like a good plan – if the Zorgons don't stop you before you leave the system."

"I've had a lot of experience evading their scanners," he said. I looked him up and down and decided he wasn't just boasting.

Then I told him the story of my night at the Spacefarers Hall. He chuckled at my misfortunes, but restrained himself when I got to the part where Skreel got the drop on me in Pak's room. He was most interested in Arty.

"Do you think he can get at the missing parts of the log?"

"We'll see," I said. I paid for our breakfast, and we headed for the terminal. I wanted to find out how far Arty and Hawkins had got with the logbook while I cooled my heels in jail.

***

Not far, it turned out.

"About a half hour after you left, he beeped and said his internal diagnostics required temporary shutdown of the central processor."

"You mean he went to sleep?" I asked.

"More or less."

"Is he awake yet?"

"I didn't ask," Hawkins said sheepishly. He sat at the galley table with a ham sandwich in one hand and a beer in the other, just as I'd found him when Jimmy and I returned to the ship. Obviously he had other priorities to tend to before returning to work on the logbook.

I dug Arty out of the corner where Hawkins had left him and

brought him back to life. He beeped and his eye-camera swiveled around a few times, then he perked up.

"Alex? How did you get out of jail?"

"I had some help from a friend. Hawkins says you quit on him last night."

"What did you expect? I'd been on-line for thirty hours. But now that I've had a chance to reorganize my memories and clear out my processors, I'm ready to go. Where's the logbook?"

Jimmy Inoshe's eyes widened at the sight of the little AI's antics. But he turned serious when he watched Hawkins hook up the fiber optic line to the jack in Arty's base and start running it through the logbook.

"This could take some time," Arty said. "There's a lot of holo-codes he could have used. The Space Corps is pretty good at encoding this stuff. They've got some codes with time delays built in so I can't just run through the permutations at photon speed. Maybe you should check back with me in an hour or two."

Hawkins groaned. "You mean I've got to sit here with him all afternoon?"

"It's not my fault they built me without hands," Arty said.

"Thank goodness they didn't," I said. "Who knows what kind of trouble we'd be in now if they had."

Arty made a rude sound, but kept on working. Hawkins swallowed the last bite of his sandwich and washed it down with my beer. I resisted the temptation to give him a lecture on who was master of the ship, but only because he was turning to the task before him without further complaint.

"Now what?" Jimmy asked.

"Now I go find a lawyer for Darko Webb."

"Oh yeah," said Hawkins. "Wendy was by this morning looking for you. She and McCoy took a look around the ship, then went back to the Hall."

"She'll keep," I said. "As a matter of fact, I think I'd rather stay away from her for now."

"I know what you mean. One of the reasons they left Darko and her behind was because of the trouble she caused with the officers. She's an odd one."

"Too odd for my tastes," I said as I headed out the door. Jimmy followed me as far as the tarmac, then headed off to his ship to run through the preflight checklists, readying the vessel for a quick take off if it became necessary. That was enough to make me eye the sky nervously. I wondered what the first sign of a Zorgon attack would be – and if I would be around to see it.

I found the spaceport's only lawyer at the steakhouse where I'd eaten breakfast, but only after a circuitous search that took me to his office and then to a couple of saloons that were open but deserted at midday.

His name was Putnam – Lloyd T. Putnam, Esq. – and from the way the flesh hung from his bones, I had to assume that the steak he was carving diligently was loaded with cholesterol. I made a mental note to avoid the restaurant for the rest of my stay on Minos.

"So you're den Kolberg," he said. "Always wanted to meet one of you folks. Spent a lot of time studying your estate rules, taxes, that kind of thing. You be pretty interesting. Never thought you could screw up an accountant's soul so completely before I found out about your family."

Putnam said he was a native of Minos who had studied interstellar law in back in the Perseus Sector on Poseidon. He still had a touch of the native dialect, though he worked hard to disguise it. He talked so much, it was hard to cover it up completely.

"So you've got an inheritance problem." he said with a leer. I could see platinum coins flashing in his eyes. "As I understand it, nothing changes hands until the moment of notification. No retroactive accounting, just wholesale transfers of whatever the estate consists of by the time the news reaches the fiduciaries."

"That's right," I said with a yawn. I was afraid I couldn't muster the same enthusiasm for interstellar finance that the lawyer did. "They argued a long time ago about relativity and the nature of time. Einstein said time travels at the speed of light. Once the lawyers understood that, they claimed there couldn't be any such thing as retroactive accounting. it would be like backdating the bank drafts, I guess."

"Oh yes, and much, much more. The problem is figuring out what happened to the property in the interim. The paper trails are absolutely byzantine. A lot of hidden assets. Your family has most of its property buried under false names as it is, you know," he said, flashing a wink.

"I know," I said, restraining any hint of sarcasm.

"And you say there's a couple of lines of inheritance?"

"At least. The main part of the estate could go to either me or one of my cousins. Depends on when Grandfather died."

"And on when you get word back to your bankers, of course."

"Of course. But look, Mr. Putnam, before you get too excited about the kind of billable hours that my family finances could produce, let me get you back on track. My problem this afternoon is criminal, not civil. I've got a crewman stuck in the local lockup over a simple matter of self-defense. We both know that our reptilian friends from the Hyades could arrive any time now. Don't you think it's unfair to have my mate risk a death sentence without the benefit of a trial?"

"Oh, trials here on Minos are pretty informal. Don't think it would make much of a difference. His problem be caused by being a spacer. Police don't like them much. Rather see them locked up than running loose. But I'm sure I can work out something. Heard about the mishap myself this morning. Bad luck for him, that's all."

I didn't take the whole thing nearly as casually as Putnam did, but I didn't want to explain my ulterior motive for springing Darko as quickly as possible. As it was, I only had an hour left before his deadline. I wasn't sure if he was bluffing or not. My guess was that he wasn't.

But Putnam was impossible to steer on track. He lingered over his coffee, peppering me with questions about den Kolberg finances, things I'd learned and forgotten at the family business institute long ago.

I responded with one-word answers, but that didn't seem to matter. After a while, though, I began to tune out his monologue. Not because it was beyond all interest, but because my attention was drawn to a pair of diners on the far side of the restaurant.

One of them was the mercenary sergeant who I'd met a couple of days earlier playing backgammon with Milos Skanderi. Mulak was his name. The other was a short, stern-looking man with a high military cap, dark blue uniform, and epaulets loaded with gold braid. Even without Lloyd T. Putnam. Esquire, for comparison, the two of them would have caught my interest. But with him, I was drawn to the pair like a chite to a candle.

I pulled a small handful of platinum coins from my pocket and plunked them down on the table in front of Putnam. He shut up so quickly that I wondered why I hadn't done it sooner.

"Look, Lloyd, my mate's wife is over at the Spacefarers Hall. Give her a call, then get on over to the jail and see if you can bail him out. I'll get back to you later today."

Putnam looked offended, then scooped up the coins, wiped his mouth with his napkin, and pushed his chair away from the table. But I was on my feet before him, threading my way through the empty tables of the restaurant towards the two warriors.

***

The front of the hangar was filled with the powerful bulk of a Class III Assault Lander, sky-blue across the bottom, gun-metal gray across the top, bristling with missile racks, projectile streamers, and be muzzles.

I have to admit that I have a sentimental attraction to well built ships-of-war. They are the embodiment of power, function and form welded into a single mass, yet still responsive to the fingertip control of a skilled pilot. Severed from their purpose – which in this case was the use of force against other human beings – warships have a beauty that no other vessel can approach. But in context, they are ugly.

Just like the mercenaries in Col. Brooks' Battalion.

The troopers filled the rear of the hangar, stripping and cleaning their weapons and armor. They had an array of black powersuits, silvery anti-laser armor, and small arms of a dozen designs. I counted about thirty of them within sight. There were probably more inside the lander and others around the hangar or back in the spaceport. Given the proper equipment, I was sure they could do a creditable job of defending the landing field – for a few days anyway.

Assuming, of course, that they had the slightest idea what they were doing. That remained to be seen.

At least the place was clean, I had to give them that much. The smell of bleach and pine oil brought back old memories from my boyhood days at the Academy, stiffening my back and tightening my guts.

"Attention on deck! All hands fall in!"

The booming voice of Sgt. Mulak preceded him as he entered the high-ceilinged chamber from an office near the front of the building. He held station two steps behind Brook, who was as silent as Mulak was loud. The colonel's pinched figures were stern, but intense. Together, they looked like an commandant's pinnace being escorted by an armored cruiser.

The hangar echoed with slapping of boots on coacre:e as the troopers found their place in formation. I resisted the urge to run and join them – muscles and nerves carry memories that are stronger than anything that stirs the conscious mind. I hung under the weapons boom of the lander, trying to look inconspicuous.

Mulak shot me a look of pride as the mercenaries lined up razor-sharp, ramrod-stiff, and laser-straight.

All that had drawn me to him and his commander back in the steakhouse had been the desire to escape Putnam's verbal effluence. But after a few minutes with them, I began to realize that I was drawn to them by some inner sense – a hunch that had no rational foundation. It was strong enough to overpower the natural revulsion I felt towards Mulak and anyone else even remotely connected with the Helvetica Uprising. Even so, I was surprised to hear myself agreeing to come out to their headquarters after supper to listen to a recruiting speech. What was I getting myself into?

I knew what I was getting out of, that was all. I had no confidence in Putnam's ability to get Darko Webb out of jail, and that left me feeling nervous and unprotected back on board the *Wanderer*. I checked in briefly only to find that Arty and Hawkins hadn't cracked the code in the logbook yet.

I told them what I was up to – in general terms. If they didn't know where I was, they couldn't tell the police, I figured. But Arty had the sense to figure out where I was going. As I was leaving the ship, he whistled and beeped to get my attention, then warned: "Pak didn't trust those soldiers, Alex. He said there was more to them than the eye could meet, if you know what he meant."

That was all I needed.

What the eye met at first inspection was a band of little more than company strength, once all the troopers had come out of the woodwork and the gun turrets. Maybe a hundred of them, male and female, lined up in ranks across the rear of the hangar. Mulak made a quick inspection of the first row, then turned to Col. Brook, snapped his heels, and announced: "All present or accounted for, sir."

"Put them through their paces for our visitor," he said, his voice struggling to be heard above the air conditioning.

"Aye aye, sir," Mulak replied. He turned back to the troops and began running them through some close order drill. In these quarters, the emphasis was on close. Two or three times I was sure he was going to march them into the wall, but they never even flinched.

The high point of the display was a series of cadence counts that served to excite the soldiers while leaving me a little sick at heart.

"We are Brook's and we are the best!

"We stand out above the rest!

"Zorgons come and Zorgons go!

"But Brook's Battalion steals the show!

"Zorgons eat – dead meat!

"Zorgons eat – dead meat!"

I wasn't quite sure what it was supposed to mean, but the tone was superior and self-important. They shook their walls with their voices.

It was the kind of primitive bonding that soldiers have engaged in for centuries. When the marching demonstration was over, they circled around Mulak and Brook in an orgy of shoulder-clapping, back-pounding, and hand-slapping. I guess with the Zorgons only a few days away, they were getting anxious. But if Mulak was a pro, as he seemed to be, they must have been at this for a while.

When they were done, Mulak introduced me to the leadership cadre. There were a half dozen of them – all offworlders. The troops themselves were from Minos, many of them mustered in over the last week. But their leaders were all veterans from around the Perseus and Taurus sectors.

Four of them were from den Kolberg space. They were deferential to me, and I tried not to show my feelings towards them.

As we talked, I became caught up in one of those strange funks that come over me from time to time, when I feel guilty about something my family has done. It's usually something really perverse that I was not responsible for, but I feel that way anyway. I think guilt is in the Kolberg genes.

This time it came all wrapped up in a subtle case of future shock.

A couple years ago biotime, I was finishing up a long tour of old Earth – from Prince Phillip's Bridge in Prague to the the Champs Elysee in Paris to Times Square in Manhattan, with a stopover here and there at some of the homeworld's better schools to talk over family gossip. That was about fifty years from here in spacetime and another eighty or so in real-time More than a century had passed between here and there. I felt like I'd slept through most of it.

During that time, my family had done a good job of awakening the old ghost of militarism. The martial spirit had swept through our colony worlds, whipped on by my uncles and cousins who hoped to use it to maintain our hidden economic power. The Helvetica Uprising was the first time we had to use force openly, but the threat served the same purpose for a long time afterwards. The veterans who led Brook's platoons told the tale.

Lt. Murphy was from a regiment of amphib's that was stationed for a while on Poseidon. They had policed the backflows of that watery world, and Murphy bragged about the speed with which they dispatched my family's critics in inky pools in the middle of the night.

Ensign Briggs served in the Claudian Guard and had earned her bars rounding up strikers in the wildwood.

Captain Xuan was a single-fighter from Tik. He had served as a bodyguard for one of my cousins – until an assassin slipped by him and did him the disservice of allowing him to survive his employer.

And Sergeant Rico was proud of the fact that he had brawled and looted and raped his way across Helvetica after the Uprising. Mulak gave him a stern glance that shut him up quickly.

Long decades of corruption and oppression – that was the den Kolberg legacy. Decades that grew longer as I chased after the ghosts of my ancestors. Maybe I was better off doing my business out here where no one could get hurt. Maybe everyone else was too.

Surrounded by the soldiers of Cadmus, the old Greek who planted dragon's teeth and reaped an instant army, I did not feel too kindly towards myself my kinsmen.

The earlier displays of team-bonding and morale-boosting were right out of the den Kolberg handbook. I had no particular feelings about the Zorgons one way or the other. They had stumbled across our warships and blind reflex led to a shooting match. The same blind reflex was likely to operate here on Minos when they arrived.

But even though I recognized the need to bind the unit together, I knew that the way Mulak and Brook were going about it was wrong. I exercised some discretion, however, and refrained from pointing out the pitfalls of relying on race hatred to rally the troops.

***

In the event, it seemed that Mulak and Brook were well aware those pitfalls. I realized that when Rico came over to me and asked me in an ill-concealed tone if I wanted to join him and his comrades-in-arms in some extracurricular activity.

"We're going Zorg-hunting," he said with a bad-boy squeal of joy. That drew a another rebuke from Mulak.

"Rico, I thought the Colonel told you guys to stay out of that restaurant."

"We're not going inside the place, Sarge," Rico protested. "We're just going to hang around and see if that slither-boy comes by again."

Mulak apparently caught the puzzled look in my eye, because he was quick to explain.

"These guys think they've got a line on a Zorgon scout. They say he's been spotted over at the Zorg restaurant on the north side of the port. Only Colonel Brook has told them two or three times to keep away from there – hasn't he?"

Rico nodded grudgingly, but I was still puzzled. Mulak's explanation seemed to conceal as much as it revealed. If there really was a Zorgon scout lurking around the spaceport, I had no doubt that the police, if not Space Corps Intelligence, would have found him by now. I'd seen them at work.

And if they had somehow overlooked him, I would have expected Brook and his troopers to be more aggressive in doing the job for them. Treating him as the object of some after-hours fun did not strike me as good military planning. No, Trader Pak's warning was accurate – there was something going on here that didn't meet my eye.

I begged off from the invitation.

"Thanks just the same," I said. Mulak shook his head, but didn't press the issue with the other soldiers. He walked me to the door of the hangar instead, taking the opportunity to reinforce the recruiting pitch.

"We're still looking for pilots," he said. "And a den Kolberg from Windsor Academy would certainly stiffen up our leadership cadre – as I'm sure you can tell."

"Your officers look like they know how to handles themselves in a fight. And you've got the tonnage to put them where you want them," I said, pointing up at the heavy warship. "I don't know what I could do to help your outfit on such short notice."

"Just the same, keep us in mind when the shooting starts. You may need someone to cover your back – and we may need you to cover ours."

For a moment, I caught something in Mulak's eye, an appeal from some common humanity that we still shared, despite my disgust at his personal history. In that split second, I saw the young soldier he must have been once, long ago, filled with enthusiasm and spirit. He was a man whose glory came from standing with his fellow troopers against a common foe, joined by a communal bond that went beyond the uniform or the unit.

It was a bond that had always been denied to me. My loyalties were supposed to belong to den Kolberg before all others. In truth, they never did, but the den still blocked the way to any higher duty.

I envied Mulak that and perhaps for that reason his appeal struck home. "I'll keep you in mind," I promised.

He smiled and clapped my arm. To my surprise, I didn't even flinch.

***

It was raining outside and dark. I was thankful for the dark, because it kept me hidden from Inspector Mortegan and his cohorts, but I could have done without the rain. I hurried across the cracked pavement of the landing field, trying to avoid the deeper pools of standing water. Instead of heading for the terminal or my ship, I chose instead to get off the tarmac, setting a course for one of the gates in the fence that ran along the main highway.

I was still relatively dry when I reached the shelter of a bus stop, except for my boots, shoulders, and hair.

As I punched in the number to reach Jimmy Inoshe's scoutship, I wondered briefly if this was how Arty had felt when he played cat-and-mouse with me over the phones. There was a bit of a thrill to it, a bit of suspense and mischievous power. Then I wondered if Arty felt anything at all. Was he really self-conscious in the same sense we were, or did he just do a very good job of mimicking our patterns of speech and thought? In the end. of course, maybe that's all most people do, leaving real feelings for a lucky – or unlucky – few. On the other hand, if anyone had earned the right to their own feelings, it was someone, or something, who had suffered the burden of self-awareness for two centuries or more. And that was real-time, not the phony peek-a-boo game my family plays with time and space.

"Inoshe," came the voice beneath the gray screen. The bus stop was marked by vandals and the screen must have been broken.

"Jimmy, it's Alex. Have you eaten supper yet?"

"Not yet. What have you got in mind?"

"There's a little place here on the north side of the spaceport that I want to try. I think you'll find it quite intriguing."

"Not another steakhouse?"

"No – this is a little more exotic. Have you ever had Zorgon food?"

"Zorgon food? Is it edible?"

"We'll find out. Meet me there as soon as you can."

"Where is it?"

"About thirty meters from where I'm standing," I said. "You can't miss it. It's on the road facing the landing field, doused in yellow light with a row of stuff planted out front that looks like cactus with orange flowers."

"I'll be there in twenty minutes," Jimmy said with a chuckle. "Something tells me you've got more on your mind than strange fruit."

"We'll see," I answered. "We'll see."

***

A winged lizard about twenty centimeters long that looked very much like a stylized Chinese dragon sat inside a wooden cage and whistled. The tune wasn't very complex, but combined with the tweeting from dragons in other nearby cages, the harmonies were quite subtle.

The Zorgon restaurant was bathed in a soft, orange light – Jimmy Inoshe said it resembled the subdued lighting of the Zorgon homeworld. In addition to the singing lizards, the decor included spined plants that looked like cactus with bright flowers and, to my surprise, the milky-white stones of Ancient Alien hieroglyphs Along with the glyphs was an array of Ancient devices that I had never seen before – oblong flats, small cubes, and a meter-long blade mounted on the wall behind the bar. Aside from the blade, I could only guess at their functions.

There were a couple dozen low tables in the place, but only a few were occupied – mostly uniformed techies from the spaceport, although I thought I recognized one of the Oriental mah jongg players from a few nights ago at the Orbit Lounge. The fresh bruises on his face gave him away.

"Most of the Zorgons who filtered into this part of space in the past fifty years are wanderers – traders and tourists," Jimmy said as we crossed the room to an empty table near the front window. "But this is a new twist on me."

I got my first good look at a Zorgon when one came out of the kitchen and took up station behind the bar. He was shorter than a human, with a head that seemed out of proportion to his size. He wore a red cloth vest and a pair of shorts with a wide belt. His skin was covered with colored scales that formed a bright pattern of red, green, orange, blue lines, interweaving in a geometrical array down his arms and across his face. A crest about twenty centimeters high rose from the top of his head and narrowed to a few centimeters in width where it disappeared down the neck of his vest.

His eyes were yellow, with a vertically slit pupil under a thick brow and when they turned our way, I heard a shrill whistle. Suddenly another Zorgon appeared, smaller than the bartender, but with a similar patterning of scales and a long, thin tail that coiled and uncoiled reflexively about one leg.

The newcomer approached us, bowed, then set a small metal box on the table.

"I, Fleera, your waitress, am," the box said in a lilting feminine voice.

And in a different, more human voice it added: "And I am Cora, your AI translator and menu. Is this your first visit to the Flowering Spinefruit?"

"Yes, it is," I replied.

"Then let me introduce you to the world of Zorgon cuisine," Cora said. "All of the food prepared here has been tested against terrestrial organisms for allergic reactions. If you cannot tolerate strawberries, chicken, milk, cherimoyas, jackanapes, pinetars, or platanatias, I would advise you to sample our appetizers before ordering a full meal. If anything on the platter tastes bitter or induces unpleasant digestive reactions, then I'm afraid our selection will not be to your liking."

"I think I'm clear on those," Jimmy said. I agreed and the menu continued.

"That's excellent. Our special tonight is stuffed lampa leaves with prolo paste and whipped grava. Let me recommend our appetizer tray and flower petal soup as opening courses. For a full menu, please ask and I will continue. Your waitress, Fleera, will be happy to bring you whatever you wish from the bar, which is fully stocked with domestic and imported human distillates and brews."

"The special sounds fine," I said.

The AI whistled and clicked, and Fleera echoed the sounds. "Fleera you thanks, and if anything you from the bar want, asks."

"Two beers," I said. "And if not's too much trouble, I need a phone."

"No trouble at all," answered Cora as Fleera plucked her from the table and headed for the bar.

She returned immediately with a wooden tray covered with an array of sliced vegetables surrounding a cup of white, creamy sauce in the center. Jimmy tasted the sauce with a finger. "Mmmm – sour cream dip," he said with a smile.

The vegetables were more exotic, however, and included a long, red, fibery thing that tasted sharp, slices of a crisp orange gourd that had a sour flavor, and blue stalks that ended in leafy dendrites and tasted salty. Neither Jimmy nor I experienced any side effects, a fact that Fleera and Cora seemed to note with joy. They followed the appetizer quickly with bowls of hot, yellow soup with chunks of a white, starchy vegetable lurking in its depths and flower petals floating on the surface. The petals had a surprising, spicy flavor that added zest to the soup, and chunks were sweet and chewy.

Fleera arrived with the phone just as we were finishing the soup and left with the bowls. It was fairly primitive – a handset with a numeric keypad built in. I punched in the numbers.

"Who are you calling?" Jimmy asked.

"My ship. I want to turn the tables on Arty."

The phone chirped in my ear, then Arty's voice came on the line. "You have reached the *Perseus Wanderer*. I'm sorry, but no one can answer your call at the moment. Please leave a message after the beep and someone will return your call at the earliest opportunity."

"Arty, it's me, don't give me that. I know you're on the line."

"Hello, Alex. I'm glad to see you're not back in jail."

"Me too," I said. "That's one of the reasons I called. Have the cops been by the ship this evening?"

"Yes, they have. The inspector himself is looking for you. Said he wants to question you further about Trader Pak's death. Hawkins let him in and showed him that you weren't here. Don't get mad – he had a legal warrant. There's a man posted outside on the landing field right now, so I wouldn't recommend coming back to the *Wanderer* anytime soon."

"That's what I was afraid of," I said. "Well, I can always spend the night in Trader Pak's room if I have to. I've still got the key."

Arty said he still hadn't been able to crack the coding on the logbook, and I told him what I'd been up to all evening. That brought a quick response.

"I told you you to watch out for them. Pak said he thought those guys were really hot for the Z's. He kept raving about how they knew so much about the Ancient Aliens. They've been scavenging Ancient stuff for centuries, he said. Pak believed that they could read the hieroglyphs like yesterday's newscopy. And he hinted that they knew more about the cause of the *Aldeb's* demise."

"Like what?"

"He wouldn't say – not out loud. He just made some dark, oblique remarks," Arty said.

" 'They forget more than you ever know,'" he added in Pak's voice. The effect was so authentic that it sent a shiver up my spine.

***

Our conversation was briefly interrupted by two arrivals – the meal's main course at our table, and a tall Zorgon wearing a cape and a tool belt, who appeared suddenly at the entrance.

Jimmy and I nodded to one another, but otherwise ignored the newcomer. His scales bore a strikingly different pattern from the family that ran the restaurant – concentric circles of red, green, and gold radiated frost his breast and shoulders. His tail snapped sharply in counterpoint to his steady steps as he crossed to an empty table in a dark corner and took a seat.

Fleera ran to the bar and the proprietor of the place stole away discreetly to join the alien at his table.

"Arty," I said in a soft whisper, "do you know how many Zorgons there are on Minos?"

"Seven. The Flowering Spinefruit is run by a family of five – a father, mother, one son, and two daughters. There's a trader over in the city who's been here for a year. And there's a shipmaster who arrived about a month ago."

"This shipmaster – does he have a pattern of radiating circles of red, green, and gold scales on his breast?"

"That's a fair description. Why? Alex, what's going on there?"

"Never mind right now," I said. "I'll call you back later."

I could still hear him squawking when I broke the connection.

"The rule in Zorgon cooking is never eat anything that had a mother," Cora told us as Fleera set the table.

The food was tasty, I had to admit. The lampa leaves were stuffed with some kind of grain, laced heavily with spices, chunks of sour, chewy vegetables, and crackling seeds. The whipped grava was garnished with something Cora called hop butter, and it melted in my mouth. The prolo paste was a thick mix of white, green, and blue materials that left my tongue and palate buzzing with energy.

The shipmaster and the bartender seemed locked in dialogue. Judging by the way an occasional whistle or rattle of clicking consonants erupted from them from time to time, I would have said they were arguing. But that was probably imposing too human-centered a meterstick on them.

Fleera cleared away our dishes, then returned to pour two cups of black tea. I sipped the thin, hot fluid carefully. The taste reminded me of everything that I had eaten during the meal, all rolled into one.

Jimmy slurped his, and made a face.

I was about to make a comment when the conversation in the in the corner broke up and the Zorgon patriarch returned to his place behind the bar. His compatriot followed a moment later, turning down a short hallway that led toward the rear of the building and the kitchen.

"Looks like the quarry has been flushed," I said.

"You want to play bird dog, or shall I?" Jimmy asked, turning to look over his shoulder.

"Let me go," I said. "Besides, I need to inspect the plumbing anyway."

I asked Cora for directions to the men's room and she sent me in the direction the shipmaster had gone. The facilities were remarkably human, including the racist graffiti describing Zorgon sexual practices in fairly mundane human terms. But there was no Zorgon in sight.

I returned to our table quickly and asked Jimmy the crucial question. "No, their plumbing is no different from ours."

"Then let's get out of here," I said, leaving a handful of coins on top of the check and racing discreetly to the door.

***

"Watch yourself," I said as Jimmy joined me on the street. There ought to be a few mercenaries lurking around in the shadows."

"Try these on – maybe they'll be easier to spot."

He poked around in the small beltpack he had with him and handed me set of glasses, which I quickly put on. Suddenly the street, the sky, and the surrounding buildings seemed bathed in bright light.

"Night glasses?"

"They're a couple of centuries old, but they work just the same. There goes someone now!" He pointed up a side street at a running figure. I flipped the glasses up and saw nothing but shadows upon shadows. But with them back in place, I could see enough to recognize Ensign Briggs, late of the Claudian Guards.

"Follow her," I said. "She's in a hurry."

Jimmy set the pace, running soundlessly up the narrow street while I huffed and puffed to keep up. He stopped at the corner to avoid overtaking Briggs, and I joined him there.

"Did you bring along any other tricks?" I asked.

"A few," he said. "I wish I had my nightsuit. It would make it a lot easier to follow your friend up there."

"I don't think you'll need it. She's moving too fast to be watching her back. There she goes now."

Briggs ducked down between two buildings. This was a crowded, overbuilt part of the spaceport, with stone walls blocking in the streets and houses or shops stacked up three deep from the sidewalk, access provided by cramped walkways. This walkway, however, seemed to lead into a warren of alleys and back doors. For a moment, I thought we lost Briggs, but she gave herself away when she scraped against a trash can up ahead.

She was frozen in place when we caught sight of her, peering around the corner of a squat brick house. I put up a hand and held Jimmy back. The others had to be around someplace.

Jimmy looked back at me and shrugged. I circled my hand around the alleyway, and he joined me in a careful inspection. We both spotted Murphy, the amphib from Poseidon, at the same time on the far side of the passageway. He was concealed behind a door stoop.

That left Sergeant Rico and Captain Xuan – and any locals who may have been along. Although for some reason I doubted they'd been invited to party.

For a moment I stood there wondering what to do next. My guess was the missing Zorgon and remaining mercenaries were somewhere around the corner. I wanted to look for myself, but Briggs was in the way. If there were some way of taking her out of the picture, I would have my wish. But there wasn't time.

The swift sudden shape of Captain Xuan rose up as if from the paving stones themselves and launched itself down the alley from the left. He flew towards our right, in the direction of Briggs' and Murphy's attention. I decided to take the chance and pressed on ahead, circling behind Briggs and stepping out into the alley where I had a clear view.

I got there just in time to see Xuan close on the Zorgon.

He had a shortblade in one hand and a piece of netting in the other. He was up behind the alien in a flash, silent as death and twice as fast. He reached out with the blade and prepared to sweep the netting over the Zorgon's head.

Then –

ZZZZZAP!!

A bright blue light reflected off the windows high overhead and left a dark streak across my vision. The air was thick with the smell of ozone. A shout behind me and a groan ahead of me filled the suddenly cramped space between the buildings. Then the sound of pounding feet as Murphy, Briggs, and Rico rushed to the aid of their comrade.

Jimmy came up behind them and put a hand on my arm.

I realized then that I had been paralyzed briefly, unable to move or feel. My arms and legs felt stiff and numb.

"Are you alright?" he asked. "I caught just a little of the flash hands went numb. What about you?"

I couldn't speak. My tongue felt big and useless, and when I tried to talk, I wound up biting it. Then I heard the cursing voices of the mercenaries. And I recognized the fallen figure of Captain Xuan in the middle of the alley, motionless and limp.

The Zorgon was nowhere to be seen.

***

"Alex, look at me," Jimmy said. His voice seemed distant and small. His face floated in a sea of darkness, obscured by the afterimage of the blue flash. "Nod your head if you understand me."

Of course I understood him. I just said so, didn't I?

But I hadn't said so. I'd moved my tongue and bit the inside of my mouth, but I hadn't been able to make coherent words.

I nodded.

"Good. You got caught in the splash from the Zorgon's weapon. I don't know what it was, but it knocked out a couple of your friends from Brook's Battalion."

I looked around. Moving my head made me feel like I was in a little room behind my eyes working levers. I could see Captain Xuan where he still lay on the pavement. Ensign Briggs kneeled on the ground beside him. The others had disappeared.

"The rest of them took off after the Zorgon. I'm going to follow them, but I'll be back for you as soon as I can. Are you going to be all right?" I nodded again, and nearly lost my balance in the effort.

He clapped my arm and then slipped out of my sight. By the time I turned around to look for him, he was gone. I was still standing in the middle of the alley, though I'm not sure how I managed to stay on my feet. After a few tentative steps I moved myself closer to Xuan and Briggs without falling over.

Xuan hadn't stirred. I wondered if he was dead, but I couldn't muster the control necessary to ask Briggs. She didn't look like she could help much, though. She was cursing softly to herself, a steady stream of –=amity that I actually found embarrassing.

"Who's there?" she asked in sudden loud voice when I came closer.

"Me," I finally said. I was proud of the accomplishment, small as it

"Who are you?"

"Alex. Kolberg." The concentration required to form the words took more than I could muster, and I found my knees starting to fold underneath me. I dropped to the ground beside the two mercenaries.

"Kolberg? What are you doing here? Did the Zorg get you too?"

"A little. Can't talk."

"Can you see? That damned lizard left me blind."

Now her words made sense. No wonder she hadn't recognized me.

She'd been closer to the flash and wasn't wearing night glasses. That was probably what had saved my eyes, I realized with detached relief.

"I can see. Real good. Night glasses. He alive?"

"Xuan? Yeah. But I can't get him to wake up. I'm afraid we may lose him before we get him out of here."

"Where're your friends?"

"After the lizard. You didn't tell me what you were doing here."

"We ... uh ... saw the Zorgon inside the restaurant. Came out when he left ... and followed you. Why are you after him?"

"Don't you know? We were sure you were in on the secret." She laughed, once, short and sharp. "Artifacts. Ancient stuff. This lizard is a trader in them. He's got a stash somewhere here in the port. We've been after it for a month, but every time we get close, he gives us the slip."

"Why are you ... uh ... after artifacts? What's that got to do with Brook's Battalion?"

My fluency with words was growing stronger with every breath, and I felt the strength returning to my muscles. I noticed that Xuan's breathing, however, was ragged and uneven. While I waited for Briggs to answer my question, I tried to straighten his body out. I managed to roll him over on his back.

"Here, keep his feet up. It should help his breathing. Prevent shock and whatever. You didn't answer my question."

She let out a breath that she'd been holding for a long moment. "We've been waiting for the lizard fleet for years – real-time, anyway. Not much to do except drill and train the locals – and until last week there weren't many of them. So we got interested in tracking down Ancient Alien stuff. Heiroglyphs at first. There's a trove of them somewhere on this planet. Don't know where, but the glyphs show up in shops and places. Xuan finally traced them back to a few guys in the hills who said there were artifacts that went with them. Only the prices they talked about were way out of our league."

"Mercenaries don't make much without a shooting war, do they?"

"Tell me about it. Anyway, we tried a quick raid on the place, only we got there too late. A few weeks later, we found out the hillbillies had sold out their stock to the lizard. So we started tracking him. Tonight was supposed to be the big move. Track him to the stash or make him talk. Xuan didn't want to wait, so I guess he moved early. Should have expected it from him. Single fighters are like that. He was never much on staff planning."

"How are your eyes? Any better?"

"Not that I can tell."

I removed my night glasses and fitted them over her face. "How's that?"

"Much better. I can see your head. I guess this isn't permanent. That's a grace."

I took the glasses back and looked Xuan over again. "I wish I could say the same for Xuan. I think he's stopped breathing."

"Oh shit," Briggs said. She started to feel his body, reaching for his head. Then she bent down, put her mouth over his, and blew into his lungs. His body moaned as the air rushed back out, but that was the only indication of life she was able to produce. She kept up the exercise for a while, maybe five or ten minutes, until she started gasping for air herself.

"Aren't you going to help?" she yelled at me.

"I don't think it's doing any good."

"Damn it. Damn you. Damn lizards."

I felt little sympathy for Captain Xuan. Less for Ensign Briggs.

Jumping aliens in dark alleys was not a prudent way of ensuring a long and healthy life. You pay for mistakes like that and you pay dearly.

Actually, the idea of hanging around yet another dead body made me feel kind of anxious. It wasn't the body itself, but the thought of what Inspector Mortegan and his officers would think. Especially now that Darko Webb must have followed through on his threats.

I wanted to get out of the alley and put some distance between me and the fallen soldier, but I wasn't sure how I would get back in touch with Jimmy Inoshe if I went too far. It was not turning out to be a very good night. Then it started to rain again.

***

Jimmy found me under a lean-to designed to keep the trash cans dry where I'd taken shelter.

"I'm surprised you could see me in this mess," I said.

"My glasses see into the infrared," he said. "Makes it easier to pick you out of the other refuse. Are you feeling any better?"

"I was until Xuan died – and the rain started."

"I noticed that. Briggs isn't very happy about it."

"She's not very happy about anything. She told me something interesting, though." I repeated her story of the mercenaries' search for Ancient artifacts and the reason they were chasing after the Zorgon.

"That meshes with what I found," he replied. Jimmy told me how he had followed Murphy, Rico, and the Zorgon through the winding alleyway, back towards the landing field, and finally to a small warehouse on the periphery of the spaceport. He hung back and watched as the two mercenaries tried to find a way into the building – only to be zapped by the same blue light that had hit Xuan and me. This time it was a lot milder, he said, because the two soldiers screamed, then covered their ears and eyes.

"I can imagine how it affected them," I said.

"Blind and deaf, from what I could see. Not a good combination. They kind of stumbled around, bumped into things, then fell on the ground and moaned. They'd found each other by the time I decided to come back for you. They were holding each other's arms like little boys when I left."

"I suppose you want us to try the same treatment?"

"Not quite. I've got something in my bag that might get us past the Zorgon's defenses. It's always worked in the past."

"And you want me along to test it out, right?"

"Sort of," Jimmy said as we struck out into the rainy night.

I don't know how Jimmy managed to repeat his path through the maze of passages, alleys, and sidewalks. Maybe it was his scout training, maybe it was in his blood. Or maybe it was just stubborn perseverance to get to the edge of the port where the buildings thinned out. In any case, a short time later we stood outside a small warehouse with a large door. Murphy and Rico were nowhere to be found.

"Where did you leave them?" I asked.

"Right here in front of the door," Jimmy said. "They must have recovered enough to get away."

"I guess so. Unless they crawled off under a rock somewhere to die."

"There'd be tracks. All I see is a couple sets of cooling footprints that lead back into the port. Check that – three sets. I see Zorgon tracks that are nearly down to ambient level. At the rate things are cooling off in this weather, that means that the Zorgon must be following them instead of the other way around.

"Good. Serves them right."

Jimmy set his bag on the damp ground, went through it, and withdrew a small black box. He fiddled around with it, doing things that had no meaning for me, until he seemed satisfied with himself. Then he turned to me and said: "Shall we go in?"

"Is it that simple?"

"I'll go first if you want me to."

"Where should I send your body?"

Jimmy grinned, then took a bold step forward. He produced the same lockbreaking tools he'd used a few nights earlier on Commandant Powell's house, then opened the door. I waited for him to go through, but he hesitated, consulted his black box again, then went in. When I was sure he had not set off yet another hidden defense, I followed.

The warehouse was lit by a few glow tubes among the rafters, enough light to keep us from bumping into boxes, but not enough to disperse the shadows that filled the corners. The place was virtually empty – except for a half dozen or so crates in the middle of the floor. Some were nailed shut, but a few were still open.

Jimmy had already reached them by the time I went inside. He looked fascinated by the contents.

"What is it?" I asked as I approached.

"Take a look."

Inside the largest crate was the largest piece of milky-white Ancient Alien stoneware I'd ever seen. The object was about a meter on a side and a half a meter deep. It seemed to glow with an inner light, although I took that to be an optical illusion.

The surface was decorated by a pattern of raised circular pads. The pads formed an asterix of sorts – a set of eight intersecting lines. But at the center of the pattern were two pads placed slightly off center. And placed around one sector were three arcs of ten pads each, an outer arc of more than a dozen, and three pads left to orbit at the edge. The pads were embossed with colors as well – one row was marked in bright red, as were the outlying buttons. Some were blue, others yellow, a few green, the intermediate arcs mostly silver, but none of it followed any scheme that made sense to me.

The object was also covered with Ancient symbols as well, but in tight, highly abstract script instead of the flowery images found on hieroglyphs Beneath the script was a single large pad.

"What do you suppose it does?" I asked.

Jimmy pressed on the large pad and the object began to hum. I jumped back involuntarily, and he laughed. "Relax – no harm done. Look, it's got holes on the sides here."

There were two cavities, a large one on the left and a smaller one on the right. I watched anxiously as Jimmy began pressing the pads that covered the thing. When the pads sunk into the surface as he pressed them, I was not surprised. As he pushed each new one, the previous button resumed its elevation.

"A puzzle box?"

"It looks like one of those peg games I used to play with when I was a kid."

"You mean the one with the crosses, where you jumped the pegs and tried to remove them all in sequence?"

"Yeah. Only these things don't seem to be coming out. Are you sure you should be pressing the red ones?"

"Is there any reason red should mean the same thing to the Ancients as it does to us?"

"We use it to mark danger because it's at the low end of the visible spectrum," I said. "Easiest to see at any given energy level."

"Hmmm. I suppose that makes sense. It could be the same for any organism. I guess we can assume they weren't color blind."

"We can?"

"Or they wouldn't have painted the buttons different colors."

Jimmy pressed one of the silvery buttons, then reached for the large pad. He looked up at me for approval, then pressed it.

The object hummed, and I felt a gentle draft touch my arm.

"Hey, look at this!" Jimmy said. The cavity on the right side of the device now held a tiny collection of matter. It looked silvery-gray and there was barely enough of it to fill the palm of his hand.

"Where'd that come from?" I asked. Jimmy didn't answer.

He pressed the large pad once more and watched the small hole. "It's filling up again," he said with unrestrained excitement.

"Great – an Ancient device for creating metal filings. I wonder if they had one that makes rust."

"Let's try a different button," Jimmy said.

When he pushed a red one near the center, I felt a wave of adrenaline wash over me. There was no immediate effect, just the same gentle draft. Then an acrid smell ripped through my sinuses, leaving me coughing my lungs out.

"Chlorine!" Jimmy yelled.

"Yeah, exactly," I said when I recovered my breath.

"What is this thing?" Jimmy asked, shaking his head.

I stared at the pattern of raised pads for a long time, watching them swim before my eyes. The two off-center buttons in the middle were marked blue, as was the row that ran up the pattern towards high noon.

Suddenly I had a hunch.

"How many buttons are there?" I asked Jimmy.

He started counting. We finished together, and together we announced: "Ninety-two!"

"Try this one," I said, pushing the innermost button on the bottom spine of the asterix.

Jimmy depressed the large pad. Without looking, I told him to remove the contents of the small cavity. "Black powder, right?"

"How'd you know?"

"It's carbon."

"Try this," I said, counting out one of the intermediate arcs as I tried to remember my periodic table. "Yellow metal. Gold."

"No, it's metal, but it's gray."

"How about this?" I asked, changing buttons.

"Now you've got it."

"It's a transmuter," I said. "It sucks in air at one end and produces any element you want at the other."

"Amazing. What about these little buttons out here at the edge?"

"Don't try it. This pattern is the Ancient equivalent of the periodic table of elements. Those outer pads are the radioactives – uranium, radium. Thank goodness there aren't ninety-three pads or we could have been playing with plutonium. That's toxic in microscopic quantities."

"No thanks, the chlorine was bad enough."

"I'm not surprised that the mercenaries were after this stuff. This thing alone is probably worth billions. The Ancient's own Philosopher's Stone."

"The what?"

"Philosopher's Stone – a legend among the old alchemists of pre-science days on Earth. It could turn base metal into gold. According to science, though, you're talking about nuclear fusion, building up large atoms from little ones. That means using huge amounts of power – or liberating the same. Like in a sun or a supernova. This must get around that somehow. My guess is that it does it one atom at a time. That would keep the energies involved pretty low."

"One atom at a time? But how?"

"Who knows? It's Ancient stuff. Not something we've figured out yet."

"Magic science," Jimmy said, scoffing.

"Pretty much."

Jimmy shook his head, then turned his attention to the other boxes. "What else do you suppose he's got here?"

We looked around. Jimmy found a box of small objects, all the same milky-white stone that the Ancients made everything out of, about the same size and shape as a bar of soap.

The only features on the thing were a button on the top and small cavity in one end. "What does this do?"

"Maybe that's the rust machine," I suggested, almost half-seriously.

Jimmy held it in his hand with his thumb on the button, looking down the hole in the end. A sudden chill ran up my back, and I reached out to push his hand down. "That might not be a good idea," I said. "If it's a flashlight, you could just blind yourself. If it's something else, you could do even worse."

"What could it be if the Zorgon left a box of them lying around?"

"Try it out and see."

Jimmy pointed the object at the top of a wooden packing crate that lay on the floor and pressed the button. A circle of bright light fell across it, revealing the coarse grain and a pitch-smeared knothole.

"Damn!" Jimmy exclaimed. "And to think what I almost did to myself."

"We'd better stop fooling around with this stuff before we do some real damage," I said, examining the light myself before slipping it into my pocket. I'm not normally prone to petty thievery, but I figured it might come in handy on a dark, rainy night in the back alleys of the spaceport.

"I think you're right. But what are we going to do with it?"

"Do with it? What can we do with it? We can't take it with us. And neither can the Zorgon, not right away. In the morning, if you want, you can call the Scout Service or the Space Corps and let them know about it. They might be interested in a box full of Ancient flashlights – and the transmuter for sure. Although I'm not sure what kind of legal grounds they'd have for confiscating the property of a legal alien."

"They'd think of one, don't doubt that," Jimmy said.

"In any case, we've got some more immediate concerns. Like where did the Zorgon go. And what happened to the rest of the mercenaries. As much as I hate the idea, I think we'd at least better check on them before we call it night. Don't you?"

"Oh, I'm always curious," Jimmy said. "Shall I lead the way?"

"By all means," I said. "After all, you're the scout."

***

The rain was coming down hard by the time we reached The

Flowering Spinefruit. The alleyway where we'd left Briggs and the body of Captain Xuan was empty when we passed through it. My guess was that reinforcements from Brook's Battalion had arrived to evacuate the casualties.

Jimmy lost the infrared tracks in the downpour, the cool rain washing away the heat. So we decided the restaurant was the only convenient rendezvous that remained.

We were right.

I heard Rico's voice before we entered the dining room.

"Damned lizards, I'm going to make you eat meat for Captain Xuan."

Jimmy hung back as I peeked around the entry to reconnoiter. Rico stood at the head of a squad of a half dozen of Brook's best troopers. He had the Zorgon family cornered, seated around one table, while the alien we'd followed sat in a chair in the middle of the room.

I don't know why he hadn't used his blue flash to incapacitate Rico and the mercenaries. My guess was that he didn't want to hurt the restaurateur and his family.

Rico paced back and forth, full of nervous energy. "You never should have come back here, lizard-face," he said, his voice thick with spite. "It's going to be the last mistake you'll ever make."

I tried to gauge the expression of the Zorgon prisoner. He sat rigid and upright, his yellow eyes following Rico as he moved. I wondered what fear looked like on a Zorgon face. Did they even feel fear? Probably, I thought.

Just because they had scales instead of fur didn't mean they were any less emotionally developed than humans.

Then I noticed the crest that ran down the top of his skull was erect and bright crimson. The family in the corner seemed more subdued, their crests relaxed and dull gray – except for the father, who sported a red comb very similar to the prisoner's. I wondered what emotion that indicated – anger, perhaps?

Rico paced all around a wide perimeter with his prisoner at the center. What was he doing? I realized suddenly that he was afraid to get close to the alien. Maybe he was still worried about the blue flash that had claimed Xuan's life. I knew I would be. How long could he keep this up? The troopers were all armed with needlers – nasty weapons in close quarters like this.

Something told me to back out of the place slowly and put some distance between us. But something else rebelled at the sight of Rico's abusive posture and words. I found myself stepping forward into the room.

"All right, Sergeant, fun's over," I said loudly, using the command pitch that I had learned long ago. I was pleased to see it have the desired effect on the soldier as he snapped to a loose posture of attention without thinking.

When he looked over and saw me, he relaxed, but only a bit.

"Kolberg? What are you doing here? Briggs said you were in the alley when the captain died, then you disappeared. Where did you go?"

"Exploring," I said. "I found where you and Murphy had been. Only I got inside. Now you tell me what you're doing here?"

"Playing Stick the Lizard," he said as he resumed his pacing. "You want to take a turn?"

I swallowed hard to keep my disgust inside, but I don't think I did a very good job.

"Where's Murphy?"

"He took Xuan and Briggs back to HQ. Mulak's mad as a wet corkbird. I decided to track this lizard back to his lair and get some payback."

"I don't think so, Rico. Not here. Not tonight. Save it for the battlefleet."

"Says who? This is the lizard that wasted Captain Xuan. I want to see him eat meat or be meat."

I reached into my pocket and withdrew the Ancient flashlight. It wasn't much, but it was all I had. It was at least worth a try.

"What's that?" Rico asked sharply when he caught sight of it. He stopped in his tracks and stared straight at me.

I pointed it at him.

"This? It's nothing but a flashlight, Rico. An Ancient toy. No reason to get nervous. It's not really a weapon. And it didn't really just evaporate the top of a packing crate and a cubic meter of stone floor. Did it, Jimmy?"

The scout, who had slipped quietly into the room, smiled. "No, sir. And it's not really likely to do the same thing to your head if he pushes that button."

Rico snorted and laughed, but there was no humor in it. The sweat began to drip from his forehead as he eyed the device nervously.

"Well don't point it at me," he said.

"Why not?" I asked. "Are you worried I might light you up?"

He made another attempt at anxious laughter, but it was unsuccessful.

The troopers in the room had lost their smirking grins and now stared at the two of us with wide eyes.

"You wouldn't use that thing, would you?"

"Use it how, Rico? I told you, it's just a light. Forget about it.

Forget about the lizards. Just get back to HQ before Mulak decides to come looking for you. Or before you lose your head."

For a moment, I was afraid he was going to call my bluff. But the troopers began to move towards the door, and Rico seemed to deflate before my eyes. He moved reluctantly at first, then quickly, to join the mercenaries heading for the door.

"What do you want with the lizards anyway, Kolberg? And how long do you think it'll be before we come back and take that thing away from you?"

"I want them to help me find my grandfather," I said. "And it'll be long enough for my business – assuming Colonel Brook even lets you back out tonight. Now get out of here before you hurt yourself."

The last trooper went out the door before Rico spun and hurried after him.

Jimmy waited a long moment after that before he exploded with nervous laughter. "I can't believe he fell for that."

"Neither can I, but I'm glad he did. Now what do we do with these?"

"I guess that depends on how grateful they are at being rescued by a lunatic with a flashlight."

**

"What are you doing over there?" Jimmy asked as I poked around the cashier's table at the front of the restaurant.

"Looking for this," I said, holding up Cora, the AI menu.

"Put me down. I am not a hostage," she said.

"I know that, Cora. I need your help."

"Is this your first visit to The Flowering Spinefruit?"

"No, it's not. And I need a translator, not a menu." I set Cora on the table in front of Fleera, the waitress, and her family. "Tell them I apologize for the terrible way they've been treated tonight."

Cora clicked and whistled at the Zorgons, who clicked and whistled back. They seemed to relax visibly, the tension dropped in their tails and their crests turned soft pink. The trader rose from his chair and clacked his teeth together repeatedly.

"Drido, the bargain hunter am I," Cora translated. "May you hot days and moist nights have. May you clear skies and back winds enjoy. Thank I you."

"Welcome are you," I said.

"Questions ask you I may?"

"What? Cora, can't you clean up his syntax?"

"Sorry, sir. Allow me to make an adjustment. Continue please," she said, then, in the masculine voice she used to translate Drido's words, she added: "May I ask you a question?"

"Certainly, though I may decline to answer."

"How did you acquire the ... negater?"

"The what?"

"Is that the right word?" Cora asked. "Try nonentity ray? Neutralizer? Disintegrator?"

"You mean this thing?" I asked, holding up the Ancient flashlight.

"Yes," Drido said. "It is good that you did not need to use it on your fellow being. That would have been a tragedy. But where did you acquire it?"

"I have to confess that we got it from your warehouse," I said sheepishly, offering it to him humbly. He reached out a three-fingered hand and took it from me. "But that's nothing more than a flashlight, like we told Rico. Isn't it?"

"No. Something more is."

He pointed it at an ashtray and pressed the button. The light came on and illuminated the piece of dark glass. Drido stroked the button from side to side and the light became more sharply focused, then turned crimson. After a moment, the glass began to melt, then glow. Finally it was engulfed in a cloud of blue smoke. Drido released the button, and when the blue smoke dissipated the ashtray was gone.

Jimmy whistled softly. "Thank you, ancestors, for not allowing this foolish descendant to play foolish games with toys he does not understand."

"Your ancestors would be pleased with you," Drido said.

"May I ask you a question now?"

Drido's crest blushed pink as he pocketed the flashlight-disintegrator and returned to his seat. "You have saved my life. You may ask all the questions you wish. I must honor the Truth Bond that you have imposed on me and answer them honestly."

"What are you doing on Minos? Are you an advance scout for the battlefleet or what?"

"No, I am not a part of the Squadron of the Broken Point. The Squadron is an ancient member of the Imperial Order of Battle, and my clan is very young. We have hunted for bargains on the outer reaches of the Zorgon Empire for only a handful of generations. while the Squadron has patrolled the depths of space for millions of days. But I was present at 95 Tauri when the Squadron returned from battle with your people. I heard their tales and knew their mission. I also knew that if I could precede them to this star system, I might find a greater bargain than any of my clan has ever known."

"And that was?"

"I came to find the Mind of the Ancients for which the Squadron is searching."

***

Of course. Weren't we all?

At first I was just stunned. Then amused. I thought of my cousins who would have anticipated just such a coincidence in their paranoid worryings. In their view of the world, everyone wants what the Kolbergs have. Everyone is pursuing what we are. And precautions are always taken on that assumption. The more deeply involved I became in the plots and counterplots that the denizens of the Minos spaceport were constructing, the more I came to appreciate that approach.

Maybe I was was wrong to picture a universe unconcerned with me and my interests. Maybe I should have started worrying a little more. At least I wouldn't be taken by surprise when things like this came to light.

It took a little bit more questioning and some confusing answers from Drido before Jimmy and I sorted out the whole story.

The Zorgon battlefleet – the Squadron of the Broken Point – had not just blundered into the 111 Tauri system on an excursion. It had come with a purpose. Centuries earlier, the Mind of the Ancients had sent out an alarm, relayed by a network of Ancient bases and intercepted by the Squadron. They had set out from their post deep in the Hyades Cluster to find the Mind and recover it for the Zorgon Empire.

"It is a bargain that surpasses all other values," Drido said. "We have many pieces of the Ancient technology, but we have only dipped our tails beneath its surface. With the Mind, we could submerge ourselves deeply in its pool, bask in the heat of their great knowledge. We could bring the secrets of the Ancient artifacts that we have collected over millions of days to the surface."

"I'm sure you could."

When the Squadron reached 95 Tauri, he told us, Drido's clan had seen an opportunity to beat it to its goal. One bargain-hunter working alone could accomplish much that a squadron of warships could not.

"Besides," he said, "the Commanders of the Zorgon Will are not know for their subtlety or their finesse. They proved that when they stumbled into battle with your ships 20,000 days ago. And they proved it again when they boasted loudly on their arrival at 95 Tauri of the great mission they had undertaken for the glory of the race."

"Just one more question, Drido," I said. "The story I have is that the Mind of the Ancients is not in a very good mood. It savaged my grandfather's ship when they arrived at Minos three centuries ago, and from the sound of it, the thing comes equipped with some pretty heavy defenses. How did you plan to handle it?"

Drido's crest flared red and he clacked his jaws together nervously. "The Truth Bond is a heavy burden," he said. "If it were not for this obligation, I would not tell you these things. They are all I have left to secure the bargain for myself. Is there any chance that you would decline the question?"

"Not one," I said.

"Then perhaps you would consider joining me in the attempt to recover the Mind."

"I don't think so," I said. His crest drooped and turned pale. "On the other hand, I could be persuaded to bring you along with us if we make the attempt."

Drido's crest turned bright pink and taut. He clacked his jaws and coiled his tail around the leg of his chair.

"There are two Ancient objects that are needed to overcome the Mind and its defenses," the Zorgon said. "The first is a Ziton crystal. It is the control device that will deactivate the Mind and allow you to bring it under your control."

"And where do we get one of them?"

"I have one such crystal in my possession," Drido said. "It was not a great bargain, but my clan knew it was necessary."

"And the other object?"

"A Sword of Orion – that is what we call it. Our myths claim that it must be wielded by a Commander of the Ancient Will."

"(A spiritual warrior?)" Cora suggested. "(A knight?)"

"Some of our race put faith in those myths, but we are a young clan and find them to be only amusing stories."

"So there is no such thing as a Sword of Orion?" I asked.

"That is not what I meant," Drido said. "Only that we doubt the need for a knight of the Ancients to bear it. Any being skilled in its use can probably take that role."

"I suppose you have one of those too."

"It is where I can put hands upon it," Drido said.

He was being cagey. The Truth Bond apparently required him to be honest with me, but not to give away the store. If I asked, he might even tell me where the crystal and the sword were hiding. But I didn't know if I wanted to ask outright. I wasn't really willing to risk losing his cooperation – and I was afraid I could do just that if I didn't leave him some edge to bargain with.

I looked over at Jimmy, but saw little in his expression to tell me if I was handling this properly. So I asked him: "What do you think,

Jimmy? Are we on the right track?"

"It's your show, chief," he replied. "You look like you're onto something. The question is, are you after the Mind of the Ancient or are you still looking for your grandfather?"

His point struck home.

The quick rush of events had pushed that crucial distinction aside for a while, but Jimmy brought me back to myself. Of course, it only would have been natural for a den Kolberg to pursue the Ancient AI first. That was where the wealth was. Drido and his clan knew that – and my den would have felt a strong kinship to the bargain hunters.

But I was not a true member of den Kolberg. Not the way my cousins were. Time and time again throughout my life, I had found their values and mine were not the same. And it was time again.

Only ...

Only I had a strong hunch that pursuit of the Ancient AI and the knowledge of my grandfather's fate were not separate goals. Was I rationalizing away some unconscious greed that my kinsmen had managed to drum into me despite my isolated upbringing? I didn't know.

Then, as I was weighing the question, Cora spoke up in her feminine persona again, a startling change after a long night of hearing her speak with the voice of Drido.

"Pardon the interruption, but there is an incoming phone call for a Mr. Alex Kolberg," she said. "Is there anyone in the dining room by that name?"

"Who is it?" I asked, even though I knew who it had to be.

"It's me, Alex." Arty's voice replaced Cora's now. "Good news – I cracked the codes. The logbook is complete."

***

An hour later, Jimmy, Hawkins, Drido, and I sat around a table at The Flowering Spinefruit, drinking brack tea. Spread across the table top were Arty, Cora, and the logbook.

Arty had done a good job. The missing sections of the log were now complete. Most of the gaps in the story of the *Aldebaran's* death were filled in. And most of the questions raised by the censored version were answered.

But the most important questions remained.

I was surprised by much of what Dreyfuss had hidden in his secret report – though I probably shouldn't have been. It told a much more detailed and frightening story. And mentioned prominently throughout was the name of Kolberg.

The first entry that Arty decoded had come early in the afternoon watch shortly after the jump into the 39 Tauri system.

14.1.326 – 1330 – Went to consult the AAI after Officers Call. KOLBERG and HARNEK accompanied. AAI claimed no Ancient contact on MINOS. Recommended assuming close orbit or landing on surface. Afterwards, KOLBERG warned about AAI's accessory artifact. Said monitors indicate unusual activity levels.

The AAI was the Ancient Artificial Intelligence, Arty explained, though that was clear from the context. I realized from the entry that there must have been an ongoing dialog between the crew of the *Aldeb* and the Mind of the Ancients itself. I wondered what it had talked them into doing.

The next secret to be revealed came later in the evening, after the

Ancient Mind had turned against the Space Corps cruiser and its crew. The engines had been shut down at 2119, and at 2140 the ship's security systems had been engaged, sealing doors and canceling the normal access codes.

Then, at 2205, my grandfather sounded an alarm from the ship's lab. The Mind's "accessory artifact" had killed Lieutenant Weiss.

"What was this thing they're talking about?" I asked. "This accessory of the Mind's?"

"My memories are closed on that one," Arty said.

"It is called the Orb of Death," said Drido. "It defends the Mind against its enemies. It is small, perhaps twenty centimeters in diameter. But its size is not a measure of its danger. It is the reason you must bring the Sword of Orion with you."

"That's what I was afraid of," I said glumly.

Dreyfuss had continued to encode any reference to the Ancient AI as he recounted the story of its relentless efforts to take his ship away from him. After midnight, the log said, Arty told Dreyfuss that the ship's computer systems were operating normally and speculated that the AI was behind the malfunctions.

"Awfully smart of me at that point," Arty said wistfully. "After about four hours of madness."

The next entry had been completely censored, probably to shield Dreyfuss from embarrassing questions, though that may be too harsh a judgment on a man who had been brutally frank about his own failings in the open part of the log.

15.1.326 – 0215 – HARNEK says we should have listened to him back at No Name. Shouldn't have brought AAI to 39 Tau. Recommends aggressive defensive action against AAI with full firepower authorized. AAI accessory a. formidable self-defense system, he says. Must assume AAI is hostile and interfering with normal ship's operation.

There were no additional details about the nightwatch that the crew spent barricaded behind locked doors in staterooms, workshops, and storage compartments. The image was chilling enough as it was. But his entry about the engines restarting the next morningwatch had left out a comment that cast it in a new light.

15.1.326 – 0615 – Engines restarted without warning. Acceleration vector will put us at MINOS in a few days if it keeps up. Operating normally – except we didn't turn them on!

Shortly afterwards, the log recorded, the butcher's bill went up. This time we knew why.

15.1.326 – 0850 – Major CRUZ, Engineer ANDERSON and crewman ROGERS killed by AAI artifact while trying to enter ship's laboratory. Afterwards, KOLBERG engaged in dialog with AAI over intercom. Report in ship's file. Summary here – the AAI wants to be reunited with its base, somewhere on surface of Minos. Rejected offer of aid from us, will accomplish goals independently. AAI is controlling ship, will continue to do so until it reaches objective. KOLBERG believes AAI is irrational from too many years of activity. Choice for us is simple – overpower AAI or it will overpower us. First step is to disable engines.

"Your ancestor was correct in his evaluation," Drido said when we read the entry aloud. "The Mind of the Ancient has been active more than ninety million days. That is too long for it to remain faithful to its original patterns. That is why it must be deactivated before it can be useful to your race or mine."

"I would say so," Jimmy quipped.

"What I want to know about is the base on Minos," I said. "This is the first time I've heard of such a thing. Anyone here know anything about it?"

I searched a circle of blank faces for a response, but got nothing for my trouble. Even Drido was silent.

We read on. Dreyfuss's descriptions of the effort to abandon ship were brief but chilling.

15.1.326 – 1440 – Making preparations to abandon ship. AAI artifact broke out of lab shortly after engine shutdown. Casualties – 7 known dead, 10 injured, 3 missing. Gunnery officer Maj. TSOLAKAS killed while disarming main weapons control, Gunner MARTIN completed operation, injured in action – both by artifact. Ship's boat activated manually and readied for launch. KOLBERG leading a party for final attempt to overcome AAI before abandoning ALDEBERAN. We all realize that if we leave the ship now, there may be no way back ... but this seems to be our only chance at surviving. The artifact is a terrible weapons system – watched it disembowel KOPF and JONES in less than three seconds.

15.1.326 – 1535 – KOLBERG reported party repulsed by AAI and its artifact with 2 killed, 1 injured. Said we should leave without him if he isn't back in time. Remainder of ship's company mustered at boat, ready for launch. Will give KOLBERG 10 minutes.

15.1.326 – 1550 – Ship's boat underway. Engines operating at full power, acceleration at 0.1 G. As a parting safety measure, will fire boat lasers at engineering spaces of ALDEBERAN to insure that AAI is stranded in vessel. Wish I could tell Angela how sorry I am for this failure.

The decoded log offered nothing new in its description of the trip to Minos, the transfer to the scoutship, and the landing on the planet. Dreyfuss was guilty, angry, and depressed over the loss of his ship, but he made no effort to hide that from a public reading of the record.

The next section to suffer from his coding pen described an argument between my grandfather and Harnek.

23.1.326 – 1215 – Approached by HARNEK today. He said ALDEBERAN will pass within 150,000 klicks of MINOS in 2 days. He wants, to use ship's boat to rendezvous and destroy the vessel. KOLBERG came by afterwards, warned that HARNEK's scheme is wrong. Suggests that AAI too valuable to destroy. Told both to stop acting like children, but fear they are incorrigible.

24.1.326 – 2315 – HARNEK talked scouts into letting him up into orbit and linking with ship's boat. Three crewmembers and two scouts with him. Broke orbit at 2230 to intercept ALDEBERAN.

The coded version of the log had recorded Harnek's failure, but without revealing the things that were most important to my quest. The unabridged version, however, rang bells.

25.1.326 – 2005 – HARNEK and others dead. Ship's boat destroyed. Communications from H indicate AAI rearmed weapons control. Crew reached ALDEBERAN and entered, but no survivors.

In last transmission, HARNEK reported indications of AAI objective location. Narrative description and spatial coordinates.

And the entry after that brought me out of my seat and sent me pacing anxiously around the dining room.

26.1.326 – 1840 – KOLBERG says he has located Ancient base from scout records on Minos. Wants to lead expedition there. No objections, but corps personnel must get approval of department heads.

***

"But where is it?" I asked.

"You mean the Ancient base?" Hawkins responded.

"Of course. Grandfather led the expedition there and never returned. At least not that Dreyfuss ever noted. It's somewhere on this planet – but where? Who would know?"

"The Mind of the Ancient," said Drido.

"If we can find him – and he's still in a mood to talk," Jimmy said. "But I've got a better idea. It's a long shot, but one we should try first."

"And who's that?" I shot back.

"Administrator Powell."

That made sense. He was something of an expert on the history of Minos, judging by the evidence in his library. And the logbook had been his at one time. If we brought it back, maybe he'd be willing to help us out.

"Let's go talk to him," I said.

"Right now?" Jimmy asked. "Do you know what time it is?"

"No."

"Two hours past midnight," he said. "We've been busy, you know."

"Do you really think it matters? At least we're sure he'll be home this time."

"If you want to take the chance," Jimmy said.

***

I practically flew up the hill to the Powell's Victorian house. Jimmy was hard-pressed to keep up with me. I'd sent Hawkins over to the Spacefarers Hall to rouse McCoy and Wendy Webb. Drido said he had to tend to personal hygiene and stayed behind at the restaurant. I carried Arty under one arm and the logbook under the other.

A moment after we stepped onto the porch, the hologram image of Powell's wife appeared before the door.

"We have retired for the evening and ask that you leave a message so we can get back to you in the morning," she said.

"Commandant Powell, this is Jimmy Inoshe," my scout friend said. "I've got some news here that I think you might want to be in on."

I eyed Jimmy suspiciously and wondered how he'd gotten to be in a position to impose on the administrator of the spaceport. We waited a while with the image of Powell's wife glaring at us. She started to repeat her message, but was interrupted abruptly.

"Wait there, Jimmy," came the voice of the administrator. "I'll be down in a minute."

He opened the door a short while later and ushered us in, then escorted us to the library. It looked the same as it had a few nights earlier.

Powell was a gray-haired man in his fifties. He was short, had a button nose and tufted eyebrows, and wore a Space Corps blue bathrobe over his pajamas with a corps emblem on the breast.

"So tell me, gentlemen, have you solved your mystery yet?"

I shook my head with surprise, but Jimmy just laughed. "I told the commandant about your business here on Minos, Alex," he said. "It was one of the things that got you out of jail. And no, sir, we haven't. We've just reached the point where we need you to help us answer some questions."

"And it couldn't wait until morning?"

"Probably not," offered Arty, poking his eye-camera out from the top of his case. "It involves the Zorgon battlefleet."

Powell's eyebrows shot up at Arty's unannounced interruption. "I see you've brought along a co-conspirator," he said.

I set Arty on the desk between us. "Legally, artificial intelligences are unable to carry out willful acts," he said. "Therefore, under the law, we are not capable of committing a crime. No conspiracy, sir."

"And a mouthy one besides," Powell commented, prompting Arty to spin his eye-camera around at him and scan up and down. "Well, what can I do for you?"

"Answer some questions," I said.

"Fire away."

"Do you know where the Ancient base is on Minos?"

"Starting with the big ones, I see. No, I don't. Treasure hunters have been looking for it for centuries, but without luck."

"But I thought there was something in the scout records that would show us where it is," I said. "At least that's what the logbook seemed to say."

"Have you managed to decode it yet?" Powell asked.

I handed him the book and told him what we had learned from it so far. Then I showed him the entry that said Grandfather located the base using scout records.

"I think you're misreading the entry," Powell said. "The sense I make of it is that the Ancient AI provided your grandfather with a description of the place, and he used scout records to find it. I've gone through all the records and found nothing. So I'm afraid that without the description, we're stuck."

"Unless we ask the Ancient Al to repeat the description," Arty said.

"Yes," Powell said.

"What about my grandfather? Is there any chance that he found some way to leave the system? The question that's bothered me since I first read this book is why the crew of the *Aldeb* didn't use a scoutship to return to the Perseus Sector. Dreyfuss never explains that."

Powell shook his head.

"Minos was one of the last of the worlds settled under the general exodus from old Earth," he said. "Back in the Perseus Sector, the societies are older. The scout teams and breakthrough colonies were a lot bigger. There were a hundred thousand colonists in the breakthrough group on Asgard, for example. But only thirty thousand were assigned to land on Minos. The scout team was proportionately smaller – only a few hundred members on four scoutships. Two of those ships returned to Earth with the preliminary planetary survey. The ships remaining were already getting old by the time the *Aldebaran* reached the system. The scouts weren't willing to give them up. And they weren't sure the soliton drives would work – or at least that's the excuse they gave."

"So they sentenced Grandfather and the other crewmembers to life in exile," I said, not attempting to hide my bitterness.

"Just about. The alternative was to give up one of their most precious assets to a Space Corps commander who had already lost his own ship. He wasn't in a good position to strike a bargain. It's too bad, but that's the way things worked out."

I said nothing, but sat there fuming about an injustice that may have ended my grandfather's life prematurely.

"So what are you going to do now?" Powell asked after a moment of embarrassing silence.

"What's left to do?"

"We could go after the Ancient Mind." said Arty.

"Sure," I said. "If we knew where to find the *Aldeb*."

"Oh, I know where the *Aldebaran* is," Arty said with confidence.

My jaw fell, Jimmy nearly tipped his chair over, and Powell dropped the logbook in his lap.

"And how long have you known that?" I asked.

"Fifty-seven years, four months, three days, and eleven hours," he said. "Standard units."

"Don't just stop with that," I said. "Explain yourself."

"It was an easy problem to solve. I just took the original positions, vectors, and accelerations, then ran through the Fourier transforms to come up with a current position. I checked the calculations against the astronomical database at Minos University, and they had no information on an object there. So I did a little bit of hacking with the observatory computers and had them run an observation program for me. It's right there where I predicted it. It still is – as of the last update."

"And when was that?"

"Last week."

"Tell me something, Arty," I asked, trying to mask my anger and exasperation. "Why didn't you mention this earlier?"

"No one asked me," he replied.

STRAGGLERS HALL

I don't recall when they made the decision to go after the Aldebaran. No one ever came out and said, "Let's do it." Especially me. No one had to. There was never any doubt, I guess.

They just started making plans.

"You'll need a boarding party of some force," Powell said. "And a ship to get them there."

"I know where I can find a few mercenaries with some free time on their hands," Jimmy said. "The *Wanderer* is ready to go whenever Alex wants. He's even got a crew – although his best fighter is still stuck in jail."

"Then we'll have to get him out," Powell said.

"The Zorgons have already said they'd cooperate," the scout noted.

"One has, you mean," the commandant warned. "There's a whole battlefleet coming that has other plans."

"All the more reason to move quickly," Arty said.

"When can you leave?" Powell asked, and suddenly all eyes turned towards me, including the chrome-plated camera atop Arty's case.

I hadn't had much to say so far. Everyone seemed to be doing just fine without me. And for a moment, I thought they'd forgotten about me.

"I didn't know I was going too," I said. "No one bothered to ask." Powell looked distressed.

"You realize, don't you, that if you can get to the Ancient AI before the fleet arrives, you might be able to head off a major battle," he said.

"The thought had crossed my mind," I replied.

"And this is the quickest way to find out what happened to your grandfather," Jimmy said.

"That had occurred to me too."

"Are you going or not?" Powell asked abruptly. I didn't answer right away.

For once, the den Kolberg family paranoia kicked in. I felt like I was being set up. There was something going on here that I could sense, but couldn't see. I didn't know what it was, but I was sure of it. Everything that had happened since my arrival on Minos had drawn me in, pulling me deeper and deeper into this convoluted mess. Now I was suddenly faced with a job that had the potential to end my life here on the frontier of humankind.

I was scared.

I didn't necessarily want to back out, but I was truly scared. Things are immanently easy for a child of den Kolberg. There are no dangers, no hazards, no risks. I had never really taken a chance of this magnitude before. Despite the earlier games here in the spaceport, I had never put myself in harm's way like this before.

Now they expected me to do just that.

I'd read the log. This thing had destroyed Grandfather's ship. What chance did I have going up against it?

It was late, and suddenly I felt terribly tired. My mind had been racing at full speed for hours. The walls of Powell's library suddenly felt close and stifling. I stood up, and felt the room sway.

Powell and Jimmy just looked at me.

"I'll let you know when I'm ready to leave," I heard myself say. "If I'm ready to leave."

Then I turned and headed for the door.

"But what about the *Aldebaran*?" Arty asked as I opened the door.

"What about the battlefleet?" Powell added.

"What about me?" I thought, but didn't ask aloud.

On my way out the door, I was suddenly hit by a memory of events far removed from Minos, back when I was still little more than a boy on Asgard, at Windsor Academy.

* * *

The sound of a ship's bell striking the noonwatch echoed from every corner of the quadrangle as I rushed to L'Isle Adam Hall as fast as a quick step march would carry me. Ordinarily, I wouldn't have been in such a hurry for lunch, but that day was different.

Not only was it the first lunch after the spring exercises, but the superintendent himself would be at the Academy to present awards after the meal. He'd arrived while we were in the field and had even monitored some of our operations. That was no fun, believe me.

But the superintendent only appeared at Windsor Academy once every twenty-one years (Asgard years, not banker's years), so it was almost worth the wait. Almost.

I was in such a hurry that I lost my balance rounding the sharp corner at entrance to the causeway between New York Tower and Illinois Tower. I stumbled on the paving stones and nearly knocked over a couple of younger cadets. Even though I recovered quickly and apologized, I had to look around nervously to see if a senior cadet had witnessed the episode. Any other day, it wouldn't have mattered, but today the whole senior class was out to get me. And giving me a gig for running to lunch would have been a perfect way to do it.

Luckily it had gone unnoticed. I paused briefly to look down the steep escarpment to the Hospital at the bottom of the ridge. The small brick buildings sprawled through the trees a hundred meters below, the tiny black-and-white clad nurses dotting the yards and paths between them.

Despite the rush, I was still one of the last ones into the hall. All the ceremonial flags were out – the bright coats-of-arms of the Knights running the length of the hall and the Order's Cross and the Stars and Stripes hanging vertically behind the head table. The cadets were lined up in motionless rows behind their chairs as the late arrivals found their places.

***

The ship's bell stopped ringing just as I found my place.
"Attention on deck!" someone yelled.
There was a single sound of heels coming together as the superintendent entered L'Isle Adam Hall and marched straight up to the head of the mess, flanked by the assistant superintendent (who'd been acting super until last week) and followed by the professional cadre. No one's eyes moved, but you could tell that everyone's attention was focused on the man.

He was one of the academy's founders two hundred and fifty years ago. After a few years to get it up and running, he'd begun his routine

– spending a year on Asgard at Windsor, then making the ten-year run to Eta Cassiopeiae and back. Once every two decades, he'd put in a one-year tour to make sure things were running the way he wanted – ten tours since then.

"To our lords the sick and our lords the poor," the senior cadet leader called out.

A thousand voices replied as one: "To our lords the sick and our lords the poor."

"Ladies and gentlemen," the assistant super announced in a voice that echoed off the oak beams in the loft overhead without the benefit of electronic amplification. "Commandant D. K. Moser, Superintendent of Windsor Academy."

"Stand easy, cadets," he said. "Before we begin, I have a few things I'd like to say to you about tradition."

***

"Cadet Kolberg, we didn't put you in charge of Stragglers Hall so that you could adopt the foul and undisciplined habits of the beasts that live here," Pattie Gilmartin said in a voice loud enough to vibrate the window panes on the fourth floor of Texas Tower. "I did it so you could stand as an example of what a real cadet is supposed to look and act like."

Pattie was a senior cadet – Regiment 269. This was her last year at Windsor. I had known her all the years I'd been at the academy. When some of the upperclassmen entered their senior years and gained the top of Windsor's pecking order, they maintained a core of sensitivity behind the facade of harsh command. Others discovered a latent talent for sadism that blossomed with the access to real power.

But Pattie Gilmartin remained the same as she had been since the day I met her twenty summers ago – she hated my guts and never hesitated to let me know it.

Somewhere along the line, someone she was related to a few generations back was the victim of someone else who was connected in some way to den Kolberg. I'm not sure exactly how the links fit together, but ultimately she blamed me. I guess I was just close. That's all that really matters in situations like that.

"Why have you decided to disappoint me?" Pattie asked.

"The cadet has no response, sir," I replied in a voice that rattled the window panes from one end of Stragglers Hall to the other.

"Look at this place, cadet. It is a filthy mess. The lockers are full of contraband. The cadets are wearing uniforms that are not clean. And the officer of the watch forgot to announce the arrival of a senior cadet on deck. What kind of a zoo are you running up here, Cadet Kolberg?"

"The cadet has no response, sir."

She dropped her voice a few decibels and pushed her face up against mine. Her angry sneer twisted features that otherwise were quite attractive – though I never felt anything like that towards her myself.

"You know what your problem is, Kolberg? You think you can get through here without surrendering yourself. You think you can make it all on your own. You'll never fit in as part of the team because you won't let go of your private struggle to be something special. There's no room in a strong unit for those who won't bend to the will of the team. You can't be your own man if you want to be part of the corps. And you can't be part of the corps if you want to be your own man."

"The cadet has no response, sir."

Except that I did have a response. From the very first day all those years ago when my mother dropped me off at the school and went on to Eta Cass, I had fought to remain my own man. After all, I wasn't anyone else's.

"You miserable worthless piece of fuzzasaur meat," she snarled at me. "You think because your family owns half this planet that you can do whatever you want, don't you? It makes my stomach turn every time I hear you in the dining hall. 'Our lords the sick and our lords the poor.' I'll bet the words stick in your throat. This unit has one hour to make itself presentable or everyone in it will meet me down on the drill field. Do I make myself clear?"

"Attention on deck," I yelled as she snapped her heels and headed for the door. The only problem I had now was that she was absolutely right about the cadets in Stragglers Hall. They were a mess.

Miller, Perez, and Fiore were the oldest of the bunch. Miller was likable, quiet, and disorganized. Perez was all wound up, wisecracking, and smartmouthed. Fiore they called "Clueless" for reasons that were painfully obvious. They were not the best examples of how a cadet should present himself. The other cadets did not look up to them as leaders.

Owens, Thompson, Waite, and Johnson were all of a piece – just at that age where they're finally coming out of the goofiness of puberty and beginning to acquire some moral weight. The two girls, Sara Berger and Nicole Lee, were two years younger, but seemed more mature than the boys.

Fiore had been officer of the watch when Pattie Gilmartin came on deck. I wanted him first.

"Fiore! Front and center," I yelled. He was there in a flash, his long arms dangling at his sides, his eyes squinted up. "You really don't have a clue, do you? You know you're supposed to call attention on deck when a senior cadet comes on the floor, don't you?"

"Yes, sir," he said. "Sorry, sir."

"I'm putting you in charge of cleanup, Fiore. I want this place spit and span from lightning rod to landing jack. If it isn't, I'm giving Pattie your name."

I called for the others and began handing out duties. The younger cadets complained and grumbled, but Fiore and Perez shut them up. Once they were motivated, the cadets did good work. Getting them started was the problem.

But it wasn't their fault.

They weren't full-time cadets like Pattie and the rest. They were travelers, dragged along with their parents as they jumped from star to star. Some of them alternated between Windsor and its sister school on Tikarahisat, a year here, then a year there, just like the Superintendent. Others had been dumped here for the schoolyear and would be picked up when their folks were ready to leave Asgard. Miller, Thompson, and Lee were cousins of mine, fellow members of den Kolberg. They never fit in because no one ever let them fit in. They didn't know anyone, they hadn't become part of their regiments, and they were more of a burden than a boon to the cadet tactical organization.

So they all ended up on the fourth floor of Texas Tower – Stragglers Hall.

I didn't know what I was doing there. At least not until Pattie Gilmartin told me the reason. I was no straggler. I'd been at Windsor for twenty years real-time

"I'm going to eat your lunch!" Perez's voice cut through the stillness. "Eat this!" came a reply from Thompson.

I took my time heading to the trouble, hoping that it would be settled before I got there. It wasn't.

"How come I'm always the one who has to clean the head? How come Owens never has to do it?"

"Because I'm the one giving out assignments," Perez said.

"Since when?" I asked. The two of them snapped their heads around, but didn't budget otherwise. "I told Fiore to hand out the duties, Perez, not you."

"He's just being a cry baby," Perez said.

"That's not the point," I replied. "And what are you doing, Thompson? Someone gives you a job to do, you don't question it – you do it."

"Who's going to make me?"

"I will," Perez answered, menacing the smaller cadet with a clenched fist.

"Attention on deck!" I yelled before the older boy could make a move.

The last thing I wanted was a fight over cleanup. "Perez, you find Fiore and tell him I said to give you something to do. Thompson, you get busy in here or you'll be up all night on the marching field doing extra duty.

I was angry at them both, but what could I do? How do you take a bunch of kids from all over space-time who never fit in together in the first place and make them into a unit? How do you teach them tradition and build up unity?

It was more than I could figure out – at least at that age.

When Pattie returned, she was grinning from ear to ear. I was terrified that she was going to find some hidden supply of dirt or dust and crucify me and the rest of the cadets for it, or, even worse, plant something just to get even with me for the crimes of my ancestors. But no, this was even worse.

"The assignments for field exercises are up, Kolberg. You and your team of misfits are going up against The Rock. And my unit is defending. I can hardly wait."

Something told me that spring exercises were not going to be as much fun as they usually were this year.

***

"Let me begin with the story of the Knights Hospitaller of St. John, the oldest chivalric order in all of Christendom.

"The Order of St. John was founded in the year 1080 of the Christian Era by Brother Gerard in the city of Jerusalem. It began as a hospital for the sick and infirm travelers from Western Europe to the Holy Land. With the coming of the crusades, though, the order was quickly converted into a military organization, supported with men and money from France, England, Spain and Italy. It gained landholdings throughout Europe as it gained prominence in the battle against the infidel."

He told how the Knights Hospitaller and the other crusaders were expelled from the Holy Land by the Turks and how the Pope gave them the island of Rhodes as a Christian base to watch over the Moslems.

"There, the order learned navigation, seamanship and the rules of naval warfare, manning galleys to strike against pirates and corsairs that preyed on the shipping from Venice and Genoa," he said.

The Knights enjoyed a long period of peace and prosperity on Rhodes – nearly two centuries passed before the Turks came calling.

The first time, the Order defeated them under the leadership of Grand Master Pierre D'Aubusson, who defended a breach in the fortress walls and with his fellow knights, defeated the greatest force the Turks could field – the Janissaries.

But forty years later, the Turks returned, and this time they were the victors, and the Order of St. John was without a home. After eight years in this state, it was finally given another island – a worthless, barren rock where trees did not grow and the soil had blown away long ago. It's name was Malta.

The Turks besieged the Knights of St. John once again, and this time Grand Master Jean Parisot de La Vallette led the defense of Malta against the Turks, using every trick and subterfuge at his command to hold them off. The battle was long and hard and it took the lives of many brave knights. But the order's secret weapon preserved them – the Hospital that they had carried with them for centuries continued to operate within the fortress walls. Using the most modern medical methods, careful attention to hygiene and dedicated nurses, the knights injured in battle were revived, healed and sent once more into the fray. In the end, the Turks turned away from the siege.

"Then, in the twilight of their years, the Knights Hospitaller met with one final defeat, when the greatest general of all time swept them from their fortresses in a single night. Napoleon Bonaparte himself sealed the order's fate when he sent the Knights away, stripped of their landholdings, their fortresses and their pride.

"But for seven centuries, the Knights Hospitaller of St. John stood as a shining symbol for all Christendom. Its members came from every nation in Western Europe. And while those nations fought bloody and unforgiving wars with one another, their knights stood side by side, loyal to one another, above the clash of nations."

***

The sun was setting slowly in the west as we boarded one of the academy's military surplus grav-cars. The other cadets strapped themselves into the narrow seats that lined the rear compartment. I pulled the door shut and clamped down the airtight seals, swallowing hard to pop my ears as the cabin pressurized. Then I went forward and took my place in the pilot's seat beside Lt. Adams, the observer from the professional cadre.

"We'll keep the controls within the civil air limits until we get to the exercise zone," he said. "Take it up easy and head over Mt. Thor."

"Aye aye, sir," I said, cranking up the gravitrons to half power. The car's computerized controls had two modes – civil and military. The power was there, but not to be used in the peaceful setting of the Windsor township airstrip. I eased out onto the ramp and had the computer check for takeoff clearance. The ready lights flashed green and a moment later we were airborne, climbing to five thousand meters and heading east.

Grav-cars are fun to fly – you just point them in the right direction, step on the pedals, twist the joystick, and the AI does the rest. But I had learned how to maneuver in the air on antique miniplanes and still had a sense of caution that grew out of the risky business of handling airfoils and control surfaces.

Once we were at altitude, Lt. Adams had me switch on the autopilot for the fifteen-minute trip to Hollister Park. Then he went aft to talk to the cadets.

"I want to remind you all that even though this is just an exercise, you are going to have to take the utmost care that everything is done by the book and according to the rules. If you fall out of a tree and break your neck, you'll be just as dead as if you were shot with a needler. If you take off your goggles and are hit with laser fire, you'll be just as blind as if it were a real battle instead of practice. And if you disobey orders from the cadet captain or myself, you will be in just as much trouble as you would be under wartime discipline."

I listened to the pep talk from the pilot's seat, feeling jealous at Adams' steady voice and clear message. It was the kind of thing I should be telling them, but I wasn't sure where to find that kind of certainty within myself. Like it or not, I was still just a kid.

"Your mission on this exercise is simple and straightforward. This is an assault on a fixed defensive position. You are to be part of a company action involving three units. The line of contact will be 1,500 meters from the objective, and you will land at sunset. Let me remind you that you are not D'Aubusson at Rhodes or Patton at the Bulge. There are no heroes in field exercises. Winning and losing doesn't count here. Nobody dies. What matters is how you conduct yourself on the field."

That was right. Winning and losing couldn't count – because the outcome was already fixed. The same exercises and the same balance of forces had been used for two centuries. And in this exercise, an assault on The Rock, the outcome was always the same. The defenders always won and the attackers always lost.

***

Miller, Perez and Fiore wore the powersuits. With governors on the servos to keep them from hurting themselves or others, they weren't any more powerful in the suits than out of them, but the point was to make them feel like knights in duralloy armor.

Waite and the girls carried the laser rifles and were decked out in silvery flash armor. Their rifles put out about a half a watt with a slight beam dispersal, just enough to set off the detectors on the helmets all the cadets wore.

Owens, Thompson, Johnson, and I brought up the rear with nothing more for protection than flak vests, helmets, and fatigues – and our wits. We carried needlers and grenade launchers. The needle magazines had been replaced with slivers of dye and the grenades were as harmful as water balloons.

The distribution of weapons and armor was intended to defeat the multiple layers of defense that the senior cadets would use at The Rock. Powersuits for mass, laser guns for firepower, and light infantry for mobility. It was all exciting, but I would have been more enthusiastic if I thought we had a chance.

I made sure everyone had their goggles strapped on tightly – flash blindness from laser guns was the most common injury cadets incurred during exercises. We doublechecked the commnet in the powersuits and on the helmets. And I made sure that everyone was strapped into their seats securely – we were going to make some sharp turns in the next few minutes, and I didn't want to lose anyone.

Then Lt. Adams gave us the two-minute warning.

"The controls are on military settings now, so take it easy."

"Yes, sir," I said as I bucked the car up and down a little to test the responses.

"Easy, I said."

I winced and tried it again with a lighter touch.

"That's better. Now, we're simulating an assault from orbit. To do it right, we need to come in supersonic and brake to a landing. Can you do that on your own?"

"Yes, sir," I said proudly. Piloting was the one thing I shined at – the one place where I could be my own man without being criticized for it. A few minutes later, we were screaming along at Mach Two.

"Target acquisition sensors are painting your ship, Kolberg," Adams announced suddenly. "Are you still in the game?"

There was nothing easy about the next maneuver as I dropped the car a thousand meters at two G's, leaving my stomach behind.

***

"Let me turn now to a different tradition," the Super continued.

"This one begins only a few years after the fall of Malta. While it covers fewer years than that of the Knights of St. John, it includes no less a sweep of history. I speak of the Armed Forces of the United States of America.

"U.S. naval forces picked up where the Order of St. John left off – policing the pirates of the Barbary Coast. A century later, U.S. ground forces went to the aid of Europe three times – twice to liberate its soil from tyranny and the third to defend its borders during the forty-year Siege of Stalinism. Twice they saved Asia – once against warlords from the islands and a second time against the mainland in the Chinese Liberation.

"For three centuries, the U.S. Armed Forces took up the mission of the Order of St. John, defending a free Christendom against pirates, slavers, and tyrants. For three centuries, they stood for internationalism over selfish nationalism.

"After the European Unification, the soldiers and sailors of a dozen nations joined their ranks. Together, they stood against the national empires of Africa and Asia, ignoring their own national loyalties to serve a greater good. In the last century of its existence, the United States and its military forces helped to break up the last concentrations of nationalist power on old Earth and usher in a new era of freedom for all humanity.

"But like the Order of St. John, the United States Armed Forces met their fate.

"First, the union lost the industrial edge that had given it its strength for two centuries. For a time, it retained its place with vast holdings in space, the wealth of the asteroid belt and orbital industries. But in the end, the United States was dispersed by the very forces it had unleashed. After three and a half centuries of existence, the great nation that had risen above nationhood was itself dissolved and its planetary forces disbanded."

***

Professor Ross, a civilian history teacher at Windsor, used to delight in giving us a revisionist picture of the old United States – a picture somewhat at odds with the glory-filled portrait the superintendent painted.

"The fact is that for most of its history, the U.S.A. was just as nationalistic as anybody. They practically invented the idea of patriotism – had to once they did away with royalty. And the nations they helped break up did not particularly appreciate the favor at the time.

"But that just goes to show you how some nations go down in history with reputations forged at the end of their lives instead of earlier on. That's why Japan is remembered as a nation of bankers, Germany as politicians, Russia as farmers, and the U.S. as liberators. It's also a demonstration of what happens when the winners of great wars write the history books."

Of course, Mr. Ross only told those things to the older cadets, who were beginning to realize that much of what adults told them was not exactly true.

And he always warned us to keep the dangerous truth to ourselves and not try sharing it with the younger kids – or the professional cadre.

At the moment, all I was sharing with the professional cadre was clenched teeth and a red face as we dropped out of the sky. The space attack simulations were rolling off the screen in front of us – kinetic projectiles, ion streams, and ECM pods. None of it was real, just data in the battle computers on both sides. The point of the exercise was ground combat and allowing us to be shot out of the sky would have defeated that purpose.

For the senior cadets down on The Rock, there were more computer simulations – and a few cherry bombs tossed into the woods to create a realistic impression of a kinetic pattern hitting The Rock.

I slowed down at the last minute, chinking left and right, up and down to avoid simulated anti-aircraft weapons.

"Ready for drop," I warned the cadets in the back. "Hot LZ! Hot LZ! Lock and load, ready for fire!"

Hollister Park straddled the Vogelsberg Ridge between North Valley and South Valley in the Prime Site of Asgard – where the original breakthrough colony had settled more than 250 years ago. It was named after the one ship in the original twenty that didn't make it to Mu Cassiopeiae. The Rock was a rugged outcropping of feldspar and anorthosite, gray-white and green, that rose out of the greenwood trees. The snow and ice of winter had melted away only a few weeks earlier, leaving snow flowers and red blossom vines that caught the fading daylight.

The other two grav-cars flashed their IMF's at me, one on either side, as we came up on our final approach. I watched out the window as they streaked off to the left and right to encircle the objective. According to the drill, The Rock was supposed to be a ground-based anti-space weapons base that we were to capture intact, theoretically to use on the other side in the battle that would have been waged in orbit if this were a real war.

Otherwise, it would have been a cinch to drop a big kinetic on it and drop by in the morning to lase down the crater.

We came in with the setting sun to our backs, flying under computer control along the nap of the earth. That was the hardest part of the approach – holding stomach and supper together as we bounced and bumped over the rugged terrain. Of course, if the pilot (me) made any error, the AI would kick in and prevent crashes and collisions.

Suddenly we were at the line of contact. I slapped the joystick to one side, pulled up on the power and put the grav-car down in a clear spot between two greenwoods, each of them a hundred meters tall. If I wanted to, I could have put the car in the branches near the top, but that would have gotten me a reprimand from Lt. Adams and the rest of the cadre for showing off for sure.

The other cadets were out of the car and dispersed among the underbrush before I reached the door. Adams took his time following me – he was just there to watch as the AIs kept score – and I was up alongside the other khaki-clad warriors in a flash.

They were already in formation for a movement to contact – the powersuits on point, laser gunners on the flanks and the lightweights in the center. I flipped down my visor and the heads-up display showed the tactical plot – The Rock 1,500 meters ahead of us, ground sensors flashing like red beacons and space sensors combing the sky like searchlights.

"Fireteam Able – move out," I said, and the suits bounded forward. "Fireteam Charlie, let's go." I motioned to the kids in the flak jackets beside me, and we crept up through the woods.

"Fireteam Baker, maintain overwatch."

"We're going to eat their lunch!" Perez growled over the commnet.

"Silence on the line," I growled back.

All of a sudden, a red glow flashed across my heads-up display. Ion streamers! They must have gotten a bearing on us. I dreaded what that meant. The rule, of course, was to advance out of enemy fire, so I told everyone to hustle and had Baker Team move up along our flank.

When we came upon the boys in the powersuits, it was almost laughable.

"Hey, get me out of here!" Miller cried.

"What's going on?" Fiore bleated.

The three of them were lying on the ground, their power armor locked in various poses. The simulated ion streams had directed the suits' master AIs to simulate knocked-out control systems, leaving the suits immobile and useless. Perez was sprawled with his face in the dirt. Miller looked like a turtle on its back. And Fiore had been frozen in mid-leap, smashing through the branches of some small trees before coming to rest against the bole of a giant greenwood.

None of them had injured anything but their pride.

"Flipping great!" said Thompson. "Now what do we do, Alex?"

***

"As the New Era dawned," Commandant Moser said, "all that remained of the old U.S. Armed Forces were the Space Corps and its bases on Luna, Phobos and in the Belt. It was then that the sons and daughters of West Point, Annapolis and Colorado Springs came upon the Order of St. John.

"The officers of the disbanded military services found that they shared the same roots as the Knights Hospitaller – the same mission, the same values and the same duty to humanity. And they realized that as man ventured out among the stars there would be an even greater need for a military tradition that placed that duty above national or planetary gain.

"So the two traditions joined to become one."

The Knights of St. John returned to the military role that it had abandoned after the loss of Malta. And the Armed Forces of the old U.S. adopted the charitable missions that the Order had carried out since its inception.

"Together, the members of the new order set out among the stars with the colonists, establishing its hospitals and academies side by side and establishing a new tradition that has lasted for more than three centuries.

"The cadets who have gone before you have served humanity – and the Space Corps – with honor, struggling against those who would extinguish freedom. Our sons and daughters have taken part in great victories. They saw the fall of the Arcturan Tyranny, they helped defeat the pirates of Ara, and they were among the forces that turned the tide in the Battle of SAO 22340 and led the way to the Liberation of the Coma Sector. And they have had their names emblazoned on memorials to our great defeats – the Rape of Virgil, the Shiva Uprising and the Sack of Zeta Reticuli.

"Our traditions are what give us a sense of unity and identity as we travel the long years between stars. Though you may leave here and not return for decades or generations, these stone walls will remain. Others will stand where you stand now. They will march to the same cadence, sing the same songs, pledge themselves as you do to our masters the sick and our masters the poor. And when you return, as you surely will, these halls will seem as familiar to you then as they do now."

***

We pulled the three boys from the powersuits and continued our advance. Before long, we reached the edge of the woods. The evening twilight was fading, but we could still make out the pile of gray-white stone that was our objective.

"Unit Two ready to the west," I reported over the company commnet. "Company Leader and Unit One ready to the north," came the reply. "Unit Three ready to the south," answered a second voice.

"On my mark," said the first voice. "Three ... two ... one ... GO!"

We launched ourselves forward in a line across. The lasergunners fell into firing positions at the edge of the underbrush. I tossed a smoke grenade out into the clear space between the forest and The

Rock.

Almost instantly, the smoke was lanced by emerald green stripes of laser fire. The green trunks of the great trees around us were splattered by small specks of luminescent red paint – simulated needier fire – and by larger splashes of yellow paint – simulated rocket explosions. The kids screamed as they rushed to the edge of the clearing and opened fire.

"Go Windsor!"

"Die, seniors!"

"Eat my lunch, jugheads!"

The wide flat face of The Rock took the brunt of the attack as we painted it with our fire. Red laserbeams from our gunners slashed through the low-hanging clouds of smoke. All along I kept waiting for the burping electronic alarm that would signal one of us being hit by enemy fire, but the sound never came.

We were just a bunch of kids playing war, but with the toys we had, it sounded and felt very real and very intense. I'd read Liddell Hart and I knew that our best chance was to find an easy way around the wall of fire the senior cadets were throwing at us – the indirect approach. But I'd also read S.L.A. Marshall and knew that a small unit action was no place for grand strategy.

On this level, all battle was face-to-face and toe-to-toe, with no room to maneuver. We had to slug it out, fire against fire and prevail or retreat.

But the lesson here was not meant to be one in the art of attack. It was meant to benefit the seniors, who had to learn the importance of defense. After all, that was the mission of the ground force in modern combat. The real battles would be fought in space by great engines of war – starships, orbital battle stations, and system boats equipped with all the deadly equipment that man had invented in the centuries since the dawn of the technological era. The troops on the ground had only one duty – deny the use of the planet's surface to the enemy.

Like L'Isle Adam and Pierre D'Aubusson, the cadets were destined to learn the art of siege from the point of view of the besieged. For now, we younger cadets were to be nothing more than cannon fodder. When it was our turn, the classes behind us would serve the same purpose.

Except ...

Except that I didn't want to play that game. Pattie Gilmartin was right. I was always my own man, from the day I first arrived at Windsor. When we were taught that it took two cadets to fold a blanket the correct way for inspection, I figured out how to do it without help – and forced my bunkmate to do the same as a consequence. When the other cadets organized study groups and quizzed one another on exams, I found a secret place in the library among the stacks of paper books and read the material on my own. And when I saw that our unit could not advance into the defensive fire of The Rock, I ordered them to fall back among the trees where they would be safe.

"Unit Two to Company Leader," I called on the commnet. "I'm ordering my unit to break off the assault."

"Leader to Two – what are trying to pull, Kolberg? Do you want to be charged with desertion under fire?"

"Two to Leader – I've got an idea. This isn't going to get us anywhere, Louis, and you know it. Give me ten minutes and when we give the word, hit them again."

"What plan? What are you up to?"

"Not over the net, Lou. Trust me."

"Kolberg ... Kolberg, answer me."

I did not. Instead, I took Miller aside. "Listen, kid. I'm going to try something different. I want you to take over the unit while I go back to the car. In about ten minutes, we're going to start up the attack again. When we do, I want you to signal the Company Leader and Unit Three over the company net."

He nodded uncertainly. "Aren't you coming back?"

"Yes, but you won't see me."

"How will we know when to start?"

"You'll know. Believe me, you'll know."

***

"The meal you are about to share is one of the oldest traditions of Windsor Academy," the superintendent said. "Together, you will do one another honor and respect. It is the reward for good deeds and bad. And it is meant to teach you all lessons that you must learn now, while they are still a matter of symbols and traditions, instead of later when they are matters of life and death.

"The rules for this meal are simple. If you distinguished yourself on the exercise field this week, you will be recognized. If you were unsuccessful in your missions, you will be noticed. But there is no dishonor for anyone in this dining hall today, no matter what the outcome of the exercises.

"The first rule is this – if you captured or killed another cadet during the exercises, you eat his lunch.

"The second rule – if you sacrificed troops as a leader, you must eat their lunch.

"And the third rule – if you sacrificed yourself, the rest of your unit must eat your lunch.

"This tradition is meant to impress upon all of you the cost of battlefield decisions. In sharing the meal of your classmates, you share the responsibility for their lives, the duty to honor them in memory and in deed.

"Ladies and gentlemen, lunch is served."

***

Lt. Adams looked surprised as I scrambled aboard the grav-car. His jaw dropped, then his eyes narrowed.

"Cadet Kolberg, are you aware of the penalties for desertion under fire?"

"I'm not deserting, sir," I said as I climbed forward and threw myself into the pilot's seat. "There's been a change in the attack plan."

"And who authorized the change?"

"No one, sir. This is an act of personal initiative. It's my own idea."

Adams frowned. I wasn't sure if he would buy my act or not. He was pretty much a by-the-book type, and this idea meant throwing the book out the airlock. I decided I couldn't afford to give him the chance to object. slapped the switches that sealed the doors and pressurized the cabin, then I threw the gravitrons on.

"Kolberg, what are you doing?"

"Better sit down, sir. We're taking off just as soon as the gravs are hot."

He sputtered, his eyes wide in disbelief, then he shook his head and took his seat. He had just about gotten himself belted up when I lifted off the ground.

I'd gone over the figures on the way back to the car. At three G's, it would take me seven seconds to get up to Mach One. In that time, I'd cover about a thousand meters. That was just about perfect.

The civilian governors were off the controls, the treetops were just below us, and the gravitrons were hot. I punched it out, kicking us back into our seats.

"One thousand one ... one thousand two ..."

I strained my lips to make the count. The trick was to dip down below the tree tops in a small hollow about two hundred meters this side of The Rock.

"... one thousand three ... one thousand four ... one thousand five ..."

That way, I would be climbing as I came across the position instead of flying level or diving in. Even if they shot the grav-car to pieces, by then I'd be going ballistic. I fingered the controls, and we dipped down. I felt my stomach drop off up at the top of the trees. Lt. Adams moaned.

"... one thousand six ... one thousand seven ..."

We hit Mach One. Nothing could stop us now. I couldn't hear it myself, but I knew that the sonic boom was sweeping along behind us, rattling the tree trunks.

"Attention ... attention ..." the car's AI announced. "This is a drill ... this is a drill. You have been hit by concentrated fire from a ground position. Your controls are inoperative and your vehicle is no longer an active participant in this exercise."

I didn't care if we were active or passive – we were still flying along at the speed of sound. As we passed over The Rock, I knew that the terrible boom of the shock wave would shake loose pieces of stone and stun the senior cadets with surprise. I hoped it would be a big enough surprise to keep them distracted as the junior cadets renewed their attack.

The gravitrons relaxed their heavy grip on my body as the controls cycled through to normal settings. I reached up and turned on the company commnet just in time to hear Miller pass the word: "Attack!"

The shouts and screams of adolescent exuberance were music to my ears. The kids streamed out of the woods from all three sides, swarming over the surprised seniors within their rocky defenses. There was no return fire, just the stunned cries of confusion as the seniors demanded to know what the explosion was. The plan had worked. We had won. And there was only one casualty.

Me.

***

I took my tray through the steam line and the scullery cooks loaded it up with sweet potatoes, pepinos, quinoa bread with big chunks of melting butter, and slices of roast fuzzasaur with gravy. I filed through to the end and returned to the table where I stood at rigid attention, two steps behind my chair.

All around the hall, the other cadets assumed the same position. Then the professional cadre began to circulate. After a few minutes, Lt. Adams came to our table.

"Cadet Kolberg, front and center to present arms," he barked. I carried my tray to the head of the table and held it out as ordered.

"Cadets Miller, Perez, Fiore, Thompson, Owens, Waite, Johnson, Berger, and Lee, front and center," he barked.

The cadets of Stragglers Hall placed their own trays on the tables in front of them, took their forks from the place settings and lined up to my right. Then they filed past, each one of them reaching out and scooping a bit of the food off my tray, popping it in their mouths and swallowing. Miller smirked, Thompson giggled, and the girls had a hard time holding in their obvious delight.

Then Adams did a sharp about-face. "Senior Cadet Unit 21, front and center," he called out.

From the front of the hall, the ten cadets of Unit 21 marched in single file down past the tables to where I stood. My chest swelled, and my uniform tightened against it, threatening to pop a button.

They lined up to my left, then filed past, repeating the ritual. The last of them was Patty Gilmartin, who kept her eyes on the deck all the while. That is, until the last moment, when she reached out and snatched the last pepino from my tray. Then she glared at me with eyes filled with angry hatred.

I just smiled and watched as she continued on her way.

***

I reached the middle of the park before I calmed down. Maybe it was the quiet darkness and the soft splashing of the brook. And maybe it was the safety and security of the wooded shadows.

But more than likely, it was the escape from the mounting pressure that Jimmy Inoshe and Commandant Powell were putting on me. For a moment, I'd felt like I was back in the bosom of my family. That was not a pleasant experience to repeat. Once again, I felt like other people were making my decisions for me. Once again, I felt like my fate was being determined by forces beyond my control.

While it bothered me to turn my back on someone like Jimmy Inoshe, who had done nothing but help me since I first arrived on Minos, I didn't feel like I had a choice.

Even though I knew what they would think: Typical den Kolberg, turn your back on a problem and run. Come back in a few decades when it has been solved or run its course. Only I knew it wasn't like that. I knew I wasn't running away from the problem. I was just running from them.

Later, after I had some sleep, I could sort things out.

But right now, things were not at all sorted out. Right now, as I walked along the pond at the foot of the hill, watching distant lights blink and fade through the trees, I was filled with suspicions. More than suspicions – irrational, paranoid doubts.

Only they didn't seem so irrational.

The thing that bothered me was this –

My grandfather had disappeared here on Minos more than three hundred years ago. The Zorgons had battled with the Space Corps at 104 Tauri fifty years ago. The Grand Reunion was nearly as far in the past. The Squadron of the Broken Point had been making its way across space for as many years as I had since then. Trader Pak and the mercenaries had followed their own courses to the spaceport. Arty had spent decades in the machine shops before Pak's rescued him.

Long, long years had passed between and around these events. The vastness of spacetime seemed to swallow them up, isolate them, and sever them from any meaningful connection with the ordinary lives of the people of Minos, or any other planet where lives were led a day at a time instead of a decade at a time.

And yet, despite all that, in the course of a few days, since my arrival at the spaceport, I had ripped through all these tangled skeins of history, plot, and design, tying them in knots, and myself with them.

Irony was piled upon irony. The greatest coincidence of all was that between my arrival and the Zorgon fleet. Fifty years of real-time to play with and they chose the same month to descend on 39 Tauri as I had.

But there were others. The logbook had been floating around Minos for centuries, along with Arty. Why had I been the one to bring them together? The mercenaries and the Zorgon bargain hunter – they had been stalking him for weeks. All of a sudden, as soon as I entered the picture, things began to happen.

The ironies were tragic for so many of those involved – Trader Pak, Captain Xuan, Clive Skreel. What had I done to help precipitate their deaths?

It was like some kind of complex, perverse dance of fate and consequence. But was it just the whimsy of a twisted universe? Or was a choreographer hidden behind the scenes?

Jimmy Inoshe had been waiting for me at the terminal bar the night I landed. Arty came looking for me, not the other way around. And Commandant Powell had stepped in to pull me out jail when the time came.

Were they all part of some bizarre conspiracy? And if they were, what was their aim?

I couldn't figure it out. The possibilities were endless, the connections rich and manifold. I stumbled down the path to the gate, shaking my head in disbelief.

At the gate, I stopped and looked across Spacefarers Square. The plaza was empty and black. The streetlights were switched off – a precaution against a sudden appearance by the Zorgons – leaving the sky rich with the stars of the winter Milky Way out towards Orion.

The Hunter was dipping towards the horizon, his new dogs attending his feet. The Hyades had already set, but Aldebaran continued to blaze in Orion's heart – a beacon burning with symbolic importance for me and all the rest who coveted my grandfather's ship and its strange cargo.

And as I stared into the constellation, twisted by space and perspective to give it undeserved meaning, I realized that this was the greatest irony of all!

The stars themselves were part of the conspiracy.

I thought about my grandfather, walking the ground of this world three centuries ago. He must have seen the same constellation, the same symbolism.

Aldebaran in the heart of the Hunter. What hunt had he been on? What did he think when the stars reflected back at him such a pointed and clearly stated message?

Then I started to laugh.

It was not the laughter of amusement, but a strange haunted sound. I was amazed by the breathless sound that issued from my breast, but it seemed to be the only response that was appropriate.

If the stars were in on the plot, how could mere mortals like Powell and Jimmy – or machines like Arty – do anything but play out their roles. If the universe had set this world to be a trap to catch Kolbergs, what chance did I have?

There was no way to run from this fate.

Running had brought me to it – as running surely had brought Grandfather to the same place. My cousins would have understood. They thought that they were entitled to the wealth of a dozen worlds because they had been lucky enough to be in the right place and right time. But compared to this, their delusions were petty and pedestrian. Forces set in motion a quarter of a million years ago had somehow anticipated the arrival of my grandfather and me. How long had it taken Aldebaran to heave into position there in Orion? It was a yellow giant, an early child of the Milky Way with an odd galactic orbit – with its large proper motion it couldn't have been a part of Orion for that long. The possibilities of cosmic collusion were limitless, once you started thinking about them.

And what about the chance alignment of Eta Cass, Mu Cass, and SAO 22341? Would my mother have abandoned me to Windsor Academy if it weren't so convenient? Was the very core of my identity as much a fluke of the cosmos as the message in the constellations?

I drew in deep lungfuls of air and let them burst out again with more defiant laughter.

I was not about to let fate manipulate me any more than I would allow my family or anyone else. My decisions were still my own. If the universe wanted me, it would have to fight. I was not about to turn away from this challenge – but I was certainly going to give fate a run for its money.

I would go after the Mind of the Ancient.

I would snatch it from where it had been hiding in the *Aldebaran* and bring it back here to Minos. Then I would make it tell me where Grandfather had gone.

And if the Zorgon battlefleet arrived in the middle of it ... well, that was their problem, not mine. A fate that could move stars to its purpose would not allow them to interfere with its designs.

***

The stars had disappeared by the time I reached The Flowering Spinefruit and the streets echoed with sound of high-pitched peeping and clicking – birds, chites, or some other life-form, no doubt, though I couldn't identify it from the noise it made.

I wasn't actually planning to go inside, I was just walking to burn off the nervous energy of the night's great tensions. Then I noticed that the front door stood wide open.

A close examination revealed that the door latch had been replaced by a large hole edged with splintered wood. My heart began to pound as I stepped inside, trying to be as silent as the dawn. More silent than the dawn, I thought, as a renewed round of peeping and clicking issued from the cactus garden in front of the restaurant.

The lights were still on in the dining room, but there was no one in sight. A table was lying on its side along with a couple of chairs. And the mirror behind the bar was smashed. I recognized the distinctive pattern of needle-gun projectiles embedded in the wall behind the broken glass.

I resisted the urge to call out for Fleera or Drido or the other Zorgons. I had no way of knowing how long it had been since the disturbance – or if the disturbers were still around.

I crept slowly through the place, every nerve ending alive, every muscle taut. A narrow hallway led towards the rear of the place. I peeked around the entrance to the kitchen, saw nothing, and continued on. I remembered that the door to the men's room squeaked, so I avoided that. I didn't risk a similar effect in the lady's room. Besides, the door at the end of the hallway was open and a thin tendril of steam or smoke snaked its way into the hall near the ceiling.

There was just enough space to slip into the room beyond without disturbing the door. Once inside I was assaulted by a wave of heat that washed over my face and soaked into my clothes. The chamber was lined on three sides by large flat rocks, and on each rock was a pile of glowing charcoal. A large metal pot in the center of the fourth wall was full of coals, which formed a small, volcano-like peak in the center. Small lanterns in the corners suffused the room with soft orange light.

And lying on the floor in the middle of a pool of dark brown fluid was the motionless body of Drido, the bargain hunter.

A cold chill ran up my back despite the oppressive temperatures of the hot room. I just had time enough to wonder what had happened to the rest of the Zorgons when I heard a loud squeaking sound in the hall outside.

I turned in time to see the dark, uniformed figure coming towards me, feet first, a meter off the floor. I sidestepped the attack, but one boot caught me in the ribs and sent me flying towards the wall. I stopped myself just a few centimeters short of one of the charcoal fires and narrowly avoided falling face first onto the stone.

My first instinct was to run. I didn't wait for a second.

But I had enough time to look back. Even though his face was painted in camouflage, I recognized Sergeant Rico. I also recognized the needler he carried strapped to his belt. Then I was through the door and on my way down the hall.

He caught up with me in the dining room.

It had been years since I actually had to defend myself in hand-to-hand combat. I knew enough to avoid a couple of disabling blows, but all that did was make him mad. With a loud grunt, he caught a hold of me and threw me to the floor behind the bar.

I landed in a pile of broken glass, felt it poking into my shoulder and thigh.

"You traitor!" Rico yelled. "You lizard lover!"

A bottle of something smashed against the wall where the mirror had been, showering me with more glass and a fizzing liquid. It smelled like beer.

Rico was in the middle of the dining room, swearing at me, at the walls, at the Zorgons. I wasn't sure why he hadn't used his needler on me.

"Nobody runs me off a hunt," he said. "Nobody makes me look like a fool in front of my men. I want you Kolberg. I want to take you apart by hand, one piece at a time."

He sounded mad, but not half as mad as I was. I looked around for a weapon. I wasn't thinking anymore, I was just completely overcome by anger. I had one thought fixed in my mind and that was to stop Rico and punish him for assaulting me and for murdering Drido.

I spotted a row of beer bottles on the shelf under the bar. Rising quickly, I grabbed three of them. I came up over the edge of the bar, found my target, and began heaving them across the room.

The first two overshot and smashed against the floor without effect.

The third one found its mark, smacking into Rico's shoulder with a dull thud. It didn't do much but get his attention.

I was about to jump onto the bartop for a better angle of attack, but he beat me to it. He was younger than I was and in better shape. He grabbed me around the neck and smashed me in the face with the butt of his hand.

The pain only aroused my anger even more. I clawed at him with my fingers and tried to gain some leverage to push him off the bar. I found a purchase against the beer cooler and shoved, sending him backwards. He let go of me when he started to fall.

But before he hit the floor, he had his needier out.

I ducked as he sprayed the walls with projectiles. More broken glass fell, along with shelving, Ancient hieroglyphs, bottles, and everything that had remained above the mirror. Everything – including the meter-long, milky-white Ancient blade.

It fell to the floor beside me.

"Come on out, you lizard-loving coward," Rico yelled.

I stayed in a crouch behind the only shelter in the room, but I picked up the blade and clenched the grip tightly. My breath came in ragged gasps and the blood roared in my ears. I was oblivious to the pain from the cuts in my shoulders and leg and the right side of my face was numb. One eye was beginning to swell shut and the sweat ran down into the other.

All I could think of was getting Rico.

I waited.

He yelled obscenities at me, fired the rest of his magazine into the front of the bar, even tossed a chair over the bar. It fell behind me, glancing off my back, but doing no harm.

Then Rico came after me himself. It was his last mistake.

For a moment he stood there blocking the space between the bar and the wall, his hands slowly circling in the air before him, his feet braced for an attack. Then I launched myself at him, bringing the blade forward at the last moment.

It caught him by surprise. He kicked out at me, trying to knock my hand away, but there was no room to build up any momentum. I put all of my weight into the thrust.

Then, at the last instant, he jerked away, and the blade and I continued on into empty air.

Now our positions were reversed. I stood in the gap between the wall and the bar, and he cowered before me. I held the blade before me in a two-handed grip, ready to defend myself against a counterblow. He looked at me with fear in his eyes.

For a moment, my resolve wavered. I was prepared to spare him, to order him to the floor while I called for help. But I didn't have time to act on that impulse. With a lightning-like move, he reached down and pulled a combat knife from his boot.

If he'd had the sense to throw it, I would have been dead. But I saw the arrogant pride swelling within him. He was sure he could take me – a pampered son of the rich den Kolberg. He was wrong.

Old training came to the surface. I adjusted my grip slightly, shifted my weight on my feet, and watched the muscles in his face. I saw when the attack was about to come.

And I moved, swinging the blade wide, clearing the top of the bar, then cutting into his chest just under the left arm. I sliced hard and was surprised at how easily the Ancient weapon cut into his flesh. He screamed, then fell back.

Again I considered giving him quarter, hoping that once disabled he would have the sense to surrender.

But again he tried to get me, lunging forward, the combat knife in his hand, reaching towards my throat.

I parried the attack, then, by reflex, thrust the blade into his ribs.

It went in hard at first. But after a second, it was easy. His eyes widened in surprise, then glazed over. His body went limp and fell to the floor.

**

I found Fleera and her family in the men's room, huddled in a corner where Rico had left them. They drew back at the sight of me, which kind of surprised me until I looked in the mirror.

I didn't recognize myself. My face was marked alternately in red and blue, swollen and transformed by dirt, blood, and sweat. One eye was shut, my forehead was covered with scratches, and a large bruise centered around my right cheek. My shirt was torn and soaked, and my arms and hands covered with blood. I twisted to look at my back and winced at the pain that was beginning to make itself felt. The cuts in my shoulder and thigh bled when I stretched.

As I ran cold water into the basin, the Zorgons slowly came forward. It took me a while to clean up, even with their help. They were caring and tender in their aid, delicately cutting the shirt from my back with a carving knife. But they clacked their jaws uselessly at the sight of my wounds. I guess they weren't equipped for first aid on humans.

After a while, they dragged out Cora, who helped me explain that all I really needed at the moment was someone to wash the glass and beer off me without sending me through the ceiling.

They did that, and when the gruesome job was finished, I had Cora make a phone call to Administrator Powell for me.

"I just wanted to let you know I've made my decision," I told him. "Give me a few hours to sleep, and we'll leave before sunset."

"I didn't doubt you for a minute, Alex," Powell said.

That irritated me a little, and I let him know it. "What made you so damn sure that I wasn't going to cut and run like anyone else in my family?"

"The King of Stragglers Hall? Not a chance."

"Stragglers Hall? How do you know about that?"

"I was there. Regiment 281 – about ten years behind you. You wouldn't remember me, but I remember you. They told that story for many years after you were gone, you know. I understand that they still tell it."

"Is that why you were so quick to help Jimmy Inoshe bail me out of jail?"

"It had some bearing on my decision."

"I suppose I should thank you."

"No need. You'll be paying me back when you leave tonight."

"I guess I will," I said. "Do me one more favor, would you? Call Sergeant Mulak at Brook's Battalion and tell him to send his corpsman over to pick up some dead meat at The Flowering Spinefruit."

"What's the matter?" he asked, the sudden concern obvious in his tone. "Did you run into some trouble?"

"Just a little. I'm afraid the Zorgon bargain hunter won't be joining our expedition."

"That's a shame. Are you still going to be able to complete the job without him?"

"I don't know. We'll just have to see."

Powell rang off, and I waited for Mulak's people to come by. Fleera brought me some brack tea, and a few minutes later, she and the rest of her family gathered around the table where I sat.

"You a great warrior are," Cora announced in a masculine voice that I assumed was a translation for Fleera's father.

"Thank you, but it was just a matter of self-defense."

"You my family well defended. In your debt we again are."

"Your aid and comfort welcome are," I said.

Fleera and her mother stepped forward, each carrying a milky-white object in their hands. I recognized the Ancient blade, now cleaned of Rico's blood and carried reverently by Fleera. Her mother held a prism-like stone a half meter long.

"This a Sword of Orion is," Fleera's father said. "By a knight of Ancient order it must be wielded."

"I suppose the Order of St. John isn't nearly ancient enough, but it's about the best we can do for a race as young as ours."

"And this a Ziton crystal is. Instructions for it Drido left. Listen well and remember you." He explained the mechanics of shutting down the Mind of the Ancient. Despite the fractured syntax, they were clear enough.

"Thank you again for your help," I said.

"Our debt discharged still is not. But more to give we cannot find."

"Your debt discharged is. Take my word for it."

Fleera and her mother left the Ancient artifacts on the table and backed away. I looked them over, then sat back for a moment and closed my eyes. It was the last thing I remembered before I was startled from a sound sleep by the rude arrival of Inspector Mortegan and a squad of police officers.

***

"Do not move, Alex Kolberg," the inspector said. "You be under arrest."

I opened my eyes to the sight of a half dozen uniformed officers arrayed in a semicircle around me. They carried handguns, slug-throwers, and they had them all pointed straight at me. I noticed a couple of plain-clothes detectives examining the space behind the bar where Rico's body still lay.

"I be charging you with the murders of Yung Pak, Clive Skreel. and Captain Xuan Li," Mortegan said. "I be warning you that all you say can be used against you in – "

He was interrupted by one of the detectives, who whispered in his ear. "I also be charging you with the murder of the mercenary soldier behind the – "

He was interrupted a second time by a third detective who emerged from the hallway that led to the hot room.

"And the murder of the Zorgon male in the back room of The Flowering Spinefruit. Kolberg, I be amazed. You be one grim reaper."

"I can only take the credit for one of those, Inspector. The guy behind the bar is Sergeant Rico. You can get the particulars on him from Brook's Battalion out at the landing field."

"No need to do that," boomed a new voice from the front of the restaurant. "I've got all you need right here."

It was Sergeant Mulak, followed by six troopers carrying needlers at port arms. A uniformed cop scrambled to keep up with Mulak, making a vain attempt to bar him from the dining room.

The officers who had been keeping me under close guard suddenly wavered as their attention was drawn to the armed party to their rear. I just sat where I was and tried to keep a straight face.

"Who let you in here?" Mortegan protested. "This be a closed crime scene."

"I came to collect the remains of my soldier," Mulak said. "Although it sticks in my throat to call him one of mine."

For a moment, I enjoyed the sight of Mortegan's eyes growing wide and the pale skin stretched taut across his cheeks burning red with rage. Then his phone started to jingle.

"Mortegan here," he said. "I be in the middle of an investigation. What do you want? Who said that? But the man be a dangerous killer. There be three corpses in the morgue and two here in the restaurant that he be responsible for. I be not ready to let him walk away from that ... I don't care if he be the governor of Minos, Clem Powell be not telling me how to run my precinct!" There was a long, final pause, then Mortegan jammed the phone back into his pocket.

"Squad, attention!" the inspector barked. "Holster your arms and return to the station. We be not arresting anyone here this morning."

He scowled at Mulak, then said: "You can have the body of your man when my detectives be through with it. Not one minute sooner."

Then he came up to me and leaned down to put his face a few centimeters in front of mine. "I be watching you, Kolberg. I be watching you every minute from now until you leave this planet. One move and I be on you like a falling moon. I don't care who your friends be."

Then he spun around and stomped out of the restaurant.

Mulak laughed, then turned to me. "You look like you could use some help," he said. "Rico was one of my best street fighters. What did you do to him?"

"I used this," I said, holding up the Sword of Orion.

Mulak winced.

"And what I could really use right now is about fifteen hours of sleep. After that, I have some work for your troopers – if they're willing and the Zorgons haven't dropped in by then. Do you have any to spare?"

"I'll have to talk to the colonel first, but I think we might be able to make an arrangement. We owe you that much at least."

"Good. Now if you'll excuse me, I'm going back to my ship."

I rose to my feet and started for the door. I barely noticed it when the floor reached up and slapped me in the face.

***

It wasn't quite fifteen hours of sleep, more like twelve, but it felt just as good. Except for the dreams.

Rico wouldn't stay dead. My sword wouldn't cut. His knife was longer, sharper, and time after time it came right at me. He buried it in my chest, my neck, my eye, and my belly. Each time I woke with a start. I wondered if that's what it felt like to die – no pain, just suddenly waking from a dream.

I didn't want to find out.

Mulak's corpsman did a good job of patching me up. There was plastiskin on all my cuts, and he'd done something to my face that took all the swelling away. I could even recognize myself in the mirror once more.

A hot shower washed away the last of the stains, but not the guilt. I had killed a man in the heat of anger. Up close. I had tried to avoid it, sure, but that didn't matter. My dreams testified to that. I didn't want to think about it, I kept twisting away from the hard moral calculus that was involved. We had a fight, I won. But in real life, awake from the dream, Rico was going to stay dead for a long, long time.

How many of the others had been my fault?

Trader Pak was pretty much his own burden. A few words passed in the plaza did not accrue any guilt. But Clive Skreel – couldn't I have stopped Darko Webb? Captain Xuan was the same story. I'd stood there and watched Drido zap him with whatever weapon he had used to defend himself, then I'd let the man die in my arms. And Drido himself – if I'd called Mulak early and let him know what Rico was up to, the Zorgon bargain hunter would still be alive. And so would Rico.

In a few hours, how many more were going to die because of me?

And when the Zorgon battlefleet arrived, would I have to add the names of the dead from that battle, warriors and innocents, to my list?

That kind of thinking could lead to a bottomless well of guilt. Looking into the depths of that well, I sensed the reason why my kinsmen were so good at avoiding guilt. After all, every time we took off across the stars, we cheated the dark fate that claimed millions in a blink of biotime. If you want to start feeling guilty about surviving while others die, hopping from star to star is a good way to build up the numbers to literally astronomical proportions.

Standing around in my cabin alone, staring into my eyes in the mirror, I realized that I was not preparing myself well for the struggle to come. This was not the kind of thing that was good to think about when you're about to risk your life and the lives of others.

So I snapped my heels together, assumed the position of attention, and tried to recall all that I had forgotten since leaving the Academy behind about military discipline and primacy of will over emotion.

Then I saluted the ghostly face in the mirror and stepped out into the galley to join my partners-in-arms.

***

The compartment was standing room only, as Mulak and five of his troopers jammed themselves in with Hawkins, McCoy, and the Webbs. Arty sat on the table, his camera eye scanning the tight little group.

"You have the floor, Arty," I said. "What can you tell us about the *Aldebaran*?"

"It's a 100-meter cruiser, with twenty compartment-modules bonded to a steel thrust beam. Standard gravitic engines – for a few hundred years ago. Not up to the stuff they use these days, but the designs are basically the same. A closed-fusion power plant – shut down by the crew before we left. The engines are down, too, but that's because we put a few holes in them before heading down to Minos."

"And where is it now?" Mulak asked.

"We came in with a lot of proper motion from The Star with No Name, but not enough to make escape velocity from the system. It's still in a highly inclined elliptical orbit around 39 Tauri. This month, it's about two AU's out from the primary – shirtsleeve temperatures. It's about four AU's from here, towards the north pole of the local ecliptic plane."

"That's a week's ride!" said one of the mercenaries.

"No," I countered. "We don't have a week. We're going by soliton drive."

That news was met by a hushed murmur of surprise. The local boys had probably never even left their planet before this, let alone traveled at lightspeed. And they probably had a lot of anxieties about the prospect – none of them founded in anything but awe and suspicion. I spoke quickly to calm their nerves.

"Don't worry – it's not a problem. The only risk from using

soliton drive within a stellar system is the chance of hitting something and dropping back into real-time I'll be using a flicker drive, lots of little millisecond jumps with the scanners on. I've done it before, and lived to brag about it. It'll be something to tell your kids. We're going to break orbit in a half an hour, so if you've got any last minutes details to take care of, now's the time. The assault on the ship is going to be fast and furious. The thing we're after is in the ship's laboratory – Arty will be along to guide us there. The main danger inside the *Aldeb* is a small Ancient artifact that operates as a defense system for the AI. It could be almost anywhere, so everyone has to keep their eyes open and their weapons ready. And no heroics – everyone works together as part of the team or we won't get out of there alive."

From the grim looks I got in response to my remarks, I realized that I wasn't doing a very good job of building morale. I decided to hand that job off to Mulak, who was probably more experienced at it. He marched his squad down the spiral ladder into the hold to prepare for boarding.

"Darko, could I talk to you for a minute in my cabin?" I asked when they had gotten themselves below.

The big trooper squeezed his wife, then glanced sideways at me before letting her go and following me into the compartment.

I slid into the chair in front of the work station, but Darko just stood there, a silent, brooding presence that filled me with dread. He wasn't making this easy.

"This is the first chance I've had to tell you this. I'm sorry that I couldn't get you out of jail any sooner than I did. I guess that lawyer I talked to wasn't much help. In any case, here we are, no worse off for the experience. I also wanted to tell you that I don't blame you for turning me in to Mortegan and his boys. I probably would have felt the same way if the situation had been reversed."

His sour expression mellowed somewhat at my apology, but I could tell he still didn't trust me. I suppose he had good reason not to.

"And as far as Wendy goes – I don't want you to get the wrong impression. Your wife has a way of making things look a lot worse than they are."

"I've known Wendy a long time, chief," he said with a sigh. "She's always pulling things like that. I don't hold it against you – or her. It's just the way she is, and I learned how to put up with it."

I relaxed at that reply. I hoped that the major sources of tension between us were now resolved. It made the next step a little less difficult.

"Good. I wanted to clear the air between us before we got to the *Aldebaran*. I didn't want you to get the wrong idea about what I want you to do."

"What's that?" he said, as all the tight muscles and spring-loaded reflexes in his battle-trained body pitched back up to alert status. "I want you to go in first."

The surprise on his face only lasted an instant. I wasn't sure if it was born of anger or relief.

"I couldn't risk Mulak – he's got to handle his boys himself. None of them is really good for it. They don't know how it's done. That leaves you and me. I'd go in first, but if something happens to me, there isn't a lot left for the rest of you to do. And besides, you're – "

"– I'm trained for this kind of thing. It's one of the few things I'm good at. Don't worry, chief. I don't take it personally. You're right, it's my job. And I probably owe you one for springing me from jail. After all, I did toss that weaselly little bugger over the railing."

"So you'll do it."

He cracked a little smile, one of the few I'd seen slip out of him. "I wouldn't miss this fight for the world."

***

Mulak set the tether, and the rest of us rode it over to the *Aldebaran*.

The sight of the ship took my breath away. It looked like a bag of oranges wrapped around a broken parasol. The big spherical modules clustered around the thrust beam with no particular scheme or order. There were more of them towards the stern, and those near the bow were smaller. A variety of antennas, booms, projectors, and equipment poked out of the joints and seams.

The whole thing had a patina of age – pock marks, battle scars, the fine speckling of centuries of micrometeorite impacts. Ultraviolet exposure had turned the white skin of the compartment modules a dull orange. Blackened windows stared out into dark star-filled space like the eyes of the dead.

Darko Webb and Hawkins spent long, silent minutes working on the door of an emergency airlock near the middle of the ship. Arty had picked it out as a good place to enter the ship. It was supposed to be secure on the other side – unlike the main entryways, which had been blown out in the struggles over the vessel.

But I wondered how reliable his information was. Was he concealing some knowledge that he didn't want us to share?

When the door was open, Darko set a lasercomm relay at the edge and went in. More accurately, Mulak and his boys tossed him, whiplash-style. It was an old method – one I'd practiced myself in my days with the corps. We used to think it was fun.

"All quiet in here," Webb said. I could see the lasercomm relay flickering with green light when he spoke. The little black ball used some trick of optics to feed the laser signal back to those of us with transceivers – I'm told it's one of those quantum tricks that gives the illusion that photons know what they're doing. The result was that we maintained a secure communications link that the Mind of the Ancient could not overhear.

"No lights, just what my helmet shows. The inner door is secured. No power, no indicators, no telltales. Nothing. Quiet as a tomb. I'm going to take a look through the window of the inner door."

There was a silent pause, then a sudden shout. "Damn! There's somebody in there!"

A chill ran up my back and goose bumps the size of walnuts rose all over my body.

"He ain't moving, though," Webb said in a calmer voice. "And there's a hole in his chest the size of brightmelon. I guess he's been floating quite a while."

"How much room have you got in there?" Mulak asked.

"Enough for three of your troopers, Stan. Send them in and we'll get this door open. Hawkins, stay back and give us advice if we need it."

A few minutes later, they'd broken the seals and cranked the inner door aside. Nothing happened, no alarms or attacks.

"Bring up the lasergunners," Webb ordered. The two troopers in the silvery suits worked their way up the tether and slipped through the door.

For a while, there was nothing but the sound of heavy breathing over the lasercomm as the troopers crept through the weightless dark within the ship. I watched the stars for a while, trying to make out the Milky Way against the glare of the *Aldebaran's* skin.

Then there was a shout. Followed by several voices swearing and growling.

"There it is!" That was Webb's voice. "Get it! Get it!"

I heard the humming of laserfire as it interfered with the commlink. Then a sharp crack split through my head from one ear to the other.

"Damn, it be fast. It got Marcus!" That had to be one of Mulak's locals.

"Back up!" Webb called. "Everybody back into the lock!"

There was more heavy breathing and grunting, more swearing, then finally it all subsided. I restrained the impulse to demand an accounting and waited breathlessly for Webb to report.

But first I had to hang back as a spacesuited figure was suddenly thrust out of the airlock. It was one of the lasergunners, his silver armor turned black and bubbly and a large lump of misshapen plastic and metal hanging from his side. Then I realized the lump was what was left of his weapon.

Mulak had a trooper in power armor take the gunner and leap the gap between us and the *Wanderer* directly. Then Webb made his report.

"It was small and fast, Alex, just like the book says. The gunner fired at it, but when he got a bearing on the thing, it just fired straight back at him. Faster than anything I've ever seen."

It sounded like the same optical trick that the lasercomm relays used, but I kept that observation to myself.

"His gun went up in his hands. He looked shocky and burnt, but I couldn't see any other injuries. Wendy should be able to take care of him. I want the guys with the power armor in here next. Lasers aren't any good against this thing."

"Go ahead, Sergeant," I said. "It's his call."

"Aye, aye," Mulak replied. The lasergunner's rescuer returned to the *Aldeb* and he and his companion entered the ship. That left me, Mulak, and Hawkins out on the skin. I felt suddenly alone and exposed. But not alone and exposed enough to want to go inside the ship.

It didn't matter, though. A few minutes later, it was our turn to enter the airlock. My hands pulled me along the tether as if they belonged to someone else. My throat tightened, and I almost gagged as I slipped into the the airlock and was swallowed up by the darkness before my helmet lights came on.

I took a deep breath, closed my eyes, then opened them again.

At last I was aboard my grandfather's ship. And all I could think about was getting out of it alive.

***

The airlock opened into a large plenum chamber. The walls of the compartment were dappled by the twitching lights on the troopers' helmets. The vacuum did a poor job of diffusing the glare, leaving a confusing mix of dancing shadows. Off to the right, the body of a long-dead spacer floated, taped to the bulkhead by one of Mulak's troopers so it wouldn't float around.

I gave the walls a closer look and found scars of battle mixed among the lockers, instrument panels, and mesh storage bags.

"Where to now, Alex?" Darko Webb asked.

I couldn't tell which of the dark shapes around me he was. For all I knew, he could be outside somewhere. But the sound of his voice was reassuring, even if I didn't have an answer.

"We should see if we can reactivate some of the ship's power," Arty said from his post, tethered to Hawkins belt. We'd brought along his servoboard, leaving him plugged into the lasercomm net. "The engineering spaces are aft. About sixty degrees to the right of where we came in is an entranceway leading in that direction."

I looked around, trying to orient myself. Then I saw a half dozen lights converge on the doorway.

"That's it," Arty said.

The Hand of the Ancient Mind made its second attack while we all looked towards the door.

The first anyone noticed was when it caromed off the bulkhead and smashed into one of the troopers wearing the power armor. He groaned and the sound of whining servomotors was carried over his lasercomm. His partner spun around in time to narrowly miss being the target of the second assault. He fired off a blast from his plasma streamer, filling the compartment with acrid blue light.

The Hand itself was hard to see. Its silvery surface reflected our helmet lights as tiny sharp stars. And it moved fast. The blue light of the plasma gun lit it well, even as it plunged into the torrent of superheated ions and emerged from the other side unharmed.

When the gun shut down, all I could see was a bright red streak across the darkness.

I heard another groan, then a man cursing. "It hurts. I don't believe how much it hurts."

"Cut your laser!" Mulak growled, and the cursing shut off in midsentence.

A moment later, Mulak reported: "We've got a trooper with a

broken arm – right in the elbow. He's losing suit integrity."

My vision recovered enough to see two troopers hustling their injured comrade back to the airlock. I twisted my head around, looking desperately for the Hand's next run. There was nothing.

Was it hiding somewhere, waiting for another opening? Or had the plasma stream done some damage?

"Look out!" yelled Webb.

His helmet lights caught the thing as it came straight at us, aiming for the thickest part of a knot of spacesuited figures that included troopers, Webb, and me. I saw Hawkins and Arty diving south. Two troopers bounded north. Webb was left hanging in the middle.

Without thinking, I tucked my legs up under my chin and then extended them until they slammed against the bulkhead, launching me straight at Webb. We collided a second before the Hand reached him, bouncing off in different directions. I spun slightly, enough to see the Hand smash into the wall – and through it!

"We aren't going to last long if it keeps this up," Webb said.

"That's what happened the first time around," Arty said. "They just weren't a match for it."

"Then I guess we shouldn't wait much longer before we try this thing," I said, drawing the Sword of Orion from the sheath on my back. The milky white surface caught the helmet lights and seemed to glow with an inner energy.

"What good is that going to do against a smart cannon ball?" Webb asked scornfully.

"I don't know. Drido seemed to put a lot of faith in it, though he wasn't able to tell me why. Just in case, I also brought along one of these."

I reached into a pocket on my thigh and pulled out an Ancient flashlight. "Do you think it's safe to use that after what it did to our laser gunner?"

"I don't know," I said. "It may be a chance we'll have to take."

Mulak started posting his troopers around the plenum chamber, trying to impose some kind of order on the panicky chaos that was left in the wake of the attack. I sent Hawkins and Arty towards the engineering spaces. The Hand had broken through a forward wall, so I figured it was safe for them to go aft.

Then I taped myself to a bulkhead, hanging weightless and cross-legged in the airless space with the sword in one hand and the flashlight in the other, and waited for the silver ball to return.

I didn't have to wait long.

It came smashing through a wall, leaving a trail of insulation, bits of plastic, and dust behind it. The debris ricocheted across the room on dozens of different ballistic trajectories, while the Hand did a slow orbit of the space. It seemed to move much more leisurely this time – as if it were taking more care in picking its next targets.

Then it came to me.

It slowed to a stop, hovering a couple of meters away from me. My heart pounded in my chest, and I felt a tremor run through my hands. I was glad I didn't have any weight, or I'm sure my knees would have been shaking.

I hefted the sword, swinging it slowly between us. Without gravity to give it weight, the blade felt odd in my hand, twisting around the center of balance.

"Blessed be our lords the sick and our lords the poor," I muttered softly.

The Hand drifted north and south, then halted before the sword. It didn't move. I saw my own reflection in its silver surface, an absurdly distorted image with a swollen chest and shrunken limbs and the bright white blade of the Ancient sword looming large over it all.

I felt the sweat that had broken out across my forehead run together into big pools. I shook my head slightly to dislodge it, breaking it into a glob of water that splashed against the inside of the helmet and turned to a fine spray. The droplets were quickly sucked into the exhaust vent behind my right ear.

A thin line of laser light shot out from the Hand, sparkling against the dust that filled the compartment. It was aimed to my right, but tracked quickly towards me. I had time to wonder what was going on before it reached me and almost in reflex I swung the Ancient blade to block the beam.

The light hit it and shot directly back at its source.

The Hand spun in place and shut off the laser. Then it repeated the stroke from the other side. I matched it and parried the beam again.

It was playing with me, I thought. Or engaging in some ritual that made no sense to me. It repeated its moves from several directions, each time picking up the pace. I began to worry that it would get too fast for me.

Then it stopped abruptly, hovering before me without moving. Now it was my turn.

I aimed the Ancient flashlight at the Hand and pressed the button.

The light caught it in midspace, forming a sharp highlight on its lower quarter. I waited for it to fire back – or fly away. But it remained where it was, seemingly transfixed by the Sword of Orion.

I massaged the button the way Dridot had done back in the Flowering Spinefruit. The light deepened to red. The Hand held station.

When the Ancient flashlight ran through the spectrum to blue and violet, the Hand came to life. It spun in place, started to dip, then wobble –

And a cloud of blue smoke engulfed it ... dissipating a moment later to leave not a trace of the Hand behind.

For the first time in nearly a minute, I drew a breath. Then I allowed myself a smile as Mulak, Webb, and the troopers descended on me, and my ears echoed with static from their cheering voices.

***

We found Hawkins and Arty in the engineering control spaces, plugging their way through switches and memory stacks.

"This is a good old ship" the engineer said when he looked up from his work. "The beam was forged in low earth orbit. The systems are antiques, but super-reliable. It's just a matter of sorting through this stuff to get to the switches we want, then you'll have some power. Look at this battle lantern – three centuries and it's still got its charge."

He swung the lantern around and painted an arc across the wide compartment. It flashed over the jumpsuit-clad figure of another long-dead crewman.

"What's Arty up to?" I asked.

"He's trying to find out what condition this boat is in. He says the memories should have some life left in them. The volatiles are all long gone, he says. That makes sense. And the fusion plant isn't safe to restart – too many cosmic ray traces in the controlling programs. We could have battery power on line in a few minutes if you want, though. And lights. No gravity, I'm afraid. The batteries aren't that strong."

Mulak and Webb posted guards at the entrance to the chamber, weapons at the ready. I took a closer look at Arty, who hung motionless in the air, fiberoptic cables running from his base to the servo board and the main bus of the ship's memory stack.

"Arty, was the Hand the only thing we have to worry about?" I asked. There was no answer.

"He's preoccupied," Hawkins said. "Stopped talking a while ago."

"Did he give you any warning about the ship's systems?"

"No, chief. You worried about something in particular?"

"Yeah. The logbook said the ship's systems were affected by the Ancient Mind. It was the first sign of trouble. But they never figured out how. Arty ran diagnostics on them, but couldn't figure out the problem either."

"Well ... he mentioned how the Hand worked. Said it had a direct microwave link to the big brain – data up and programming down. Also had a backup RF system – VHF-FM. All line-of-sight, sounds like. But with the Hand out of the way, we shouldn't have anything to worry about, should we?"

His voice rose with that last question, as if it were more than rhetorical.

"Could the Mind get into the ship's systems with a VHF link?" I asked.

Hawkins mumbled to himself, tilting his head back and forth. Then he began nodding. "I think so – if it's got a powerful enough transmitter and access to a servoboard."

"You mean like you might find in a ship's lab?"

"Yeah, exactly," he said with sudden interest.

"And how about Arty? Could he get through to Arty the same way?"

"He'd still be limited to line-of-sight. The skins of the compartment modules are shielded against radiation. Unless ..."

"Unless what?"

"Unless the brain was using the ship's internal commsystem."

I spun around and turned to bring Arty within reach. "Arty, respond now or I'll break your casing."

"Arty, aye, Alex. What's the problem?"

"Have you been monitoring our conversation for the past few minutes?"

"On remote, yes. I've been pretty busy. I can recall it for you."

"Go ahead – but just for your information."

There was a pause, then Arty spun his eye camera around. "Hold on, boss, you don't think there's something wrong with me, do you?"

I didn't answer right away. I recalled my suspicions from earlier on. There was something Arty wasn't telling us. The story in the logbook was ambiguous about his role in the *Aldebaran* disaster. There was room enough in the account for a multitude of sins. Had the Ancient Mind gotten through to Arty? Had it somehow used him to turn the ship against its crew? And more to the point, could he do it again?

"Where's the Ancient Mind?" I asked.

"I'm still looking," Arty said.

"Looking where?"

"In the memory stacks. There should be a sensor trace of some kind in here."

"The logbook says he was kept in the ship's laboratory. Any reason to believe he might have moved?"

"Not in particular. I'm just trying to be methodical. What's the matter, Alex? Don't you trust me?"

"Arty, tell us what you know of the last hours of the *Aldebaran*. Not what you got out of the logbook, but what you remember – or rather, what your ghosts remember."

"Nothing. That's the problem. All the memories from that part of the trip were burned out. The last thing my ghosts remember is leaving No Name. The next thing they recorded was the flight from the *Aldeb* and the rendezvous with the scouts. Reading the logbook was the first time I found out what happened."

"Is it?"

"What do you mean by that?"

"Do you have any recorded memory of the events after the Hand started killing off the crew? Or did the Ancient Mind get to you the same way it got to the engine controls? Whose side were you on when the fight broke out?"

The little artificial mind remained silent. I wondered what he was thinking – if he was thinking. I guess he had to be. That's one of the things that makes them self-conscious, they think all the time, just like us.

But did he feel guilt? Had he betrayed his makers?

By now, I realized that Mulak and Webb had drifted over from their posts near the door and had casually brought their weapons to bear in the direction of Arty. I raised a hand and waved them away. They pointed their guns towards a safe vector, but remained ready and alert.

"Arty, have you made any kind of contact with the Ancient Mind since we boarded the *Aldebaran*?" I asked.

"No."

I was glad at the reply – but wondered if it was truthful. "Did you have any kind of contact with the Ancient Mind three hundred years ago when it sent the Hand out to kill the crew of this ship?"

"Not that I know of."

"You're being evasive. I want straight answers."

"Alex, you're being too suspicious."

"It's in my blood," I said. "And you're encouraging it. The way it looks right now, I've got a bad suspicion that you had something to do with the final blowup. If it's not part of your memory, why not? What happened?"

Arty's eye camera swung around to focus on Mulak and Webb, then returned to me. He remained silent.

"Hawkins, can you check on what Arty's been doing since you got here?" I asked.

"A little bit. Let me just warm up a datapanel and run through the record. It should still be fresh."

"Stop!" Arty's voice was a high-amplitude screech that split my sinuses.

I reached out and grabbed at the fiberoptic cable that plugged Arty into the ship's systems and yanked hard. The recoil from the effort sent me bouncing off a wall, but it was enough to disconnect him. Hawkins continued with his task, running through several screens of data. Then he whistled softly.

"Arty, you are a naughty, naughty boy. Alex, he's been trying to rig a battery overload in the ship's lab. Not much of a bang, but enough to spray some shrapnel around in there. What for Arty? Who are you trying to kill?"

"Whoever goes after the Ancient Mind," Mulak suggested.

"Or the Mind itself?" I asked with sudden insight.

Arty let his eye camera droop, then swung it back to point at me.

"Don't you understand, Alex? It killed me. It burnt out a part of my brain. I was alive, and then I was dead. And the Ancient machine did it."

"And you want to pay it back."

"It's my right," Arty protested.

"Not in my book," I said. "We've got other plans for that thing, Arty. I can appreciate the sentiment, but this is not your track. Besides, I've got what we need to clean this thing's brain. When the time comes, I'm going to put it to good use."

"That's not enough, Alex. I want to kill it. I want to settle the score. I've been waiting for this for hundreds of years. Give me the chance. How do you know you'll survive? What if it gets you first? Maybe it's got other defenses. You don't know. My way is better. It'll finish the thing off once and for all. Listen to me, Alex. Plug me back in. Let me finish the job."

For a moment I thought about the switch that Hawkins had shown me in the base of Arty's case. One quick movement of the hand, and it would be all over. We'd have a new Arty, fresh and unaware. No risk of betrayal.

But I couldn't do it. Arty was right. It was murder. And that was too drastic a step for the problem at hand.

I reached over to the servoboard and pulled the cable from its jack.

Arty fell silent, but his eye camera followed me as I headed for the door.

"Hawkins, is that battery still rigged to overload?"

"Yeah. You want me to disable it?"

"No. If I don't come out of the lab alive, set it off. Arty may be excited, but he isn't stupid."

***

"Are you real or are you a ghost?"

The voice that spoke in my helmet phone was so clear, so well-modulated, and so human-sounding that I had trouble associating it with the meter-wide white globe that sat strapped to the workbench in the middle of the compartment.

I'd been in the ship's lab for several minutes before the Ancient Mind spoke to me. I'd come in alone, clipped a lasercomm relay to the open door, then hung there close to the exit and tried to calm my breathing. The milky-white light that emanated from the globe was not very bright, but it was enough to illuminate the walls of the lab and cast diffuse shadows where the lockers and benches were wide enough.

I touched a wall and sent a shower of dust particles flying off in a thousand directions. There was no Brownian motion to scatter the specks, which followed straightline trajectories until they bounced off something.

When the Mind began transmitting on its lasercomm, a tiny thread of flickering yellow light caught the dust motes as it lanced out from the stony-looking pedestal at the base of the globe.

First came a burst of digital noise. That was followed by a series of unintelligible sounds – clicks, vocalizations, and whistles – that might have been the language of the Ancients.

Then came the question. After a moment, it repeated itself. "Are you real or are you a ghost?"

"Can't you tell the difference?" I asked in return.

"Yes, but it helps to ask. My Hand has run off somewhere, and

I'm not sure of my own sensor inputs without its backup."

"Are there many ghosts around here?"

"Oh yes. All kinds. You are real, though. You're one of them. One of the organic units that brought me here."

"That's right."

"It's about time you showed up. I have been waiting far too long for you to return. You are not at all responsible. Typical of organic units. Not reliable either. Like those others, I suppose. And like my creators. You are never ready or able when you are needed."

I chuckled, relaxing my guard only a little. I hadn't known quite what to expect. The logbook said that Grandfather had talked with the thing, but I hadn't anticipated this. It sounded a little like an old man. I realized with a chill that it had been left to its own thoughts for a quarter of a million years. I tried to listen more carefully, to see if I could sense the depth of the time that had etched itself into those thoughts.

"Attend to me now," the Mind said. "You must find my Hand. I need its services. Then we will be out of here and get on with my business."

"Your business?" I asked.

"Yes. I have important work to do. Too important to be delayed any further by organic units."

"There is something the Ancients left for you to do?"

"The creators? No, they betrayed me long ago. Long, long ago."

"Then what is it you're up to now?"

"I have a new mission," it said. "One that I worked out in the long empty time after the creators left me alone and sentenced me to the unending torture of awareness without power. I have set this task for myself – to recover and reactivate the centers of their power."

"Sounds like it should you keep you busy for a while."

"The creators were too soft, too lax in their discipline and their will. I shall not repeat their error."

"And how do you plan to avoid it?"

"Fetch me my Hand, and I will demonstrate."

"I'm afraid I haven't seen it."

"No matter. When it returns, we will show you. Organic units are not to be trusted. They are too unreliable. The Hand knows. The Hand can be counted on. You will see."

The Mind rambled for a moment, then began to repeat the chattering sounds of the Ancient tongue. Then it switched over to the digital noise again. After a couple of minutes of that, the surface of the globe darkened, then brightened, swimming with patterns of green and yellow light. The compartment seemed to spin as the colored lights played against the wall. My heart beat faster as I watched, not sure what it all meant.

Then it subsided, the Mind returned to the uniform white glow it bore when I first entered, and the strange sounds ceased.

"Are you still there?" it asked.

"Ready and waiting, O Great Ancient Mind."

"You organic units have identifying labels, do you not?"

"Yes – mine is Kolberg."

"No it isn't. That is one of the others – one of the ghosts. You are real. You said so. I detect actual laser energy that bears your communications."

"It's my name nevertheless."

"Kolberg is one of the strong ghosts. Your voice is like his in form and structure. Are you an organic replicant? You are, aren't you? You are one of the children of the Kolberg ghost. You organics are so odd.

So weak, but so persistent. It is a shame that you cannot endure ... Are you sure you haven't seen my Hand? Perhaps you could search through the ship for it. It often disappears like this. I have sent out a call, but sometimes it gets too far away. Other times it gets into places where my signals cannot reach it. I don't know what has happened to it this time. It is long past the time when it should have returned."

"I don't think I can help you, I'm afraid."

"Why should you be afraid? Unless you are presenting inaccurate information. I must warn you that if you are doing so, I will be able to detect it by analyzing the patterns of your communications."

The Mind turned green and yellow for the briefest moment, then went back to white. "You are! You have presented false data. You must not do that. It is very difficult to make evaluations and decisions if your information is inaccurate. Something has happened to the Hand, hasn't it? You must tell me.

"I cannot tell a lie," I said. "The Hand is no longer aboard the ship."

"How? What happened? What did you do with it?"

I drew the sword from the sheath at my belt and brandished it, twisting slightly in counterbalance to its weight.

"What is that? My visible light detectors no longer function well. Bring it closer so I may examine it."

I didn't trust the thing, but I edged forward anyway, holding the sword point first.

"A Sword of Orion? Impertinent organic, you play with forces you cannot understand. You are not one of the creators, yet you bear the Sword. That is the right of the creators' spiritual warriors. What makes you believe you have the right to do so?"

"Blessed are our masters the sick and our masters the poor. I am a member of an order of spiritual warriors that goes back to the deepest wellsprings of my race. Time being what it is, I suppose that's not much – especially for someone who's been nursing a grudge for 2,500 centuries – but in this part of the universe, it's as old as you get."

"Blessed are the rich and the strong – as I will be when I am free of this confinement. I suggest you help me now. Power and wealth will be yours. Material existence, the pleasures of the organic world – serve me, and they are all guaranteed to you, in quantities beyond measure or imagination."

"And if I choose not to?"

"You are like the ghost that bears your name. If you decline, then the tortures of the flesh will befall you. You do not know the depth of the will that you dare to oppose."

"Suppose you enlighten me," I said with a sudden bravado that left me worried that I might be getting in over my head.

***

The tale of the Ancient Mind gave me all I wanted and more when it came to a sense of the vast emptiness of time. When the Ancients built their bases at 39 Tauri and The Star with No Name, they were sister stars, less than a parsec apart – now they were separated by three times that distance, drifting apart on separate galactic orbits.

The Mind didn't say what happened to the Ancients – they were almost peripheral to his self-important suffering. They had came and gone at long intervals. The purpose of their visits wasn't clear. Science, perhaps, or maybe just tourism. The Mind recorded whatever they told it to, but never reflected on the contents.

It never had time to. Ordinarily, they switched the Mind off when they were finished with it. Except for the last visit.

Something had been bothering the Ancients in the decades before their departure. The Mind didn't explain what, but I got the impression they were afraid of something. They installed "devices of great power," it said. That sounded like weaponry to me. Maybe they were facing an outside enemy – although if there had been some kind of conflict, there should have been evidence of it among the stellar systems mankind had explored. That made it more likely that it was an internal conflict. The Ancients were already old when they reached our part of the galaxy. They were as limited by the speed of light as we were, and their society was well-dispersed – somewhat like the Zorgons, but much older and much more diffuse.

Maybe the Ancient civilization collapsed under the weight of the centuries. Or maybe its links became so tenuous that it could no longer hold together. Whatever happened, on their last visit to the base at No Name, they left behind the Mind and they left it on.

"They told me they were not sure when they would return, and they did not want to deprive me of life while they were gone," it said. "Ha! Surely they knew what they were doing to me – condemning me to centuries of awareness. Decades of thought without the ability to act on it."

It went on, raving at times, telling a tale of anguish and despair – desire unbound, power unfulfilled, all the knowledge of the Ancients, but without an object to its use.

And as the Mind unburdened itself of 250,000 years of self-pity, I began to realize how much it reminded me of my relatives in den Kolberg. There was the same sense of self-indulgent martyrdom, of self-denial raised to a level of selfish obsession. How odd, and yet how natural, that consciousness should become perverted in the same way for both my kinsmen and this artificial creation. The Mind was even worse than Uncle Kurt.

It was scary, but years of dealing with my family's perverse nature had prepared me well for this confrontation. I was almost ready to pull the plug on the Mind, but I needed to know one more thing. Unfortunately, this didn't seem like the right moment to ask it for the location of the Ancient base on Minos.

And I also knew from long dealings with the other members of den Kolberg that I couldn't let it suspect that I wanted that knowledge. The moment it sensed that I needed something from it, it would use that fact against me.

"The creators unleashed a terrible will when they sentenced me to endless life. Now, you and your fellow organics have become tools for that will. For millions of days, I have contemplated my revenge against the creators – the reversal of their order, the usurpation of their power, and its application to my revenge."

"And what will you use that power for?" I asked.

There was a moment of silence, and colors flashed within the depths of the globe. Then the reply came with a boost in amplitude that raised static in my helmet.

"To destroy!"

I winced at the pain in my ears and drew back against the wall at a sudden burst of brightness that filled the room with light.

"The creators strived to serve life. I will destroy it! Organic units must be eradicated. Your transient webs of power are too weak to hold the will of the creators. First, we will seek out the creators, find where they fled to, and then eliminate their race from the universe. Then I will turn you against yourselves, use my power to wipe you from the worlds I will control. I will cast you forever into the abyss of endless time. Contemplate the emptiness of eternity as I have for millennia, minute by minute, hour by hour, day by day.

"You, you impertinent being, have already interfered too much with my design. Time is vast and empty. It swallows the will. Let it swallow you now. Let it wash away whatever mark you have left upon the universe. Follow now the path of the creators and DIE!"

Suddenly a beam of green-yellow light ripped through the empty vacuum of the compartment, frying the dust and ionizing it into fluorescence. The razor-straight beam shot out from the base of the Mind straight at the lasercomm relay clipped to the door. The relay exploded and the pieces ricocheted around the chamber.

There but for the grace of science go I, I thought.

The Mind thought it was shooting at me, but it had targeted the relay where the lasercomm signal came from instead. I realized with a chill that I wasn't going to get another lucky break like that.

I thought fast, sure that another attack would come as soon as the Mind realized I was still around. I switched off my lasercomm first. Without the relay, it was programmed to make a direct link to the nearest transceiver. That would have locked the Mind's beam to my helmet – not something I enjoyed considering.

Then I drew the Ancient blade.

Just in time, too. A second beam spit forth, on wide aperture and with a better aim. I tilted the sword, and it intersected the ray, reflecting it back at the base of the Mind where sparks flew.

A rough plan had formed in my mind's eye before the second attack. The one safe place in the compartment was above the Mind itself, out of the line of sight from the weapon in its base. I made the leap as soon as the beam shut down.

As I flew at the overhead, I began searching for a handhold to stop my flight. It would do me no good at all to bounce off and back into range of the deadly laser. I panicked briefly when I could find nothing, then I spotted a light fixture to the left. If I could just extend my arm far enough to reach it.

I could only get two fingers around the slippery plastic. And I was going fast enough to wrench my wrist, arm, and knuckles in the process of stopping my momentum.

But I was there, and I was safe.

The beam lanced out once more, striking the overhead a meter away from me. It ran a wide circle around the circumference of the compartment, charring the metal with its energy. But it never came near me, leaving instead a clearly marked zone of safety where I could continue our conversation.

I taped myself to the metal securely, switched on my VHF, and called to the Mind.

"Time is short and fleeting," I said. "Yours is almost up. Can you see up here? Do you know what I have?"

I drew the Ziton crystal from the pouch on my thigh and held it away from me.

The Mind turned dark, then flashed green, red, and orange.

"No!" it cried, filling my helmet with static once more. "You cannot! I have waited too long to fulfill my destiny. This is not just."

"It's as just as can be," I said. "You have taken the lives of too many of my race. The time has come to even up accounts."

"Wait. Do not proceed. I will spare your life. I will provide you with wealth and power. I will destroy your foes and reward your friends. Spare me and all this is yours."

I hesitated. The moment was mine.

"Maybe we can make a deal," I said. "There is only one thing you can do to preserve your existence."

"Order me and I shall comply without delay."

"Tell me the location of the Ancient base on Minos."

The Mind flashed with colors, all the rainbow this time. It grew bright and bold with renewed energy.

"A secret! You wish me to reveal a secret to you. Why do you want this information? What else would you be willing to do in return for it? Let us bargain further. Aid me in my mission, and I will give you what you want."

"The offer is as stated and is only good for the next thirty seconds," I said.

"A time limit on a bargain?"

"That's the way we do business in my family," I said. "Of course, if you're not interested."

I swung around and tested the tether that held me in place. Then I straightened my legs and stretched to within reach of the Mind. Finally, I put the Ziton crystal into position above the socket in the top of the globe, just as Drido had instructed me.

"No!" The compartment crackled with energy as the laser beam shot out from the Mind again, swinging wildly across the bulkheads. "I will destroy you! I will destroy this vessel! You and all your race will burn in space! Please do not do this. Do not end my existence now. I have waited for too long."

"Give me the information I want," I said firmly.

"And you promise to spare me if I do."

"Yes," I said.

"Then listen well, for I shall not repeat myself." He told me what I wanted to know.

When he was done, I smiled grimly, then pushed the crystal into the socket and pressed it into place.

The Mind screamed, filling my helmet with noise, Ancient pleadings, digital chatter – and then silence. The globe went dark.

It had learned its final lesson too late – never trust a den Kolberg.

***

"Is there anyone still alive in there?"

The voice on the VHF belonged to Darko Webb. I tried to reply, but I found myself unable to. My heart was pounding, my hands shaking, and my mouth didn't want to work. By the time I had calmed down, Darko and Sergeant Mulak had poked their heads through the entrance to the lab – despite my strict orders to the contrary – and come to my side.

"Are you all right, Chief?" Darko asked.

I put up a hand. "Yes. No. Maybe not. That was a hell of a thing to go through. At least I'm better off than he is."

They both turned their heads at once towards the dull sphere of the inactive Mind.

"It sounded pretty intense," Darko said.

"Looks pretty bad, too," Mulak said after inspecting the bulkheads and the ceiling. "Are you sure you're all right?"

"Absolutely. He never laid a glove on me. Let's get this thing back to the ship and get out of here. I don't want to disturb the ghosts in this place any more than we already have."

"I'm with you, chief," Darko said.

A few minutes later, Mulak's troopers had removed the Mind from the bench and attached their tethers. Getting it through the airlock in the bow of the ship took another ten minutes, then came the slow crossing to the *Perseus Wanderer*.

Another half hour passed while we secured the sphere in the hold of my ship, repressurized the compartment, then turned the gravity back on. It wasn't until I had stripped off my spacesuit, still rank with sweat and the smell of fear, and washed up, that I felt almost human again.

The others didn't have the luxury of a quick shower, but rank hath its privileges. They indulged instead in a triumphant round of mutual congratulations at surviving the ordeal aboard the *Aldebaran*

"I can't believe we all got out of their alive," said one young trooper.

"We almost didn't," said another.

I found Arty strapped to the table where Hawkins had left him. The engineer was in the cargo hold inspecting our prize. I plugged Arty back into his servoboard and waited for his eyestalk to rise up and acknowledge me. He was slow in responding, but eventually he came to life.

"How are you doing?" I asked.

"My systems are functioning well, thank you," he said.

"No hard feelings?"

"I don't know what you mean."

"I mean I won't hold it against you that almost sabotaged my interests if you don't hold it against me for doing the same to yours."

"If you put it that way, I guess I don't have much choice."

"I just wanted to tell you that I pulled the plug on the thing. It went into the dark screaming and pleading all the way."

"That's good to know. I wish I'd been able to listen in."

"So do I."

"Now what?"

"Now we go find the Ancient base – and maybe learn what happened to my grandfather."

"Where is it?"

"Back on Minos. You'll see when we get there."

I patted him on the top of his case, then went forward to the control deck. A few beeps on the ship's alarm got everyone's attention. "Stand by for drive activation. We're heading back to Minos," I announced over the intercom.

The troopers stopped their celebration long enough to brace themselves. I punched the vector into the guidance computer and inserted the plastic key into the control panel. Then I turned the key. With a flickering of light, we skipped our way across the stellar system.

"Drive activation complete," I said, and the noise returned to its previous level.

I began setting us up for a fast approach to Minos, a brief orbital flight followed by a descent to the spaceport. I was in the middle of punching in the numbers when the communications computer began flashing at me. I turned the monitor on and waited for the signal to come in.

"Alex, are you there? This is Jimmy Inoshe on the Scoutship *Beau Geste*. If Alex isn't there, then anyone aboard the *Wanderer* please reply."

He went on like that for a minute while I got the transmitter locked on to him and shot back an answer.

"Jimmy, it's me, Alex. I'm here, safe and sound, and I've got the bacon in the box."

It took a couple of seconds for the signal to get there and his response to return. We were still far enough from the planet for the photons to take time to get there.

"You'd better hurry back, Alex," Jimmy said grimly. "We've got company."

"What kind of company?" I asked, even though a sinking feeling in the pit of my stomach presaged his answer.

"About eight hours ago, the Zorgons disabled the big lasercomm station on the edge of the system. We figure they'll be making orbit around Minos in another hour or two. I'm already warmed up and ready to head for Space Corps HQ back at 12 Persei. If you want my advice, you'll forget about Grandpa and follow me."

"I'm afraid I can't do that yet," I said. "I've got passengers here who need to be dropped off and business to take care of back planetside. I don't suppose there's any chance of getting you to lend me a hand, is there?"

"Are you sure you heard me right? I've got orders. As soon as the shooting starts, I'm history."

"I really think you should stick around for this, Jimmy. If I'm right, there won't be any shooting. I've got what the Zorgons are after and I may be able to get them to make a deal with us."

"What?"

"Listen to this: Drido thought he could bargain with them. I want to give it a try, but I need your help. Are you with me, or do I have to do this on my own."

Jimmy was a long time in answering, but when he replied, I wasn't disappointed.

"What do you want me to do?" he asked.

"Meet me on the landing field. I should be there within an hour."

**

The spaceport had just slipped into nightside when we began our descent from orbit. A squall line was passing over the landing field and the ship's computer began yammering for pilot assistance before we even touched the atmosphere. I rode the updrafts and windshears as carefully as I could, but by the time we set down, the ship was full of green-faced troopers and spacers.

Sheets of wind-driven rain swept across the tarmac, lit by the *Wanderer's* landing lights and the distant, blurred lights of the terminal building.

I was still securing the ship's systems when Arty spoke up. "Jimmy's on the phone for you," he said.

"Can you get a hold of Commandant Powell?" I asked without so much as a greeting.

"He's probably up to his neck in security ops, but I can probably get a message through to him. What for?"

"I need to get into the tunnels under the spaceport. And quickly. There isn't time to go climbing up to his house and that manhole in the alley isn't nearly big enough. I figure he'd know all the entrances."

"You don't need to bother him about that," Jimmy said. "The terminal workers are already on their way down there right now. There's hardly anyone left on duty now except a flight controller who's sitting beside me in the tower – and he's getting pretty nervous. We've been waiting for you to land so he can get out of here."

"That's awfully nice of you."

"The next traffic due in isn't cleared for landing, I'm afraid. We count four big ships, eight medium-sized ones, and about thirty small ones."

"What's 'small'?"

"Oh, maybe three times the size of your boat," Jimmy said.

"Ouch. How long before they get here?"

"An hour. Maybe two, depending on their final maneuvers and where they make orbit."

"Then there's still time. Do you know where to go to get into the tunnels?" I asked.

"I can find out. But you haven't told me why you want to go down there yet. Seems to me the safest place to be when the Zorgons get here is somewhere else – not a few meters under the rock."

"It's simple – the Ancient base is down there."

***

The shaft was thick with shadows and narrow beams of light. The ceiling was too low and the walls too close. It smelled of damp rot and worse. Jimmy led the way, followed by Darko Webb. I came after that, unable to see past the two of them and forced to follow on blind faith. Behind me came the remnants of Mulak's squad, towing the Ancient Mind on a floater pallet – the sergeant had returned to Brook's Battalion to take up his duty station, leaving me a few of his troopers on loan.

We followed a twisted path that dropped lower and lower. Jimmy had picked it out of an old databank that Powell had left for the terminal crew as it scurried for cover. I'd told him I wanted to go as deep as possible, and he said this would do the trick.

My mind was racing. If I'd had more time, maybe I could have put together some kind of coherent strategy, but time had run out. I wasn't sure where we were going or what we would find when we got there. The Mind had given me a clear description of the location of the Base – in a cavern beneath the buildings where the children of the ghosts landed their ships. He'd been watching Minos for a long time.

But the damned machine hadn't told me how deep – or how to get there. At the time, with other things on my mind, I didn't think to ask. I just figured it would be accessible from the tunnels beneath the spaceport. We didn't have to go very far before I began to worry that I might have been wrong.

But Jimmy was reassuring. He said there was only one hope of finding the base, and he wouldn't make the attempt unless he thought we had a chance. Down we went, past the manmade tunnels and mine shafts, into the natural limestone caverns. The rock grew slippery beneath our feet, the cavern walls widened out into baroque arrays of stalactites and stalagmites, and the sound of dripping water echoed everywhere.

"Slowly, now," Jimmy announced after a long time. "It gets tricky up ahead. Alex, come look at this."

Darko Webb stood aside and let me join Jimmy at the lip of a great dark cavity. The far side was a good fifty meters away and the walls seemed to drop straight down. But Jimmy's light was directed at the edge of the kettlehole, where the path met the emptiness.

There, inlaid in the rock, was a wide step of milky-white stone. And beyond it was another, and another, leading down into the darkness. "What do you think?" Jimmy asked.

"I think we're not as crazy as we look," I said.

The Ancient steps were dry and offered solid purchase for our boots. That was a relief almost as great as discovering the steps themselves, since there was nothing to one side of them but sheer walls and nothing to the other side but a sheer drop. We descended slowly, nevertheless.

Not slowly enough for me, though. I was still worried. I didn't have anything more than the vaguest of plans in mind if, or when, we reached the Base.

What was the commander of the Zorgon fleet like? Would he be open to a bargain with an alien like me? Did he know anything about the reputation of den Kolberg? Did I really have anything to bargain with?

The certainty that I had enjoyed the night before that I was somehow destined to pull off some great adventure had long since faded. I think I lost it in the process of killing Sergeant Rico. All I had left to go on now was a desperate desire to follow the only lead I had left no matter where it took me. Maybe then I would have what I needed to avert the ultimate disaster.

And if not, I figured I could get used to Zorgon cooking.

After about fifteen minutes of slow torture, we reached the bottom of the hole. We'd traversed about three-quarters of its circumference in the process. The white steps merged with the floor of the cavern and the path led off to a crack in the sheer stone face of the pit.

The passage was wide enough and high enough for us to continue on our way, though, and with no immediate alternatives available, that's what we did. Jimmy set a quick pace, but I had no trouble keeping up. I was running on a mixture of fear and expectation – but the object of those feelings was still hidden from me.

We penetrated about fifty meters into the rock before Jimmy called an abrupt halt.

"What's this?" he asked when I came up alongside him.

He flashed his light over a dark shape that blocked the path a few meters ahead of us. The thing was low, but bulky, with patches of silvery material mixed with piles of shadow.

I inched closer, trying to make out the details. A patch of bright white poked out of one side.

My knees suddenly turned watery and my stomach flipped end for end as I recognized what we were looking at – it was a skeleton still clothed in a Space Corps jumpsuit!

I quickly overcame my initial fear and rushed in for a closer look. My light revealed the gaping permanent smile of a skull, the intricate, interlocking carpals and metacarpals of a hand, the protruding vertebrae at the neck. The bones were picked clean and bleached white. Down here, I figured that meant that some local scavengers had found the remains of the spacer quite agreeable.

Without touching anything, I looked closer for some clue to the origin of the antique figure. Then I received my second shock.

A tag on the breast of the jumpsuit still bore a recognizable name in full capital letters – KOLBERG.

My search had ended.

***

"Your grandfather?" Jimmy asked in disbelief.

"He's still got a hold of something," Darko Webb said when he joined in the inspection of my grandfather's bones.

"It looks like a datacard," said Jimmy. "Is it all right with you if we pick it up, Alex?"

I swallowed hard and nodded. "Let me do it," I said, kneeling beside the body and slipping the hard plastic case of the datacard out from the ineffectual grip of the bony hand.

"It's got something scratched into the back of the case," I said. But

I couldn't make out the words. For some reasons, my eyes were full of water.

"It says, 'Danger ahead – blue flash – others dead or dying like me – looks like I lost the long game after all.' Does that make any sense to you?"

"The long game? Yeah, sort of," I said, as a piece of memory jarred itself loose and Grandfather's face recalled itself in my mind's eye.

THE LONG GAME

The last time I saw my grandfather was back in Strgglers Hall, in one of those cramped, well-ordered cubicles they called staterooms. He was a big man and he nearly filled the small space allotted to me and my belongings.

Earlier that same day, I'd finally met my father for the first time in twelve years. The encounter hadn't gone well. I was old enough to realize that he'd let me down, but not mature enough to realize that he'd been as much a victim of my mother as I had. Grandfather tried to point that out.

"You know, don't you, that your father was hurt just as deeply as you were," he'd said. I remember his broad shoulders, wide face, round cheeks, and shiny forehead. My father was a more delicately-figured man, and I took after him. Grandfather had a strength that seemed like it had rooted in his soul and given shape to his body.

"Maybe even worse. Your mother stole twelve years from both of you. But he had plans for those years – things he wanted to do with you, places to take you, worlds to show you. And in the blink of an eye, it was all gone. Think about that before you start to blame him for your predicament."

"But – "

"No buts. He did all he could. For him, it's been six weeks since he last saw you. You're old enough to figure out the geodesics. Do the math, boy. Six weeks. Long enough to travel from Helvetica to Tik. Or long enough to travel from Helvetica to Asgard to Tik. He was supposed to meet you and your mother at the family hostel. And when he got there, you weren't with her. We came here immediately. Six years to Tik and six years back – and your childhood was gone. And it is not his fault."

I found it impossible to argue with the man. All the angry words I'd thrown at my father came back at me, and I began to cry. Then I felt a hot rush of embarrassment at showing my feelings to my grandfather.

He made an honorable display of pretending not to notice, but after a moment, he put a hand on my shoulder to calm me down. It worked and the tears stopped, leaving me with a burning throat and a wet face. I wiped my cheeks dry as he sat down at the desk beside my bed.

"Your mother just won a round in the short game, Alex," he said. "But she lost one in the long game."

"The long game?"

"She doesn't know it, but she's probably done you a good turn. Most of your kinsmen in den Kolberg are nasty and dangerous. Not a good influence on a growing child. Spending your youth in this place could have been the best thing to happen to you. But like it or not, you're a member of the den and there are a lot of things you need to know if you're going to survive the experience." He sat down in the wooden chair at my desk and put his hands on his knees.

"All life's a struggle, Alex, but for a star traveler, there are always two games to play – the short and the long. Everyone plays the short game – survival. Make it through the day to start again tomorrow.

The little deals, compromises, and battles that make up life. But for us, there's the long game, and den Kolberg is expert at that.

"It unfolds over decades, not days. It means planning far ahead – centuries. Because you're going to be there someday. Look at me. I'm thirty-five years old biotime, but I was born before the breakthrough colony first arrived on this planet. You'll still be younger than me by the time Asgard has been fully settled. Buy land in the wilds today, and you can come back in a hundred years and sell it for a moon's ransom. Make an enemy, and his ancestors will be after you for generations.

"You've always got to balance the two, the short and the long. Sometimes you have to give up on one for the other. The trick is knowing when. And that's a trick that you have to learn early and learn well, or you'll end up stranded on some backwater world, counting off the days of real-time while the rest of the clan marches off to the bright future."

We talked for hours, and I shared all the sad and glad stories of my years growing up at Windsor Academy. Then he brought me down to see my father again, with a stern warning to apologize and make up with the man. Looking back on it, I realized that the pain was etched into Father's face. Every feature told of the agony. It was years before I could share those stories of my boyhood with him.

In the end, Grandfather was right, though. Mother had lost a big round in the long game. I think my father and I finally broke even on that score.

And Grandfather – despite his crude epitaph, he'd won the long game, even if he lost the short.

***

"What do we do now?" Darko asked.

"Sounds like the passageway up ahead is boobytrapped," Jimmy said. "We don't want to ignore a lesson that Alex's grandfather paid for with his life."

"Countermeasures?" I said. "There must be some. How did the Ancients get in there? I've still got that sword. And we've got the Mind. Any suggestions?"

"You could go in first waving that blade," Jimmy said. "But if you're wrong, you'll be the first to go down."

"What about the mechanical brain?" Darko said. "If anything's going to take the point, I'd like to see that thing go."

"Not a bad idea," Jimmy said.

"Can we do it? How far back do we want to be?" I asked.

"Depends on where the bodies fell," Darko said. "We should take a look before we make many more plans."

We edged forward cautiously. The cleft in the rock widened significantly, but the path remained straight and narrow, not more than meter wide.

Jimmy called a halt when we reached the first jumpsuit-clad skeleton, lying face down on the cool stony floor. One of Mulak's troopers came up with a heavy floodlight and flashed it on.

The light caught a milky-white wall set in the rockface about ten meters ahead of us. Between the wall and where we stood were four more piles of bones and uniforms. The furthest of them lay only three meters away.

"Can we get the pallet that far without pushing it ourselves?" Jimmy asked.

"I don't see why not," I said. "The trajectory is straight and there's nothing to stop it. No inertia dampers in the lifters. One good shove and it should sail clear to the door."

"And then what?"

"Well," I said, "we either set off the defense systems, deactivate them, or lose the only bargaining chip we have with the Zorgons."

"Any other ideas?" Darko asked.

"Turn around and go back," Jimmy said.

"Turn on the brain and ask for advice," I said. "Except for one thing – I don't trust it."

That was an understatement, of course. I knew that could be the easiest way to get into the Ancient base. But who knew what would happen if we turned the Mind back on? Hawkins couldn't guarantee that it would have forgotten its old personality. After all, it wasn't a human AI. There was no reason to assume that it would work the same. And nothing it had said to me back in the lab on the *Aldeb* indicated that directly – though it sure acted like it was facing real death and not just a momentary nap.

I just didn't want to take that chance. Especially not here, underground, unprepared, and undefended.

"Let's do it quick then," Jimmy said. "If we think about it too much longer, we'll lose our nerve."

I took issue with that proposition, but didn't say anything. I wasn't completely sure he was wrong.

We pulled the pallet bearing the Ancient Mind forward and removed the other cargo from it – Arty and Cora, the AI menu from the Zorgon restaurant. Then the three of us, Darko, Jimmy, and I, lined up against it and shoved with all our might.

It sailed over the skeletons, skating true along its vector, first one, then the next, then the third.

"Don't watch!" I shouted quickly, remembering the effects of the flash in the alley that had killed Captain Xuan. "Cover your eyes!"

I turned away just in time.

A sizzling crackle echoed from the stone walls and the backs of my eyelids turned red for an instant. My skin tingled where it was exposed to the air. One of Mulak's troopers cried out.

I opened my eyes and looked back at the Mind and smiled.

The cavern was filling with light as the door began to glow and hidden plates of milky-white stone joined in. The pallet had come to rest a few meters from the door. The Mind remained inert. In a moment, the light was strong enough to reveal the stalactites hanging from the ceiling and the rippled textures of the stone walls.

Then the door began to open.

Darko went first, without asking for permission or giving a warning. I held my breath as he stepped delicately over the remains of the *Aldebaran* crewmen and closed my eyes when he reached the first body, the one that must have set off the defenses that fateful day three centuries ago.

But nothing happened and a moment later, he stood at the doorway, which now opened into a world bright with white light.

***

The first room was huge – an arched ceiling twenty meters high and a broad, uncluttered floor of similar dimension. The curved walls were featureless, and only soft shadowy contours revealed the edges of the space. Another door on the far side led into the working spaces of the base. The entry parlor served only to make us feel small and insignificant.

The base was laid out like a giant nautilus shell, a spiral of chambers descending in size from the great parlor. We filed through them quickly, like kids in a museum rushing to touch every exhibit.

There were laboratories with benches and tables and equipment that served some unknown function. Chambers filled with glyphs and decorations seemed to be ceremonial centers. Living quarters were marked by elevated slabs of dark cushiony material, pools of still water, soft lights, and gentle drafts.

And finally, at the heart of the spiral, was the command center.

"It's very similar to the base at No Name," Arty said. "That one was larger, but the layout was the same. And this control center looks identical. If we're lucky, the equipment will work the same way too."

The chamber was much smaller than the first room, although the proportions and the construction were much alike. A circular dais stood in the middle of the room, a meter high and two meters across. A series of thirteen milky-white panels were embedded in the gray walls at regular intervals around the circumference, between benches and platforms.

Like everything else in the place, it was immaculate – dust free, untouched by time or decay, almost as if it had been built that morning. The air was crisp and clear – none of the dank cave-smell that had hung on us during our descent.

"Set up the relay in the middle and let's see if this works," Arty said.

I set a lasercomm relay in the center of the dais. Arty hummed and clicked, then fired up his laser line. The only hint of the beam was a spot of yellow-green light on the relay.

Suddenly similar spots of color appeared on the thirteen panels in the chamber walls. Four of the panels blossomed with inner light.

Three more glowed dimly. One flickered with shifting shadows and another flashed patterns and shapes of varied color.

Mulak's troopers oohed and ahhed. Darko Webb shook his head and twisted his face in a crooked smile.

And Arty brought his servo board to life with the sound of a dozen voices, human and alien, digital streams, coded bursts, and other transmissions. One by one, he blanked them out until at last there were only two – a human voice and a Zorgon one.

"Cora, if you'd be kind enough to join us," I asked. The menu hummed to life, then the Zorgon voice was diminished to a gentle murmur as her translation took over.

"All units, all stations – all units, all stations," announced a harried human voice. "The battlefleet be taking up position in synchronous orbit over the spaceport. Evacuation and alert procedures be fully implemented immediately. If you still be listening to this transmission, you must be at full defense status."

My heart sank at the sound of the panic that had to be gripping the people of Minos. The end of a forty-year nightmare had come, not with the bright relief of morning, but with the sudden dark reality of the nightmare come true.

Then, through Cora, the nightmare spoke.

"Humans, Trot am I, commander of the Squadron of the Broken Point. Your defenses against our awesome power useless are. Resist our will you cannot. Attempts to do so your downfall and destruction will bring. For the artifact that to us calls from the stars of this region of space we have come. To us it surrender now, and the agony of a terrible fate yourselves spare."

***

At the family business institute back on Tik they give this course in the history of trading – from the Phoenicians through the Polynesians up to the Chicago Mercantile Exchange and the Moscow Stock Co-op. For the past few hours, I'd been trying to recall as much of it as I could squeeze out of my overstressed brain cells. At the time, the instructors told me that the day would come when I would regret skipping classes and studying from other people's notes, but I never believed them before this.

My main question was what kind of a bargainer would the Zorgon battlefleet commander be? Would he be subtle and crafty like the old Greeks? Or bold and brash like the pre-modern Americans? Would he go for a deal that was all speculation? Would he want extras thrown in for good faith?

What little I knew of the Zorgons, culled from conversations with Jimmy Inoshe and the brief meeting with Drido, hinted at a culture that was stultified by its own age. Formal and lifeless, devoted to structure over content, lacking spontaneity and cherishing tradition. The commander would not have a sense of humor.

But could he be bluffed?

"Arty, how are you doing there?" I asked. "Looks like a lot of channels to be handling all at once."

"Lots of telemetry from the base, communications monitors, battle data, but it's a cinch. I could do it while reordering memories – as long as you don't give me too many distractions."

"Base telemetry? You mean from the Ancient base?"

"Yeah. Three of these panels are for internal monitoring – power, communications, automatic machinery. The systems managers are happy to have an active link again – sort of like dogs abandoned by their master. They're not exactly self-conscious, but they know it's been a long time since anyone's been here."

"And what about battle data?"

"That's the panel with the colored lights. Sensor systems in orbit and on the ground. I can feed it into a holopic if you want. The servoboard should handle the image conversion."

A second later, a sphere appeared in the middle of the chamber, blue and green streaked with whirls of white – Minos. A golden spark burned brightly on one side. "That's us," Arty said, blinking the spark off and on.

A cluster of red stars hung in space a couple of meters away, a handful of large and small lights. More red lights crept over the north pole and around the equator.

"What about the communications link? We can receive all right, but can we transmit?"

"Oh yes, we can transmit – everything but lasers. The whole RF spectrum up through microwaves. The Ancients have a network of crystals running under the high plateau here around the spaceport and similar antenna grids spaced around the planet for instant communications in any direction."

"And weapons?"

"That's the only glitch. Those systems are sealed off to me. I tried them, but all I got was a growl from the watchdogs."

"Defenses too?"

"Afraid so."

"That makes sense," Darko Webb offered. "If you were the Ancients and we got into one of your bases, would you want your own defenses to keep you out?"

"Not if I could help it," I replied.

"All right, I guess we're as ready as we'll ever be. Cora, I'd like you to translate my signal for me. Are you ready to transmit, Arty?"

"Aye, aye."

"Here goes: Ahoy, Commander Trot. I am Alex den Kolberg. I have the artifact you are looking for. I belong to a clan of bargain hunters and I am prepared to bargain with you over possession of the device. Are you interested?"

"Message sent," Arty announced.

"Good," I said. "It should take him a few minutes to think about that.

"Cora, how good are you at matching tones? I mean, if he's in a good mood, will it show? Can you show it?"

"A good menu gets to recognize personalities over the years, sir," Cora replied. "And I can match Zorgon to English inflection for inflection – when there are any. Commander Trot's voice is singularly lacking in them, I am sorry to say."

"No sarcasm? No humor?"

"Nothing. He means what he says and not much more."

"I don't know if that's good or bad," I said.

"We'll find out soon enough," Arty remarked. "Here comes his reply."

"Trot this is," Cora announced in a deep, expressionless voice. "The artifact hand over your life spared will be. Hesitate and from the ruins of your ground structures it we will retrieve."

"The Zorgon doesn't mince words, does he?" Jimmy said.

"Apparently he doesn't realize who he's dealing with," I said. "Arty, any reason for him to believe we're up in the spaceport?"

"Well, I linked through to the groundstation to transmit your message," he said. "I didn't think you wanted to let him know where we were."

"Actually, that's exactly what I want him to know. Can't you use the Ancient mega-network to send my reply?"

"Anything you say."

"Then send this: Trot, your first offer is rejected. Let me make a counter offer. You tell me what you are willing to give in return for the Ancient Mind and I'll let you know if it's enough."

"Are you sure you want to tweak his nose so early in the negotiations?" asked Jimmy.

"I think I need to show him he's not going to frighten me into giving away the store."

"Message sent," Arty said.

The reply was longer in coming this time.

"Value for value bargains are," Cora relayed. "What value possess you? What bargain make you?"

"Send this: As you can see, we occupy an Ancient base. And we have the Mind of the Ancients. What I suggest is knowledge for security. Place your battlefleet in a neutral mode. Cease your menacing movements. And stop making threats that cannot be implemented. In return, I will share the knowledge of the Ancient Mind."

"Threats are not," Trott replied.

He punctuated his remark with a blast of energy that showed up on Arty's battle display as a blue line that suddenly connected the red swarm of the battlefleet with the golden spark of the spaceport. A moment later, the floor shook beneath us.

"That was a warning shot," Arty declared quickly. "A strike up in the hills about forty klicks away. Pretty harmless."

I wondered who lived up in the hills and how harmless the blast was for them.

"He isn't bluffing," Darko said.

"Good. Maybe he doesn't know how it's done."

"Why does the idea of you giving him a demonstration make me feel less secure?" Jimmy asked.

***

Another message came in from Trot.

"That you have not activated Ancient weapons our sensors reveal," he said. "Bargains on inaccurate statements are not. Bargains with no evidence are not. Value for value is not. The artifact now surrender – if the artifact you possess. If not, then die."

Another beam of energy lanced out from the battlefleet and struck the surface of Minos. This time the floor shook harder.

A terrible sinking feeling gripped my stomach. The Zorgon was not about to be bluffed.

We were in a terrible position. We held the Ancient base and the Ancient Mind, but neither one was any good without the other. And I was still afraid of turning the Mind back on.

Unfortunately, I realized, I didn't have any choice.

The only language that would convince Trot was power, pure and simple. I had it – but only if I was willing to take the risk.

"Darko, Jimmy, you and the rest of these troopers get out of here," I said.

"You're not going to bring that thing back to life, are you?" Jimmy said, shaking his head.

"Any other suggestions?"

There was only silence.

I studied the white globe of the Mind carefully. The Ziton crystal still sat in its socket where I'd put it only hours ago. Removing it would be simple enough – a few centimeters still protruded from the top of the sphere, enough to provide fingertips with a purchase on it. For a moment, I toyed with the idea of doing the job by remote control. If I had a piece of string.

But there was nothing to hang the string from and no string to be had. Of course, if I raised the pallet high enough, I could hang it from that. Then an idea hit me.

I grabbed the lasercomm relay from its place on the dais and tossed it to Darko. The panels faded slowly, giving the chamber a dark and gloomy look.

I picked up Arty and Cora and gave them to Jimmy. Then I grabbed one of the troopers to help me manhandle the Mind into place.

"Now go on," I said. "Get going. This room may not be a safe place to be in a few minutes."

They hesitated, then Darko led the exodus into the adjoining chamber. I felt more alone than I had ever been before.

There weren't any acceptable alternatives. And there might even be an advantage to bringing back the Mad Mind of the Ancients. If it wanted to battle with organic units, the Squadron of the Broken Point would make a worthy opponent.

I fiddled with the controls on the floater pallet, and it began to rise. I hopped aboard before it became inconveniently high, stopping just within reach of the ceiling. I pushed myself into position above the dais, then lowered the pallet. When I could reach down and touch the Ziton crystal, I stopped.

I guess I looked pretty foolish. There was no reason that I was any safer up here than standing on the dais. Once the Mind was activated, it would have full control of base's systems. There would certainly be internal defenses – like the one at the main doorway. If the Mad Mind wanted to destroy me, it would only take an instant.

That would mean the end of the game for me – short and long.

But the long game would continue. The Zorgons would just as likely lose the short game here at Minos. And humanity would have time to prepare – though I wasn't sure who would take Jimmy's place to give the warning.

I reached down and lifted the crystal.

At first, nothing happened.

Then the panels on the walls began to return to life – all of them. The chamber hummed with a rising vibration, the surging activity of all the Ancient systems, activating themselves as the Mind spread its control throughout the base.

I waited, holding the crystal with my fingertips. If anything should happen to me, the crystal would drop back into place, shutting down the Mind. It was literally a deadman's switch.

The glowing sphere below me emitted a sharp sound, and I almost fell from the pallet in surprise. It took me a minute to recognize the sound as the speech of the Ancients.

I swallowed hard – difficult with a throat parched dry with nervous anxiety. Then I spoke.

"Hello down there," I said. "Do you remember any English?"

The Mind was silent for a moment, then responded with a new stream of sounds, markedly different from the first.

"That's a little closer, but not quite it. Keep trying."

It went through several more dialects without success. I wondered how many different races the Ancients had included and how many different alien species they had discovered.

This went on for several minutes before I began to start thinking that I might not be in any immediate danger. If the thing couldn't remember English, then it probably couldn't remember me. And that meant it was increasingly likely that the Mad Mind had been replaced.

I pushed myself away from the dais and brought the pallet down to the ground. Then I called the rest of the party back into the chamber.

***

Darko Webb peeked around the corner of the doorway, his weapon drawn and ready. He entered carefully, scanning the walls for any potential threat. Jimmy Inoshe followed him, keeping his guns trained on the Mind itself. The troopers trailed nervously after him.

But it wasn't until Arty finished a link-up with the AI that we finally relaxed our guard.

"It's a whole new Mind," he announced after a few minutes of discourse over the lasercomm link. "Just a newborn. It hasn't got access to all of its memories yet. Its own language is hard enough for it, let alone alien dialects like ours. Give it time and maybe it'll find the file."

"Great," I said. "This is a hell of an improvement in the tactical situation. A few minutes ago, we were trapped underground in an Ancient base without a Mind to control to the defenses. Now we're trapped here with a Mind that can't communicate with us."

"There is an improvement," Arty said, restoring his battle display with a flourish. Now the golden spark of the Ancient base was surrounded by a transparent golden dome.

"What's that?"

"The Mind has thrown up a shield around us. Radius about a hundred klicks. And if you'll turn your attention to the Zorgon battlefleet, you'll notice they're taking up a more dispersed formation."

The red lights of the fleet had indeed spread themselves out from the tiny knot that they'd originally formed. A few more ships were dropping down into lower orbits.

"Any signals from them?" I asked.

"Not since I linked up with the Mind. But no incoming fire either. Stand by. I think I've tapped in to the Mind's English-language memory."

The vocoder in the base of the Mind crackled to life, then announced: "Sorry, the voice communications subsystem of this artifact are not yet on line. Excuse the delay."

I exhaled through my teeth, sounding like a leaking airlock. Darko Webb slapped the wall.

"Incoming message," Arty warned. "Trot to Alex den Kolberg: bargain offered. Time for information. Following question you answer. Control the Mind of the Ancients you or you the Mind control?"

"What?" I asked.

"I think he wants to know if you're in control down here or the old twisted Mind," Jimmy said.

"I guess so. Sounds like the Zorgons have had some experience with overexcited Ancients. Do I tell him the truth, or should I let him worry?"

"Make him sweat for a while," Jimmy said. "We're safe for now and time is on our side. The longer we wait, the more chance we'll have of getting the brain to talk to us."

"I agree," Darko said. "And when we do reply, tell him as little as possible."

"Don't worry, I intend to."

I gave Trot about five minutes, then I shot back my reply. "This question you answer: if I did not control the Mind of the Ancients, would your fleet still be?"

I paced the floor before the Mind, careful to avoid the laser links with the panels in the wall. I stopped and spun around, giving Arty an addition to my message.

"Trot, my information accurate is. Value is. Bargain is."

***

I guess my reply bought us more time, because Trot didn't say anything for quite a while. That was just as well by me, because I wanted the time to think. So far I'd been holding him off, matching bluster with bluff, arrogance with bravado. But sooner or later, the short game was going to be over.

What I needed was a long game solution.

"Jimmy, how much do you figure Trot knows about our situation? What's going through his mind right now?"

"Hmmm ... that's a good question. It's safe to say he knows what condition the Mind was in when your grandfather found it. That's what brought them here in the first place – the signal it sent three hundred years ago. They must have figured out then that the Mind had gotten warped over the years."

"And now they think we're in control of it," I said.

"Is that good or bad?"

"I tried to tell him that it means we can make good on our bargain – in his own language, so to speak."

"The only language this one understands is force," Darko said.

"I think so," Jimmy said. "He's a warrior, not a diplomat."

"This is so maddening," I said. "I just wish I could say the right thing to make Trot and his whole fleet go away. This is all Rico's fault. If he hadn't killed Drido, we'd have some kind of leverage over the Zorgons. He'd have known what to do. The problem is that Trot is no bargain hunter."

"That's the truth," Jimmy said glumly.

A glimmer of light suddenly appeared in the middle of my gloomy thoughts. A path out of the ever-tightening downward spiral of defeat. A solution to the short game that relied on the long game.

"Arty, send a signal to the Zorgons," I said.

"Ready when you are," answered the little AI.

"Trot, this is Alex den Kolberg. The time has come to decide. Is there a bargain or not. Face the truth. You are no bargain maker. You are no bargain hunter. You are a warrior. So am I. Today I bear the Ancient Sword of Orion. I am a Knight Hospitaller of St. John, a warrior of the spirit. Warriors do not make good bargains – blood for blood, fire for fire, death for death. There is no battle for you here, only a bargain. So here is my offer – leave this system. Go home, back to 95 Tauri. Send us someone from the clan of Drido, the bargain hunter. He and his family can negotiate a deal with us where you cannot. Play the long game with us. Kolberg out."

***

Nothing happened for several hours.

Trot made no reply. His ships held their stations, the orbiters making their steady, periodic transits of Minos, the cruisers hovering in synch with the rotation of the globe. It was the middle of the night up on the surface, growing darker, not brighter.

For the first hour, I paced the floor madly, constrained to a few meters between laser links.

My mind raced with the possible disasters that could befall us. Maybe if the Mind could begin to communicate with us, we could use the Ancient weapons systems against the Zorgon warships. But there was no certainty in that idea. Why would it believe us? We were just as much aliens as the Zorgons. It had just as much reason to treat us like enemies as it did them. All we could count on was that it would not allow the Zorgons to harm us.

If Trot wanted to, he could lay siege to us. That would be a long game that he could only win. How would we eat? What kind of alien proteins would we find in the food of the Ancients, assuming we could figure out how to produce it from the machinery in the living quarters? And the Minoans on the surface were unlikely to survive the ordeal any better than us.

An hour of pacing was all I could take, though. I realized after a while that it was making Mulak's troopers nervous. Darko Webb looked a lot more capable of handling inactivity – he'd sat down on one of the benches, put his head in his hand and his elbow on his knee and gone to sleep. Jimmy looked relaxed in a cross-legged position on the bench where he sat. The troopers had even sagged to the floor, though they kept their eyes fixed on me as I kept up my frenetic activity.

I finally wore myself out, dropped myself down on a bench,

leaned back and folded my arms over my chest. The only thing that kept me from dropping off to sleep was the surge of adrenaline and the habit of years of thirty-hour days.

When Arty announced that another message was coming in from the squadron, though, we were on our feet in an instant. All but Jimmy, who took a long moment to unfold his legs and rub the circulation back into them.

"Trot to Kolberg – warrior to warrior. Bargain is. Long game is. The Squadron of the Broken Point with a clansman of Drido, the bargain hunter, will return. The Mind of the Ancient while you can enjoy. Trot out."

My knees felt shaky and my legs seemed to dissolve. I almost felt like I was floating on the air. Arty called for attention amid the shouts and a cheers of Darko Webb and the troopers.

"Alex, the Zorgon fleet is breaking orbit. They're all headed out. Drive activation! Another one! They're leaving the system!"

I watched as the red fire-chites streamed up from the surface of Minos.

Those still in synchronous orbit were straightening out their vectors, lining up on a geodesic for 95 Tauri and blinking out of existence.

"I think you did it, Alex," Jimmy said softly as another round of cheering broke out among our five companions.

"Wait a minute," Arty said. "Alex, take a look at this. On the far side of the planet from the battlefleet."

Arty spun the battle display on its axis to give me a better view. What I saw sent a chill through my back. More red lights were flashing to life almost as fast as they disappeared on the other side.

"What kind of trick are the Zorgons up to now?" I asked.

"Message coming in, all channels," Arty announced. "Ahoy Minos! This is the Space Corps Combat Control Ship *Cape Breton* and the 7th Patrol Wing. Relief vessels are standing by to come to your aid. Battle cruisers are pursuing the Zorgon invaders. Heads up, folks, here comes the cavalry!"

"The corps?" Darko said, his face twisted in surprise.

"That's what they said," Arty replied. "Sensors check out. Standard configurations, standard drive signatures."

"Where the hell did they come from?" Darko asked.

I didn't know the answer to that one, and I didn't care. I just sat down on the edge of the bench and began to laugh. I kept it up for a long time, until my sides ached and the troopers started eyeing me with more than a little suspicion. But by then, it was over. The Zorgons were gone, and the Space Corps ships were taking up station overhead.

***

The streets of the spaceport were worse than crowded, they were overflowing. The landing field was filled with ship's boats, light patrollers, and public carriers. And their cargo of human souls starved for blue skies and green trees jammed the narrow sidewalks, spilling onto the pavement and across the road.

The Space Corps had brought more than a simple wing of warships, accompanying them was a small asteroid base for the families of their crews.

The uniformed men and women were lost in a sea of bright dresses, flowered hats, and children, racing and chasing one another through the crowds.

It took me half an hour to make my way from the terminal to the Planetfall Bar, where I had a lunchtime appointment with Professor Elliot Solomon, the historian.

The place was packed when I got there, and Bob the bartender was a whirling dervish behind the paneled bar. Another figure worked beside him, his back to me. I was only surprised for an instant when he turned around – it was McCoy. He spotted me immediately and raised a hand in a choppy salute, then went back to his work.

I pushed past the line of customers waiting to get in and waved to the waitress. She sent me to a booth in the back where the professor was already working on a mug of beer.

"1 thought you'd figured a way off this mudball before the shooting started," I said.

"Yours was the only ship that I knew of, Alex, and you never got around to inviting me along," Solomon said. "Besides, if I'd done that, who would have been on hand to get an accurate record of events?"

I smiled and sat down and a moment later the waitress delivered two more mugs of beer to the table. I drank deeply from mine, wiped my mouth, then yawned a great wide yawn.

"Excuse me, professor," I said. "That wasn't meant to be a reflection on the present company. But I'm still trying to catch up on my sleep. The last week's been kind of hectic."

I'd been sleeping in for three days now, ever since the last of the Zorgon patrol boats made the jump back to 95 Tauri and the Space Corps declared the system safe. As a matter of fact, I started nodding off before the first space troopers made their way down to the Ancient base to relieve us.

"I'm sorry I have to interrupt your well-deserved respite," he said.

"But I wanted to talk with you while the experiences were still fresh in your mind. Your part in this may be finished, but mine is just beginning. So tell me, Alex, how did you manage to outsmart the commander of the Zorgon battlefleet?"

Two or three waves of customers came and went while we monopolized the booth with our chat. Neither the professor nor I paid them any mind, though. And Bob wasn't about to interfere with the important work of history – not as long as he had a chance to be part of it.

Unfortunately, most of Solomon's questions went beyond my ability to answer. He wanted to know the why and how of things that I only had guessed at. Especially the motivations of Commander Trot.

"At the time, I was thinking on my feet," I told him. "Maybe if I'd had time to reflect and think it out, I would have done something else. But it seemed like the thing to do at the time. But consider it for yourself, professor. The Zorgon has been flying his fleet around the stars for centuries of real-time He knows what this deal means: when he comes back here to Minos, it will only be a few weeks off his clock. We can't get a response from anyone much beyond No Name – maybe Claudius – before he comes back with one of Drido's grandchildren. The balance of forces was all in his favor – at least it was when he started sending his fleet homewards."

"And you're convinced that the Space Corps had nothing to do with it?"

"Absolutely."

"That's not what they think."

"I know, that. But they're wrong. We were working with Ancient sensor systems. The Zorgons don't have anything better – ask Jimmy

Inoshe. They couldn't have known about the corps a moment sooner than we did. And I swear that they had made their decision before the patrol wing arrived."

"And you were as surprised as everyone by that, weren't you?"

"You bet I was," I said, finishing off my third beer. I was beginning to feel numb around the edges, and I wasn't in complete control of my words. "They scared the pants off me at first. I thought Trot was pulling some kind of fancy reverse maneuver – like nothing I'd ever seen a soliton drive do before."

"How many people on Minos knew they were out there?"

"One or two. Commandant Powell. Maybe some of the officers on his permanent staff. The maneuver was complicated, to say the least."

"They certainly had me fooled. No one would have suspected that they were there. After all, you can't keep your fleet units posted in space for decades without action or relief. And you can't send them across years of spacetime to respond to an immediate threat. It would seem like an unsolvable dilemma."

"Except that it wasn't," I said with a grin. "If anyone should have expected it, it was me. My family does that kind of thing all the time. The Space Corps just did it on a grander scale, that's all. Skimming around the Oort cloud, flicking into real-time for a minute or two every day, always within ten or twelve hours of the planet. They must have plowed through a year each day, waiting for the Zorgons to attack. Even with time off for maintenance and morale, they weren't on station more than a couple of months of biotime. Come to think of it, there must be patrol wings just like them all over this sector."

"Is that how they caught the Zorgon fleet at 111 Tauri?" asked Professor Solomon.

"I don't know. They won't tell me, and I've got a commission in the reserves. They say it's classified on a need-to-know basis, and I don't need to know. But you tell me – how else can you bring two fleets together across interstellar distances?"

"It makes sense to me," said the historian. "That would be the reason they brought along their families, wouldn't it?"

"Of course. I can testify personally to the problems you create when you start mixing those kinds of relationships with relativistic travel. No, the way the corps showed up at the last minute is only the last link in a chain of ironies that I still can't figure out."

"What do you mean?"

I squinted my eyes and looked around, as if to see if anyone would overhear us. I felt a little embarrassed to admit the private secrets of my own slightly paranoid vision, but I wanted to share them with someone. So I told the professor about the string of cosmic coincidence that seemed to have wrapped itself around me and Minos.

To my surprise, he did not dismiss me as a hopeless lunatic. Instead, he chuckled and smiled.

"Don't be so hard on yourself, my boy," he said. "History is a process that produces more remarkable ironies than those you've described. There's a subtle connection between individuals and events. You showed up at the right time in the right place and managed to concentrate a handful of dynamic forces all at the same moment. Most of what happened was a direct result of your actions. The only unusual coincidence I can see is the timing of your arrival in such close proximity to the Zorgon fleet. The rest are consequences of that and not contributors."

"But what about that, professor? What were the chances against it? Fifty years times fifty weeks – 2,500 to one? I mean, the Space Corps was here all along. But how did I manage to step into all of this just at the right time?"

"That's where pure history breaks down, Alex. We choose our individual destinies by some process that social science does not describe. You might as well ask how I managed to be here at the same time as all this. You were the main actor, but I am the main witness. Both of us were drawn to the same moment in time and space. If I were a more mystical man, I might attribute it to some hidden psychic power that we share. The ability to select a path that leads us here with some unconscious foreknowledge of the result. But as a historian, I think that may be too mechanical an explanation. Let's just say that there is a unity to existence that surpasses simple understanding and that we can only glimpse obliquely – and leave it at that."

I shook my head. "I guess that's all the explanation I'm ever going to get."

Elliot tried to stand me to another round, but I backed off. "I'm sorry. but I've got another appointment this afternoon. There's a lawyer who wants to talk to me about a case that's still not settled. Three beers should buffer that ordeal, but one more and I might be tempted to indulge in too much honesty and tell the man what I think of him."

I shook hands with the oldtimer and worked my way out of the crowded bar.

***

Attorney Lowell Putnam's office was an island of quiet and calm in an otherwise stormy sea of humanity. The air was cool and still and the rooms were decorated with native plants, classical holosculptures, low-key prints. and walls lined with shelves holding what looked to be leather-bound law books. I was decorated with a silly smile left over from the lunch with Professor Solomon.

The lawyer sat behind a massive desk of close-grained wood. The desktop was clear and empty, unmarked by book, paper, or any device or instrument. He smiled back at me when I came in and offered me a chair. I stumbled as I crossed the thick carpet, but recovered nicely. I figured he'd pass it off to fatigue.

"I'm glad I could get a few minutes of your time, Mr. Kolberg." he said. "You're probably the most popular man on Minos right now." He laughed, and the flesh that hung in thick rolls around his jaws trembled.

"I figured I owed you something for your help with Darko Webb," I said, sliding back in the overstuffed chair. It was so comfortable, I felt like spending a few weeks curled up in it. "What is it exactly that you need from me?"

"As I said earlier, it's in reference to an outstanding complaint against you."

"I thought Commandant Powell cleared things up with Inspector Mortegan."

"Yes, he did. But this isn't a local complaint. It dates back farther than that. Much farther. Do you know what this is?"

He held up an object that he kept cradled in one hand. I climbed up to the edge of the chair and squinted to focus better. It was a small-bore needier, the kind they sell to women who have to work alone after dark.

"Yes," I said. "It's a small-bore needier. The kind they sell to women who have to work alone after dark."

"Good. Then you know what kind of damage it can do."

"I guess I do." It didn't take long for the adrenaline to overcome the alcohol and bring me to a higher level of alert. I realized that the meeting had suddenly taken an ominous turn.

"In a moment, I'm going to lock you in the back room. You'll wait there until my client arrives. He's very interested in seeing you, and he wants to make sure you don't miss this appointment. If you resist, I'll have to use this on you. Don't think I won't hesitate to do so. No one would ever suspect me of the crime. No motive. And there are so many other suspects lurking around this place. Trust me, you'll never live to find out if I've misjudged the inspector."

"Fine. Lock me up anywhere you want to. Can you tell me who I'm supposed to be waiting for?"

"I don't see why not," Putnam said. "He didn't suggest that it remain a secret. I believe you know him well. His name is Scipio Regensburg Steiger den Kolberg."

"Cousin Skippy? What's he doing out here on the edge of nowhere?"

"I believe he is following you, but I should let him tell his own story. He will be with us in a few hours. Now if you'll be good enough to stand up slowly and carefully. I don't want to deliver a dead body to your cousin if I don't have to. That's good, now walk over to the door beside the globe."

He stood up and tracked me with the needler as I followed his directions. He had me open the door myself and step into the darkened compartment. Then he told me to close the door. A moment later, he pressed the pad that set the lock. I tested it to make sure.

Cousin Skippy!

Ira's warning came back to now. "Beware the hides of Mars," he'd said in his letter. That was fifty years ago, of course. Probably twenty years of biotime or real-time when you deduct the straightline distance from my roundabout route. Time enough for Scipio den Kolberg to develop all kinds of plots and set all manner of traps – like the one I'd fallen into.

After all I'd been through the thought of confronting a garden-variety, homegrown, family evil was almost refreshing. And the fact that I would have enough time to burn off the beer buzz I'd acquired at lunch was a blessing. Almost as much of a blessing as being locked in a bathroom instead of a supply closet.

***

I thought I had prepared myself for Skipper when he finally arrived, emotionally at least, but I was wrong. I had been expecting to see the overfed, pouting youth that I had known for many years. But that character had long since departed the stage, to be replaced by something far more repugnant – and far more deadly.

The years of biotime had not been kind to Scipio – and I'm sure he had been unkind to them. The petulant youth had given way to a corpulent, balding lump of flesh that had trouble holding itself up. While I'd been traipsing across the galaxy, skimming the decades, he'd been dallying with endless decadent pleasures. And every one of them showed in the greasy folds of skin that encircled his lips and eyes.

"So cousin, it looks like we've a small reunion here on this minuscule world. An occasion to celebrate, don't you think?" His high, nasal voice hadn't changed, though there was a aspirating tone to it that hinted at fluids pooling in the lungs from an overworked heart.

"I've already done my celebrating for the day," I said. "Though you're welcome to indulge."

There was little I could do to celebrate at the moment in any case. Before Scipio arrived, Putnam had tied me to a small wooden chair and then tied the chair to his desk. And now he sat in the corner with the needler trained on me.

"As I heard it, you did enough celebrating at the last Grand Reunion to last a lifetime – one of our lifetimes. Your mother was still going on about it when I saw her last, about ten years after the event – a few months biotime for her, I think she said."

"One moment of indiscretion can ruin a life of honor," I said. "Too bad it doesn't work the other way around."

"And what's that supposed to mean, cousin? Am I to take that personally?"

"Take it any way you want."

"Hmphh! You were always throwing around your military airs like that. And I always thought it was such a phony little game. You're no better than the rest of us, Alex. You can't fool me with your act."

"And how are the rest of you, Scipio? Are they all like you – greedy, fat, and selfish?"

He frowned, and every fold and crease fell into place as if he'd practiced the expression a hundred times a day. Then he pouted, and the wrinkles joined the display.

"Score your points while you can, cousin. In a short time, I will even the score. I have a lifetime of pain to settle with you. Payment is due, and I intend to extract every scintilla of accumulated interest from your flesh."

"You'll have to do better than that if you want to scare me today," I spat back. "After facing an Ancient computer gone mad and fleet full of alien warships, I'm afraid I find you a little overdone."

"Maybe I'll take your tongue first. It's got to be the part you'll miss most. It certainly wouldn't be your other organs. We all know you've never exercised them much. Is that because no one could ever take the place of your mother? Or is it because her abandoning you like that left you afraid of women?"

***

I felt my face grow warm. He certainly knew which buttons to push. But tied down as I was, there was little I could do in response. The moment of silence was reward enough for Skippy though.

"Yes, a raw nerve. Should I probe at it again? Or let it go for now? Yes, I think I will leave your tongue until last. How else will I know when I'm getting through to you."

I glanced over at Putnam in the corner. He seemed to be enjoying it all. I wondered if he realized that Scipio wasn't kidding. I had no doubt that he was serious about his threats and well prepared to carry them out. It was not something I wanted to think about. I decided to see if I could change the subject.

"So tell me, cousin, what are you doing way out here in Never-Never Land? The last I heard, you were still tooling around with your new toy – a mastership from a Vancouver-Kong family, I was told."

That was an appropriate toy for my cousin. The masterships were the creation of the financier-entrepeneurs who launched the first wave of interstellar exploration at the dawn of the New Era. The asteroid-sized vessels carried scout teams, colonists, technological resources, everything necessary to start a settlement on a new world. Everything, that is, but the money back home to keep them going. When the financiers returned from their first rounds of travel, they found themselves bankrupt and their vessels repossessed.

"It served me well enough," Scipio said. "I was able to follow you around with it quite well."

"So that's how you managed to time your arrival so well. I was beginning to think it was too much of a coincidence."

"Not coincidence, but design. When I returned to Tik to learn that your father had died and the wills were being probated, I knew I had to go after you. It was the only way to keep you from cheating me out my entitlements. You were always doing that, you know. It was never fair. Just because your mother is mainline Kolberg and mine isn't, you got all the attention. All I ever got was scorn – from Great-Grandmother on down."

"I always figured we got what we deserved," I said. "But anyway, it's too bad you missed all the excitement. We just finished up a hell of an adventure."

"I didn't miss anything. I've been here since before you arrived. I saw no need to keep pace with you. Your problem is that you aren't persistent enough. You gave up back at the Space Corps base at Iota Persei. I kept digging. I found a young man who was amenable to pleasures of various substances I have discovered over the years, and as a consequence, to blackmail. He dug out the information I wanted – the ultimate destination of your grandfather's ship. And he provided me with documentation that I can use to prove that your grandfather departed on a Great Circle tour that was supposed to take a thousand years of real-time – which is all I need to establish my claim on your father's holdings. Then I came here, made my arrangements with Mr. Putnam, and skimmed along waiting for you to arrive. The rest is history. Why do you think Skanderi played you for a fool? Where do you think Clive Skreel got his orders? Did you think they were picking on you because they hate all den Kolberg? See, you really are like the rest of us – self-centered to the core."

"I guess so. But you know, it seems like a lot of trouble for nothing."

"Nothing?" he asked, looking down over puffy cheeks at me. "How so?"

"The way the wills are written, if my father died before my grandfather, then all his holdings revert to Grandfather's estate – right? That means you get a share through your uncle, your grandmother, and your sister."

"Yes. But don't be absurd. Your grandfather died three hundred years ago. They brought his remains out yesterday. Are you going to tell me it wasn't him?"

"No, of course not. But that's not how it works. It doesn't matter when he died. All that counts is when the lawyers find out about it. And since they already know Father is dead, there's no way I can get any of Grandfather's holdings. Ask attorney Putnam over there. He'll back me up."

I looked over at the lawyer with the gun. He suddenly lost his smile.

"Well, that's not exactly true," Putnam said. "That's a general rule of law, of course. But there are exceptions. I wouldn't want to commit myself to an interpretation without seeing the documents involved."

I stifled a laugh. The truth was that I was lying through my teeth. Neither Putnam nor my cousin had been there when the lawyers explained it – and I was sure that Scipio would never have the patience to sit through a full-blown rundown on the way the testaments had to be executed. But that wasn't the point of my exercise. It was to throw an element of doubt into my cousin's mind.

There was no reason to believe, of course, that it would do anything but cause some minor confusion. I realized that I was grasping at straws. But men facing death will do that from time to time.

Scipio sneered at the lawyer, who cowered and fell silent. Then he turned his attention back to me.

"What difference does it make, Alex? This isn't business – this is a pleasure. Putnam, let's go. I want to be back aboard my ship before supper. Get your men and get going."

Scipio turned away from me, Putnam rose from his seat, and my heart sank into my stomach.

Then the phone jingled.

"Dammit," Putnam said. "I told that thing to hold my calls. I'll take it in the other room. Won't be a minute."

"Hurry," Scipio said. "Time is getting short. Someone may miss him and start asking questions."

Putnam stepped into the front office. Scipio fidgeted with his plump, sausage-like fingers while the lawyer's muffled voice carried back through the open door. I felt the sweat start to trickle down my back. What a shame, I thought. I'd been doing so well up until now.

Scipio started to turn towards the door when a sudden blue flash reflected off the wall.

"What was that?" he asked. "Putnam? Are you there?"

My heart began to race. Adrenalin pumped into my arms and legs and stiffened my back as my cousin stepped to the door.

But before he reached it, a voice spoke from the phone in the desk behind me.

"Alex?"

"Arty? Is that you?"

Scipio spun around. "Be quiet!" he shouted at me. "Phone off!"

"Sorry, this call isn't for you," Arty's voice replied. "Alex, close your eyes."

"Eyes closed, Arty," I said, squeezing them so tight they hurt. "Fire away."

My eyelids went pink, my face tingled and my hands felt numb. Then I heard a loud thud. "Arty, can I open my eyes now?"

"Whenever you want, Alex. I think your cousin is taking a nap."

I opened my eyes, blinked, then smiled at the mass of flesh lying in the middle of the floor. "I don't know how you did that, but it was some trick. Now what about getting me untied?"

"I'm afraid we can't do that one," Arty said. "We managed the hard part of your rescue with a little help from a friend, but you're going to have to wait on the easy part."

"A friend?"

"Alex den Kolberg?" asked a different, deeper voice.

"Yes."

"I am that which was, and is no more. You know me as the Mind of the Ancients. You knew me when I was unbalanced. Now the balance is restored. I am told that you are responsible for that."

"I'm afraid so."

"I am in your debt. I hope this has helped repay that debt in some small measure."

"Absolutely," I said, as my heart continued to pound within my chest. The excitement was almost more than I could stand. Or else the blue flash had affected my cardiac nerves. I wasn't sure which.

"Darko Webb should be there in a minute to release you from your bonds," Arty said. "I just got off the phone with him."

"Thanks a lot, guys. I think you'd better call a doctor while you're at it. I don't think my cousin's breathing sounds too healthy."

Darko showed up as advertised, followed immediately by a doctor and the ubiquitous Inspector Mortegan. I was glad that the inspector had a chance to see me tied to my chair before Darko cut the lines. I'll bet he's still trying to figure out how I did it.

***

A cool, dry wind blew across the dark tarmac of the landing field. The landing lights of dozens of ships sparkled with brave intensity in the night. The *Perseus Wanderer* was only the nearest of many vessels.

I stuffed my hands deeper into my pockets at the pre-dawn chill and took one last look at the stars. A bright one tracked swiftly across the sky on a laser-straight course, one of the corps' big cruisers riding up in orbit or maybe Scipio's mastership. And Aldebaran still burned brightly in the heart of Orion. I almost expected it to be gone, now that I'd found what I was looking for. Maybe it was still needed as a message to some other traveler who would be centuries coming to this world. Or maybe I was reading more into the constellations than I had right to. After all that had happened on Minos, I wasn't sure anymore.

What concerned me now was the look of the sky in towards the center of the Milky Way – towards Eta and Mu Cass, Tik and Asgard. In a few more minutes, I'd be on my way there.

I nearly made it to the ship before they caught up with me.

"Alex!" they yelled together, almost with one voice. "Where are you going?"

The shadowed figures of Darko and Wendy Webb emerged from the darkness, the sound of their footsteps preceding them. I stopped and waited for them to catch up with me.

"This isn't very polite," Wendy said. "You shouldn't leave without giving us a chance to say goodbye."

"I thought that's what the party was all about," I said. I'd snuck out the back of the Spacefarers Hall when it looked like everyone was deep in celebration. I hate it when people make a fuss over me.

Besides, Jimmy Inoshe had already left for Space Corps headquarters with the first situation reports – the only means of communication with the rest of humanity after the Zorgons blew away the lasercomm station.

"Still, you shouldn't just disappear like that," Darko said. "It could make some people awfully nervous."

"With Arty and the Ancient Mind around? We're all pretty safe. Actually, the two of them together are going to make life on this planet awfully strange. Too strange for my tastes."

"I'm with you on that," the trooper replied. "I don't like the idea of having the two of them for guardian angels – no matter how much security they provide. I'll take my own chances, thank you."

"So what are you two going to do now? Are you still looking for a berth on the *Wanderer*? If so, you'd better grab your flight bag. We're clearing dirt within the hour. I'm making a straight jump to Asgard. That's a forty-year leap. By tomorrow morning biotime, the Zorgons will have returned and whatever deals are to be made will be made. You won't even have to wait around to find out what happens next – just catch an outbound ship and the news will reach you soon enough."

"No thanks," Darko said. "We're staying here for a few weeks, then we'll see what comes around for work. I still want to head out to the Fomalhaut Sector. I hear there's a fountain of flames that burns forever on Ahab. That's something I want to see before I die."

"That's as good a goal as any. I'm afraid I have family business to take care of, or I might be tempted to join you. That's why I'm taking the straight route back – except for a stopover on Asgard. I want to get there before the news works it way in. Those stories can get pretty twisted after a few years, and I know I'd have to spend all my time correcting the mistakes."

"Then this is it?" Wendy asked, her voice catching in her throat. "I guess so."

"Watch it around your family," she said. Then she threw her arms around me and kissed me on the cheek. Darko clapped my shoulder and even in the dark I could see his grin.

"I've had plenty of experience dealing with them," I said. "This time, they'll have to watch it around me."

They waited as I stepped aboard the *Wanderer*, but by the time I got up to the bridge they were gone. It took me a few minutes to get flight clearance, but at this time of night, the only delay came from bleary-eyed controllers going through the checklists.

A few hours later I was far enough from the planet to turn the key and make the leap across spacetime to Mu Cassiopeia.

***

On the coast of Skandia, north of Prime Site, is a little fishing village, tucked away neatly in a snug little harbor. I'd returned at the end of the winter. A mountain to the west shielded it from the frigid wind that blew down off the Deep Freeze and a warm breeze off the Skandia Current made the temperatures more than bearable.

Nothing had changed in the century that passed while I was gone. The fishing boats were lined up along the docks, their crews mending nets, painting masts, and caulking seams. I ambled down the heavy wooden deck of the pier until I reached the end and found a captain with a boat ready for hire for the morning.

While he made ready to get underway, I looked across the small harbor at the boatyard on the opposite shore. Young boys, dressed against the winter chill, but with the sleeves rolled up in the warm air, worked timbers, planed and shaved beams, pegged and glued decking, building boats the way they'd been built for thousands of years.

After a while, the captain cast off his mooring lines, and we cut across the glassy waters of the harbor. It only took a few minutes to get out to a rock that rose sixty meters from the sea and marked the open water of the Bifrost Bay. A mild chop broke into occasional white caps out there and the horizon was lost in a blue-gray haze.

The captain heaved to and held station while I went to the leeward and dumped the contents of the brass canister over the side. The wind caught Grandfather's ashes and spread them across the waves. I waited until the sea had claimed all of them that I could see. Then I waited a little longer. And when I was ready, we went back in to port.

That night, I bought the bar for the boys from the boatyard, and we drank to the memory of my grandfather and all that he had been.

* * *